A JOURNEY THROUGH THE PLANES OF DOMINIA

"Festival of Sorrow"
Robert Vardeman

Gormank, a wandering ogre, lived a life free of sorrow—until he came to Coraleon and discovered a tragedy uniquely his own.

"Chef's Surprise"
Sonia Orin Lyris

As if her name didn't cause her enough trouble, now Asmoranomardicadaistinaculdacar has a hungry Pit Lord on her hands. But perhaps there's one thing she can do to keep from becoming his next meal. . . .

"What Leaf Learned of Goblins"
Hanovi Braddock

A wise elvish elder seeks to discover whether goblins are deserving of pity, and learns instead "the folly of wisdom."

MAGIC ™
The Gathering

DISTANT PLANES

AN ANTHOLOGY

Edited by Kathy Ice

HarperPrism
An Imprint of **HarperPaperbacks**

This is a work of fiction. The characters, incidents, and dialogues are products of the author's imagination and are not to be construed as real. Any resemblance to actual events or persons, living or dead, is entirely coincidental.

HarperPaperbacks *A Division of* HarperCollins*Publishers*
10 East 53rd Street, New York, N.Y. 10022

First printing: January 1996

Interior illustrations by Elizabeth Danforth

Cataloging-in-Publication Data is available from the publisher.

Printed in the United States of America

HarperPrism is an imprint of HarperPaperbacks. HarperPaperbacks, HarperPrism, and colophon are trademarks of HarperCollins*Publishers.*

❖ 10 9 8 7 6 5 4 3 2 1

Acknowledgments

The editor gets her name on the cover, but the truth is that every anthology is a team effort—and the *Distant Planes* team is the best around. I'd like to take this opportunity to thank my teammates.

My first readers: Brett, Jana, Jessica, JoAnn, Julie, Rhias, Sean, Steve, Sue, Tara, Tom, and Wayne.

My anthology cohorts: Adam, Beverly, Casey, Dave, Ellie, Janna, Lisa, Shirley, T. Brian, Thea, and Vic.

The continuity guys: Rev and Scooter.

The team from HarperPrism: Caitlin, Carolyn, Christopher, John, and Julie.

And Nancy, who copyedits above and beyond the call of duty.

Thanks, team. You guys you-know-what!

Table of Contents

DISTANT PLANES

Insufficient Evidence

by

Michael A. Stackpole

I felt as if I'd been shuffled, cut, dealt and discarded. It rather amazed me that I was not blind, what with white-hot embers grinding around in sandy grit where my eyes should have been. My body ached—not hurt as if I'd been wounded, but *ached* all over as if my bones were one size too big, my flesh one size too small, and everything in-between had grown elbows and used them to fight for leftover space.

Grover set a steaming, bubbling container of a black, tarlike fluid on the bar before me. "Drink this."

I raised an eyebrow at him—a major effort for which I paid dearly. "What kind of a sap . . ."

Grover, being one of the Ironroot Treefolk, rustled branches at the pun he'd heard at least once for every creature that ever darkened the doorstep of his wayhouse. "For you to stoop so low . . ."

"No height puns," I snapped shortly.

"You really do need this." He nudged it toward me. "Drink up."

A leaf floated down from one of his upper boughs and landed in the effervescent soup. It promptly dissolved.

"You expect me to drink this?"

"Yes, Loot. Drain it."

"Cannibal."

The treehost laughed, which is usually a pleasant sound, but not to my ears in my condition. I picked the cup up, less concerned by the fact that the beverage was being served in a gold-encrusted skull-cup than I was by the sensation that the steam was melting my eyebrows. I hesitated for a second as I considered using a spell to cool the liquid. I decided cooling it would mean I'd have to chew it, and that wouldn't work. So, unable to recall if Grover had a reason to want me dead, and uncertain I had any particular reason to want to live, I drained the drink to the dregs.

Not being able to recall ever having drunk molten steel, I am not certain how Grover's draught would compare in terms of heat or sheer agony. I do have to admit that it made me forget all the other aches in my body. In a fit of jealous pique, the embers burning in my eye sockets extinguished themselves and the grit melted into tears that glazed a path down my cheeks.

About the time the liquid hit my stomach I determined that I would do all I could to keep it down, because I was pretty sure I didn't want it coming back up. It tasted horrible—halfway between grave dust and sewer fungus, but without the redeeming features of either—and gastric-distillation was not likely to improve the flavor. Moreover, I was convinced my vomit would have liquefied the bar.

And I refused to even think about the problems of future elimination of the drink.

That's less out of willful disregard for myself than knowing I'd survive it. After all, I'd survived the drinking and purging each day for the last fortnight. I didn't think I'd ever get used to it, and part of me knew if I did I'd be in serious trouble.

I tried a smile on and it didn't hurt. "Thanks, Grover."

He scooped the skull away. "Where did you end up last night? I didn't see you after Sopti Borth came in looking for you. Did she find you?"

"I don't remember, but I guess she must have." I shrugged my shoulders and felt surprised that my arms didn't feel ready to fall off. "I ended up about a mile and a half due east of Junktown. I brought that group of Llanowar elves in, so it was a good thing I was out there."

"Loot, as I recall it, the elves brought *you* in."

"Oh, sure, take *their* side."

Grover's description had been as accurate as my reply had been facetious. For the past two weeks I had proceeded, starting in the morning and continuing into the night, to consume a variety of fermented beverages in quantities that stunned newcomers and won not a few wagers for those who had been around a while. Not that I normally drink like that, but some people at Grover's had memories that worked the way they were supposed to and remembered my last midsummer binge.

My memory does *not* work the way it is supposed to. Of my life before my summoning I remember nothing—and the summoning is an act I have determined must have happened, though I have no recollection of it, either. The fact that no one at Grover's has seen anyone who looked like me means my people—though apparently human—are unknown in the more heavily populated realms of the world, making solutions to the mystery of who I am a bit more rare than even my people are.

Everything I have and am dates from when Kyyrao Grrenmw, a Cat Warrior of fearsome aspect and fierce spirit, and her pride-mates found me wandering around in the wilderness. Strong drink had not been the cause of those peregrinations—the blow that stole my wits and left the crow's-foot scar on my forehead was still fresh when they found me.

Kyyrao and her friends adopted me and named me. While they stood ready to do what they could to help me ferret out clues to my past, they didn't care about who or what I had been. To them it was enough that I was Loot Niptil and I was one of them. As my lover and companion, Kyyrao also became a rudder for me. In times when the desire to know what I could not remember overwhelmed me, she would steer me away from the frustration and make me forget that I wanted to remember.

Once a year Kyyrao and her pride-mates headed off to the eastern mountains, on past Junktown by nearly a week. At the top of the highest peak, at the dawn of midsummer's day, they greeted the sun. They offered it an accounting of what they had done in the last year and made sacrifices to it. In return they felt the gentle kiss of a breeze, a sign they took as approval by Lord Windgrace of what they had done with themselves.

Kyyrao had invited me along on both of these outings, but I had chosen to remain at Grover's instead. The fact is that I think I'm an atheist. Kyyrao has always been tolerant of this attitude—ascribing to ignorance what I put down to reason. I felt that if I went while I did not believe, I'd be blaspheming. Since I didn't think any gods existed, I wasn't particularly worried about divine retribution. Even so, I didn't want to mock the beliefs my friends held dear.

Grover deposited a mug of water and a hard roll on the bar in front of me. "I think we can move you to solid food now. Your bingeing should be over today, shouldn't it?"

I smiled and actually liked how it felt. "Should be, yes. Kyyrao's due back today sometime. I can't wait."

"Neither can I. I had entertained visions of you getting into serious trouble in her absence."

"Every one of those Benalish heroes I baited I could have handled."

"I don't doubt it. You managed well last time."

I frowned and it didn't hurt at all. "And what was different this time?"

"The blackouts. You had me worried a number of times, including last night."

"Sorry about that."

"Apology accepted, on condition." The treehost tapped a twig on the bar. "I will give you a week to settle back in, then you and Kyyrao are going to have to head out on an expedition."

I jerked a thumb at the elves. "I brought them here. Doesn't that count?"

"They were only three miles away, Loot. You've staggered home from further than that."

"Good point." I broke a piece off the roll and stuffed it into my cheek so it would soften. "Just don't have us round up war mammoths for another feast. That was hard work."

"That's because you're supposed to slaughter them *after* you drive them here."

"Hey, I know that, but you sent me out there with a pride of Cat Warriors who hadn't killed anything very big in over a month and Malkean Feorr and Sopti Borth, with both of them intent upon seeing how that mechanical butcher she created worked. . . ." I turned toward my right as I heard a murmur working its way through the early morning crowd. "Speaking of whom . . . "

Malkean Feorr stopped short of joining me at the bar and stiffly posted his fists on his hips. Taller and thicker than I am, with bright blue eyes and blond hair, my friend the Argivian archeologist looked utterly ill at ease. I thought, initially, this was because of the two men standing behind him, each clad in a hodgepodge of armor manufactured from different metals and comprising a dozen different styles.

Then I noticed the thick clockwork medallion hung from his neck. It had a pair of scales on it that dipped down on one side, then back up again, clicking slowly and precisely as they did so. He had once told me that it functioned because of a spring that got wound tight, and until it ran down, the person wearing it was a marshal for Junktown and the closest thing to a judiciary system we had in the vicinity of Grover's. Marshals were appointed when needed and generally chosen because of their knowledge of the quarry they pursued.

"Are you the man known as Loot Niptil?"

I felt a cold chill pucker my flesh. I slid from the bar stool, resting my left hand on it to steady myself. "I am."

"By the authority hung on me, I place you under arrest."

"Arrest?" Grover planted two branches on the bar. "What crime has he been charged with?"

Malkean shot Grover a side-glance, then looked back at me. "Where were you last night, past mid?"

I shook my head. "I don't know."

"Did you see Sopti Borth last night?"

Again I shook my head. "Grover said she was looking for me, but I don't remember meeting her."

One of the Llanowar elves stood. "We found him about three miles from here, dead on to the east, two hours before dawn. He was sleeping in the dirt. We thought he was a child lost."

One of the two men behind Malkean moved forward, bumping the archeologist-cum-marshal with his shoulder as he did so. "Let's take him."

Malkean grabbed the man by his cloak. "I am the authority here, Vlorik. I will handle this."

"Get on with it, then."

Life drained from Malkean's expression and his lips became a thin line gashed across the lower half of his face. "Last night, near one hour past mid, Sopti Borth was murdered in her workshop."

I caught myself on the stool when the news buckled my knees. "Dead?"

"That's what happens when ye murder someone, they end up dead."

I glared at Vlorik, wishing my daggerish stare was lethal enough to test his thesis on the spot.

Malkean frowned. "The truthsniffer chose you as the guilty party. If you ever hope to establish your innocence, you must come with us."

Vlorik snarled fiercely at me, giving me full view of the scattered yellow teeth in his jaws. "If ye run, I'll hound ye down."

A piece of the fauna inhabiting his scraggly beard chose that moment to leap out at me, convincing me that even as satisfying as scattering teeth *out* of his jaw might be, there was no way I ever wanted to touch him. "The only reason I would have to run is to put you and your menagerie behind me—*far* behind me."

"Afraid o' me, are ye?"

"No." I plucked his flea from my shoulder and flicked it back at him. "I do not fight with those who have reinforcements living on them."

Pleased to have his pet back, Vlorik said nothing.

I turned to Malkean. "You have witnesses that saw me kill Sopti?"

"No, but we have evidence, physical evidence."

I nodded. "So my guilt or innocence will be decided by the Justiciar?"

"I'm afraid so, my friend." Malkean gestured back toward the door to Grover's. "Will you come, or must we bring you?"

I knew in my heart that I'd not committed murder, though remembering nothing about the previous night did leave me with a fair amount of doubt. Still, truthsniffers were not known for making mistakes. If it had picked me out as the guilty party, something was significantly amiss. The only way to sort it out was to go to Junktown. Malkean, I had no doubt, would make sure any trial was conducted fairly. "I'll go."

Grover caught my sleeve with a branch. "What will I tell Kyyrao?"

Vlorik sucked at his teeth and answered before I could. "Tell her the murdering little man got his fill o' justice and she can have what's left o' his hide in a month."

Junktown is not, of course, what the inhabitants call the wide spot near the crossroads to the east of Grover's. To them it's Automatown, and they cling to this name with a certain amount of pride. Over the years, just as people have gathered at Grover's, artificers, inventors, traders, collectors and the curious have come together at Automatown to invent, investigate, repair, and trade in all manner of magical, mechanical, and clockwork creatures, and items.

Now I happen to consider Kyyrao rather more exciting and interesting than gears that cannot be seen by the naked eye. This attitude marks me as something of a mocker within the society present in Automatown. Their nearly orgasmic joy at being able to clean the corrosion off some ancient, twisted lump of pins and wheels, springs, cogs, and gears is all but incomprehensible to me, which is why I call the place Junktown. If you want one—and it doesn't matter what it is that you want—you can buy it in Junktown. And if you want to get rid of something—even something that was trampled beneath the feet of war mammoths stampeding away from slavering Cat Warriors—you can sell it in Junktown.

I don't want to make it sound as if Junktown is just some giant midden where trash is traded between hermitish creatures that make Vlorik appear intelligent and cognizant of the concept of personal hygiene. Many are the nice folks who live there, for the general bazaar-like nature of the town demands support industry like inns, taverns, and stables. There is even a temple there with a clockwork godling that exchanges blessings for gold.

Sopti Borth was one of the nice folks. Though she was an artificer of great skill, she realized there was more to life than tinkering. While she was no Teeka, her creations were highly prized among collectors. Her nearly encyclopedic knowledge of how devices were created in the past enabled her to make very exact copies of famous pieces—though she always did manage to improve them—and she signed each by imbedding a black pearl in the brow, just so her creations would not be mistaken for authentic antiques.

The butcher thing she had created had been an example of her creativity. The butcher had been as slender as a sapling, with steel blades snapping out and whirling around when she set it in motion. It had only one leg and moved by bouncing along on a spring mounted at its base. The whirling blades seemed somehow to keep the thing upright, and it was able to stay upright even after it had sawed halfway through the first stampeding mammoth. The other beasts stomped it into so much rust-fodder, but its ultimate failure had not dampened the smile planted on Sopti Borth's face by its initial success.

Malkean lowered the sheet back over her waxy, gray face, then looked up at me. "She's dead, you see."

I nodded. "Single dagger thrust to the heart?"

"So it seems."

"Where?"

Malkean pointed to the doorway leading to her workshop. Closest to the doorway the rectangular room had a table with two chairs, one of which had been toppled over. I could see a dark brown stain on the stones which I knew to be blood. I tried to remember if I had been there last night, but I got nothing in response to my efforts.

"From the way that cup is tipped over, it appears the murderer lunged at her across the table and stabbed her. She fell back; he vanished."

I smiled half-heartedly. "Thanks for not saying 'you vanished.'"

"I don't want to think you did it, Loot, but we have evidence." Malkean crossed his arms. "The truthsniffer picked you out."

"From the knife?"

"No, we don't have that. The killer took it with him. If he had not, well, the act of murder would have made enough of an impression on the knife that we'd have had him in a heartbeat." Malkean dropped down onto his haunches and snapped his fingers. "The sniffer has been here since we found the body, looking for new clues, but you're it."

From deep in the cluttered far end of the workshop, a bronze-and-onyx creature came trotting. It looked for all the world like a small dog, though with each step the springy tail wagged in a most unnatural way. The truthsniffer had no mouth, so it couldn't bite, but it did have a somewhat exaggerated nose that had been carved out of a single piece of onyx. Its ears lay flat against its head and its eyes had been fashioned from little pieces of yellow topaz that glittered wetly.

The truthsniffer was a cunning combination of mechanical parts and magic that made it very useful in the pursuit of fact. Within magic there are two Laws—Similarity and Contagion—that posit a connection between items that appear to be the same, or items that have spent time in close proximity to each other. The fact that the truthsniffer looked like a dog was an example of Similarity—its very shape was meant to enhance its ability to follow a trail.

The Law of Contagion would have meant that the murderer, through the act of committing the murder, would have left a very great impression on the murder weapon. Had that been available for the truthsniffer's examination, the little whirligig beast would have pointed the culprit out straight away.

"Malkean, the presence of one cup suggests there was another, doesn't it?"

"Just as the presence of the knife wound suggests a knife, but we have neither. The murderer was careful."

"What about the chair?"

"Too many impressions to get a clear one. It would be easier to find the people who had not sat in that chair than to find those who had." Automatown's temporary marshal shrugged uneasily. "I have to believe the murderer also undertook a scapegoat ritual to sever the connections between himself and the evidence."

I winced. Even the few psychometric spells I knew—taught to me ironically enough by Sopti Borth—would have been unable to counteract a scapegoat ritual. In such a ritual, a person, in effect, magically filtered his essence through another creature—often a goat or sheep. That animal, in a magical sense, would become them for the purpose of tracking. Such rituals are most often used to shift a curse from the victim to the animal, then the animal is slain, breaking the curse. Killing the animal in this case would leave the murderer with no link back to the victim or evidence.

I felt confused. "If all that has been done, then what is the evidence you have against me?"

We walked back over toward where someone was drawing a pint of blood from the corpse and beyond to a small side table. Malkean opened a small wooden box and drew from it a cameo brooch. It looked old, and the worn gold setting even older. I'd seen similar styling and symbols, but only in pictures of such items that Malkean had drawn into one of his journals.

"Sopti had this clutched in her hand. The sniffer picked it out when we asked for the strongest clue to the identity of the killer." He handed it to me. "You can see why we have to suspect you."

They might not have had an eyewitness, but the cameo was as good as having a dozen of them. The creamy white image on the black background was of me, from the neck up, wearing some heirophant's miter. On the headgear and against the background all sorts of arcane symbols had been excised from the surrounding shell.

I looked up at him as I turned the brooch over in my hands. "What is it, besides the obvious, I mean?"

"This brooch is very rare and very valuable. More importantly, if I read the symbols right, the figure is a representation of the last and greatest of the Tchokta war-priests. His name was given as N'ciczli, but I doubt that it really was since *nysikzly* is a predynastic Sarpadian word meaning inhuman. It was a religious term and carried with it implications of being savage, barbaric, blasphemous, cruel, and arrogant."

"They packed a lot into one word."

"They meant to. The Tchokta were a nasty people. They had their own little empire and used their subject peoples to feed an unending need for sapient sacrifices. This N'ciczli was their last war-priest. He used to vanish from time to time and came back telling of grand battles he saw and fought in when the gods summoned him to their sides. He used these godspats as inspiration for his battles and supposedly never was defeated by another army."

I raised an eyebrow. "Even allowing for my lapse of memory, I've never heard of the Tchokta Empire."

"You wouldn't have. N'ciczli was summoned away and never returned. His empire was ripped apart like his victims. His people, who were wiped out by the progenitors of the early Sarpadian empires, maintained the gods made their N'ciczli a god himself. Cameos like this were supposed to have marked the occasion of his elevation, and to be discovered with one in your possession was to be slain outright by Sarpadian authorities."

"You don't think this is me."

Malkean shrugged. "You'll notice you don't have your scar in the cameo."

My fingers traced the puckered crow's-foot above my right eye. He was right, the cameo was unblemished. "Is it possible for someone to be summoned from the past?"

"I have no way of knowing, Loot, but there are stories about legendary warriors being summoned. From then to now, or just within their own time, I have no way of knowing. Even studying the folktales doesn't do much good, since few of them are datable."

"So why would I murder Sopti?"

Malkean took the brooch back from me. "This cameo proves you were the leader of a black-hearted people. She held the key to your identity and it was an identity most foul."

I shook my head. "But if I murdered her to prevent her from spreading that sort of thing about me, why would I leave the cameo behind? You can't think I'm that stupid."

"N'ciczli would have protested the same way." Malkean shrugged. "I don't want to believe you murdered her. I don't believe you are N'ciczli, but if you are, then murdering Sopti is exactly the sort of thing you would have done. Because you were found in the area last night and cannot remember anything about it, I have no choice but to bind you over to trial by the Justiciar."

Malkean conducted me from Sopti's workshop straight across the town square to Justiciar Court. I had been there once before, on a day when no trials were being held. The court was comprised of an open square courtyard with a wall six feet high on the interior. The spectators' gallery started right behind that wall and continued on up at a sharp angle to the top of the twenty-foot tall external walls. Sand covered the floor of the courtyard, and the plastered walls matched it in color, with the red of the wooden spectator seats making for a nice contrast.

Centered in the courtyard, seated on carved throne of granite, was the Justiciar of Automatown. When on its feet it stood ten feet tall, with long slender legs and long slender arms, with two sets of the latter starting with one pair of shoulders being mounted just above the first. As short as I am, I was just above waist high to the beast.

Though its body was proportioned as a man's might have been—the spare set of arms notwithstanding—the hands and feet had only three digits, each of which ended in a sharp claw. The head was, from the front, a triangular affair with a bulbous back, looking much as an insect's head might, if it were scaled up and given enough cranium to house a fair head of brains. The mandibles had been deemphasized and blunted, though they looked more than capable of crushing something.

Like my throat.

This was because, just like the rest of the Justiciar, the mandibles were made of well-weathered hammered copper. The verdigris staining the hollows and edges of its broad torso and the long limbs gave it a patina of antiquity. The styling was simple and Haspian Chastoril—more a salvager than an inventor—had tried repeatedly to convince people that it was an old Imperial device he discovered and refurbished before he took up residence in Automatown. The fact that he had subsequently produced a number of things "modeled" on predynastic primitives had confirmed suspicions that he'd created the Justiciar himself, and because it served such a useful purpose among the artificers, Haspian was valued for his eccentricity to the same degree to which the provenance of his devices was assumed to be fake.

Haspian, a large, ample-bodied man, looked almost entirely like a bear with mange. He growled at me as Malkean led me to the center of the court. "The Justiciar has dealt with murderers before. Your predations are at an end."

"I thought this was a trial, not an execution."

"Thus hope all who are guilty." Haspian patted the automaton on the side of the head. "Almost ready."

Haspian reached up with fat fingers for a cut-crystal oval that served the cyclopean creation as its eye. He plucked it from the center of the Justiciar's forehead, just below and between the two crystalline horns that curved up from the creature's brow. "Justice must be blind."

I glanced at Malkean. "I hardly thought that was meant to be taken literally. . . ."

The marshal shrugged. "It is the way of things here. Bare your right forearm."

I complied with his request, though I did not know why he wanted me to do so. The people filtering into the gallery apparently did, and cheered as a result. Before I could ask what I was to do next, the Justiciar's top two hands reached out and took solid hold of me at the wrist and elbow. The mandibles hissed apart and a needle telescoped out. It pierced my flesh just shy of the joint.

The piercing stung and I tried to pull away, but the mechanical thing held me solidly. To my dismay I saw a decidedly sanguine hue entering the rightmost horn on the beast's head. The pain in my arm and the dizziness washing over me left me no question about what was filling the vessel, but before I could initiate a spell to free myself, the Justiciar's head reared back and the needle made a rude noise as it sucked the last of my drawn blood into the horn.

I clapped my left hand over the hole in my arm, then stepped back when the metal monster released me. It turned its attention toward a man approaching with a bowl of blood, and I faintly recognized the man as the one who had been taking blood from Sopti's body. The Justiciar greedily sucked it all up, filling the left horn.

Haspian held his hand out and into it Malkean deposited the cameo. The Justiciar's inventor slid the brooch into the slot that had previously housed the eye lens. Haspian gave me an appraising gaze, then sneered. "You'll pay for your crimes, you will."

I gave him a fiercely mocking stare and let it go at that. I tore a strip of cloth from the hem of my tunic and used it to bind the hole in my arm. I knotted the cloth with hand and tooth, then drew in a deep breath and found myself all but alone in the Justiciar Court proper.

Malkean stood over by the wooden ladder that groaned beneath Haspian's bulk as he climbed out of the arena. "Citizens of Automatown, the man known as Loot Niptil has been accused of murdering Sopti Borth. Were there living witnesses against him, a trial would be conducted by the living. Loot stands accused by physical evidence and automatons. His trial shall be by his accusers."

My friend gestured toward the Justiciar. "Blood of the victim and the accused have been drawn into the crystal horns. Evidence of Loot's guilt has been provided the Justiciar. If Loot survives the draining of the horns, his innocence in this matter is established. The evidence against him will be destroyed immediately and never again will this crime be spoken of. If he does not survive, his guilt and his punishment will be unquestioned."

"Justiciar," Malkean called from the top of the ladder, "seek the guilty."

The automaton came up out of the throne more smoothly and swiftly than I would have guessed possible. I had expected jerky movements and clanking, but instead the whoosh and hiss of hydraulics meshed with the rustle of well-oiled joints to produce a fluid motion that would have done credit to a Cat Warrior. Arms flung wide, the creature loomed over me and quickly sought to embrace me.

Being short is seldom thought a virtue, especially in consideration of martial contests. Lack of size generally equates with lack of power. Though speed may compensate somewhat for this lack, a faltering of speed can have lethal consequences, whereas misapplied strength still hurts.

Speed I have, and combined with my lack of height, it enabled me to duck beneath three-quarters of the Justiciar's hug. The one quarter that did hit caught me in the left shoulder and cartwheeled me over toward where Malkean had pulled the ladder up behind him. I managed to roll to my feet and get my back against the wall, which gave me a close view of furrows the Justiciar's talons had gouged from the stone in previous trials.

As it darted forward, I tucked and rolled off to the right, then ran back around to where I could keep its throne between me and it. The Justiciar surprised me in that it did not immediately move to attack me, but instead raked all four of its paws across the stone where I had rested for a moment. That seemed stupid, but something began to niggle at the back of my mind because of it.

Haspian had blinded the Justiciar, but it had known where I was when it first attacked. Then, when I had been by the wall, it had attacked where I had been, not where I had moved to. I knew it was not tracking me by sound—the noise of the crowd was sufficient to render that impossible. Touch, taste, and scent seemed likewise out, so I decided it had to be comparing the sense of my essence it got from my blood with my essence in the court. It attacked at first because I had been standing in one place, letting the air and the dirt absorb my essence. The wall, where I touched it, likewise had a magical connection to me.

When it turned toward me, it started on an arc along my route of retreat, then oriented on the stronger impression I'd created by staying in one place. I backed quickly and cut right and left, assuming distance would weaken its ability to track me. I had to be careful to avoid a corner, for I didn't want to trap myself, but I realized that as long as I kept moving, it was always a step or two behind me, flailing wildly before it with the quartet of arms.

Two things occurred to me as I moved around the court. The first was that, despite the catcalls from the stands, I could continue to run and dodge for as long as necessary. I knew I was not guilty, and if surviving this thing's assaults was what I needed to do to prove my innocence, I could and would do that.

The second and far more important point, to my mind, was that proving my innocence would not point out who actually *had* murdered Sopti Borth. An altruist might have been concerned about this in terms of realizing an injustice in this matter generally weakened the fabric of society and started things on an inevitable slide toward to anarchy, or, worse yet, stagnant democracy in which progress moves at a glacial pace in a direction dictated by the pendulum of public opinion. Avoiding that sort of dire future was ample reason enough to want Sopti's killer brought to justice.

I, on the other hand, am a firm believer in the deterrent effect of vengeance. The murderer had killed a friend of mine, and for that he deserved to die. He had also managed to frame me for that murder, which made me want to use the adverbs *slowly* and *painfully* to describe the manner in which he would die.

The thought struck me, as I dodged away from the Justiciar's clawed groping, that the only evidence that had a chance of revealing the identity of the murderer was the cameo that rested in the Justiciar's brow. Because it and I looked similar—similar enough, perhaps, to prompt the truthsniffer to equate it with me—I wondered if I might employ a spell to let me see what it had seen. If so, I could use it to show who really killed Sopti.

Of course, the fact that the evidence would be destroyed at the end of my trial rendered that exercise rather moot. The only way I could employ the spells I possessed would be to touch the thing—allowing a convergence of similarity and contagion—and study the result long enough to see what there was to be seen, if anything. Doing that while the Justiciar was after me was impossible.

Unless. . .

I cut past its outstretched arms and ran to the side of its throne. I spun around there, filling a little circle with my essence, for a heartbeat and another, then ran off around the back of the throne to the far side. The Justiciar chased around itself in a circle, like a dog preparing to lie down, then stopped with its back to me and sought new clues to my location.

I sprinted straight in at the metal beast, vaulted off the stone chair and slammed both feet square into its back, right between where all four shoulder blades would have been on a living creature. The impact propelled the Justiciar forward for a few steps, then the restraining wall stopped it abruptly. The metal beastie stumbled back, then dropped to its knees and fell forward on all sixes.

I immediately leaped onto its back and hooked my left hand down where the flexible neck sank in past the backplate. As the Justiciar came up and began to turn to find me, I hooked my right hand over his head and slapped it firmly over the cameo. Closing my eyes, I invoked my spell and commanded my body to hang on for dear life.

The psychometric magic instantly brought to me a vision that I knew had to have been through the eyes of the cameo because all I saw was darkness and the occasional ridge of finger or palm. At first I thought I was seeing what it was seeing at the time I had invoked the spell—making the palm mine—but flashes of myself and Malkean dissolved back into another hand that I took to be Sopti's.

I had help in making that conclusion. The sharp sensation of surprise, wrapped up in pain and anger, that accompanied the image told me it came from the time of her death. The brooch had not seen the killer because Sopti had clutched it tightly in her hand, as she might if she were brandishing evidence of perfidy on the part of another.

Almost invisible because of that sensation was the fact that something was missing from the whole image. The anger swam in and out of focus. Some of it I sensed as being directed at herself for putting herself in such danger, for having underestimated her murderer. That was clear, but the object of the rest of the anger remained hidden. Its lack was evidence of the fact that the murderer had, indeed, performed a scapegoat ritual to erase connections between himself and the crime.

The cameo, therefore, could tell me nothing about the killer.

I was fairly certain my analysis was correct, but something else left the door open—a door I almost slammed shut prematurely. My hand lay in contact with the cameo *and* the Justiciar. Though I concentrated on the impressions from the brooch, the Justiciar's impressions still sought to interfere with what I saw. My hand worked back into the brooch image, clearly drawn from the Justiciar, and I sought a way to push its interference away.

I don't care what the Justiciar saw.

Then it struck me that what the Justiciar saw might have, in fact, been very important. The arched gateway to the Justiciar Court looked out directly at Sopti's workshop. It was possible that the culprit had been spotted when he left the scene. Though the ritual might have removed traces from the Justiciar, the more I could learn, the better my chance at figuring out who the killer was.

I shifted my focus and pushed back the pain of Justiciar's elbows battering me from one side of its back to the other. My consciousness sucked in all the impressions it could from the automaton. It struck me that I might find the memories of a predynastic artifact overwhelming—my appetite for impressions could be sated by a century, and I had no desire to become a glutton. Fortunately for me the Justiciar was of recent manufacture, and the majority of its impressions came from the series of trials in which it had fought in the dozen years since its creation.

This twelve-year history proved useful in one thing only. It showed me that getting in close to the creature, as I had done, was a tactic best described as suicidal. I shoved this dour news aside and tried to focus on last night, but the most recent and strongest impression came from when Haspian blinded it and the Justiciar drank in my blood.

"Loot, look out!"

The warning cry blasted into my brain. As I withdrew from the impressions I felt myself and the Justiciar sailing backward at a high rate of speed. Without truly thinking, I kicked both feet down into the small of its lower back and pushed off. Arching my back, I pulled my body up above its head just as the Justiciar slammed itself spine-first into the courtyard wall.

But for the warning, the beige plaster dust curling up to choke me would have *been me*—though, in that case, it would have been a mist and a damned sight more scarlet than beige. The Justiciar jerked spasmodically as if hitting the wall had briefly knocked its hydraulic pumps out of synch, then it began to recover itself.

The impact had loosened my grip on the backplate, but the Justiciar's rebound from the wall didn't carry it far enough for me to lose touch entirely. I shifted my hands around to where skull met neck and tightened my grip, then I kicked off the wall itself, projecting my body up and over the Justiciar's head. As my feet reached the apex of the arc and started down, my grip shifted so my palms hit its jawline and I continued on over.

Though I am not big, the Justiciar remained unbalanced enough that my weight was sufficient to start it forward into a somersault. When I landed on my feet, I tucked my head in, bent at the waist and heaved, pulling the Justiciar up and over the top of me. The metal creature flew as I had flown, but since I controlled its travel, its landing was not nearly as smooth as mine.

Slamming into the ground jarred the Justiciar enough that the cameo popped out of the creature's eye socket. I snatched it out of the air, thinking that using it without the Justiciar being in contact with it would be much more convenient. Neither thing had an impression of the killer, but the brooch clearly possessed more in the way of useful impressions.

Suddenly everything came together. What I had seen was not as important as what I had not seen. I knew who had killed Sopti, but without a link between her and him and the cameo, I had no way of proving his guilt.

Then I looked up into the bright amber eyes of Kyyrao Grrenmw. The lady clouded-leopard sat poised on the edge of the wall, ready to leap into the court and rip the Justiciar apart, but would only do so if I gave her leave. A wink, a nod, and she'd enter the fray—*and her tendency to stand and fight would leave her dead like the others this thing has fought.*

"The warning was enough, Kyyrao." I flipped her the cameo and she caught it deftly in one hand. "Get me the one who did not hunt mammoths with us."

A snarl and flashed canines cleared the crowd around her of everyone save Malkean and Vlorik. She ignored the marshal and dropped Vlorik with a backhanded clout that dented his ego a bit more than it did his helmet. Past him she leaped from row to row on a straight line for Haspian Chastoril.

The fat man stood, clapping his hands and snapping his fingers in a pattern too quick and odd for me to make sense of. He held the crystal lens from the Justiciar over his own right eye and stared hard at Kyyrao. "Kill the cat! Kill the cat!"

The Justiciar rolled to its feet and gathered its legs beneath it. It leaped upward toward the gallery and would have easily cleared the wall except that Malkean heaved the ladder at the automaton. Tangled up in it, the Justiciar fell back to the ground, trapping its lower left arm beneath it. Metal screamed and I heard a snap.

The Justiciar reared up on its knees and ripped the ladder apart with the three whole arms it had left. The broken limb aped the motion of the others, but succeeded in doing nothing more than spraying me with hydraulic fluid, which I found to be as hot and black as Grover's hangover cure, and a damned sight more flavorful.

I spat the taste of the liquid from my mouth as the Justiciar reached for the top of the wall and started to haul itself up and over. I leaped for the creature and resumed my place on its back. The pumps thudding beneath its copper flesh matched speed with my pounding heart, and I hoped they might explode, because it certainly felt as if my heart would. The Justiciar showed no sign of cardiac weakness and went over the wall as if my weight were as inconsequential to it as the weight of a flea is to a dog. It stalked forward and up, ignoring the menace in Kyyrao's snarls.

"Get Haspian, Kyyrao!" I grabbed the Justiciar's neck and hung on as it ducked a shoulder and tried to slide me off. Kicking wildly, I connected with an arm and managed to secure my position again. "Go on, I've got this thing."

"It does not seem worried, my precious."

"That's because it's all brawn and no brains."

Kyyrao ducked beneath a copper-clawed swipe that reduced a red bench to kindling. Powerful muscles in her legs and haunches bunched, launching her down two rows in a pounce that cut off one avenue of Haspian's escape. "If you had any brains, Loot, you'd not be clinging to its brawn."

She had a point, but I felt my energies were better spent maintaining my position than acknowledging the wisdom of her analysis. I felt certain there was a way to stop the Justiciar, and provided some time, I was fairly certain I would find it. A sudden reversal of its direction on the stands pitched me precipitously toward Justiciar's head and I realized my time would probably run out before the hydraulic horror would even begin to slow down.

I have to do something! I licked my lips, thinking furiously, then smiled. "Get the toymaster, Kyyrao, I've got his toy!"

Jamming a toe in a shoulder socket, I twisted around enough to slap the Justiciar on the back between its four shoulder blades with my right hand. I pumped a spell into the copper monster, then ripped my flesh free from the steaming patch of white and kicked free of the Justiciar's back. A shuddering twitch from the monster helped vault me higher into the air and propelled me further than I had intended on going.

It was probably just as well, since I flew safely above the courtyard's interior wall instead of smashing into it. I realized, as I slowly tumbled through the air, that the courtyard's sandy floor would soften my fall, though I did not expect it to be as gentle as my landing actually turned out to be. I also didn't expect the sand to say "oof" when I landed; it seemed somehow no stranger than anything else that had happened that day.

When I rolled clear of my landing spot, I realized the ground had not made any noise. I had landed on Haspian Chastoril, compounding the damage done to him when Kyyrao tossed him from the gallery to the courtyard. To be more specific, I'd cracked ribs on him when I hit, which would have been painful for him if he'd not already been unconscious from *his* courtyard landing.

Malkean dropped over the wall and Kyyrao crouched beside him seconds later. She straightened up, letting the Justiciar's head dangle from her right hand by a horn. Malkean appeared surprised by what she had done, but he shouldn't have. He knew her predilection for decapitating dead foes and the Justiciar *had* been after her at the last.

The marshal looked back up at where the Justiciar's body remained stiff-limbed like an insect caught by a frost. "What did you do to it?"

I held up my raw right palm. "It functioned through hydraulics, using a hot liquid to move the limbs. The taste of the liquid brought to mind Grover's hangover cure and the spell I almost used on it this morning. The spell chilled the Justiciar's main pumps, freezing the liquid, and it, in place. I also froze a layer or two of my skin to its back, but the exchange was worth it."

"I would agree." Malkean narrowed his eyes and turned toward Kyyrao. "After Loot tossed you the cameo, you went straight for Haspian. Scent?"

"Yes, which was what brought me here in the first place. I cut across Loot's scent to the east and came into town, then to the court here." Kyyrao's tail flicked and danced. "The cameo had only a few scents on it. You, Sopti, and Loot were there, but weak. Haspian was strong on it. He has spent much time with it."

"It could be that he discovered the cameo."

I shook my head. "He created it."

"What?"

"Everyone here thought his predynasty artifacts were poor forgeries, which led them to believe Haspian's artistic skills were limited and clumsy. He contributed to that idea and played the buffoon so he could trick everyone later. He created this cameo, and probably has a lot of similar pieces that he's put together over the years. He put my image on it because he wanted that to distract Sopti. If she authenticated the piece as being Tchoktan in manufacture, he could use that endorsement to legitimize an entire trove of forgeries. Then all he had to do was sell them and make a fortune."

I took the cameo back from Kyyrao. "The impressions I got from this brooch indicated I'd held it twice. Haspian had given it to Sopti, and she came to me at Grover's last night to show it to me. I probably pointed out to her that there was no way, no matter who I was, that I'd have been a priest of any stripe, war or otherwise. I may not know *who* I am, but the way I act and the things I do are clues to the type of person I am. In making his forgery Haspian had overstepped himself, and Sopti confronted him with that fact. She threatened to expose him and he killed her."

"But you couldn't have gotten that from the brooch since his scapegoat ritual would have destroyed all links to him."

"Right, that was the key. The brooch showed me nothing of the murderer." I took the Justiciar's head from Kyyrao and slipped the cameo back in the eye socket. "The impressions from the Justiciar showed me nothing of the murderer, either."

Malkean frowned. "I don't follow."

"The Justiciar bears no link with Haspian before last night."

"But he created it."

"Yes, twelve years ago, yet there is no link to him." I smiled. "The scapegoat ritual broke *all* links between him and other things prior to last night. The question was, why wouldn't he be connected to something he had created? The answer was that the links had been broken, which meant he'd performed a scapegoat ritual. Since the only image of him connected with the Justiciar came from today, that means his ritual was performed last night. He might have argued that he just happened to perform such a ritual last night by chance, but I think a search of his home will turn up other fraudulent Tchoktan items."

The marshal nodded. "Then the truthsniffer picked up on the brooch because, after the ritual, the impression you left on it was the strongest present, aside from Sopti herself."

"It would seem so." I shrugged. "Of course, my guilt was assumed by everyone because of the image on the cameo and the dire things it suggested about my past. Had Haspian not made it in my image, using my amnesia as a way to deflect people from a true examination of its origins, you would have had no suspect. Had he not involved me, I'd not have stumbled across the absence of evidence that proves him guilty."

Kyyrao squatted down and pressed her clawed hand to Haspian's throat. "The Justiciar cannot deal with this crime. I can, if you so desire."

"Thank you for your offer, Lady Grrenmw, but no."

A low growl rumbled from Kyyrao's throat. "Postponing justice rewards the criminal."

Malkean nodded. "I know, but until we find evidence of the fraudulent items Loot suggests exist—and I have no doubt that we will—only his word implicates Haspian. You could see how his denunciation of Haspian and your killing of him could be seen to serve Loot's interest."

I smiled at Malkean. "Framing an innocent man is just the sort of thing a notorious Tchoktan war-priest would do, isn't it?"

"Exactly."

I hefted the Justiciar's head up onto my left shoulder. "Come on, then, Kyyrao, let's head back to Grover's. We can mount this trophy on the wall and tell lies about how we got it."

She stood and her tail twitched. "We have no need for lies."

"Oh, but we do." I looped my free arm over her shoulders and steered her toward the street. "I don't think anyone will believe I froze it to death on a hot sunny day, all to prove a man was a murderer based on insufficient evidence of his guilt—including his failure to hunt mammoths with us last year."

Kyyrao frowned at me for a moment, then lightly cuffed me above the crow's-foot scar on my forehead. "That blow to your head did more than just steal your memory."

"Scrambled my brains, no doubt about it." I gave her a quick kiss on the cheek. "That's why, without you, I get into all sorts of trouble."

Kyyrao used no words in her answer to me, but in her purr I found sufficient evidence of all that really mattered.

FESTIVAL OF
SORROW

by

Robert E. Vardeman

Gormank moved slowly, huge muscles straining the blood-red sleeves of his shirt. Bent over, his knuckles almost dragged the ground as he moved along the shoulder of the road. From beneath heavy bony ridges peered two piglike eyes that betrayed no hint of intelligence.

"You, ogre," called the tall, well-built Benalish hero from the rear of a caravan filled with war wagons and handcarts pulled by scaly purple creatures of no obvious breed. "Come fetch my gear. I need a servant to carry a heavy load into yon city."

"Coraleon?" croaked Gormank. He ambled forward and shifted his mass slightly to keep a heavy cudgel dangling in the center of his back.

"Where else, dolt?" The hero reached into a pouch and tossed a few copper pieces into the dust at Gormank's hairy feet. "There. That ought to be pay enough for the few leagues we need to travel."

"Why Coraleon?"

The Benalish's handsome face turned dour. He inhaled deeply, his broad shoulders rising and his chest expanding. It failed to match the girth of Gormank's thick torso by a huge margin.

"I have fallen on hard times, through no failing of my own. My last fights were lost by others, not my fault, not at all, but now none will hire me. My life is blighted by the perfidy of others."

Gormank frowned as if thinking hard, his face turning into an ugly twist of flesh. One heavy hand lifted to scratch himself.

"You pay to get me into Coraleon?"

The Benalish hero's mood lightened and he chuckled. "Of course I shall, if that fine city and its festival interest you. Though what you would have to commemorate is beyond me."

"Festival?" Gormank held down a surge of fear. His plans might be dashed against the rocks of forbidden magic. He had not realized any festival was being celebrated this fortnight—certainly not in Coraleon.

He needed unobserved entry into the city if he was to do what was necessary. Gormank fingered the translucent blue disk held in the special pouch dangling around his neck. That magical artifact had been ripped from the gizzard of a giant flesh-eating crow and would serve as payment for a special task once he reached Coraleon.

"Come along, ogre, and take care with the large green box. The caravan to Coraleon leaves us far behind, and I am loath to spend a night alone in these woods. Rumor of a craw wurm nearby sends shivers up and down my spine."

"Some hero," grumbled Gormank as he shouldered the Benalish's belongings and settled box and pack on either side of his gnarled cudgel.

"Ha! You are the fool if you do not fear the wurms. They are ferocious creatures and will bring you only grief."

"Slew one last night," Gormank grunted as he began to walk, stumbling under the weight.

"What? You claim to have killed one?" The Benalish's eyes narrowed as he studied the ogre. "Where do you hail from?"

"Not slew one, *flew* from one. Last night. In deep woods. When I first laid eyes on it." Gormank studied the Benalish hero closely to see if the momentary slip changed anything. It did not. The Benalish was too caught up in his own concerns to notice. Gormank hoped such inattention would get him past Coraleon's gate guards, with the blowhard Benalish hero drawing attention from a *true* fighter and hero. Once in the city, he could find the wizard, Boxx, or at least Boxx's ghoul.

"Step lively. It is imperative we reach Coraleon soon." The Benalish strode off, not waiting for Gormank or noticing the ogre left the paltry few coppers in the dust, walking on the coins as he followed.

All afternoon Gormank struggled onward, bent over from the weight of his load. But he had little trouble keeping up with the Benalish or the others in the caravan bound for the distant city. Gormank's dark eyes widened a little when he saw the shining prize on the horizon as insidious twilight stalked the countryside.

Coraleon gleamed like a precious gem, radiant on the cliffs above the gunmetal gray ocean and promising him his heart's desire. She was there. If only time did not run away from him. Unconsciously, Gormank's stride lengthened and his back straightened. The ponderous load lightened as he became intent on reaching the gates of Coraleon.

He had to find Boxx and hire the wizard. Soon. So soon.

If only the oracle had not lied to him. If only . . .

"Hey, do not get ahead of me!" the Benalish hero called. Gormank immediately slowed and leaned forward to assume his role of humpbacked servant.

"Sorry," he said. "Saw city."

"Ah, fair Coraleon, once a prosperous port with a sheltered harbor until the very land swelled beneath its foundations. Such a battle that was! Now it serves as a beacon for those rounding Cape Tempest on their way south to warmer climes."

"And festival," prompted Gormank with his broken grammar. "What of festival?"

"It is a sorry plight to be unwanted by those you have served nobly and well. Left behind to fend for myself, no friends, nothing but endless empty road stretching before me. I might have spent my time at Grover's drinking away my sorrow, but no, I am made of sterner stuff. Take the future into my own hands and mold it to my liking! Yes, the festival will do much to lighten my mood."

Gormank grunted in disgust. He had wanted to learn more of this festival before arrival. All he got was self-pity from the hero. Assembling the knowledge and the bribe for the wizard had taken longer than expected, and now an unforeseen detail rose to thwart him. Out of the corners of his eyes, Gormank saw how pilgrims flooded into the city, coming from every direction. The accursed festival drew them like flies to a rotting carcass.

"Entry for one, dear lady," the Benalish hero called to the city guard. Gormank dropped the luggage and stared in anger at the tall man. He twisted, bringing the heavy cudgel to his hand. He would have crushed a Benalish pate save for the presence of so many guards from the city moving through the crowd of pilgrims to keep the peace.

"You have been paid well, ogre," the hero said, hefting the load himself and staggering through tall gates of the purest jade. He went on his way without a backward glance.

Gormank had intended to sneak into the city so that he could work unopposed and unobserved. The Benalish had dashed such hopes by drawing unwanted attention to him.

"You would enter Coraleon for the Festival of Sorrow?" came a soft voice.

"I would find someone within," Gormank said, eyeing the woman carefully. Dropping all pretense of being doltish, he knew he had to rely on his wits now. He tried to define her origins and failed. A slight greenish skin tone hinted at elven heritage, but her eyes were of a deep sea blue and her hair hung like fine strands of seaweed. A delicately boned hand with too many fingers lifted to beckon Gormank to one side. He vacated his spot in the line of people paying their admission to enter Coraleon.

"Is it a long lost love you sorrow for?" the woman asked. She straightened and towered above Gormank. Try as he might, he was unable to match her height, even by standing on his toes.

"I regret nothing," he said sharply. "I *will* find her."

"Ah, it *is* a lady. I thought as much." She moved, trailing a thin wrap around her slender frame. Gormank saw her in profile against the last rays of the sun. Another might have found her gorgeous. To a mountain ogre with different notions of beauty, she was only . . . graceful.

"Must I have a sorrow to enter?" demanded Gormank.

"You need only pay one piece of gold. If you truly sorrow for this lost love, I will be happy to advance you the coin." Shiny gold appeared from the thin folds of her dress. The coin flipped along the backs of her fingers in a controlled movement that hinted at even greater dexterity in other pursuits.

"I can pay," Gormank said, fumbling to show a handful of gold. He was mindful of the small pouch around his neck cradling the blue disk. Something warned Gormank not to reveal the magical artifact to his would-be benefactor. "I shall be no burden on the constables or innkeepers."

"You surprise me, Mountain Born. I had thought you indigent. Were you not carrying *his* luggage?" She inclined her head in the direction taken by the Benalish hero. A soft evening breeze from the ocean blew her fine green hair into a veil. Through her hair Gormank saw an impish smile and eyes like limitlessly deep pools of limpid water.

"Many here do not appreciate my kind. I had worried my greeting at Coraleon's gates might be somewhat sharper than open arms."

"In Coraleon, during the Festival of Sorrow, we permit all beings to exalt their sadness. I am Dolores, Lady of Sorrow. It is my duty to see that the pilgrims entering Coraleon examine their sorrow most carefully."

"What is this festival?" Gormank asked. His fingers tensed around the handle of his cudgel, anxious to get on with his quest to find the lost Eorra. Gormank remembered the prophecy of the oracle all too well. He had only until dawn to find her, or she would be lost to him forever. But first he had to find the wizard.

"In Coraleon we celebrate all the emotions, not merely love and joy. Those are important, true, but the other emotions refine, define, give texture to our existence. We have festivals of reverence for doubt and fear, as well as sorrow."

"A curious place," muttered Gormank. He scratched himself, finding a nit avidly chewing at his thick hide. He squashed it and flicked away the offending bug to stick wetly on the city's pristine wall.

"We ask that you examine your sorrow, not forget it or hide it under a stone, never to be seen again. It is a part of you, as is love."

"And hatred," mocked Gormank. "*That* is more to my liking."

"The Festival of Hatred was observed three months ago, at the end of winter," Dolores said, as if not noticing his irreverence.

"I have only to pay my admission and I shall be free to explore your fine city?"

"The Hymn to Tourach has been sung already," Dolores said, "marking the beginning of the festival. There will be three days more of observance and reflection."

Gormank chafed at this and what it might mean. "What of magic?" he demanded.

"No magic may be performed during the festival."

"And combat?"

"When we are called to arms, so be it," Dolores said easily. "Your scars attest to the fighting you have seen."

Gormank tensed his muscles, causing his shirt sleeves to moan in protest. Barrel chest shoved forward, he swung the cudgel about as easily as if it were a mere splinter. A single blow could have crushed the Lady of Sorrow's bones to powder.

"Such prowess," mused Dolores, "and yet you claim to have no sorrow locked within you even for your lady?"

"None," Gormank said hotly. "Anger, yes, and other emotions, but I regret nothing of my existence."

"You might consider remaining outside Coraleon's walls until after the festival," suggested the tall woman. Her eyes bored deep into Gormank's soul. "Sorrow might not seem important to you, but to many, including me, it is an essential part of existence."

"What do you regret? What causes you sorrow in the depths of night?" Gormank asked sharply.

"You may enter, though you claim not to feel any sorrow. Perhaps you can learn its value, Mountain Born," she said lightly, avoiding his question. Dolores pushed away the gold piece Gormank offered as admission. "Go into the city and seek the one you have lost."

"She is here," Gormank said firmly. "I know it."

The Lady of Sorrow said nothing as the ogre turned, pushed to the front of the line and strutted into the town on his bandy legs.

The instant Gormank passed through the jade gateway, he felt as if hundredweight stones had been piled onto his shoulders. He sagged under the palpable sensation of regret around him. Everyone he saw sported a somber look of introspection.

Such a course was not for Gormank. He had to find Eorra quickly. And the edict against magic only added to the feeling of uneasiness plaguing him. No magic might mean his trip—his life—would be for naught unless Boxx desired the translucent blue disk more than he feared transgressing festival rules.

"No!" he bellowed. "I will not be cheated again. I will not!" Gormank spun about, cudgel in hand, defying anyone to challenge him. No one even noticed his outburst, so lost in self-misery were they.

Gormank spat. Coraleon was beautiful on the outside and rotten within, with people abandoning themselves to wretchedness and regret. He refused to partake of those heady, self-consuming emotions. He had told Dolores he was not one to dwell on emotion. He was brave and strong and the best fighter in the land. Those were the traits he relied on, not pity of his condition.

The Benalish was taller and even handsome in his way, but Gormank knew the hero would fall to him in single combat, if they were ever to fight. Gormank was that good, that confident. The Lady of Sorrow showed agility and speed in her movements. Gormank was quicker. Battle after battle had proven that. Fast. Brave. Skilled. He had nothing to ache over during the long nights. Only one victory was lacking in his life, and that would soon be his because he did *not* wallow in regret.

Where would he find Eorra? That would be Boxx's quest—if only Gormank could find the wizard.

Slinging his cudgel over his shoulder, Gormank set off in search of a particular tavern in the ragged section of town that he knew was frequented by Boxx's ghoul. Small religious rites were conducted openly all around him as he walked, curiously shaped candles burning and filling the nighttime air with heady incense. He wondered if Eorra had ever smelled such fragrances and thought soft, loving thoughts. Or did such remind her of the coppery tang of blood spilled in battle?

Gormank's feet moved into darker quarters. A smile crossed his scarred lips when he spied a swinging tavern sign proclaiming this to be the Gutted Cockatrice. Inside the oak door he stopped and took a deep sniff of the air. The heavy incense did not penetrate this far. Stale beer and spilled ale mingled with charred meat and freshly baked bread. Eyes adjusting to the dimness, Gormank strode over to a table in the corner, rested his cudgel against the wall, and dropped a silver piece onto the table.

"Bring me ale and food until the coin is spent," he ordered. From behind the bar a one-armed Vodalian who once might have been a fighter nodded glumly. The food and drink came, and Gormank gave in to ravenous hunger. The Benalish hero had not given him so much as a crumb all day. To his surprise, both food and drink remained after sating his mammoth appetite. He pushed them away, belched, and rocked back on his stool to scratch himself. He studied the others in the tavern. Boxx's ghoul—or any ghoul—was nowhere to be seen.

Only when the tavern owner bellowed at the rear of the establishment did Gormank's interest build. Looking past the Vodalian to the alley beyond, he saw a murky figure clad in rotting garments being shooed away from the garbage. Gormank finished his ale in a single gulp, belched again, and grabbed what remained of his meal.

Leaving the tavern, he stepped into the street. Somber music floated on the increasingly brisk trade wind whipping down the streets. No one watched him. With sureness of purpose, he went to the side of the building, then ducked down the alley. It took only seconds for him to find the scavenging ghoul huddled in an alcove. Gormank stopped in front of the skeletal creature and tossed it the remains of his meal.

"That ought to be dead enough for you," he said.

The ghoul reacted with blinding speed, grabbing the haunch of roasted meat and swinging it at Gormank, intending to break his knee. Gormank lifted his leg from the path of the blow as he stepped forward. His huge fist crashed down squarely atop the ghoul's head. The creature jerked back, stunned by the powerful blow.

"The wizard Boxx," Gormank said. "Where do I find him?"

"He is my master, but what do you want of him? He is powerless during the festival."

"Is that your sorrow?" Gormank laughed. "That Boxx cannot use his magic to resurrect a good meal from the graveyard for you?"

"You mock me," grumbled the ghoul.

Gormank kicked hard. His bare foot might have been sheathed in heavy boot leather for all the power delivered to the ghoul's frame. The creature rattled as if made of nothing but bones hung together with wire.

"Of course I mock you," Gormank said hotly. "And I will rip you apart if you do not take me to your master."

The ghoul took a tentative bite at the bone thrown him. Then powerful teeth broke the bone, and the ghoul avidly sucked the marrow.

"More, and old, dead, decaying," promised Gormank, hunkering down so he could look the ghoul squarely in the face. Cold eyes that saw nothing but death peered back at the ogre. Gormank had found his source of information. "And something for Boxx." Gormank fished out the blue disk and held it carefully. The ghoul's eyes widened.

"Boxx," urged Gormank.

"This way," the ghoul said, never taking his gaze from the disk between the ogre's fingers. Gormank smiled. He *had* brought the right reward to find Eorra quickly.

Gormank shifted impatiently, the blue disk in the palm of his hand. The ghoul had brought him to a barren room. Only a simple polished iron-wood box on a table interrupted the dust and emptiness.

"I can crush the disk," Gormank threatened. "Where is—?" He swallowed hard when the container began to glow. Bright beams of green and red shot from colored disks on opposite sides of the box and bathed him in light. Somehow, although he heard no sound, he *knew* that the wizard was speaking to him.

"Yes," came the words that were not words inside Gormank's head. "I am Boxx. And you bring me another window onto your world. The blue disk. Insert it into the empty slot."

The container swung about under its own power, showing a gaping hole the precise size of the translucent blue disk Gormank held.

"No, no payment until you deliver the one I need! She . . . she is dead, an elf buried in Coraleon."

"Elf? One of two fine cemeteries, that's where she would be. Sometimes an elf is sent to one, sometimes to the other." The words boomed within Gormank's head until he wanted to scream. Dealing with wizards was never easy.

"But using your magic, you can find her, " prodded Gormank.

"True," said the wizard. "The casting is easy enough, if this elf is newly interred. While those of the burial guild might direct you to her grave for a huge bribe, they are thieves. You need someone such as I to direct you properly."

"Her name is Eorra," Gormank said, studying the container and the dancing red and green rays shifting about from the twin portals. "She was killed in a recent battle. I have only until dawn to resurrect her magically or she will be lost for all time." Gormank closed his eyes and rubbed his furrowed forehead to ease the throbbing within. The oracle was never wrong about these matters. Less than a day to pull Eorra back from the dead. Less than one day.

"Then truly will you have something to celebrate during the Festival of Sorrow," observed the wizard.

Gormank never paused as he sent his heavy hand crashing into the ghoul's putrescent face. He pulled back and wiped the defiled hand on his soft leather trousers. Black streaks remained wherever he had touched them. The trousers would have to be burned. Later. After he had dragged Eorra back from the grasping, cold fingers of her grave.

"Your ghoul will be destroyed first," Gormank promised. "Then I shall destroy this." He spun the blue disk in the air, catching it deftly. "Never again will you have the chance to add power to your already considerable arsenal of spells."

"I will not lie," Boxx said slowly. "The disk will enhance my power, but I am powerless at this time to help you."

"I will not let her perish forever, to lie dead in a grave!" bellowed Gormank. He lowered his voice and leaned closer to the wizard in a box. "Your magic will bring her back to life for me."

"The festival code prevents that!"

"Then we shall break the rules of the festival this night, after we find Eorra's burial site."

"You will protect me against . . . her?" came the wizard's unexpectedly timorous plea.

"Against Eorra?" Gormank laughed. Then he fell silent at the reply.

"No, not her. She is nothing but dead. You will protect me against Dolores, Lady of Sorrow?" Twin beams of light focused on Gormank, pinning him in place.

"This is not right," the ghoul protested. "It is almost dawn." The ghoul clutched Boxx to his bony chest.

"Four hours remain until dawn," Gormank said brusquely. He tried not to show his fear as they wandered through the cemetery, which was littered with tombstones marking the resting place of fallen heroes and villains. Each had a special story, Gormank realized, but he had no desire to partake of them at the moment. They would only duplicate what went on in Coraleon. The continual moaning and breast-beating in the city had lingered through the night. People of all races eschewed sleep to wander the streets, exploring the depths of their personal sorrows.

Gormank spat at the weakness of those fools. He felt not a shred of sorrow for anything. If a problem presented itself, he wasted no time lamenting what might have been. He worked to correct it. Battles were to be fought and won. It was that simple.

Looking around nervously, he tried to find Eorra's resting place. Amid the graves it was a difficult task finding the right one.

"There has been a fight recently," he said, more to hear his own voice than to bring forth any truth. The large number of new graves made it apparent a fierce battle had been fought.

"Good eating," the ghoul said.

"Silence," commanded Boxx. "I must use my powers sparingly to avoid drawing unwanted attention." The flashing lights from the iron-wood box darted into the murk, lingering here and there on tombstones and markers before flickering away in a hunt for Eorra's resting place.

"That way," the wizard said suddenly, the beams brightening through the two disks in the sides of his case. "Take me that direction." The dark creature with the tattered clothing hefted his master and made its way through the graveyard, dancing with practiced ease over the markers.

"Where is she among all the fallen heroes?" muttered Gormank, trailing far behind.

He jumped as a soft touch caressed his cheek. Grabbing at his cudgel, he spun, ready to do battle. His heart almost exploded when he realized he faced not a fighter but Dolores, the Lady of Sorrow.

"You think to find sorrow here, Mountain Born?" she asked in her deceptively sweet voice.

"I, uh—yes!" he blurted. Gormank dared not turn to see if the ghoul and his master remained in the cemetery. To be seen with a wizard able to conjure necromantic spells would alert the keeper of tradition for Coraleon's ridiculous Festival of Sorrow.

"There is a hint of magic in this cemetery," Dolores said, drifting around him, as if her feet did not touch the ground and the brisk sea breeze alone carried her about like an unconstrained balloon. "You would not break the festival covenant by a conjuration?"

"I am a fighter," Gormank said truthfully. "I command no magic of any import."

"The city fills with many who do," Dolores said lightly. "The punishment for violating the rules can be quite harsh."

"I am out for a stroll and nothing more," Gormank said lamely. Why did his mind and tongue tangle in Dolores's presence? He cursed his inability to find the right lies to soothe her suspicions. All he needed was a few more hours.

A few hours or Eorra would be gone forever.

"A curious place to take a walk," Dolores said. "You should return to the streets of the city and share sorrow with others. But I forget! You lack any sorrow. Perhaps you can take the load off another and help find accommodation with grief."

"A splendid idea," Gormank said. "However, I prefer to . . . meditate."

"Ah, yes, solitude helps," Dolores said. "I shall follow your progress with interest, Mountain Born. I have taken a fancy to you and your plight."

"Plight?"

"Not having any sorrow in your life is a true misfortune. It prevents you from soaring to the fullest heights of joy if there is no standard for comparison."

Gormank closed his eyes and sighed as the Lady of Sorrow reached out her long-fingered hand and caressed his cheek. When his eyes opened, she had vanished.

He spun about, forcing back a mixture of rage and curiosity. He could not find Dolores, but did see the ghoul eagerly scavenging a freshly dug grave. Gormank's short legs pumped as he hurried to the grave site. His cudgel swung about, and he lightly tapped the ghoul on the head, sending the rotting creature tumbling into the grave with its meal.

"If that is Eorra, you will die here and now," promised Gormank. He peered past the fallen ghoul and saw the body of a misshapen purple creature akin to those in the caravan entering Coraleon.

"What of the lady?" asked Boxx, his container on the ground near the open grave site. "She spoke with you. What hideous torture did she promise for violating festival statutes?"

"She seemed to take a fancy to me," Gormank said.

Boxx laughed, and it was the sound of the netherworld erupting. Gormank swung his cudgel again, this time stopping it just above the top of the wizard's container.

"Do not mock me," snapped the ogre. "I will not tolerate it. Now, find Eorra's grave and perform your diabolical ritual to resurrect her. Do it or I smash this to dust." He drew forth the blue disk. Somehow, magic now touched the glass and caused it to glow with an inner light. Gormank almost threw it from him. Only Boxx's question stayed his hand.

"You love her so much you would risk the wrath of the Lady of Sorrow?"

"She seems a gentle woman."

The wizard laughed, and this time it carried the shrill pitch of a creature close to insanity.

"She is anything but that. Dolores takes her duty seriously. Many's the fool who crossed her. Just a little spell, that's all. And whoosh! Up in smoke they go, their souls frozen in pain for ever and a day."

"Eorra," Gormank ordered. "If it comes to pass, I will tell Dolores everything is my doing. You will be held blameless."

"So be it, but I need the blue disk. Now, ogre, now or I order the ghoul to take me back to my quarters."

Gormank hesitated, then thrust out his hand with the precious artifact. The container spun about on its own, presenting the gaping aperture for him. The ogre realized he had to trust the wizard at some point—as much as any could trust those born to magic.

The wooden container vibrated and pulsed with raw energy when the translucent disk was dropped into place. Where there had been two beams, one of red and the other of green, now three played across the cemetery.

"How long ago did your lost love Eorra die?"

"A week, no longer. Rather, it will be one week at sunrise."

The prophecy had been precise on this point. If Eorra dwelt beneath her tombstone longer than one week, she would be consigned to the lower depths for eternity. Gormank experienced a moment's tightness in his chest as anxiety rose. He *had* to rescue her. He *had* to!

"She must mean the world to you for you to take such a risk," said the wizard in his words that were not words.

"Find her."

The ghoul grabbed up its master's container and scampered off, trailing gore from his meal. Gormank stepped away from the spilled blood and flesh and glanced around, thinking to see Dolores. The sensation of being watched proved strong, but he caught not a glimpse of the Lady of Sorrow.

A hound scenting its prey would have behaved no differently than the ghoul as it made its way in and out of fresh graves. The wizard's light rays touched the ground and seemed to bore holes in the earth, but every time Gormank thought Boxx had found the proper grave, the wizard ordered the ghoul onward. For an hour the ghoul snuffled and lapped and sniffed until Gormank's patience wore as thin as a whore's virtue. But when the ghoul stopped and the particolored beams focused into a single bright white spot on a small marker, Gormank was ready.

"This is her grave?" he demanded. His keen eyes read the elvish curlicues on the tombstone. Only after he translated the inscription did his lips move in silent tribute: *Eorra.*

"Your lost love," the wizard declared. "You *will* assume blame should Dolores discover us?"

"Yes, yes," Gormank said impatiently. "Now raise Eorra from her sleep."

"Almost sleep eternal," Boxx said. "I can feel such things."

Gormank dropped to one knee and delicately brushed away dirt from the tombstone. The dirt had hardened around the stone, showing it had been almost a full week that she had lain here.

"Perform your magic," he said. "Be quick about it." Gormank moved away, cudgel whistling restlessly through the air. He had no wish to watch the foul necromancy, yet it intrigued him. He tried to force his eyes past the ghoul and its master to the streets of Coraleon, where the festival-goers moved in solemn sorrow.

Gormank shook himself free of that and looked beyond, out to the limitless sea. All he had ever wished for was soon to be his. Perhaps afterward, an ocean voyage would be a fitting reward for his diligence. He shook off the notion. He was a creature of rock and mountain and cave. Resurrecting Eorra would be reward enough.

The almost audible spell twisted evil strands of magic through his brain and tugged, pulled, cut like a hot knife. A hairy hand flew to his eyes, shielding them from the brilliance dancing about the edge of the grave. Gormank steeled himself and widened his stance to prevent the rush of air out of the now open grave from staggering him.

The ghoul swayed like a willow in a high wind as he held high the box containing the wizard. Then somehow, Boxx remained suspended in midair, no longer supported by his foul servant. The ghoul's bony hands rose to challenge the night sky, then dirty talons plunged into soft dirt. A cloud of soil erupted into the air and a new layer of grave lay open. Delicate hands now showed.

Eorra, Gormank mouthed silently. His hand tightened on the cudgel. So close, he was so close to resurrecting her!

The spell built in intensity until Gormank shivered. He hoped Dolores was occupied with her duties at the festival. Even he, a fighter and not a mage of even modest ability, could feel the potent magic required to raise the dead.

The ghoul spun about, corkscrewing into the ground until its knees were drilled into the loam. A final spell by Boxx and the ghoul threw its hands upward and exploded from the ground like a skyrocket arrowing into the heavens. But the ghoul did not glow or explode. That was the province of the wizard.

Boxx's wooden vessel rivaled the sun in radiance, beams arrowing forth from the three colored ports in the sides to rip through the dark night. As Gormank watched, the eye-searing light died and the wizard's container lowered. The ghoul readily accepted the home of his master and protectively tucked it under his arm.

Gormank shifted his attention to the grave and the dirt remaining over Eorra. The soil blasted out in a sudden, fierce cloud. As it settled, Gormank saw the elvish woman sitting up in the grave, a dazed expression on her face.

"Eorra!" he cried.

"She is not as you knew her," cautioned Boxx.

"What do you mean?"

"She recovers from the malady of . . . death. It is never easy throwing off such damage. The longer in the ground, the harder it is."

Gormank knelt beside the still dazed elf and drew forth her weapons. The bow and arrow she had used with such skill—and her sword. That sword had taken a dozen lives and more. Gormank pulled it from the grave and thrust it into Eorra's hand. Mechanically, her hand closed on the hilt. She turned vacant eyes in his direction.

Gormank sprang back, cudgel ready for battle.

"Stand and fight!" he shouted. "I will kill you this time, Eorra. Twice before you bested me. Not this time. Not now!"

Eorra stood, sword dangling limply in her hand as if she did not understand its use. She stepped from the grave, stumbled, and fell to one knee.

"What's wrong with her?" Gormank moved around, ready to fight, thinking this another of the ferocious elf's clever tricks. Eorra watched him with eerily unseeing eyes. "She was the finest swordswoman in the land. She could kill anyone—and did. I fought her twice and twice came away with scars. No one else has ever come close to being my equal in battle. What's wrong with her?"

"The spell," moaned the ghoul, when Gormank advanced on it. "The resurrection spell. Let me explain!"

Gormank stepped up and shoved Eorra. She sat down hard, the sword falling from her hand.

"Will she recover her wits? Her strength and skill? What of them?"

"No." The wizard spoke, silencing his frightened assistant.

"What do you mean?" bellowed Gormank. "You say she will not!"

"The resurrection took much of her life force. For a lover, she need have little more energy than this. But for a fighter? She will be this way ever more." Colored lights of obvious warning flashed in Gormank's direction as the ogre swung his cudgel about. Gormank's anger rose like a new sun, but found no focus.

"I wanted her brought back whole. How can I kill her now? It would be a farce, a joke, a travesty! She was the best ever to swing a sword or shoot an arrow. Can she draw her bow?"

Gormank kicked away the elvish sword with its razored edge and placed bow and arrow in Eorra's hands. For a moment, he dared hope. She nocked the arrow and drew back—but only halfway. Her strength faded and prevented the full draw required for a kill.

"She is no good to me this way. I wanted to kill her! I had to. She is the only one who ever defeated me in battle."

Gormank sat heavily and stared at the elf. Some animation came to her face. Her cheeks developed roses as circulation returned to her once dead body, but he saw Boxx was right. Eorra would never regain the spring in her step, the sharpness of eye, the strength of her arm, or the flashing skill with her sword. Another had bested her in combat and robbed Gormank of his vengeance.

The ghoul whimpered as Gormank stalked past. Then, clutching the wizard's case, Boxx's ghoul rushed into the darkness to become one with the shadows. Behind him, the ogre heard Eorra's first words as she realized life once again flowed, albeit sluggishly, through her veins. Never would Eorra be a threat to any fighter. Gormank knew then his scars would go unavenged.

His pride was forever a crippled thing—as was Eorra.

Gormank whirled, his cudgel swinging up when he sensed someone nearby. The Lady of Sorrow stared at him with her unreadable blue eyes.

"You used magic to bring her back," Dolores said mildly.

"It was my doing. Any punishment to be meted out is mine and mine alone."

Dolores drifted about him, studying him from all angles. Gormank closed his eyes and wallowed in self-pity.

His eyes shot open to find Dolores only a few inches away. She touched his cheek again with her cool, teasing fingers.

"Poor Gormank. You came into Coraleon bragging you had no sorrow in your life."

"I do now."

"Yes, I know. I permitted Boxx to perform the resurrection."

Anger built inside Gormank, and he almost used his club on the Lady of Sorrow. He lowered his arm once again.

"Sorrow is neither good nor evil," Dolores said softly. "Study it, find its place in your life. Perhaps it will make you better for that knowledge."

"And if it doesn't?"

"Then I have allowed festival rules to be broken for naught."

"Would that fill you with dejection?" Gormank asked.

The Lady of Sorrow did not answer. She receded, as if flying away at a high speed. In seconds Gormank stood alone at the edge of the cemetery. From the city streets came the sounds of festival-goers examining their own lives and afflictions.

Sadly, sorrowfully, the ogre who would have been the greatest fighter, went to join them.

CHEF'S SURPRISE

by

Sonia Orin Lyris

The night sky was painted the sort of black that does not rest the eyes but instead brings to mind small chitterings, wet sounds, and nightmare's unpleasant spawn. Cold it was, too, the wind having picked up, hissing like a cat through the trees and promising to freeze the world before dawn.

Inside the tavern, though, a high, crackling fire burned at one end, filling the room with a warm, bright orange glow. Tables were scattered around the room and in every chair was a human. Mugs of ale and wine cluttered the tabletops, surrounding the cards and stones that were the game of choice on this long winter night. Laughs and curses and songs drowned out the wind's insistent howls, making winter seem just a little farther away.

The front door opened with a crash, pouring in stabs of icy cold air.

"Hey there," yelled a man near the door. "Come in or go out, but shut the cursed door . . ." His voice trailed off as he turned to see the newcomer.

The figure became solid out of the night's shadow, cloak snapping against the winds. He ducked to pass through the tavern door and stood there, tall and wide, blocking the door and making no move to close it.

At his side hung a sword nearly as tall as some of the villagers. His hands clenched and unclenched, fists as thick around as the mugs of beer popular at harvest. His face, twisted and lined as it was, with sharp fangs and pale red eyes, was unmistakably not human.

Except for the crackling and hissing of the logs in the firepit, the room was utterly silent. From somewhere, someone spoke aloud. Quietly, once, and with respect, the voice said what everyone was thinking: *ogre*.

Just coming out of the kitchen was Big Frenna, who would routinely remove large, rowdy men from her tavern by simply picking them up in her arms and dropping them into the mud outside. Now she paused at the door of the kitchen, took in the scene, and vanished back inside.

The ogre did not look friendly, but who knew what a friendly ogre should look like? While the wind's icy fingers cooled the room, the ogre's gaze swept across the villagers' faces, his fists still clenching and unclenching.

When he spoke his voice came slow and deep, like a growl out of a large cave.

"I'm looking for someone. The name is Asmor-ano-mar—" he exhaled frustration "—something." Into the long silence that followed he repeated, "Asmor."

A young boy made a small, whimpering sound. His older sister touched him, warning him into silence.

On the fire a log shattered and fell in. The sound would never have been noticed in the usual din, with songs and yells and howls of outrage at particularly lurid jokes. But now when the log fell, villagers jumped. And then there followed a sound that froze the blood of many. Those old enough to be veterans of the wars groped reflexively for weapons long gone, sold off, or left at home to rust as relics in this small, peaceful village.

It was the sound of metal being drawn, and taking a very long time to be done.

The ogre's blade point seemed to float in the air. Every eye watched. Were those bloodstains along the edge? One sweep of the long blade and the ogre could take the five people nearest him. Another sweep and it would be five more.

No one moved.

Then, from the back of the room came the sound of chair legs scraping against wooden floor. A small, slender woman stood, head up, eyes challenging. Beside her a brown-and-gray-haired man whispered fearfully at her, "Sit down, sit down."

"You," the woman said to the ogre, "have found me."

The ogre made a hiss, a sound of surprise.

"You are Asmor?"

"I am."

He nodded slowly, returned his sword to its sheath. As the sword sighed into the scabbard, an echoing sigh came from all the villagers.

"You," the ogre said to the woman, "are dead." He pulled a small, loaded crossbow from under his cloak, held it up, aiming high.

"Is that so?" she asked.

"Very dead. But first I want to talk to you about one of your recipes."

A humorless smile came to the woman's lips. "Oh? Which one?"

"Gray ogre toes in a sweet black sauce."

The woman's smile widened. "No one uses enough clove. The meat can be so gamy. The sauce makes all the difference."

The ogre howled his outrage and aimed the crossbow bolt at the slender woman. All those near her dropped to the floor, flattening themselves like rugs.

The woman began to laugh.

*　　*　　*

That summer's day so many seasons ago had been as warm and sweet as it could be, with soft breezes and deep scents of things quietly growing under a blazing sun.

With meadow grasses and yellow and blue flowers up to her knees, Asmor cut the air with loud curses. Then, hand to her temple, she mumbled, "By the thousand hells, my *head*."

"Too much for you?" chided a disembodied whisper in her ear.

She ignored the voice, shielding her eyes from the sun as she searched the sky in vain. She cursed the wind now, for having picked up at just the wrong moment, whisking away all her wasps.

Their buzzing was audible, but fading. Each of them was as big around as a man's skull, yet still they fled eagerly with the breeze. She had not thought them quite so bright.

Light, mocking laugher floated by her ear on the warm summer breeze. She felt a sick chill at the sight of the shattered remains of the wasp's hive, now a flat, crumpled mess on the green grass.

"Got you," came the whisper. "You're going down, Asmor."

She forced herself to snort, to sound amused. "Not yet."

"I shall invite you to respond, then," came the whisper.

Behind her was a large rustling. Another problem. This time her curses were entirely silent.

"You called me forth," came a voice so deep she could feel it in her bones, "with a promise to feed me."

Slowly she exhaled and turned. He stood far above her, muscle and sinew exposed, all twitching, pulsing, filled with some dark liquid. He was the sort of creature that didn't believe in skin. Or didn't need it.

Damn the sunlight and the breeze, and damn the whispering voice who had forced her to this moment.

"Greetings, Dark One. I am honored to be able to welcome you to my world—"

"You're not the first, little wizard. Don't bother with so many words. Where's my food?"

"It—got away, lord."

She was breathing hard. So was he. She from fear, and he from— anticipation, perhaps? Asmor tried not to notice how bad he smelled.

"You are in some trouble, little wizard."

"I know," she said quietly.

"Stupid little human. You should stay in your cities and play your stupid little games there. You shouldn't tangle with the underworld, human."

Asmor swallowed. "Yes, Dark One. You are right."

"Too late now. I ask you one more time: where is my food?"

She glanced around, desperately seeking something live that she could catch with what energy she had left. The wind tickled the meadow grasses and flowers, but nothing else moved. The wasps were gone, seeking out a new home somewhere else.

"Give me some time, lord—"

"I'm hungry now. There is no time."

"Surely there is something I can offer you, besides myself." She licked her lips. "You must be so bored with the same suffering, day after day. I can tell stories—ah, the places I have seen!—I can tell you—"

"I have all the stories I need. I like to watch small things suffer. Like you. Why else do you think I would allow myself to be summoned thus?"

"Ah. You are clever, great lord."

"And you are weak, little wizard." He chuckled, like the sound of rocks being ground together. "If I take what is rightfully mine, you will die. Am I right?"

"Please—"

"Yes, beg. You will beg and then you will die. Am I right?"

Her lips thinned. "Yes."

He smiled, revealing long teeth that dripped something sticky and brown.

Asmor brushed back sweat-dampened hair. "All right, no stories, great lord, but listen: I can turn spells, I can sing, I can weave five different kinds of rope braid—"

"I'm *hungry*."

"I can cook."

"You can cook *what*?"

"Anything."

"Ah," he said slowly. "Anything? Indeed?"

"Certainly."

"I eat a great deal. And truly, I grow bored, age after age, of the same food. Grub and potato stew. Pressed kittens. If you can do better than that—"

"I can. I'm an amazing cook."

His eyes seemed full of white flame as he stared at her for long moments.

"You may have won yourself a second chance at life, little wizard."

Asmor swallowed hard, forced herself to keep meeting his gaze.

"What are you offering?"

"Anything is better than death, is it not, human?"

"Many things are better than death. I want to make sure that what you are offering is one of them. *Before* I accept."

He laughed, and the sound echoed in the ground below her feet.

"You are brave and foolish. You had better cook very well for all that nerve, little wizard. Here is the offer, then: seven years and seven days you will be mine. For that time, all that time, I expect to be amazed. If a day goes by in which I am less than amazed, I will eat you, rather than what you have prepared."

"That doesn't seem quite fair."

"No, fair would be for me to kill you now, since you failed to keep your part of the bargain."

"I had food for you, lord. My wasps escaped."

"That is your problem. And this is your choice: life as my chef, or death as my dinner."

Asmor rubbed her head, which ached terribly, and gave a long sigh.

"I think I'm going to regret this."

"Do you accept or not?"

"I accept."

He spread his wings a little and tilted his head back, showing the skinless muscles of his neck.

"Fish is good," he said. "I've always liked fish. But I'm sick of elves and dwarves and goblins, and as for humans—" He turned his glowing eyes back on her. "I can eat humans. But I abhor asparagus. You should be taking notes, human. Are you ready to go?"

Asmor took a long look around at the green meadow, the flower-speckled hills beyond, and the blue sky above. She inhaled deeply the smells of summer. It could be a very long time before she would know summer again.

"As ready as I'm going to get."

The scratching at her door turned into a click as the latch was turned, then a creak as the door was pushed open. Asmor grumbled, wished yet again for a lock or a binding spell. She rolled over in bed, pulling the thickly woven blankets up over her head.

"Mistress?" came the all too-familiar voice, always irritating, even now, when it was soft.

"Go away," Asmor said. "I'm not awake."

"But you *sound* awake, mistress," said the voice, gaining both confidence and volume as the door opened all the way. Two sets of long claws dragged across the floor.

"Mistress, we hate to disturb your sleep, but the Dark Lord, he—"

"He's hungry," came the second voice, equally irritating. "He wants an early breakfast."

Asmor summarized her feelings on the matter into her pillow.

"She doesn't wake easily," said the first.

"Not at all," said the second.

"Shut up," said Asmor.

They were silent. Asmor sighed, sat up in bed, and regarded the two naked, pinkish-winged creatures in the wan light that sufficed for daylight, here in this strange land which the natives called "our lord's domain."

One of the imps was slightly older and a bit larger. He had more veins shot through his translucent wings, making the wings a deeper shade of bruised violet.

"I would think that after a year here it would become easier for her to wake up, wouldn't you?" the smaller one asked, wings folded back, leaning toward its older companion.

"I would think so."

"But apparently not."

"No."

"Learn to whisper, imbecile pests."

"Yes, mistress," said the first.

"Yes, mistress," said the second.

She threw the covers back, got out of bed, and stood looming over them. They looked up with bright eyes, their long ears twitching with uncertainty.

The Dark Lord had assigned them to her, so they called her mistress, but there was never any question in her mind who they were really loyal to.

Irritating, they were definitely that.

In the year since she had arrived, she had learned a great deal about cooking. Indeed had learned most of what she now knew, specifically about cooking for the Dark Lord. She had found out how much variety he liked and how much he could stand, and she always walked a careful line. Lastly, she had learned that to the Dark Lord a meal always meant meat.

Fortunately, meat was everywhere.

She turned to her dresser, pulled out clothes, and began to dress.

"Imp stew," she said thoughtfully. "No, no. Not enough taste and too stringy. Maybe I could use it to fill out a cream of serpent soup. Or use shredded imp wings as a garnish for tonight's merfolk fillet."

The imps glanced at each other then back at her.

"Perhaps we should leave you to dress, mistress."

She gave them a hard smile and pulled on a sock. "Good idea."

"She doesn't wake up easily at all," the first said as they scampered out the door.

She hurled one of her boots at the closing door.

                              *   *   *

The door to Asmor's room opened slowly.

"Is she gone?" asked the younger imp from behind as the elder crept into her bedroom.

"Yes. Gone to the kitchens."

"Well, it's hardly surprising she has such a temper, I suppose. Didn't she used to be a mage?"

"So she says."

"Yes, and now . . . well."

"Yes. Well."

The elder imp began to open drawers in the dresser while the younger one flattened himself against the floor and crawled under the bed.

"Dirty socks," he said. There was a ripping sound. "There are worse things than being her servant, I suppose."

"Much worse." The elder imp scooped out a glittering rock from a drawer, held it up to his eye, then put it in his mouth, crunching loudly.

"Not," said the imp, voice muffled from under the bed, "that our Dark Lord is anything but the finest lord."

"Indeed, the finest lord any creature could hope for."

"I would sing his praises every moment of my life if I were only free to do so."

"If we had not been assigned to serve her."

"Our lord is great, is he not?"

"Yes, and very powerful."

"More powerful than Asmor, certainly."

"Certainly."

The younger imp pulled himself out from under the bed, unfolding his wings and shrugging his shoulders. A strand of sock-colored twine hung from his mouth. "Have you heard her talk about how the wind shifted that day?"

"I have."

"Do you think that the wind could really have prevented our great lord from overcoming her?"

"Of course not."

"She says she had the sun in her eyes, when she was battling our great lord. Sun! Can you imagine having it in your eyes?"

"I would never battle our lord."

"Nor would I. I would sing his praises every moment of every day, if I could."

"I would not even sleep, so that I could sing more," said the elder. "If I was only free to do so."

The younger imp pulled out a pair of underwear from another drawer. The elder pulled it away from him, ripping bits loose with his teeth. The younger one pulled out another pair.

"It's hardly surprising she has a temper, I suppose," he said, as they both chewed. "If she used to be a mage."

"So she says."

"But our lord is much stronger, or he would not have been able to enslave her. Isn't that right?"

"Yes. I'm glad that our lord is so much stronger."

For a moment they both paused, looking at the shreds they held in their hands.

"But she does have a temper."

"Yes."

"We'd better not eat them all."

"No. We'd better not."

"Cubed Pegasus," Asmor said, announcing the dish. "In red sauce. With a dragonfly garnish." Behind her two serving ghouls carried steaming dishes into the great dining hall.

She stood to one side of the door as the ghouls stepped into the room and set the dishes down on the long table. At one end sat the Dark Lord. All along the sides sat his guests.

A more disgusting, slimy, and rancid mix of beings she could not imagine. She used to summon creatures like this. It was a bitter thought.

"Basilisk eyes in Jasconius paste," she added.

The ghouls removed the covering platters on each of the dishes. One of the guests, horned, fanged, and blinking an extra set of eyes, was drooling onto the table in long, thick strands.

"And great wurm soup with basil."

A shadowy shape at the end of the table turned to the bald man next to him and said, "I hate that fishy taste. Can you eat this stuff? I can't. Wurms just taste like fish to me. I hate fish."

Asmor pretended not to have heard.

"And for dessert," she said as more dishes were squeezed onto the table, "Frozen Sprite Delight with chocolate sauce."

There were exclamations of happy anticipation as everyone reached for their dessert. Asmor struggled to keep her expression neutral.

The Dark Lord gave her a warning glare. She was sure that she had not even cracked a grin, but sometimes he could tell. She nodded at his unspoken command, though she was unconvinced his guests would notice even if she laughed outright at them.

Asmor retreated to the kitchens, put her hands over her mouth, and allowed herself the laughter she had been denied. Underworld creatures took themselves so seriously, but after seeing them eat, she found it almost impossible.

The skeletons who served as her staff were moving around the room, casting flickering lines of shadow against the grimy walls. When she had first arrived Asmor had directed them to scrub the walls for hours until she was finally convinced that the stone itself was made of mold and dirt and gave up. Now one of them was wiping up a spill on the floor while another pulled a large pot from the stove and put it in the sink.

At least the place had running water.

"Hey, what are you doing?" she yelled at the drudge, backhanding it away from the pot.

Their expressions never changed.

"Cleaning, mistress," it hissed, wind through bones.

"Well, stop it. That's dragon foot marinating for tomorrow night's feast. You know how expensive that stuff is? Idiot."

"Yes, mistress," the drudge wheezed, turning away from the pot.

She grumbled, heaved up the big pot, and put it back on the stove.

Even so, aside from having kitchen help with the intelligence of— well, of skeletons—having to live in this particular one of the thousand hells wasn't so bad. Indeed, over the three years she had been here, the worst of it had been the boredom. Planning meals simply didn't take that long. She ended up with hours each day to do nothing.

She would never admit it to him, but she found herself looking forward to the Dark Lord's visits to her kitchen after feasts like this.

After a while the lord's guests were invited into another room for a show. Tonight's entertainment consisted of a double cage, one side of which held starved sprites, the other side bits of flowers and aromatic herbs—just the sort of stuff that the little creatures craved. Separating the cages was a dryad with a small hole drilled through her navel. The hole was big enough for the sprites to see their goal, but not big enough to get through. Yet.

Asmor sighed and mentally began planning tomorrow morning's deep-fried dryad bark, which would be pounded into pancakes, then doused in thick maple syrup. And if the sprites left any leaves, she could add stuffed dryad leaves to tomorrow night's dinner.

But not as a main course. The key was variety. The Dark Lord got testy if he ate too much, too often, of any one kind of critter.

Now her drudges were standing around, motionless.

"Get out there and clear the dishes. And I don't mean onto the floor this time. Bring them back in here."

They moved, sluggishly at first, then faster as she growled at them. Two bounced into each other, clattering against the walls as they tried to get out of the kitchen.

There were just no two ways about it, you couldn't get good help in Hell.

When the Dark Lord at last strode in from the other kitchen's entrance, Asmor was struggling to teach the drudges—yet again, they were constantly forgetting—how to wash dishes. His wings brushed the kitchen's high ceilings and swept the floor, his bulk nearly filling the room. The drudges folded themselves into corners, confident that Asmor would not object to their idleness while she was engaged with the Dark Lord.

He looked around, his eyes glowing in the flickering light.

"Another fine meal, Asmor," he said, his voice like the sound of small rocks being pressed for a strange wine.

The howl of a banshee echoed distantly off the edges of the room like the sound of a knife being sharpened on stone, only much louder and an octave higher.

"Can't you control your creatures?"

He gave her a strange look. But then, all his looks were strange. "I like the sound. I find it relaxing after a fine meal."

She glanced at the dishes in the sink, all of them picked clean.

"No leftovers again. Your guests are pigs, Vincent."

"My guests have a good appetite, chef. Yes, another fine meal. How do you do it, human?"

"Desperate fear," she drawled, stifling a carefully planned yawn.

He grinned, or at least that's what she thought it was when he showed so many of his teeth all at once. Or perhaps that was the expression he used to frighten his prey into submission.

"Come now, little chef. You have a special way with food. When I first brought you down here, I had no idea what you were capable of. I admit that I thought you were lying about being able to prepare edibles. I assumed then that you would say anything to save your little life."

"I would have. In fact, I did."

He brushed away her words with a gesture, long claws leaving traces in the air. "You made good on your word. I am pleased with your efforts."

She shrugged.

"Come now, chef, can you not find it within yourself to even say, 'Thank you, lord'?"

Asmor made a thoughtful sound as she picked a bit of horse meat from between her teeth with her nails. She was considering becoming a vegetarian.

"I don't remember making a deal that included my groveling to you, Vincent."

"And a good thing, too. You're lucky you're so good with food."

"Of course I'm good. I'm still alive."

"And will be as long as you keep doing such splendid work."

"I live in fear," she said dryly.

"It's a shame I can't eat you for lack of respect."

"How you must suffer. And besides, who would prepare me? I'd be stringy, tough, and quite bitter, I assure you."

"I believe you. And it would be a shame to lose your fine cooking. Not quite worth the satisfaction. But I must tell you, Asmor: I do worry."

She snorted, took the bait. "About what?"

"About what I will eat when you are gone. In some four years I'll have to find myself another chef. Clearly I cannot go back to the tripe to which I have, by your hand, become unaccustomed. Perhaps if you were to somehow record how you make those dishes of yours, it might save me effort when I begin to train my next chef."

"And save some chefs their lives as well, maybe."

"Indeed. Have you considered recording your recipes? I would be happy to provide you with materials. Quite durable materials, ones that are only found in the underworld. It would be a testimony to your prowess."

A cookbook. That could, she reflected, be a fun way to use her free time while she was stuck in this dark servitude.

She made a doubtful noise. "It sounds like a lot of work."

"I will assign ink imps to write for you. All you need do is dictate."

Ink imps. She had seen the strange creatures, regurgitating black goopy stuff onto their flabby bellies and then dipping pointy nails in the foul stuff to scratch words on vellum. Or whatever. Idiots they were, good only for translating speech into little scratching sounds.

"I will need twenty."

"Twenty imps? What for?"

"I'll write you your cookbook, lord," she said, pointedly using his title, "but only if I can have twenty copies made. Then I'll sell the extras and keep the profit for when I get out of this hellhole."

He considered, then nodded. "I accept."

"I'll start on it when I feel like it."

"Some might say, 'Thank you for your generosity, my lord.'"

"Doubtless."

His lips pulled back again, revealing long, sharp teeth. "Another fine meal, Asmor. I look forward to a breakfast to rival even this feast."

She met his glowing eyes. "You'll have it."

"I am sure. And tomorrow night I'll have a handful of demons as guests. Something tasty, chef."

"Barbecued throat wolf ribs with corn bread and baked beans."

His eyebrows raised. "Throat wolf? How did you manage that?"

"Almost anything can be had for a price, Vincent."

"Very true. I shall look forward to it. Good night, chef."

"Good night, Vincent."

Under the wan midday sun, in the Dark Lord's domain, tucked away in a crevasse halfway up the side of a cliff, sat two imps crouched over a small bag of swamp slugs.

The elder imp picked up a slug, pressed it tight between sharp, long nails. The slug contracted, trying to fold itself. The imp put it in his mouth, teeth squeaking as he chewed.

"Do you remember," the younger one asked as it fingered a slug idly, "when she was working on a sesame hydra salad, chopping up the mushrooms and pecans, and the baby hydra slipped out of the cage and tried to make a run for it?"

"I remember," the other said, mouth full of white slug meat.

"The thing never even went into the pot. There wasn't enough of it left when she was done with it."

"I remember."

"Asmor certainly knows how to use sharp knives, doesn't she?"

"Yes," the elder said crossly. "I said that I remembered, didn't I?"

"Sorry." The younger picked out a slug, held it up to his eye, sniffed it once, and put it back.

"Do you think Asmor will be very upset?"

The elder took another slug, grunted, tossed it down his throat, swallowed. "About the books not selling, you mean?"

"Two of them sold."

"In five months."

"That's not good, is it?"

"No."

"Then Asmor will not be pleased?"

"I doubt it."

"Will she be, quite, quite upset, do you think?"

"I fear so."

"Who will tell her, do you think?"

"Not I."

"Well, not I."

"Neither of us, then."

"It is not our task to tell her, is it?"

"I hope not."

"Someone will tell her, though."

"Someone will have to."

"But not us."

"I hope not."

"If Asmor finds out, she'll be furious, won't she?"

"I think so."

The younger imp let go a sigh. "I'm tired of swamp slugs."

"I am, too."

"Asmor will be expecting us soon, to wash her clothes and polish her boots. Should we be getting back?"

"Yes." The elder imp reached for another slug, wrinkled his nose, shut his eyes, and put it in his mouth.

"Perhaps," said the younger, "just a little while longer?"

"Yes," said the elder, swallowing with distaste and reaching for another. "A little while longer."

There was a bad moon out tonight, so the Dark Lord was in a fine mood. Which was fortunate, because Asmor was not.

She stood at the kitchen counter, punctuating every word with a squeezed lemon as she lectured two ghouls and a drudge.

"You are idiots. Half the babies are sick, the others are dead and rotting. There are two—*two*—carcasses that I can use. You know how many of your Dark Lord's ravening, disgusting guests that will feed? I should use you instead."

They watched her attentively. Fearlessly. She wouldn't use them, of course; they had no meat. Sometimes she suspected that the Dark Lord had arranged for just such help so that she would not be tempted.

She hurled the lemon across the room, where it bounced off one of her imps, who had just scraped into the kitchen, its wings folded tightly into a shield.

"These," she said through clenched teeth, "are lemons." She took a deep breath, forced herself to calm. "You squeeze them into this bowl here. *Not* onto the floor like last time. Understand? No seeds, no pieces of lemon rind, and no mud. Wash your hands *first*." They all stared at her blankly. "*Now*."

They moved sluggishly toward the pile of lemons. Asmor turned back to the counter and started mincing sprigs of mint furiously. Maybe if she used enough mint in the sauce, the Dark Lord would not remember that he had had Ghazban ogre tenderloin just last night.

"Mistress?" came a small voice from behind her. Small and insistently irritating. And deferring. Too deferring, and that meant that something was wrong, and she didn't need it, not tonight.

"What?"

"Perhaps we should come back later," the first imp said.

"Yes," agreed the second. "We will come back later."

She rounded on them, knife in hand, fury threatening to boil over inside her. A spell almost came to her lips, but she swallowed it. The Dark Lord would not forgive her if she used her mage's abilities in his domain. He could afford to be quite vindictive in his own realm, with his power greater than she could hope to match.

"I do not have time for your little impish games. Tell me fast or I'll make you the main dish tonight."

The imps paled, eyes on her knife.

"Your mother bought one," the younger imp blurted out, taking a step back, right into the elder imp, who put his hands firmly on the younger imp's shoulders, holding it between him and Asmor.

Her mind was still half on the meal. Would the lemon sauce clash with the stronger taste of the ogre in mint? Would the Dark Lord's guests notice? *He* would, and that was what mattered. Maybe more marjoram on the Benalish babies.

"What?" she asked the imps, trying to understand.

"The other was bought by our gracious lord," said the elder imp from behind the younger. "That's all. In six months, mistress, no other cookbooks were sold."

"You," she called to a drudge. "Check to see if we have any Vodalian caviar left." That would hold them for a little while. "And just *look*, don't touch anything." She looked back at the imps. "My cookbooks haven't sold?"

"No, mistress."

"But—why not?"

"We don't know, mistress."

"Perhaps because most cannot read, mistress?"

"Imbeciles! Half-wits! I don't believe it! All that work, all that effort, for *nothing*?" With a cry she hurled the knife across the room where it sunk deep into the wall.

Every creature in the kitchen froze. Asmor stood a long moment, clenching her now empty hands into fists. Finally she turned a coldly furious gaze on the trembling imps.

"Burn them," she said quietly. "Burn every one of them."

"Mistress?"

"Which word don't you understand? Aren't your ugly ears big enough already? Perhaps I should stretch them." She reached past the knives for kitchen clamps.

"We'll burn them. Of course, mistress."

"As you say, mistress."

"*Now*."

The imps scrambled over each other to get out of the room. The ghouls and drudges turned empty stares on her, their hands falling limply at their sides.

"Bone stew," she said simply.

They turned back to their lemons.

Tonight the Dark Lord dined alone. Since it was a smaller meal she saved herself the trouble of dealing with kitchen help and served him herself.

"Atog paté on honey-soaked ironroot bark," she announced.

He frowned, looked suspiciously at the dish.

"It's only the liver, lord, which is quite edible. It's the rest of the critter that tastes like sawdust and grease."

Or so the imps had gleefully told her when she had given them pieces to taste the day before. At least nothing went to waste around them.

She put down another dish. "Crisped Serra angel wings, breaded with crumbled bees. Shanodin salad."

"Ahhh, and dessert?"

"Sugar-frosted cockatrice giblets in marionberry sauce."

"Ahhh."

He began to eat. Asmor backed into the kitchens, beginning to clean. A short while later the Dark Lord joined her.

"A little over a year left. My time with you grows short, Asmor."

She smiled. "It sure does."

"I shall miss you, Asmor. More than I can admit."

"I wish I could say the same."

"I've always liked that about you, how you don't show me false respect. You've done good work, you know, chef."

"Yes, I know."

"And no false modesty. Admirable."

She glared at him.

"Good meals. No—fantastic meals, Asmor. Year after year."

"You will understand if your praise does not mean to me what it does to your many subjects."

"Of course, little human."

"I will not be your little human for much longer."

"No, indeed. Have you given thought to what you will do after? You could stay on. I would pay you well."

She brushed her trousers, trying to get rid of the black dust that seemed to be everywhere down here. "You could not pay me enough."

"I thought you might say that." He picked up a small, hard pod from a bowl. "What are these?"

"Pepper berries. For cheddar and dragon egg omelets. Tomorrow morning's breakfast."

The Dark Lord made a happy sound through his teeth, his lips pulled far back, showing a hungry smile.

"Breakfast. What a lovely word."

The deepening twilight cast fuzzy shadows across the two imps in the cliff's crevasse. Together they crouched over a small bag, not full of swamp slugs this time, but of envelopes. They watched it fearfully, as if it might move and bite.

"Do you think Asmor will be in the least bit flattered?"

"No."

"But didn't she want the book to be popular?"

"Not in the overworld. Not, I think, to be shown about by a zealot as an example of the wickedness of the underworld."

"She will be very upset, then, you think?"

"I think so."

"Surely it was not our fault that the line to the incinerator was so long that day."

"No, surely not."

"And not our fault that the garbage chute spat the books up into the overworld."

"No."

"Or that the books were not even singed from the molten lava."

"We could not have known."

For a moment they were both silent, staring at the letters in the bag. Then the elder imp reached in and pulled out an envelope which he held between long nails. He turned it over, his eye up close to the vermilion circle of wax.

"The imperial elven circle," he said. "Perhaps Asmor will be flattered after all."

"Do you think so?"

"No." He put the envelope back into the bag, took another. "The dwarven high council."

"Do you think, if we give her the bag, she'll figure out what happened?"

"Yes."

"Perhaps she will be forgiving."

"I do not think so."

"Then what shall we do?"

"Perhaps Asmor does not yet have need of these missives."

"The post is often delayed, is it not?"

"Often. Sometimes long delayed. When her time here is over she may be in a better mood. Perhaps then she will find the attention of the overworld lords flattering."

"Perhaps under the sunlight of her own world she is a sweet and for-giving woman."

"Perhaps we should bury the mail now, for safekeeping."

"Here?"

"Unless you feel that we should give it to her."

"I do not wish to."

"Nor do I."

"Then you think that Asmor can wait for these letters?"

"Yes," said the elder imp, beginning to scratch a hole in the back of the cave. "I think Asmor can wait."

Asmor surveyed the room where she had slept, woken, and dressed every night for seven years and six days. Was there anything here worth taking?

A knock came at the door. For the first time the Dark Lord entered her room, his wings brushing the high ceilings. There was a good reason that all the ceilings in the palace were so high.

"Tomorrow's dawn comes quickly," he said. "Are you ready to end your stay in my domain?"

"More than ready."

He looked around the room. "All packed?"

"What is there to pack? I came with the clothes on my back."

"I have had clothes fashioned for you during your stay. Don't you want to take any of them with you?"

"They all stink of hell and are full of dirt that never comes out."

He nodded. "Yet you went through them quickly. I never knew humans used up clothes so fast."

"They kept disappearing. Maybe my imps were stealing them."

He made a thoughtful sound. "Asmor, I want to say, about the cookbook: I am grateful. Your book will save me from eating slime muck when you're gone."

She snorted. "If your underlings had your taste I might have sold the rest of them."

"You were just aiming at the wrong market, little human."

"What?"

He laughed a moment, then sobered, staring down at her.

"You would honor me to stay. I could make it worth your while."

She snorted, shook her head. "I doubt it. And why should I want to stay here in this disgusting little hell, which is just one of many, many disgusting little hells?"

"Do you think to soften my heart with flattery, woman?" He chuckled. "But consider: even my disgusting little hell could provide a great deal of power, both in underworld and overworld, to my reigning queen."

"Queen?" She looked up at him, let her gaze fall all the way down to his feet, each longer than her forearm. She looked up again. "What are you saying?"

"The offer will not stay open long."

She exhaled. "Vincent, I— Really, that's very—"

He smiled wide, showing many sharp teeth. "Am I about to hear appreciation?"

Asmor scowled. "—very stupid of you. An overworlder ruling an underworld. Of course I refuse."

"Of course. For a moment I feared that you might show me some tenderness. I am reassured."

"You could let me go tonight."

"And miss my last meal? My last chance to find you wanting? I think not."

"Of course not."

"And what will you be serving me for my last meal, little human?"

"Tonight—Hurloon tartar with horseradish."

"You remembered how much I liked that," he said softly. "I am touched."

"Don't be," she said, more harshly than she intended. "And I've prepared a few jars of Takklemaggot jam for you to have on your toast, in the mornings after I'm gone."

They were both silent for a long moment.

"Will you join me for dinner tonight, Asmor?"

"As a guest or main course, lord?"

He chuckled. "Depends on how tender the minotaur is."

"Then I'd better make the horseradish extra strong."

"To cover the bitter taste of human?"

"So you won't forget me. One way or another."

"Not much danger of that. And now I will leave you to your preparations." He strode to the door. "Oh, I have something for you. My demons came across it last month." He held out a small, dirt-covered bag.

"What is it?"

"A bag full of letters. Addressed to you. A little delayed, I'm afraid, but I think you'll find them interesting."

The road was a dusty, lazy companion, leading her past long stretches of golden fields and lush orchards. Asmor inhaled the smells of summer, of fruit and vegetables, of farms and dust.

She had taken off her shoes and tied them over her shoulders along with the bag of letters that she had yet to open. These things could wait, wait for the bright day to wash away her memories of the dark world and the sentence she had just finished serving.

In time, she reflected wryly, she might even come to view that service with fond nostalgia, remembering the great Dark Lord and his appetites, the irritating little imps who had at the very last seen her off with a shy wave and wishes of good luck in her next job. Whatever that meant.

She rubbed her sunburned nose, adjusted her new hat. She had traded a magic flea ward for new clothes a few villages back, exercising her mage's energy again after so long.

But for now it was enough to simply drink in the scents of the overworld, to taste the sun's hot touch, to feel the ground beneath her feet. She could not imagine anything, not even the occasional stone that bit into her tender feet, or the pain of her red nose, disturbing these sweet moments.

A shadow passed over her, then passed again, larger. She looked up.

The creature was slate black. It drifted down as if it were a feather finding the ground and not a winged animal made of stone. She had never actually seen one fly before, had never imagined that they could land as gracefully as birds.

Once landed, the creature stood before her, tall enough that she had to look up. When it spoke it was with a deep, whispery voice.

"Are you the one known as Asmoranomardicadaistinaculdacar?"

It was rare to find one who knew her full name, let alone who could pronounce it correctly.

"Yes."

"I have a bone to pick with you, chef."

"Oh?"

"Your cookbook has made me a hunted delicacy. I have had to destroy whole parties of orcs who had been erroneously informed that my flesh was worth more on the plates of the high courts than on my own bones. This is not good; I have other things to do with my time. Listen: my brothers and sisters and I are not happy with you or your book, chef. I am going to kill you."

"What? But that doesn't make any sense. All the extra copies of my cookbook were destroyed, years ago, by my . . ." She trailed off, then swore.

There was a sudden sound, like stone cracking. Shadows danced across her face.

Asmor ducked down, hard and fast. Where her head had been passed a gargoyle's paw, not once or twice, but three times, each successively lower and much too fast.

She rolled away on the ground and snapped up to her feet. She dove her senses deep, seeking her magic, but the spells wouldn't come. It was the wrong place, the wrong time, or she was just plain rusty. She might be able to call up a wind, but not much more.

"Wait," she cried out. "Let me explain."

"No explanation is necessary. We want you dead."

She desperately tried to recall what she had written about gargoyles in her cookbook.

"This isn't what you think. Let me explain—" Breathing hard, she jumped back as the gargoyle's paw cut air again, missing her by a finger width. "Have any of your kin actually been caught?"

"That is not relevant. We do not appreciate being advertised as food."

"By the moons and the thousands hells, *wait*. That recipe wasn't meant to be taken seriously."

At least not by overworlders. It had never been meant for over-worlders to see at all.

"Explain."

"It was a joke, damn it. Not serious. Do you really think there is a carving implement in the world that can cut through your flank?" She had had one in the underworld. They were quite rare.

The gargoyle paused.

"It was," Asmor went on, pursuing what she hoped was an opening, "intended to put other chefs to shame. Because they could not hope to make the described dish. You see? To put the high houses to shame. I never thought that they would actually try to prepare honey-baked breast of granite gargoyle."

That much was true. She herself had only done it once. It hadn't been any fun.

The creature cocked his head at her, stone eyes blinking slowly.

"It was a *joke*," she repeated. "What high house has eaten gargoyle? None! But they will keep trying." She forced herself to laugh. "You see? It's hilarious. What fools!"

"They disturb our matings and frighten our young."

"By now they are surely convinced that preparing the dish is impossible. They are probably so embarrassed that they will never set foot in your mountains again. You know how ground-dwellers are."

"Foolish and cowardly."

She swallowed. "Exactly. I may even have helped you, by putting the fear of your kind into them."

"That I doubt. Foolish creatures like you do not learn."

She held her irritation in check. "Yes, of course. Exactly."

After a long moment he said, "Accepted. You may live. But if you are lying, if our kind are sought again, we will come after you, my brothers and sisters and I. And the next time we will not let you change our intent with clever words."

"I understand."

As he leapt, his wings cut the air with the sound of the wind through high mountain crags. Only when he was a small speck on the horizon did Asmor let herself exhale.

Without question it was time to practice her magery again, to remember how to find the power when she needed it.

And, she reflected, glaring at the bright sun, this might also be a good time to open her letters.

The only noise in the tavern was Asmor's chuckle. On the floor the villagers trembled in silence.

"You're not the first, you know," she told the ogre. "I doubt you'll be the last. You might think about that for a moment."

The ogre growled quietly. "My brother has no more toes, because of you."

"I don't think you have that quite right. I've never even met your brother."

"Just because I'm big doesn't make me stupid, chef."

"Who actually cut off his toes, then?"

"It doesn't matter."

"I think it does. Don't you want to know who is picking off the meat from your brother's large toe bone, dipping it in sweet sauce, popping the tasty tidbit into their mouth, and reaching for another?"

The ogre's face was turning red.

Asmor's smile vanished. "It's not my fault that you're food. We're all food. And it's not my fault that I can make you taste good." She glanced around the room at the villagers on the floor and those sitting in their chairs, seemingly frozen with fear. "I can make anything taste good."

"Make yourself taste good."

"It's been suggested a number of times. Indeed, I appear to be a favored meat among some overworlders these days. Someone is writing a cookbook with recipes that only feature me."

"*I* would eat you *raw*."

"You would have to catch me first. And frankly, despite your size and obvious intelligence, I doubt you could."

The ogre let loose a deep howl of fury, his hands tensing on the crossbow. Suddenly the air around the bow shimmered. He yelped in pain, dropping the bow to the ground where it smoked, charred black.

Asmor rubbed her head, mumbling, "There has got to be a better way."

The ogre launched himself at her. Villagers threw themselves against each other to get out of his way. Those nearest the door dashed outside. The rest tried to become part of the walls.

Big Frenna peeked her head out of the kitchen again and pulled back.

Asmor held up her hand and the ogre was back at the door, as if he had never moved. The few villagers still left in the tavern froze again, trembling, eyes wide.

"Ah, by the moons, my head. Listen, ogre, believe it or not, I sympathize with you. Being hunted isn't any fun. There just isn't much I can do."

"Give my brother his toes back."

Her lips curled. "I'm only a mage. I don't do regeneration."

"Then I want *your* toes."

She gestured with a hand and the ogre tensed for a moment.

"Look here, ogre, I'm going to tell you who's eating your brother. It's the goblin princes, the dwarven high council, the aristocracy of the sea. Even the elven conclave has offered me a job as court chef. Don't you understand? The world has gotten fat and bored. My cookbook is the latest entertainment. You want vengeance, ogre?" She shook her head. "I'm the wrong target."

He growled. "I want those who have eaten my brother's toes to be hunted for their own toes."

Asmor's eyebrows raised. "Do you, now?" She cocked her head at him. "Now *that's* something I can perhaps help you with."

Motioning at a nearby table while the last of the villagers slipped out the door, she said, "Why don't we talk about this over some ale?"

"I will not drink with one such as you."

"Suit yourself. Frenna," she called. "Bring out a couple of ales. You're safe, woman, and I need an ale. I need it, you understand?"

The ogre pulled up a stool and sat down gingerly, as if he were afraid the small bits of wood and nails would not hold him. In moments Big Frenna came out with two large mugs, set them down, and left.

"I don't know why I'm even talking with you, chef."

She sighed. "I understand you being upset about the gray ogre dish. But the real problem is those who are making my book popular, who are not, coincidentally, listed as main dishes."

"Why not?"

"Because the Dark Lord was sick of them. They were standard fare for so many millennia that he would rather have eaten swamp mud, and sometimes did. This is part of why those races' civilizations have succeeded so wildly over the last hundreds of years, I suspect. In any case, I think I can help you achieve your goal, but you're going to have to help me, too."

"Why should you want to help us, when just a little while ago you were cooking us?"

"Everyone is food," she said wearily. "And I'm getting tired of fighting rocs and dragons and gargoyles. Sea journeys are entirely out of the question these days." She rubbed her head. "I'm a little too popular for my own good."

"But—" He looked back at his smoking crossbow on the floor. "You're a mage."

"And your brother is an ogre, big and powerful, and now he hasn't got any toes. No one is invincible. There's always a way to take someone down; it's only a matter of time. Listen, here's what I'll need: get together as many of the other 'main dishes' as you can, and prepare yourselves to go around to all the big cities. You'll be selling a new book which I'll arrange to have delivered to you when I'm done writing it."

"A new book?"

"I suspect it will sell very well, but I'm prepared to split the profits with you to make the deal even more attractive."

"*What* new book? I don't think I want to see you writing anything new, chef."

"You will want to see this one, I'm certain. It's a cookbook with some new recipes, ogre. Very new."

He made a thoughtful sound. "What, like maybe 'elf toes in green sauce'?"

"You have the idea. Or perhaps goblin cobbler in sauce of 'most sincere' zealot."

He began to smile.

"I think," she said, "that when *The Underworld Cookbook, Volume Two* hits the great houses, your toe problems will be over."

He was nodding.

"Will you drink with me now, ogre?"

He laughed. "Oh, yes, I will drink with you now, chef."

FOULMERE

by

Stonefeather Grubbs

The thatched roof of the Naturalist's shack was barely distinguishable from the gray-brown grassy islet it was built on. Though accidental, the effect pleased him. He felt as invisible as a thrush in the brush.

The Naturalist ... it was not merely what he was, it was *who* he was. Nearly everything he did anymore was a matter of function, not personality. His calling had become his identity. Only occasionally, and only with a few, was it otherwise.

It was a chill, rainy morning. Weather like this always made him a little wistful. It had been on such a day one autumn long ago when ...

No, let the past sink into the sediment of time. Let old sorrows lie to decompose slowly in the muck.

The slender elven fingers smoothed the blank sheet of homemade papyrus as he turned his attention back to the present. Before lunch, he would catch up on this week's cataloging, and then this afternoon ...

The knock on the door startled him. The only visitors he usually ever had were the Eub Hlut, and they never knocked. In keeping with traditional Eub Hlut manners, they would stand silently and wait for him to come out (if they knew he was in, and they always did. Come to think of it, he always seemed to know when they were out there, too.)

So, a foreigner, then, and more than that. ... He set his cup of spicebush tea carefully down on his wickerwork desk, but before he could reach the door, it was thrust open from without. Very bad manners indeed.

The traveler's clothes were journey-stained, but of good cut, middle class. Human. Meaning to pass for a merchant, maybe. A handsome gray cat paced back and forth in his wake.

"Do I have the honor," the traveler began, "of addressing Dr. Peter Langwynd, late of the university at—"

"You do," the Naturalist snapped. "As well you know that you know, sorcerer!"

"No, no, my good doctor," the man protested. "I am a trader, a simple, honest trader, and I come in search of—"

"Rare herbs, exotic lore, yes, yes ... I have heard all the standard deceptions, planeswalker! It was to get away from your sort that I left Akkat's golden domes and marble boulevards, to never see your decadent kind again that I extinguished a most distinguished career. At the university, yes. Don't remind me: always the regents insisting my studies serve the end of practical commercial exploitation of nature, yes, that was bad enough! But being probed by prying necromancers seeking new metaphysical linkages for no nobler purpose than their insane, infernal warfare. . . . I mean, is that something they teach you in sorcery school? Find the most civilized place on a mostly uncivilized world, find somebody at the former who's made a career of studying the latter, grab a teat and suck? After twenty years I could take it no more! And so I came hither to the Fens of Foulmere, to devote my remaining days to pure research."

The traveler's expression, at first a seething mix of vexed and perplexed, relaxed at last into a generous chuckle. "Well done, Dr. Langwynd! But how did you know? Am I that poor an actor I cannot personate an ambitious entrepreneur?"

The Naturalist shook his head. "This swamp is inhabited by a primitive but stealthy people called the Eub Hlut. I believe them to be descended from the wood gnomes of ancient Havenwood, displaced centuries ago by the pestilent thallids that disrupted, and finally vanquished, the sylvan communities of that halcyon epoch. At first but a desperate refuge, the swamp little by little became their home, where nothing now moves without their knowledge and consent. You could not have penetrated this far into their domain, unmarked and unscathed, without the aid of enchantment; nay, more, a quality of spellweaving well beyond the shoddy magics of common practitioners confined to a single plane."

The traveler nodded. "Yes, I see you know something of We Who Walk Between, beyond mere legend and glamour. It is easy to forget, I will admit, in this rustic, dank, forlorn morass, that you actually hail from a somewhat more sophisticated land: Akkat the Mighty, Citadel of All Knowledge. Not even a whistle stop in the larger scheme of things, believe me, but neither is Akkat completely bereft of lore. That is how I came to be there, where in casual converse with one of your forsaken colleagues, your name came up as a repository of vast and obscure learning, exactly as I desire."

"And exactly what I have no desire to provide you!" the Naturalist shot back, wondering who at the university had betrayed him. Then with a jolt of startled discomfort he remembered his own casual mention of the Eub Hlut. Evidently, some sort of charm was at work here, lurking in the man's dissembling patter.

The wizard frowned. "But if you know so much, you know that your life is at my disposal."

"I said I didn't want to," the Naturalist replied coldly. "I never said I wouldn't end up doing it anyway."

The traveler grinned and stuck out his hand. "Vram's the name. And this," he glanced toward the cat, "is my familiar, Mao."

"Yeah, right," grunted the Naturalist, and walked toward the door.

The clouds were already breaking up as Dr. Langwynd sat on his porch bench to pull on his hip waders. "You'll want to conjure yourself up a pair of these," he remarked to his unwanted guest. "It's pretty messy out there. And I'd appreciate your not meddling with the weather, thank you."

"A little rain more or less won't harm anything. And you do have a boat, I see." Vram looked distastefully out over the bleak prospect before them. "You really do like this place, then?"

"It's all the home I have," the Naturalist said, scowling. "But yes, I do like it. It is so full of life! Yes, I say life, though you see only death. But it is shot through with life: abundant, varied, beautiful. Oh, yes, snicker away, Lord Vram! It is not flashy, like a garden, titillating to the casual glance. It requires a close, long, and most of all, *intelligent* kind of looking to see the intricate interactions, the rich but subtle harmonies. But even a layman like you, if you saw it in high spring—"

The Naturalist gasped, Vram chuckled. It was suddenly full spring, the sun blinking merrily in a clear sky. Every shrub, tree, and water plant was in full flower, every bird on wing and singing. A bedlam of color, a rainbow of sound.

"Stop it! Turn it back! You fool, don't you understand a violent change like this could kill them?"

Vram looked disgusted, snapped his fingers, and autumn returned. "Very well, but no rain till I leave. And," he glared sharply, "you are never to call me a fool again!"

The Naturalist nodded helplessly. "Let's get on with it."

Vram seated himself in the punt as Mao, his cat, sprang into his lap. The Naturalist stood in the stern and poled them out into a shallow channel that emptied into a wide pool covered with duckweed and lily pads.

"Is this the part of the fen where the . . . the Yube Lute, I think you called them, live?" Vram blandly inquired while Mao, the cat, peered warily from the bow at the gurgling black-brown water.

"Yes," the Naturalist said, nodding absently, "though of course they are familiar with and make use of all its sections." *Curse all this sneaking spellcraft,* he thought, catching himself.

"This section of the fen would naturally be their preferred habitat, as it is of all that is backward and stunted," he hastily dissembled, in hope of shifting the mage's attention away from the Eub Hlut. "You see, Foulmere is really several places all at once, converging around the many-branched mouth of the Kron Lu River. This area, for instance, is a shallow freshwater swamp, wet but fairly open, where bog and marsh intersperse with shrubs and small trees: willows, alders, and the like. The slow-running outermost channels north and south of the delta are like this, an interlacing of small streams, struggling to find the sea, backing up into stagnant pools or joining into large ponds like this one. Ah, look there, a heron! Wading beside those cattails. . . ."

"Dr. Langwynd, I appreciate the lecture, but I'm afraid I haven't paid my tuition," the bored Vram interrupted. "What I want from you is something of practical use in the magical battles I am forced from time to time to wage. Mao! Get back from the edge of the boat!" The cat obediently returned to its master's side, making the Naturalist suspect that the animal really was a spirit familiar and not just a glorified pet. "He didn't mean real cat's tails," Vram whispered to the animal. "It's a kind of tree, I think."

"Further in, where we are heading," continued the Naturalist ruthlessly, "the channels of the Kron Lu run deeper. The lands to either side of them are dry enough most of the year to support larger trees: moss-covered oaks, lichen-clad cedars. . . . It is a dark place, in many ways, and not even the Eub Hlut venture there after nightfall. There used to be a lake, many years ago, that was blocked off by accumulating debris from lands to the west, where the forest was being cleared for lumber and farmland. The lake gradually became a huge peat bog, while the river carved itself a new channel several kilometers to the north. We will be there in an hour or two. Now off to your right—"

"I am tired of this," Vram announced. He made a motion and the boat was lifted up out of the water and above the treetops. Mao gave forth a yowl that sounded more like a sound of glee than terror. Vram smiled serenely at the Naturalist (whose stomach wasn't quite sure where it wanted to be right then) and said, "Just think about where you want to go."

The Naturalist looked around to get his bearings. Yes, there, where the swamp gave way to tidal marshes, sandbars, and finally the ocean, that was east. He mentally turned the boat starboard and piloted them through the sky, south toward the very middle of Foulmere Fen.

Ten minutes later, the punt settled gently down onto a thick carpet of sphagnum moss. Big Bog *was* wide—fortunately, as the dense brush surrounding it would have been impossible to land the boat. Normally, the Naturalist would have pulled his vessel up in a marshy arm of the new channel he'd mentioned. From there he would have slogged through the muck, bashed through the bulrushes, ripped his way through the black-berry brambles, et cetera, then hiked nearly a kilometer through a wide belt of thickly wooded land, just to reach the spot where the enchanted craft had set them down so easily. He was a little sorry about that, because his teacher's instincts didn't want this to come so cheap for his pupil, an easy study but a slow learner if ever there was one. But nothing, seem-ingly, could be rendered arduous to a planeswalker, and to his thinking, that in itself was the nub of the problem.

The Naturalist climbed out onto the spongy peat. The cat leaped nim-bly out beside him. Vram gazed dubiously down at the moss. "You're sure this will support us?" The Naturalist rolled his eyes, and then jumped vigor-ously up and down a number of times, which set the whole surface to bob-bing like an All Hallows' apple upon the pool beneath. Mao looked startled, but then began hopping, too, as if it wished to try the trick for itself.

Vram climbed awkwardly out, clutching frantically to the gunwale for support. Apparently, the wizard had no Disembark spell to assist him. The Naturalist smiled, then snapped his features back to a neutral aspect as Vram turned round to regard him with obvious scorn.

"What," he asked, sweeping an arm emphatically around, "do you expect me to do with *this*?"

"Not *this*." The Naturalist shook his head and pointed to a large lump at the edge of the bog. "That!"

As Vram stared, his boredom and annoyance gave way to curiosity, and at last to recognition and awe. "It looks . . . like just a big lump in the moss . . . until you recognize the shape for what it is. By Gemini, though! It's by far the biggest I've ever seen, and I've . . . well, been around. . . ."

"Over four meters long," the Naturalist recited, "three wide, and two high at the shoulder. *Rana palustris giganticus*: Big Bog Frog."

Vram looked thoughtful. "I want a closer look at this."

"I wouldn't get any closer than this, Vram. Hold onto your cat, too. She's cold-blooded, naturally, and thanks to your weather meddling, she'll be a bit more active than she would otherwise. She is one of about only a dozen that live in the bog here, though they wander around elsewhere in the fens from time to time. There is a related subspecies, *Rana palustris familiaris*, the Common Bog Frog, which, despite its name, is found only in Foulmere. Now, I am investigating a hypothesis that—"

"Dr. Langwynd!" The Naturalist looked startled. "What can it *do*? Does it jump?"

"Yes, but generally not very far or high, owing to her great bulk. It's really more of a waddle."

"Then what—?"

"Let's get out of sight. Then you can pretend that you are a naturalist like me. You can watch . . . and wait . . . and hope that something happens. . . ."

Vram looked disgusted, but decided to play along . . . for a while. As they waited by the bank in the shade of a large water oak, he began to notice that the Naturalist was right, this place *was* full of life. The mosquitoes were annoying, large, and thirsty, but there were dragon-flies and butterflies in abundance, as well. The plant life, too, was far more varied when one sat still than it appeared to the preoccupied glance. The hodgepodge hedge of trees encircling the bog hosted as many kinds of birds. And something else, small, moving about in the peat . . .

But after a half hour of this, Vram began to suspect he was being made fool of. Then he gasped as an instantaneous feathered bolt from the blue struck the bog and carried away a squirming bit of brown fur about six inches long. "Marsh hawk, bog lemming," the Naturalist whispered. Then there came a strangled screech as the airy predator vanished sud-denly into the mouth of the Big Bog Frog.

The Naturalist beamed proudly. "Her tongue is a marvel. It has a reach of over six meters. Fast as a rattlesnake, strong as a python. I've seen her and her kind take down hawks, ducks, cranes, herons, and once even an osprey."

"Oh. Certainly." Vram looked thoughtful, then smiled. "That will do very nicely. I'll take it. Mao! Stay with Dr. Langwynd."

The cat rubbed itself against the Naturalist's legs and whimpered in alarm as Vram calmly approached the gargantuan amphibian. He hummed a low mesmeric chant, while the frog made noises of helpless anxiety as, little by little and contrary to all instinct, it fell under the planeswalker's enchantment. By the time the wizard rested his hands upon the creature's lowered forehead, it was utterly vanquished. The trail was blazed, the gate-way opened.

A peripheral glimmer of motion caused Vram to glance at his feet, where he saw his familiar, with the legendary curiosity of its species, pok-ing a tentative paw at the cold flesh of the Big Bog Frog. "Mao! I told you to stay— Oh, damn!"

He whirled around in alarm, scooping up the cat and carrying it over to where his disgruntled guide waited. "You! Hold onto Mao for me," he snapped, thrusting Mao into the Naturalist's arms. Then Vram went bounding across the bog, setting the whole surface to rocking beneath him. The Naturalist was startled to see him transform . . . see *her* transform . . .

And Mao lay caterwauling in his arms until, at some indeterminate moment, the sound turned into the sobbing of a frightened child.

"Heyah, Pete! Wha' gives wi' guy not guy no more, huh?" Perched on the Naturalist's shoulder was Peft, the Eub Hlut's chieftain since the first of the month and for the next few days until the New Moon Lots. "An' who's kid in ya lap use t' be cat?"

"Bigger's a magicker, a *dobéhm*, magicker," the Naturalist answered in the same dialect, "an' this-un be her daughter, betcha." He had never heard of a *dobéhm* being a planeswalker before. But the world was so full of things he had never heard of that it didn't particularly trouble him.

He watched Vram's suddenly long, lavender hair streaming back from her butterscotch-colored face as she ran toward the middle of the bog, where now another figure stood, white robed, golden haired, black faced, streaming with pearly light. The Naturalist shook his head and looked down in his lap. There lay a young *dobéhm*, about five years old.

The most notable peculiarity of the *dobéhma*, besides their unique coloration, was that they were a race of women and girls only. They had no known homeland, and traveled hither and yon across the continent, usually singly or in mother-daughter pairs, more rarely in adult couples, or with two or more daughters. They were little trusted and eked out a living as best they could among many peoples, from among whose males they found mates, though seldom husbands, and so renewed their generations.

Legend has it that during the brief dark age that followed the collapse of the ancient Sarpadian civilization, diligently carrying the torch of ignorance and privation through the land until the Ice Age arrived to finish the job, there was a particularly cruel Neo-Ebonic priest-king named Vetro, a man so vicious that he was held by some (himself included) to be Tourach reincarnate. He was finally murdered by his slave-wife, Dobeh. To ensure that his evil seed should not endure, she also killed their sons (whom she thought of as his alone) and fled the land with her daughters. It is said that Vetro then placed a curse on her from beyond the grave:

Maize and lilac stain thy seed,
And may it only daughters breed;
Thou shalt give sons to no man other,
While mine lay murdered by their mother.

Modern skeptics debated whether a lack of male offspring was the result of a curse or a continuing tradition of infanticide. The Naturalist felt sure that enchantment played some part, at least, in the *dobéhmi* makeup. According to the heretical experiments of the mad Mendil a century before (with whom the Naturalist secretly concurred) there was no heritable trait, such as their distinctive pigmentation, that could in any natural way pass exclusively and invariably down a given female lineage. Despite this, the *dobéhma* transmitted the stain of "maize and lilac" from mother to daughter perpetually. Therefore, if this impossibility were nonetheless so, wouldn't it be idiocy indeed to implicate every member, without a single known exception, of an entire race of humanity, however small, in a practice sickening even to contemplate?

The *dobéhm* child was weeping against his belly, so he hitched her up into more of a sitting position, turning her toward him so she wouldn't see the combat. He rocked her and whispered words of comfort as he watched her mother do battle. Several creatures had been conjured on both sides now, and the air crackled with lightning bolts, brimstone, and fire. "It will be all right," he lied. "I won't let anything hurt you."

The little girl looked up at him and saw Peft eyeing her curiously. The crying stopped, and her eyes grew very large at the sight of the Eub Hlut hunter, barely eight inches high, with the tiniest bow and quiver she had ever seen. "What is that funny little man?" she asked. "Can I pet him, will he bite me?"

"Actually, he is a she. Her name is Peft, and she is a person like you or me, so you should really ask her about the petting business. But if I were you, I would ask to shake hands instead."

"Do you want to shake hands with me . . . Peft?"

The Eub Hluta considered briefly and offered her hand. "Please meetcha."

"I am Peter," the Naturalist said. "Is your name really Mao?"

"*Name* is a word for who somebody is?"

The Naturalist nodded. The child deliberated. "I don't think Mao is the really word, but it's the only word Mommy will tell me till I get bigger. There is a really word, but only Mommy knows what it is."

The Naturalist wondered if this was a *dobéhmi* custom or just a manipulative game of the mother's devising. "Is Vram your mommy's really word?"

Mao laughed. "Mommy has lots of words. Vram is her word for telling to people when she thinks she'll prob'ly kill them when she's done using them . . . unless she changes her mind."

"Does she usually change her mind?"

The answer was barely audible. "No."

An unpleasant shiver ran down Peter's spine. "Well. Mao, do you understand what your mommy is doing out there?"

"She has to fight the bad trickers. The bad trickers make us have to leave all the time, unless Mommy can beat them. She makes tricks, too. She gets the juice and she makes the tricks with the juice."

Peter nodded. Mana. "Your mommy calls it juice?"

"She doesn't call it anything. That's just what I call it, 'cause I think it's like juice is in fruit, only this juice is from way down in the ground."

"Can you see the juice?" He'd had a few encounters with planeswalkers himself, and found he could tell when one was drawing mana from the earth, like a sixth sense. Even from the edge of the bog, he could feel the twinges coming faster and stronger now as the battle out on the heaving peat progressed.

Mao nodded. "Not really *see*, but I don't know how else to 'splain it. I like the spicy juice best. You get the spicy juice from the woods, where the animals live, and I like animals."

"I like animals, too, Mao. I try to learn all I can about them, and how they like to live." A sudden appearance out on the sphagnum battleground caught Peter's eye, and he cringed. *No, Vram, one doesn't conjure mammoths onto a bog.* . . . With a gulp and a belch, the mighty creatures broke through the peat mat and sank into the lifeless depths beneath, carrying with them a half a dozen screaming goblin warriors. Mao hugged tight to Peter's neck.

"Pete, heyah!" cried Peft, just as a particularly powerful mana surge tingled him to the marrow. "Wha' gives, huh? Whoah!"

"Huah! Wha' matter, Peft?"

"Whoah? Don' cha feel, boy? Stupid magicker pullin' skooker outta fen!"

Pulling out the skooker? Peter knew that *skooker* came from the actual Eub Hlut language, of which he knew little, and that it seemed to mean both "dream" and "memory" at once, but was probably really a mental state unique to the Eub Hlut. It was the closest they had to a concept for "soul," though in fact a very different . . .

Pulling the skooker out of the fen!

He felt the blood drain from his face. He gasped, shook his head in a daze. "This is very bad."

Mao patted his cheek comfortingly and whispered solemnly, "I know. I hate it, too, when she does bad tricks with the stinky juice. But she has to do it, or the bad trickers will get us."

"Yes, I hate it, too, Mao. I hate all the tricks. But your Mommy has just done something so very foolish and dangerous . . . to her, to you, to me, to Peft—"

"Hey!" cried Mao, distracted by the sight of something back behind him, over his shoulder. "What happened to the big froggy?"

Peter could see the answer straight ahead of him. The Big Bog Frog had popped from out of nowhere into the midst of battle. She looked half dead, a woozy mass of migraine and dyspepsia. Peter sympathized, remembering the feeling of transport shock. He imagined how it would be for her, the enormous tongue lolling inside her mouth, suffocating her. As if on cue, she let it flop out onto the moss and gave voice to a violent croak of agony.

"Peft callin' archers!" the chief of the Eub Hlut declared in outrage. The archers of the Eub Hlut would have been much feared if anyone had ever lived to tell of their prowess abroad. Their skill with the bow was mostly employed in hunting large game (such as marsh sparrows and bog lemmings) and in keeping a check on Deep Foulmere's population of the animate undead. Against more normally corporeal intruders, they had arrows tipped with the poison that flowed through the pulsing veins of other vile things that dwelt in the further depths of the dark mire.

"No!" warned Peter. "Ya shoot magicker, even poison, she getcha by skooker!" Any attack on a planeswalker could, in theory, establish a metaphysical linkage that could later be keyed, just as the frog's had been. The Eub Hlut had never before attracted the attention of the mana benders, and Peter wanted it kept that way. That, he explained to Peft, was why he had led Vram away from their habitations in the outer marshes and into the Deep Fens, where he had hoped to satisfy her with the frog.

"But bogfrog she fen chief!" objected Peft.

Yes, the Eub Hlut, when they drew lots each new moon to choose a new chief, also randomly chose one kind of plant or beast to be the symbolic chief of the fens. Or, at least, Peter thought it was symbolic, just as he thought the lots random. But the shrillness in Peft's voice made him uncertain. He had felt guilty himself for offering Vram such a rare species, but it was the only thing he could think of, besides the Eub Hlut, that could have satisfied the mage. But he knew something that neither Vram nor Peft could guess.

"Don' cha fret, gal! Fen take care its own chief, betcha."

Yes, as long as there *was* a fen. . . .

The Big Bog Frog was jerked and jolted into action. Although she'd only just had lunch, she had a sudden nonhunger urge to snap up that odd flying creature heading more or less her way. *Zip-plook!* Soon the air was empty of Scryb sprites once again.

The little girl in Peter's lap, bored with a conversation she couldn't understand, was squirming around, trying to see the battle. *Oh well,* Peter thought, letting her look, *it's not like I'd be shielding her from something she's never seen before. . . .* Like that was any excuse.

"Ooh! I never saw that tricker before! He's making his bad tricks with spicy juice, and squishy juice, and shiny juice. Mommy uses the squishy juice, too, when we play dress up and I get to be a animal if I want to, like today, or when she wants to talk nice so people will help her. And she uses the shiny juice to make me better when I get hurt."

"And when she fights the bad trickers?" Peter prompted.

"Then she uses the spicy juice . . . and the noisy juice . . ." Her voice dropped to a shamed whisper. "And sometimes, the stinky juice."

"She gets the stinky juice from places like this?" Peter asked, beginning to get a feel for the child's self-made nomenclature.

"This is a stinky place," Mao agreed. "After Mommy uses the stinky juice, she gets angry at herself, and says she's bad for doing bad tricks, and she'll never do it anymore. And then she sends all the bits of the stinky places away, and I tell her she isn't bad, 'cause she's the bestist mommy in the whole worlds."

Though nearly as heavy as a mammoth, a Big Bog Frog interfaces the sphagnum with nearly fifty times the surface area provided by the broad soles of the departed shaggy pachyderms. This is why Big Bog Frogs can not only squat on the peat without breaking through, but actually find it very conducive to jumping, which is why they live along the edges of Big Bog in the first place. Landing doesn't hurt at all on the moist mat of spongy peat, so they're able to put more power into their leaps than elsewhere. Also, once the waves really get going, the whole bog can be used like a springboard.

A young soldier, Ladric by name, translated through space and time from ancient Icatia, glanced up with shear dismay as a shadow from

above abruptly engulfed him. A sudden, early nightfall, but plunging from
the zenith instead of rising from the horizon. And so to hasty sleep . . .

"That's going to cost her," Peter remarked to no one in particular.

"Oh, no!" Mao gasped, as her mommy doubled over in apparently
sourceless pain. "That big froggy put his stinky juice in Mommy's
pocket! Why? And how come it hurt Mommy?"

"I don't know why," Peter replied, "but when a . . . a tricker makes
this kind of froggy go fight somebody, well, that's just what it does. And
your Mommy didn't know what to do with the stinky juice in her . . .
pocket, so it . . . the juice just . . . bit her."

Mao looked at him sharply. "How did you know it would do that?
And why didn't you tell Mommy?"

*Okay, watch yourself here, Pete. This kid's a little unsophisticated,
but not a bit stupid.*

Mao's mommy was not in a pleasant mood. She'd lost her mammoths and
goblins, her enemy had stolen control of her dwarf, and now the only
fighter she had left was the damned toad, and that was hitting her with
mana burn. That fool Langwynd was going to get it, and he'd better be
taking damn good care of Mao. . . .

What really had her fury going, besides the obvious, was guilt. The
death magic. Swamp mana. After every battle, she swore she would never
use it again, and she would divest herself of every source she had of the
vile, putrid stuff. And acquire more at the next opportunity. But this
meant she never had enough to do much with. Right now, for instance, the
mana from Foulmere itself was all she had to work with, not counting
what Langwynd's toad was tossing her, too fast and slippery to use before
it burned her. There was, however, one spell she did have a certain felicity
with.

"Yes, Mao, I did know. I know because I saw another tricker use one of . . .
the big froggies . . . that way. He got stung with the juice, too, just like your
mommy, when he was trying to learn what the frogs could do and how to
make them do it. But when a tricker uses juice like that, especially if the
juice comes from another world, all the trickers in the world they're in now
can tell they're here."

"I know *that*," said Mao scornfully. "That's why I use only just the juice from the world I'm in, so Mommy won't know I do fun tricks when she isn't looking. But *please* don't tell," she added with hasty anxiety. Peter's eyebrows shot up in mute concern, but he solemnly nodded his assent. Relieved, the child went back to her original line of questioning. "When did you see the tricker do that?"

"It was long ago, when I was a boy. I'm not a tricker, but my father could do little tricks, like help the garden grow better, and I could feel it inside whenever he used his juice, but it wasn't the deep down juice like your mommy uses."

"Puddle juice." Mao nodded. "It lies on the ground and gets sticky and dirty." She paused, puzzling over Peter's words. "What's a father?" she finally asked.

Peter Langwynd was truly dismayed. Hadn't the mother . . . ? No, of course not. There was no point, not yet, since the child had probably never seen her father and never would. And she was too young, maybe, to have the mysteries of reproduction explained to her. He, for one, was not about to try it.

"My father was . . . a man I lived with when I was little, like you do with your mommy. I had a mommy, too. But they were both taken away to fight by a tricker when I was . . . bigger than you are, but not as big as I am now."

"Was it a bad tricker?" asked Mao.

"He didn't think he was bad. He thought he was very good. But what he did was bad. Bad to the people he took away from their homes and children so they could fight for him."

"But why did he take away your mommy and your father-man?"

"Because he thought that being a tricker made him more important than anybody else. He came to the island where we lived and did wonderful things for us. He cured sickness and destroyed the giant sea monster that sank our fishing boats sometimes. But he only did those things so he could think it would be fair for him to use us any way he wanted later on, so even his good tricks were bad."

"I think he was one of the bad trickers, then."

Peter Langwynd sighed. "All trickers are bad trickers, Mao," he whispered.

The Big Bog Frog was waiting with eager anxiety for her next assignment when the spell hit her. Fear, horror, terror, panic, dread! Fear of yonder radiant mage! Horror at the rampant battlefury in her stomach! Terror at the churning green beneath her! Panic at the looming blue above her!

Dread of the sudden, unprecedented awesome, comprehension of the concept of eternity, arising spontaneously like a volcano in her tiny amphibian brain! Something deep in the midst of her broke, and the expanding bubble of darkness carried her away.

He threw it back at me! The dirty, no-good ratfink killed my *toad with* my *spell!* The sorceress who called herself Vram badly needed to conjure up more fighters to defend her from her foe, but the proper spells eluded her as she scattered bolts of lightning among the rallying enemy forces now swarming around her.

Inspiration! She could use the same black mana spell that had backfired last time, and even if her opponent could again manage to ricochet it back, it would do so to no effect, as it was not the sort of spell that could hurt a planeswalker.

There is a truism among sorcerers that Peter had come across in his reading during his undergraduate days, as he worked to piece together the truth about planeswalkers: "Tap not the land on which you stand." That this saying was unknown to Mao's mother is not surprising, since planeswalkers spend so much more time fighting than talking to each other. Most of them, though, are intelligent enough to figure it out for themselves.

The mana was drawn, the spell was cast. . . .

The eyes of the Naturalist had observed the destruction of the most magnificent amphibian specimen they had ever beheld with guilt and dismay, but deeper down, the soul of Peter Langwynd paid little attention. He was remembering his first coming to this accursed spot over forty years earlier. *He had been born in a mixed community of elves and humans on the Isle of Indigo, possibly in this world, more probably not. His father, Ruannon, was a fewman[1] deep-sea fisherman; his mother, Alandrah, an almost-but-not-quite-completely human captain of the Volunteer Archery Corps of Indigo Isle. It was just before he turned nine, the same year his granny died, that the high mage, Nimbys of Tharkair, came to dazzle Peter and his fellow Indigents. When he left them, he left them all feeling grateful. All except Peter. He feared and distrusted Nimbys, and due to his peculiar mana sensitivity, the mage's high-powered spellcasting gave him headaches and nightmares.*

---

[1]elf-human

Then people began to disappear, his father among the first, vanishing from the boat one sunny morning, harpoon in hand, while his partners screamed and rushed to the side of the craft, not believing at first what they had seen. By the time they again reached land, they had themselves convinced that Ruannon had fallen overboard, struck his head against the side, and sank at once, so they were shocked to find his body already returned to Alandrah, heaped with gold and an enchanted dagger for weregild, and a letter praising Ruannon's valor in service to the Cause.

"He said it was for the Cause," Peter murmured aloud; then catching himself, he added, "which is just a grownup way of saying he didn't want us to think it was just for him. I didn't understand what the Cause was, and I still don't."

"You mean like my mommy does tricks *'cause* she has to take care of me?"

"Exactly, Mao! But trickers need juice, and they need other people and animals and things to do their fighting for them. And the more they use, the more they need. The more they do their tricking for a Cause, the more that tricking is the only Cause they have anymore."

After his father's death, Peter's own Cause had been to protect his mother. Since vanishment occurred without warning and was impossible to prevent, this only made him anxious, obsessive, and frustrated. He refused to leave Alandrah's side, ate little, and seldom slept. One morning while they were dressing, the moment finally came. As soon as he felt the first nauseating metallic shiver of the summoning fill the air, he threw his arms around his mother's waist, screaming, spittle foaming through his clenched teeth. The spell didn't want him, though; it wanted Alandrah and tried to wrest her from his grasp, dislocating one of his shoulders in the process, but still he held on, fighting with all his will.

As the portal shock had begun to fade, he found himself groggily sprawled beside his mother on the violently quaking bog of Foulmere Fen. In the midst of the slaughter surrounding him, he recognized Nimbys of Tharkair dramatically gesturing and chanting. He could feel the mana in the air around him, tingling all his nerves, but without the sickness and pain it usually caused.

A bolt of lightning sprang from the unclouded sky, badly searing a monstrous huge spider that was lumbering toward the mage. Then he saw Alandrah leaping into the gap, dressed not in the everyday clothes she had been donning, but in the uniform of the corps, bow drawn, arrow nocked.

As the arrow buried itself in the arachnid body, the monster was upon her, lifting her with its horny, black fangs, breaking her spine and filling her body with poison as it, too, crumpled beneath the gleaming teeth of death.

The mana was drawn.

The spell was cast.

And Foulmere Fen erupted. The warring mages were swallowed up in a flash of blackness. Balls of flaming gas hurtled through the darkened sky. Grasses withered. Rocks shattered. Trees burst into flame, or toppled with a crash. Birds exploded in midflight. Beasts screamed with pain and confusion.

Peter Langwynd grabbed hold of Peft and Mao and scrambled onto the shore as the surface of the bog began to pitch and churn. Once on solid footing, he paused, struggling to keep the two of them in his grip. "No place is safe here!" he screamed through the tumult. "If you run, it will only be to your death!"

Peft could see that her friend was right and relaxed to the eventualities of the fate which awaited them, but Mao was entirely given over to that totality of terror that only a child can know. "Where's Mommy!" she wailed, thrashing back and forth against him. It was not so much a question as a howl of agony, rage, and despair. "What! Happened! To! My! Mommy!"

"I don't know!" He wept, rocking her, hushing her, while Peft resumed her perch on his shoulder. "I really, really don't know. . . ." But to some degree, he knew he did. Looking back out onto the bog, he could see the battle's only survivor, Vram's blamelessly treasonous dwarf, hopping around on the heaving peat, as the bog began to boil away beneath him. Peter watched until the rising steam, seeping up through the porous mat, obscured him from view.

I should have let her kill me, Peter thought. *She'd have gone away empty-handed, and the fens would not be ruined.* The fens. The frogs.

Oh, gods! The Eub Hlut!

He looked toward Peft. Silent tears poured from beneath slitted lids. It was the first time he had seen an Eub Hluta weep. "We'd better leave now," he said softly. Peft nodded, said nothing.

Hours later night was coming on, and they had made little progress, though the upheavals had abated within an hour of their beginning. The brush areas were a tangle of fallen trees and blighted undergrowth. A thorny new variety of poison ivy and a reeking, ravenous fungoid parasite that Dr. Langwynd had never seen before covered all, save for where the overgrown tangle opened onto smoldering ember fields, still too hot to cross. The waterways they had formerly traveled were a sticky morass of accumulated muck, mixed with occasional patches of quicksand, drained of their running water, impassable either by foot or boat. Standing pools swarmed with mosquitoes and no other living thing. They had seen fish lying in the lily pad-littered glop, gills gasping helplessly, and now the fishy stench was a curse and a lament in their nostrils. The birds and beasts that were able to had fled, and the land was mute of life.

Then, finally, they arrived at the new channel of the Kron Lu and saw where all the water had gone. "We'll never get across this without a real boat," Peter muttered to himself. "Even the punt would be no good; this is too deep and too fast now for poling." They stood there in dreary dejection for what seemed to be several hours, was likely not more than ten minutes, and then turned wordlessly around and began to retrace their steps.

Mao had lost all of her vivacious geniality, plodding without complaint in a sullen daze. Peter had tried to cheer her with encouragements and praise for her stoutness of spirit, but to no discernible effect. Peft's mourning, too, was tempered by exhaustion. Peter grew frightened by the approach of night. The unclean things of the deeps would come forth then, as usual, he guessed, but probably never to return to their places of rest with the dawn. They could all be wanderers and refugees together.

The bog, when they got to it, was a dry bowl of hardened peat, which they easily crossed. They paused in the middle, and Peter cut them hunks of mammoth meat that was so well done, the flesh fell away from the bone with but the gentlest hint from Peter's dagger. Suddenly Peft frowned and scrutinized the farther shore.

"Is guy wi' fire," Peft mumbled, her first words since the cataclysm.

Peter looked to where Peft was pointing. He could make out no figure from this distance, especially in the failing light, but did see a distant spark, a wisp of smoke. "Let's make for it, and quickly," said he, swallowing a mouthful of mammoth meat. "It may be our deaths, but it's also our only hope."

"Maybe is both," reflected Peft.

The dwarf had not been idle. A cord of firewood had been cut, split, and stacked. A haunch of what looked to be some kind of venison was spitted and roasting. He greeted them civilly when they arrived, offering them a mouthful each of wine from his skin, while keeping a wary eye on them.

"Where be you from?" the dwarf asked Peter, once they had established that their only common language was Old Sarpadian, the ancient common tongue of both Icatia and realm of the Ebon Hand, and for over a millennium since, the lingua franca of the continent and surrounding islands, which neither Peft nor Mao could speak or understand. Though the dwarf could make out most of their Modern Sarpadian, if they spoke slowly enough (except for Peft, whose dialect he couldn't understand at all), he couldn't speak it himself. "Where from, sir? From what world taken, on which side fighting—not that it matters anymore—or are ye local folk?"

"Local." Peter nodded. "And thou, sir?"

"From a land with no star like to that one," he said, pointing to Jinuoe, the evening star. "My name is Ingvik. I am not a professional fighter, though I served my proper hitch. I am a metalsmith of the City of Deep Keep." He raised his fifteen-kilo hammer as if in evidence. One face was flat, the other wedged. Peter realized that this hammer was what the smith must have used to cut and split the wood for their fire.

"Thou could have dug some peat coal more easily," Peter remarked.

Ingvik nodded. "I prefer wood. It gives off the brighter light, which will be as important as heat tonight, I fear."

"But how did you escape the boiling bog?" asked Peter, remembering how quickly the heat had intensified. The dwarf's skin looked as if he'd been out in the sun a bit too long, but no worse.

"I found a little boat, a most unusual little boat. I climbed into it, hoping to steal another half a minute of life away from death, and lay down in the bottom, wishing I could get my head up above the scalding steam. Soon I found breathing easier. I sat and found myself floating in a cloud. I wished I could get out in the open, and in short order it was so. I found that I could move this vessel through the air with my thoughts. But I was nervous that the enchantment might wear off, so I landed it here." He pointed to a stand of wilted willows, where Peter saw his punt stuck in a tree. "I have never been too handy with boats."

Together Peter and Ingvik pulled the boat down out of the tree, but it wouldn't fly for them at all. Peter hadn't been able to understand why its enchantment hadn't dropped away with the Vram and kitty disguises, as utility spells almost always do when planeswalkers turn their minds to combat.

He shrugged it off and turned his mind to combat.

The dry, crusty peat was crumbling, heaving, as the dead emerged with the fullness of night. Even after millennia, the anaerobic environment of the bog had preserved the physical integrity of flesh so well that corpses buried in the thick peat sediment, by chance or design, tended to forget they were dead, forget that they had no need of exercise, forget that they were not, in cold fact, ravenously hungry for the flesh of the living.

It was Peft who first heard the squeaky, leathery sound of their approach and extrapolated its meaning. The ghouls of the bog had been, that day, effectively mummified. Better and better. She alerted Peter and hustled the morose Mao into the boat, about which they had already planted a tight ring of several dozen of the torches they had prepared by wedging dry peat moss into the cracked ends of long stakes of split wood and dipping them into the bitumen that issued freely from a crack in the earth nearby. Surrounding both this inner keep and the campfire, they had piled up peat coal and brushwood smeared liberally with the tar. This Ingvik and Peter soon set afire, and then they all waited.

The undead, it is true, feel no pain despite any kind of physical harm that may befall them, but they can be harmed. As their dehydrated bodies began to amble clumsily through the outer ring, they burst into flame, but didn't stop. Peter and Ingvik fell on them, Peter wielding a heavy club, and Ingvik the same in his left hand, with his smith's hammer in his right. So armed, they smashed the bog mummies asunder, thrusting the hapless, thrashing pieces back into the blazing outer ring, where they served as additional fuel. Peft, from behind the second ring of as yet unlit torches, shot arrows with razor-sharp flint points, severing hamstrings and jamming knee joints, while keeping an extra eye out for intruders. It would have been so easy . . . if there hadn't been so *many* of them . . . and if it wasn't for the bear.

Though in life a strict vegetarian, in undeath the giant cave bear is all carnivore—or, to be perfectly precise, all *vivivore*. Peter screamed as he saw the mummy bear walking through the fiery ring, bursting into a furry, furious blaze. Ingvik ran to Peter's aid, while several burning man-shapes shambled unopposed into the ring. Peft hollered a warning and lit the inner ring of tourches on the side farthest from her comrades. Then she readied her last four arrows. These four were tipped with a swift-acting poison, which would have been gilding to the lily, as far as the mummies were concerned. But these arrows were not for mummies.

Next to Peft, Mao lay huddled on the hull, waiting for death. She was afraid, but more exhausted than fearful . . . until she looked up into the towering face of the burning bruin. The flesh was mostly scorched into a sooty patina on its skull, and Ingvik and Peter were falling back through the closing second ring of fire, still swinging. The bear was missing its right forelimb, and Ingvik's beard was singed to the skin all down the left side of his face. Looking back over her shoulder, Mao could see four or five dead things beginning to push through the inner wall. Peter and Ingvik tripped over the gunwale and tumbled back into the boat on top of little Mao, knocking Peft's shot awry, one arrow lost. How now could the Eub Hlut archer have the heart to release only three, while leaving one of their company, the last alone, to face this horror?

"Get up! Get up!" screamed Mao from beneath Peter. Startled, he began to move, but was checked by a shuddering shock of vertigo. The boat was a good five meters from the ground and still rising. Ingvik sat up and grinned through his burns.

"'Ware!" Peft screamed, and Ingvik whirled about, hammer smashing sideways into the skull of the mummy that had managed to climb into the boat in the midst of their ascent.

"*No!*" Peter screamed, lunging for Ingvik's hammer arm. He was nearly thrown from the boat, but Ingvik and Peft were just able to nab him by his blackened tunic and pull him sobbing to safety. In his hand he clutched the charred insignatory lanyard of a captain of the Indigenous Archery Corps.

"No!" he had screamed fifty years earlier, scrambling to Alandrah's side, only to find that she was as dead as the broken bow laying beside her. Rage filled his throat, overwhelming the strangling anguish rising from his thundering heart. His eyes fell upon the enchanted dagger hanging from her belt, his father's weregild, and he snatched it up with both hands. As Nimbys loosed his final fireball against his sorcerous foe, Peter sprang up and, with a strength vastly enhanced by the magical blade, buried it in the mage's heart.

Nimbys looked down at him, startled, while his yonder enemy vanished in a puff of humility and defeat. "How does thee come to be here, lad of Indigo? I called not for thee."

"You son of a rabid dog!" Peter screamed. "You killed my father, and now you killed my mother!"

"But how . . . ? Ah! You forced your way here alongside your mother, I suppose. That shows a powerful force of will. As does this." *Without appearing to think much about it, Nimbys drew the dagger from his heart. There was not even a drop of blood on it, nor a single severed thread in the long white tunic.*

Peter's hate froze solid in his belly. "Your letter claimed it was enchanted!"

"And so it is, else it could never have touched me to the heart like this. But once it did, I had the power to heal myself."

"Make my mother alive again!" *Peter savagely demanded.*

"That would do her no good now, lad. Her soul is gone from here. I'm sorry, but she has given her life for the Cause."

Peter said nothing, feeling a disgust too strong for mere words. Nimbys sighed. "I must send you home now, along with your mother's remains."

"Don't you dare!" *Peter fumed.* "You keep your filthy spells off her and me both. I will bury her myself. I will get home myself. I refuse your so-called help. But I will take this for my father," *he added, snatching the dagger away from the mage,* "and for my mother, I take this!" *He shot out his free hand and grabbed a finely inscribed brass medallion from the wizard's breast, pulling it free from its golden chain.*

The wizard smiled appreciatively. "You have a powerful will for a lad your age. It is possible, though not very likely, that you could become a mage yourself. I always wanted a son like you to follow in my path. The Cause has such need of us!"

"You're crazy, old man! I know nothing of your stupid Cause and care less! I hate all magic and them that use it, and you most of all!"

The mage of Tharkair scrutinized Peter. "You remind me of that giant frog I was experimenting with when trouble showed up and had to be dealt with," *he said at last.* "A fair fighter, that frog, but stings you with swamp mana, I almost think on purpose."

"I'd sting you with a lot worse if I could," *Peter fumed as, without another word, he stormed off across the still-heaving peat to give his mother a sea burial in the dark deep below. Nimbys declined to follow.*

Mao lay huddled against the chill of the autumn sky with Peter in the low bow of the flying boat. Peter had removed his tunic and wrapped the *dobéhm* child in it. They had then landed briefly and gathered many armfuls of the stiff, dry papyrus reeds and crushed them as best they could into a coarse bedding in which to burrow themselves for the night, while they drifted aimlessly in the ironically gentle breeze. Ingvik lay sprawled against the stern gunwale, attempting to converse with Peft. They both seemed to enjoy the distraction from grief and pain that the futile activity afforded them.

Flying the *Sky Skiff* (as Peter had dubbed her) low over ruined Foulmere—a name still only half true, but now inversely so—they had found no Eub Hlut refugees, but plenty of the undead, now permanently expelled from their marshy graves. It would be impossible to tell anything for sure until the morning, but Peft already feared the worst.

Nor would the swamp ever return to its former state. From the floating punt, Peter had seen that the Kron Lu now was running in one deep, straight channel to the sea, as if a giant plow had been driven right through the middle of the fen. All the land was changed, and he could no longer even tell where his shack had been. Maybe in the light of day. . . .

"I'm bad," Mao murmured into the ear lying next to her tiny lips. "I did the bad thing, and now Mommy went away. . . ." She began softly to moan again.

"No, child," said Peter. "I don't know what happened back there, but it wasn't you playing at putting the flying trick back in the boat while your Mommy wasn't looking that did this to the fens. That was dangerous, but only dangerous to you, because the tricker might have noticed and then done bad tricks to hurt you because he was afraid. I see now you must have stopped at an island somewhere since your Mommy brought you back to this world."

He could feel Mao's head nodding beside his cheek. "I got the bits of the island in my pocket, so I could get the squishy juice when I wanted to," she whispered, and shuddered.

"But why didn't Mommy take me with her? She always takes me when the bad trickers make her have to go away. Why doesn't Mommy come back?"

That was a puzzler, not because he didn't at least partly understand, but how to explain to a young child the concept of matrix feedback loops and explosive sub-planar disruptions when, in part, they were only so many words to him, too? But as for the rest . . .

"Something your Mommy and the other bad tricker did threw them right out of this world. Threw them hard! They didn't just go by themselves. I don't think your Mommy would ever leave you on purpose." *Though you don't know that for certain, do you, Pete? Not much you* can *know for certain when it comes to planeswalkers. Especially not this one.*

And? Better tell her, Pete. "I don't know where your Mommy is. I don't know if she will ever be able to come back. I don't even know if she is even still alive." He held the child tight as she began to sob quietly in the heap of reeds.

"But what will happen to me now, Peter?" her voice quavered in the dark. "I never didn't have my Mommy before."

"I will take care of you, Mao," he said as gently as he could with such strong emotion welling inside of him. "You will come with me."

"Then you will be . . . my father-man?"

"Yes, Mao. For a little while, anyway, I will be your father."

What kind of convoluted karma loop have I landed in? he wondered later as he lay in the *Sky Skiff*, buried in reed-stubble, with a child snuggled beside him that he, suddenly destitute, could care for now no better than her mother had. So powerful, in theory, was Vram; in reality so power-less, even to the extent of giving her daughter a stable life and a secure home! He wondered if it was due to her *dobéhmi* legacy, the politics of planeswalking, or some trait of personality inherent in her own unique being.

And here he was, as indirectly the cause of Mao's orphaning as Nimbys had directly been of his own. And here he was, too, in a good position (if he kept his promise to Mao, to be her "father-man") to lure her away from magic use, just as Nimbys had tried to lure him into it. Did he have the right to? Did he have the right not to try? What was now only an innocent amusement, he knew, could easily grow into the vicious, destructive obsession so manifest in the mother. And yet he owed his life to that "amusement."

To be honest, too, he knew nothing of child-rearing. Mao had origi-nally taken to him, he guessed, because he treated her as an equal, but fatherhood had a different flavor from friendship, and he didn't know if he could live up to what he felt that difference ought to be. Maybe it would be better to find Mao's kin, if he could, but he had know way of knowing if Vram was even originally from this world, let alone which continent.

He felt the tiny breathings breaking like the surf of a miniature sea against the beach of his breastbone, and knew one thing for sure: until he could come up with a more able replacement, he was now all she had in the world to defend her, to provide for her. There was no way to undo the day's events, for however many reasons he might wish there were. This day was catastrophe unmitigated, and in comparison, this new burden of responsibility was minuscule. He could not save the fen, or the Eub Hlut, or his own mother, but he could do this one thing. For a little while, any-way, he would be her father.

GOD SINS

by

Keith R. A. DeCandido

The island hadn't changed very much in the thousand years since I'd been there last. For some reason, this surprised me.

Then again, there are limits. After all, the island was remote, physically isolated from the rest of the world, populated mainly by humans who survive primarily by the fishing trade, secondarily through farming. Very little of that was likely to change when you got right down to it.

I returned home by boat. It had been a long time since I traveled in so mundane a manner; I must confess I had completely forgotten about its deleterious effects. The first trick we learn is control over the body, so for my body to so thoroughly rebel against me in response to the ship's bucking and weaving was something of a shock.

I could have eliminated the queasiness, but the point of this was to move away from my past life, to get away from the madness once and for all.

We are a rare breed, if "breed" is the right word. In any case, we are few. The names for us are manifold: *mage, wizard, demiurge, planeswalker, demon, gatherer*. Choose which one you prefer. Long ago, I mastered the art of understanding any form of communication I was presented with, so the intricacies of language hold no interest for me.

Of course, the most common word is *god*. It's also probably the most accurate.

Occasionally, and apparently at random, someone—human, elven, dragon, whatever—is born with the ability to harness the forces of the earth. Again, the nomenclature varies depending on who you ask, but it's basically *power*. Very few have the power, and those of us who do tend to use it to better ourselves. It's when one of us tries to better ourselves to the detriment of another of us that the problems start.

I was as bad as any of them. I clashed with many a fellow wizard, but I always won in the end. I was unstoppable, invincible, insatiable. I used and abused anything I felt I needed at the time, from the noblest elf to the dimmest orc, from the craftiest goblin to the most savage sea serpent.

Sometimes I would rule a land overtly. I may have even done it here on the island where I was born. One loses track. So many centuries, so many conquests, so many times growing bored and moving on.

In a sense, that's what happened now. Except there was nowhere to move on to. I had reached the stage where I could do *anything*.

Who would have thought that one with the ability to do anything would find himself with nothing to do?

Semantics again. Perhaps it's part of my new worldview.

You see, I've given it all up. That's why I travel home by ship, nausea and all, rather than simply traveling there under my own power. From this day forth, I shall no longer be a god or a king or a wizard. I have been all that and more in a thousand years of life. Now, I shall be a simple human among other humans.

It isn't as easy as it looks.

My vow not to use my power fell by the wayside fairly early on in my endeavor. For one thing, finding arable land that I could take over would have been impossible had I not taken a stretch of barren land and made it farmable. The island (which was now called Kartya; indeed, that may have been its name when I grew up here) had had a bad run of crops over the previous years and had stayed solvent mainly through the fishing trade.

So I used my power a bit, pushing the soil in the direction *I* wanted rather than the direction nature had ordained. Then again, changing the course of nature is what we do.

However, I only did it up to a point. I made the land ready to be farmed, and I manipulated tools more efficiently than a normal person could—but I *farmed* that land.

And I got results.

Fruits, vegetables, herbs. I even grew Girs'elm artichokes (an odd name, that: they are neither from Girs'elm, nor do they remotely resemble artichokes), which are difficult to grow, and harder to sell because the majority of humans can't stand the things. But I knew the elves were fond of them, and so was able to arrange to have my yields sold to the elven boat captain who brought me to Kartya.

Within a couple of years, I had a viable farm. I didn't really require the food or the money that selling the crops brought in, but I got immense personal satisfaction from the whole endeavor.

However, even personally satisfying work grows tiresome after a while, year after year, so I decided to vary the routine by hiring some locals to do the actual work on the farm, while I supervised.

We always fall back into the old patterns, don't we? Here, I'd intended to become just like every other ordinary person on the planet, and what happens? I find myself becoming the lord of the manor again, the king, the ruler, the supervisor—the god.

Or, at least, that's what I'd intended. I ran into a bit of a snag when the two young brothers, Firal and Dovroder, agreed to work for me, then arrived at the farm and asked where the plow was.

I stared at them blankly. "The what?"

"The plow. You know, to, uh—to plow the fields with."

"What purpose does that serve?" I asked.

They exchanged confused glances, then they stared at my farm, as if it would provide answers. "You can't farm without plowing the fields."

I finally realized what they meant. "Oh, you mean a machine! Well, that's hardly necessary, really. After all, I simply—" I hesitated. On those rare occasions when I actually communicate with mortals, I use the language in their own minds. But the Kartyan tongue had no words for the concepts I needed to convey. Lamely, I finished, "—*do* it."

Again Firal and Dovroder exchanged glances, but their expressions were more—confused? strained? It was hard to tell. It had been so long since I paid attention to mortal body language.

"Sir, if you please—what is your name?"

I blinked. A name? I had so many, it was hard to choose. The one I was fondest of was Rafe—and, fortuitously, there was an image in Dovroder's mind of someone named Rafthrasa that I reminded him of. Rafe was a legitimate abbreviation for such a name, so I said, "Rafthrasa, but most simply call me Rafe."

Before I even finished the sentence, their eyes widened, and they fell to their knees.

"What are you doing?" I bellowed.

"It is You, my Lord," Firal said, "returned to us as was prophesied!"

"I beg your pardon?"

Dovroder replied, "Please instruct we who have sighted You, that we may bring Your word to all who worship Your greatness."

This was starting to annoy me. "Will you *please* get up?"

They rose.

"What are you blathering on about?"

"You have returned to us, my Lord. Please, instruct us that we may do Your bidding."

I couldn't believe it. "Get out of here!" I bellowed. Behind me, thunder cracked the clear sky.

This time, I could read Firal and Dovroder's body language quite clearly: they were scared. They practically tripped over themselves fleeing my wrath.

Once they were out of sight, I dispelled the brewing storm my anger had started. I didn't want a rainstorm right now; it'd be bad for the crops.

A god. They thought I was a god.

After a moment's thought: *Of* course *they thought you were a god, you idiot! You created a farm from nothing, by yourself. You don't even know what the proper tools for such an endeavor are, you just guessed! How else is a mortal supposed to interpret that?*

As it turned out, it was much worse than I had imagined.

Firal and Dovroder didn't mistake me for their god.

They didn't mistake me at all.

I put up wards around the farm, then changed my appearance and traveled the island. (Changing my appearance turned out to be a more intricate process than I'd thought. I'd never done it before—no need, really. Wizards can recognize each other by ways other than sight, and what possible need would I have to tailor my appearance to the needs of a *mortal*? But still and all, I managed it.) Wherever I saw a place of worship, it was to the Great God Rafthrasa. The statuary throughout these temples were all unmistakably of me. Shoddy workmanship for the most part, but definitely me.

The religion got its start a millennium ago, so obviously I *did* set myself up as a deity here before departing. I don't remember it, but that doesn't mean it didn't happen.

One priest was very helpful in showing me some of the sacred texts; it was so rare, he said, to find someone, outside the priesthood, who could *read*. However, none of the religion's tenets had any significance to me—though some of them sounded like the kind of idiotic thing I was fond of making mortals do in my youth. For example, one of the rules was that no fish would be eaten on first day of the month. The texts claimed this had something to do with sacrifice to show piety or somesuch, but one childhood memory I did retain was that, by the time I reached my teen years, I was well and truly sick of fish and wanted there to be at least one day a month where it would be no part of any meal. Obviously, I had made my wishes manifest when I deified myself.

The part I was most curious about were the texts relating to Rafthrasa's Return To His People (every single reference to me was capitalized, which also sounds like the kind of thing I would've insisted upon). Apparently, Rafthrasa would return in secret, disguising Himself as a commoner until one of the devout would recognize Him. Rafthrasa would then bless this one—called the first disciple—and he or she would go forth and proclaim His Return.

Well, Firal and Dovroder did their parts just fine, and so did I up until we got to the blessing part.

More overt questioning of the priest—to wit, by forcing truthful answers out of him rather than the religious gobbledygook he usually gave to the devout—revealed that the texts relating to the Return were written after the Departure by the priests who desperately didn't want to lose the faith of the devout just because a god who had been so tangible was now gone. Apparently, I went on a Great Quest, and I would return when the Goal was found. The exact nature of this goal was something the priests and the devout would argue for centuries and proved to be the subject of some of the livelier philosophical debates in the church. Several priests devoted their lives to trying to learn what the Goal was.

I slammed the book shut in disgust, which elicited a cry from the priest. (The book was old, and that kind of treatment could irreparably damage the fragile paper. Not that I cared; I was half tempted to burn all the texts to cinders.) These people were pathetic. I'd probably come to this conclusion before, a thousand years ago, and left in disgust.

But there was nowhere left to go this time. And dammit, despite the fact that it was populated by imbeciles, Kartya in general and that farm in particular were my home now. I'd continue to farm on my own. I'd gotten more satisfaction out of creating that farm than from any of the inane conquests I'd manufactured over the last millennium. I'd keep growing my vegetables and herbs, keep picking fruit from the various trees, keep selling Girs'elm artichokes to the elves, and that would be that.

Except when I needed to sell off crop yields, though, I would stay away from the Kartyans themselves.

Once again, my plans were skewed by reality. When I returned home, I found a huge crowd of people—led by Firal, who stood on a rock—gathered just outside the wards I'd placed. Odd that no one had broken through them, which would've alerted me instantly to an invasion (and also incinerated whoever penetrated). I gazed at them, using my power, and found that a black-haired woman wearing the garb of a priest standing near Firal had a very minor facility with the power of the earth. That meant she was able to see the wards, invisible though they were to the naked eye, and thus prevent anyone from actually going through.

I hadn't changed my appearance back to my usual looks, so I decided to blend with the crowd and see what nonsense Firal spouted. (Dovroder, by the way, was nowhere to be found—obviously he had actually listened when I instructed them to get out.)

"At last He has been Returned to us," Firal was carrying on. "Rafthrasa has come to save us from the pestilence that has gripped our soil! He has come back, as was prophesied, and I am His first disciple! Let us all join hands and pray to Him."

"Oh, *please*," I said. Somehow, Firal heard me. Then again, the devout were so silently hanging onto his every word (not surprising; he was one of the holiest people on the island right present) that any other words would be like a beacon.

"What was that?" Firal bellowed. "Who interrupts the Holy Word?"

I sighed. *Getting a bit full of ourselves, Firal?* Projecting my voice, I said, "I do! What proof do we have that you are truly the first disciple?"

Firal looked at me as if I'd sprouted another head. "I have brought the devout here to the place of Rafthrasa's Return."

"We only have your word that this is the site of the Return."

Firal sighed with feigned impatience. "His Holy Guards have been erected to protect this Holiest of Holies from being defiled by the unworthy. Sister Gillmin has seen the Holy Guards with her Sight."

"How do we know that you and Sister Gillmin haven't conspired to deceive us?"

"What purpose could that possibly serve? What is your name, that I can tell Rafthrasa who you are so He can smite you for daring to doubt the word of His first disciple?"

"My name is Grex," I replied, choosing an alias at random. "I tell you this freely because I don't believe you will ever be able to bring that instruction to Rafthrasa, because I don't believe you are in a position to tell him anything. To answer your question, your motive is obvious—you were just a farmhand. Now you're a holy man. Quite a jump in status."

"I am telling you, Grex the Heretic—" wonderful, I'd already gotten my own title "—that I do not lie. Rafthrasa has Returned, and I am His first disciple."

"I require proof."

"The devout should require no proof."

"As I said, we only have your word that the Holy Guards are in place. I see nothing that would prevent me from walking past that rock you're standing on and entering the farmland."

Firal smiled. "What proof is it that you want, heretic?"

"The Holy Guards keep the unworthy out, yes?"

"This is true."

He wasn't lying, either, since the unworthy were basically those who should not be in sight of the god. I could allow certain people passage through the wards, if I so desired, and those were probably the priests, since they were my contact to the devout. (At least that's probably how I did it. It would certainly make the most sense. I *wish* I could remember the details.)

I said, "Then you should be able to pass through the Guards with no trouble, yes?"

Firal hesitated.

"You are the first disciple," I continued. "If you are not worthy, then who is?"

"Of course, but—"

"But what?"

Firal straightened, cleared his throat, and said, "Of course I am worthy! I shall prove it to you, then we shall hang you where you stand for your heresy!"

Then he took several steps backward and was incinerated before everyone's eyes.

A collective gasp rippled through the crowd. The order that Firal had maintained with his theoretically holy words evaporated as people panicked, cried out, fell to their knees, and started backing away from the rock.

I quadrupled my size so I towered over everyone, but kept the "Grex" disguise, since I didn't want anyone to associate me with all the statuary floating around Kartya. *"Silence!"* I bellowed.

Everyone was very quiet after that.

"I am *not* your god! Rafthrasa's Return has not yet come! All of you will leave this place now, or meet the same fate as the pretender Firal! *Begone!*"

They scattered. Within a few minutes, no one remained. I decided to leave the wards up, and I went back to my farming.

Sadly, peace was not mine to be had. Within a few days, another smaller crowd gathered. I managed to frighten them off, but a few days later, more came—some the same as the previous crowd, other new faces.

Again I scattered them. Again they came back.

I tried expanding the wards, but the idiots always seemed to know where they were and stayed just outside them. Only once did one of them try to pass through, which is what alerted me to their presence on that particular occasion.

After about the eighth time, I was ready to commit violence. Still in the guise of Grex the Heretic, I stepped through the wards and cried out, "Begone from my sight!" I punctuated this request with a lightning bolt, which singed the hair of a few of them. As they ran off, I yelled after them, "Anyone else I see invading my demesne shall be destroyed!"

"That'll just renew their faith."

I turned to face this voice, surprised that there was one who hadn't run screaming. The voice belonged to a woman, leaning comfortably against a nearby tree. She was tall for her gender, with long, flowing black hair: Sister Gillmin, the one with the minor talent who could see the wards. This explained why only one person broke through them, if she had been here to detect the boundaries. As before, she was dressed in priestly robes, though she obviously had not cleaned them since her initial venture here with Firal.

I asked her, "What are you blathering about, woman?"

"The more You display Your phenomenal power, the more they believe that You are Rafthrasa. I don't know if You've noticed, but the crowds have grown larger each time."

I hadn't, actually. The numbers didn't concern me; their presence alone was irksome.

"Why do You deny Yourself, my Lord?" she asked. "You are obviously Rafthrasa. The prophecies have all been fulfilled."

"Those 'prophecies' were made up by your predecessors when Rafthrasa left this island a millennium ago."

"Nevertheless, who else could do what You have done? Who else could so change His appearance?"

I glowered at her. "What makes you think I have changed my appearance?"

She smiled. "I can see it, the same way I can see Your Guards, my Lord."

I returned the smile. "Ah, yes. You're what Milos used to call a 'hedge' wizard." And I chuckled.

"I fail to see the humor, my Lord."

"You wouldn't," I said, realizing that Milos's Bandrati pun didn't translate into the Kartyan language. "In any case, you possess a fraction of control over what I control absolutely."

"Yes, I have been granted a small blessing of Your holiness. It is why I chose to live in Your service, my Lord."

"Stop *calling* me that! I'm no god! I'm just a simple, ordinary human being like everyone else—"

"—who can call lightning from the sky, operate a farm with no outside help, not even machinery, who—"

"*Enough*! You're trying my patience, woman!"

She pushed herself off from the tree and approached me. "So are You! I've spent my *life* dedicated to Your service, waiting, sacrificing, praying, hoping against hope that You would come back and save us from this miserable famine! Instead, I find that You're nothing more than a selfish, brutish bully who cares nothing for what His people are going through!"

I grabbed her by the shoulders. "*Yes*! That's *exactly* right! *Finally* someone on this misbegotten island *gets* it! Sister, I will say it again, I am not a god. Apparently I once set myself up as a deity on a whim here, but that was a thousand years ago. I am a simple, ordinary human who was unlucky enough to have supreme power."

"Unlucky?" She seemed stunned by this. "I would gladly give up *everything* to have power such as Yours."

"Would you?" I chuckled. "Yes, perhaps you would. I'm sure when I was young and stupid I thought the same thing. I must have, if I went to all the trouble of making myself the focal point of my home island's religion. But all a thousand of years of supreme power have given me is a complete and total sense of waste and frustration. That, and a tremendous amount of chaos in my wake." I laughed. "You're a perfect example, 'Sister' Gillmin. You said you've devoted your life to worship of 'Rafthrasa,' yes?"

She nodded.

"Ridiculous. Absolutely ridiculous. You've taken something I used as entertainment, as sport, and magnified it into something grotesque. My coming back here was whim, not the conclusion of the Great Quest."

"Wasn't it?" she asked.

This brought me up short. "I beg your pardon?"

"It is written that Rafthrasa—that You left when You grew weary of Your holy duties, and so went on a Great Quest."

I chuckled again. "Well, I certainly did grow weary." At least I assume boredom was the reason I left. It was the only reason I ever did *anything* new, really, whether it was arriving someplace or leaving another one.

Gillmin continued, "What the Quest was, we were never told. But when the Quest was ended, You would Return."

"Yes, I know, I've read those texts. None of it has anything remotely to do with reality."

"No? You *did* leave on a quest, yes?"

"No, I simply wished to get as far away from this place as possible. An urge I'm coming to feel again, truth be told."

"And do what when You left?"

"Find somewhere else to conquer, somewhere else to rule, find other wizards to gain power from."

"So You had a goal in mind?"

"Not a specific one, but—well, yes, I suppose I did."

She smiled. "What do You think a quest *is*, my Lord?"

I sighed. Semantics again.

But she didn't stop there. "Or perhaps Your Quest was to find something more fulfilling—and, as You just told me, You didn't find it. Nothing fulfilled You, so You decided to Return to Kartya. When You lost Your sense of fulfillment, You came back to Your people. I'm sorry, my Lord, but, save for the fact that You killed Your first disciple, as far as I'm concerned You've fulfilled the Prophecy of the Return to the letter."

I found myself unable to respond to that. How could I? The mind of the fanatic could easily twist anything to meet its needs.

"Fine," I said. "You want to believe those texts? By all means, believe them. Go right on believing them. You want to believe that Rafthrasa has returned? Fine." I allowed my face to return to the one I was born with, which elicited a gasp from Gillmin. "Rafthrasa has returned to his people! And his first command to the devout is for the devout to *leave him alone and stay away from him*!"

Sadly, my wrath had little effect on her. Then again, I *had* been going to great lengths to convince her of my lack of divinity. . . . She said, "That shouldn't be too hard, my Lord. A few years are as nothing to someone like Yourself, and that is all it will be before the devout are all dead."

"It'll be a lot less than that if you keep milling about outside my farm, believe me."

She turned on her heel to walk away, but continued speaking. "I will bring the Holy Word of Rafthrasa to the devout. I will tell them that Our Lord has indeed Returned, for He wishes to observe the slow death of His people firsthand as they starve to death. I will tell them that He has forsaken us."

Well, it's about time *someone* figured it out.

The "famine" story was ludicrous, of course. It had simply been a bad run of crops. These things happen, and run in cycles. It usually results in an apocalyptic panic. People start running around proclaiming that the end of the world will come on the next solstice, deterred only slightly by solstice's arrival with comparatively little fanfare.

I certainly wasn't about to let some idiot hedge wizard convince me that I should do anything other than what I had been doing: tending to my farm, and damn little else.

Months passed in blissful solitude. The only other animal life I saw were the girl who brought my items to the marketplace, the elven captain who took the Girs'elm artichokes, and the collection of bugs that that tried to eat through my vegetable crop.

One afternoon I stood on a ladder, picking fruit. I didn't need to do it manually, of course, but I rather enjoyed it. I was generally trying to do more things with my hands—though for some reason I still couldn't bring myself to obtain a plow—and I found it more gratifying. At last, I could live in peace.

No such luck.

Just as I tossed a badly bruised fruit into the wheelbarrow I used for compost, I felt a disturbance in the wards. Some idiot had once again tried to penetrate them.

Sighing, I finished removing the fruit from the trees and separating the good from the bad with my power, which took all of a second, then moved myself to where the disturbance was.

A score of the devout had gathered, laying offerings. Upon seeing me, they all fell to their knees.

"Give us Your Holy Word, my Lord," one of them said.

I shook my head. "You people are staggeringly stupid. You believe my word to be holy law, yes? Fine. The last time you imbeciles invaded my land, the oh-so-holy words of Rafthrasa were: 'Anyone else I see invading my demesne shall be destroyed!'"

To their credit, a few of them realized what, exactly, this meant. Most of them, however, burned to a pile of cinders from my fireball in complete ignorance.

I then directed the ashes to the compost heap. May as well put them to good use.

Then I summoned Sister Gillmin from wherever she was on the island. She appeared before me laying down, asleep, dressed in night-clothes. I woke her up.

"What, exactly, does it take to get through to you people?" I asked her without preamble. "Do I have to kill all of you to get you to leave me alone?"

"The people are desperate. On top of everything else, an infestation destroyed what little crop there was this year."

I blinked. "Infestation?" *Of course, you idiot,* I admonished myself, *if you were ravaged by bugs, it stands to reason that the rest of the island would be as well.*

"They thought Your anger would be assuaged by offerings. I tried to convince them that it would be foolish, but they thought they had nothing to lose."

"Interesting perspective. They, in fact, had everything to lose, and have now lost it."

Her eyes widened. "You killed them?"

"Of *course* I killed them! You were there, you heard me promise that I would. And we *can't* have Rafthrasa's holy word being broken, now can we?"

Gillmin started to say something, then stopped. "You know, I was about to utter an oath, praying that the devout who came here would not be dead. But that oath would've been to You. And there's little point in swearing such an oath, is there?"

"None whatsoever," I replied, my voice hard.

"They won't be the last, You know," she said after a moment. "More will come, with bigger offerings. Offerings they probably can't afford, but that won't matter to them. All they want is succor from their Lord."

I looked at her, my mouth hanging open in amazement. "You're serious, aren't you? Even if I kill more of them, they'll keep coming back?"

"They're *starving to death*! What would You have them do?"

"The same thing everyone does when famine strikes. The same thing you mortals always do. Either live on a little while longer, or die."

"That's it?"

"What do you think *mortal* means, Sister? Some time very soon, they're going to die, whether it's at my hands or not."

"So their suffering means nothing to you at all?"

I laughed. "Why should it? The only thing on this world that means anything to me at all is being left alone. And, it seems, even that is being denied me."

Silence fell between us. I wondered why I had even bothered to summon her and was about to send her back to her bed when she spoke: "There is a way to get them to leave You alone."

"Oh?" I said, skeptical. I couldn't believe she'd thought of something I hadn't.

"Answer their prayers."

"What?"

"Do as they ask! It's not beyond Your power. Your farm alone has been immune to the ravages that have plagued us. Would it be asking so much for You to extend that blessing?"

I started to angrily point out that it wasn't a blessing, then decided it wasn't worth it. Instead, I said, "No."

"Why not?"

"I am not a god! I am a human being who is trying to live out his life in peace."

"The only way You will get peace is if You answer the prayers of the devout, my Lord."

I stared at her. It was the first time she called me "my Lord" since I summoned her.

And then I considered her proposal, and realized that she was absolutely right.

"Very well," I finally said.

I closed my eyes to concentrate, then I altered the soil across the island. It took a bit more effort than I'd been expecting, but the process still was quick. I also wiped out all of the island's bugs as I had already done on my own land. "It is done. The infestation has been eliminated; the soil is at its richest. Now I want you to go back to the devout, and I want you to carry a message from the almighty Rafthrasa. I can promise that Kartya will know more prosperity than it has ever known, but it is conditional. And that condition is that *I be left alone*. If so much as one person breaches the Holy Guards uninvited, I will sink the island into the ocean forevermore. Is that understood, Sister Gillmin?"

She fell to her knees. "Perfectly, my Lord. I will carry Your Holy Word to all the devout. And I thank You for Your kind indulgence."

With that, I sent her home.

I wouldn't have believed it possible, but the morons actually had the wherewithal to leave me alone after that. A few people did wander accidentally into my land, but I had altered the wards so that it would only repel those coming in search of Rafthrasa. Lost souls desperate for a roof would not be incinerated.

And so I continued to till the soil, to cultivate the flowers, to pick the fruit off the trees. One year, I even obtained a plow in exchange for a yield of vegetables.

Sister Gillmin rose to a position of prominence within the church, which wasn't terribly surprising, since she alone had heard the True Word of Rafthrasa and brought it to the devout. I even occasionally sent donations to the church, under the name of Grex.

My captain died in a shipwreck, and I lacked the interest to obtain another mode of transport to elven lands, so I finally let the Girs'elm artichoke crop die out.

One day, decades after I first came back to Kartya, I looked out on my farm and smiled. Finally, for the first time in a millennium, I was happy.

A Monstrous Duty

by

Kathleen
Dalton-Woodbury

Torya Longshanks hacked at the ground one more time and then put the hoe down to look at her hands. She'd have thought that all these months of winding a crossbow would have hardened them so blisters wouldn't form. Not to mention all the years before that working the farm. But the balls of her hands ached anyway, and one blister had opened, smearing into the dirt on her skin. It stung worse than some of the wounds she'd taken from goblin blades. She rolled her shoulder at that thought, but the joint throbbed no more than usual.

So she sighed and picked up the hoe again. Why of all the tools did the hoe have to be the one to outlast the fire? Not that it was in much better state with its handle gone than the scythe with its broken blade or any of the others. At least it was straight and still had an edge. Maybe not as good an edge as the one on her dagger, but she couldn't bring herself to dig with that.

What did other people use to make a grave? King Rogan had never let his army rest long after a battle, desperate as he was to conquer, so she never saw how the casualties were buried. Perhaps the healers took care of it after dealing with the wounded left behind.

She scooped the dirt into her helmet and stepped out of the hole to dump it. Not much of a hole, not nearly deep enough, but she could cover the bodies with the stones piled near the house. Stones that she and her father plowed out of the fields last spring and intended to use for fences before she was called away to fight in Rogan's war. Best not to think about her father, or any of the others, though. She stood up and brushed off her knees. The bodies lay behind her in their wrappings of thatch from what was left of the roof of the house. Soon enough she'd have to turn around and look at them again. Thatch didn't seem right, but the goblins of the Flarg didn't leave much behind. No blankets, no rags; she couldn't bury her family without giving them some kind of covering.

She swallowed and wished again that the goblins hadn't filled the well. Her waterbag was almost empty, but she'd wait until the bodies were in the hole before she walked to the spring on the hill behind the farm to refill it. She wiped her forehead with her arm and stretched. No good in putting it off any longer. The smell wouldn't be any easier to bear later in the day.

Pull on the thatch around the first body. Don't think about who it is. But long yellow hair slid out as she pulled the thatch closer. Long yellow hair, the only thing left to tell her she was pulling her sister Jess into the hole. Don't think about her that way. Think about her laughing and running and singing and fixing the meals. Better yet, don't think at all. She lifted the yellow strands, almost the same color as thatch before it weathers, rubbed their silkiness between her fingers, and dropped them into the hole as she moved toward the next body.

Don't think about the hands, strong and gnarled, that patted her on the back and assured her they'd be all right while she was gone. The solemn gray eyes and the thinning gray hair. He would have gone, too, to fight for their king, but someone needed to stay and watch over things. Torya sat on the edge of the hole and coughed. If she'd stayed, if she hadn't gone off to fight. . . . No, she couldn't think about that, either.

The last body was the smallest and the hardest to move. She'd gathered the pieces and arranged them on the thatch, but one small bone or another would roll off with each move toward the grave. After stopping several times to push something back inside the thatch cover, Torya finally roared her anguish and jerked everything that would come into the hole. She couldn't bear arranging them again, so she just pushed the laggards in after the rest. Delly was past feeling anyway, thank the Goddess.

Torya jumped to her feet, grabbing the waterbag, and set off for the spring. She wished she were past feeling, as well, but that didn't bear thinking of either. Let her get her father and sisters buried and then she'd worry about such things.

The waterbag full, her face and hands washed, and her back rested in the long walk to and from the spring, Torya felt as ready as she was likely to be for the next effort. Should she carry one stone at a time to the grave and put it in place, or should she carry as many as she could until she was tired and then place them once she had a pile? Somehow it didn't seem to matter, so she did it first one way and then the other. The soft crunch of a skull collapsing under stoneweight sent her to her feet. "I didn't mean to!" She picked up a stone and shoved it willy-nilly into the hole. "I came home as soon as I could!" Another stone, and another. "I didn't want to go! I wanted to stay! I'm not a soldier, I'm a farmer!" In her frenzy, she pushed more and more stones into the hole, until the pile near the grave was gone. She fell to her hands and knees, coughing and sobbing and retching. "I should have died with you!"

"Well, you didn't die, did you? Happen there's a reason for that."

"Huh?" Torya raised her head, trying to silence her gasping breath. Who? She leaned back on her heels and looked around. A healer, cloaked and hooded in the official green, a woman, perhaps, stood on the other side of the cairn.

Yes, it was a woman. She pushed back her hood to reveal a tired, ordinary face. Her hair was black and simply styled. Nothing to make a man look more than once. She smiled, but with more bitterness than anything else. "Happen you've been chosen." She gestured toward the cairn. "Would you like revenge?"

Torya almost said "huh?" again, but stopped herself by swallowing. "Revenge? How?" Against King Rogan, who wanted to be like Lacjsi and the Knights of Thorn, going off to fight goblins and win glory? The king who found out he wasn't Lacjsi and his soldiers weren't knights, and that goblins of the Flarg were always ready for battle? The coward who was hiding in Angremur city while those goblins, who had never bothered this land before, now ravaged it?

The woman moved toward Torya around the cairn. "Yes, how?" Her smile changed to a snarl. "Happen I told you, would you be brave enough to do it?"

What was bravery? For all the battles she'd fought, for all the fear she'd felt before them, and all the nightmares she'd had after them, the hardest thing she'd ever done was to gather up the pieces of her family where the scavengers had dragged them and put them in that cairn. She didn't feel brave. She just felt tired. "Do what?"

"Help me lay a curse on him."

Torya snorted. She was a practical woman. She knew healers didn't lay curses. Besides, hadn't she already wished every terrible thing she could think of on that treacherous serpent?

The woman smiled. "Serpent. And a treacherous one at that." She tilted her head back to look at the sky. "That would do nicely." Then she snapped her head back down to stare into Torya's eyes. "Give me your hand! Your left one."

Torya blinked. Healers couldn't read thoughts, either. "You're ill. You don't know what you're saying. Let me get you some water."

She laughed. "Just give me your hand."

"Healers don't lay curses."

"Happen I'm no longer a healer. Happen I've no more to give. Happen I'd rather end my life cursing someone who's destroyed all I ever tried to do than go on watching everything else die." She stepped up to Torya and grabbed her hand, lifting it to her mouth before Torya could pull away. When she did pull away, it was with a cry because the woman had bitten the ball of her thumb, deep and hard. She stared in amazement as blood flowed out across the dirty skin and onto the ground.

Torya grasped her left hand in her right and squeezed against the pain, staring at the woman who now clambered to the top of the pile of stones. She wanted to stop her, but the pain in her hand rose up her arm and spread through her body until she dropped to her knees, barely able to stay conscious.

The woman stood facing east, toward Angremur, Rogan's stronghold, and raised both arms in the air. "I spit my curse on you, King Rogan, serpent of treachery! I spit the blood of this land on you. You have betrayed your trust as its king. And your people have followed you, wanted you to do it. You deserve each other!" She turned slightly toward Torya and then back toward Angremur. "Only this blood will bring trust back. By the pain and blood of your victim I declare it. Nothing will protect you now."

Torya's skin crawled and her nose ached at a bitter smell, just as lightning struck the top of the cairn. The noise and force knocked Torya onto her back and darkness took her.

When she awoke, the sun had set and the moon risen. Though she searched the farm, the only trace of the healer were the bits and pieces of charred green material caught in the blackened rocks of the cairn.

The bite had scabbed over, but it burned and itched worse than her shoulder, worse than any wound she'd ever gotten in battle. As she walked around the farm, gathering her few things, she noticed that the burning eased whenever she faced east, toward Angremur. Toward the king. She stood staring in that direction. Why should she go back there, though? Rogan's army was scattered now. What good would it do for her to join the slow, trickling return? She glanced around her at what was left of her home. What good would it do for her to stay here, instead? At least if she went back to the king there might be a chance to take her own vengeance, vengeance she could understand.

She settled her pack on her shoulders and started down the road. It was time to report back to duty.

Word of the newest trouble came to Torya as she sat in an inn halfway to Angremur, listening to the other customers complain with the innkeeper about the food.

"Think I'd serve this if I could get better? If you don't like what we've got here, you're welcome to go elsewhere. Or you can go up to Angremur and offer to kill the king's monster. Get rid of that and the food'll get better."

"If we could kill that monster, we'd have no need of your food. I hear the king's offered a reward to anyone who'll rid him of the monster."

"What kind of reward's he got to offer? Half the kingdom? Half of nothing. If you'd travel as much as I do, you'd know theren't anything worth having out there. Might as well go off and join the rebels trying to fight the usurper Mairsil and restore Lord Ith to his throne for all the good it will do. This land is as near dying as that land, and this monster'll deliver the deathblow."

"I hear it's a lurker, with eyes like lightning that'll turn you to stone."

"With all the burning, maybe it's a coal golem. I heard it set the whole north side of Mount Shadow on fire."

"Nah, nah. No lurker that thing, nor golem neither, but a fire drake, sure's I'm sitting here. My cousin used to live in Angremur town, and he said he saw it one night, flying over the fortress. Great, big fire drake."

"Well, whatever it is, I wish someone'd get it. Then I can go back to my farm and start again. Planting season'll be starting soon, but I hear nothing will grow where that beastie's done its damage."

"Goddess's luck on finding any seed. The goblins take all they find. If they don't eat it, they burn it. No point in staying 'round my farm. Going to have to take my family clean t'other side of Angremur, where my brother lives—if he's still alive, that is."

Torya got up from her table. The stew had no meat in it, and the bread was stale, but for all that it hadn't been as bad as some she'd eaten. She hated to give up the mug of ale she'd been holding in her left hand. The coolness of the mug eased the itching. But it was time to go. If a monster was attacking Angremur, they'd need all the soldiers they could get, injured or not. She promised herself that if she saw the thing attack King Rogan, she'd manage to get her crossbow ready too late to do him any good.

In the press at the city gate, someone pushed Torya from behind, knocking her into the small, green-robed figure in front of her. She grabbed at the robe, catching the healer before they both landed in the dirt. "Oh, pardon my clumsiness."

The healer turned in her hands until the face under the hood appeared. Torya, at the same time, pushed herself and pulled the healer upright, bracing her feet against the surging crowd. The mouth spoke and a hand tugged on her cloak. Though Torya couldn't hear the words in all the clamor, she understood the message and followed the healer to a niche in the city wall just inside the gate.

"Your clumsiness was not your fault, so no pardon is needed." A hand came out to sweep the hood back, and Torya saw gray hair in a braided crown, and gray eyes set in wrinkled skin. The madness she'd seen in the other healer's eyes was replaced here by sorrow and weariness. "But something else is wrong." A frown darkened the woman's eyes, and the hands came out. "Let me see your hands."

Torya hesitated, then put out her hands. The healer reached for Torya's left hand and brought it up to her eyes. Her touch was cool and soothing, and for a moment, the itching eased. "Where did you get this?"

Torya glanced down at the scab in its nest of red, angry skin. "From someone in a green robe."

Gray eyes turned up to meet Torya's gaze. "It will not heal until you lift the curse."

"Until I lift the curse? But I didn't lay it."

"It was laid with your blood. Only you can lift it—the healer who laid it is no more."

Torya didn't answer. That last had not been a question. Instead she pulled her hand away and put it behind her back. "I can bear the itching. I've borne it for several days now."

"It will get worse. The scab will spread. Do you think it is for cursing alone that a healer is destroyed? It is also for giving pain and illness to another in order to lay the curse." The woman shuddered.

"And if I'm willing to pay that price? What have I got to lose, after all?"

The healer shook her head. "Consider it, at least. You are strong and young. You have lost no more than any of us have lost. If you feed the curse with your hatred, you will let your very soul die. No revenge is worth that."

Torya leaned against the wall. What if the healer were right? Was revenge on King Rogan worth the cost? The itching in her hand was fiercer now that the healer no longer held it. She didn't look forward to trying to sleep that night. But the thought of rescuing him from something he deserved made her gorge rise. How else to make him pay?

"And how would I go about lifting this curse, then? The monster is part of it, isn't it? I don't know how to fight monsters."

"You've been a soldier long enough and fought goblins enough. Are they not worse than one monster?"

Torya shrugged off that thought. What she'd seen made her want to agree, but she couldn't let herself think about such things. "If I can do it, then why can't any of the others who've tried?"

The healer pulled at Torya's left arm. "Because you are the only one."

Torya sighed and pushed away from the wall. "Well, I'll think on it.

Right now, my stomach complains more loudly than my hand." She forced her way back into the crush of bodies and let it carry her away from the gate toward the inns and taverns that waited to take a traveler's money.

King Rogan liked to review the new members of his garrison, or so the officers told Torya. As he sauntered along the short line of recruits, some returnees like her, others desperate for any work at all, Torya wondered if he did it because he didn't have anything else to do, pompous beast that he was.

When he stopped before her, she stiffened, not out of respect, but out of habit. And she kept her position out of pride—she hadn't been the one to ruin the country, after all.

He looked her up and down, and though she stared over his shoulder, instead of back at him, she could see enough out of the corner of her eye. He was taller than she, though just barely, and broad, with muscles that might turn to fat as he aged. His hair was long, with the sidelocks braided, and his eyes were green. He sported no beard or mustache, and she could see a small scab where someone had scraped his skin shaving him. She wondered how many lashes that had cost the poor barber.

"Another soldier? What company?"

"Vortex Riders, sire."

He turned to the officers who accompanied him. "I thought that company was wiped out. Died gloriously in battle and all that." He didn't wait for a response, but swung back to face Torya. "How did you survive?"

"Cursed, sire."

He stepped back, his green eyes widening. "What do you mean by that?"

"I was wounded and left for dead, sire. I'm not much of a soldier: I was born a farmer—used to hard work, but not much good for pain, sire." Torya resisted the urge to twitch her shoulder where the wound still bothered her during a rainstorm.

"Why didn't you report back sooner than this? That battle was over months ago."

Torya thought about those months. How had he spent them? Her vision filled with the image of her hands around his throat, his face changing color, and his eyes staring from his head. She was a practical woman and knew better than to try such a thing, but it didn't hurt to think about it, as long as she held herself very still.

He stepped forward, moving very close to her and frowning as he waited for her answer. She took a deep breath and blinked to clear her vision. "It took me a while to heal enough to travel, sire. And then I passed by my farm on the way back. Goblins had destroyed it and killed my family. I had to gather the pieces and bury them, sire."

He cleared his throat. Torya stared back at him. Why, he was younger than she was. For all his size, he wasn't much older than her sister Jess—than Jess would have been, that is. She gritted her teeth. He was old enough to be a better king.

"So now you're back and ready to soldier again?"

"Yes, sire."

"Heard about Our curse?"

"Which one, sire?" Her father'd always told her that her tongue would get her into trouble, but she couldn't resist. This boy didn't deserve her respect.

The soldier next to her started coughing, and she had to grit her teeth again to keep from smiling.

Rogan's countenance took on a darker shade, but he didn't say anything for a moment. Then he took a deep breath. "The monster, the one that's tearing up the countryside, that curse."

Torya narrowed her eyes. Maybe he was growing up a little. She felt herself relaxing and stiffened again. "I've heard a little, sire."

He took another deep breath. "I never thought it would be like this." His gaze softened as he stared at her. "How many were there in your family, soldier?"

Torya's mouth dropped open and she shut it with a snap. It was her turn to take a deep breath. She inhaled Rogan's scent, warm and reminiscent of trees and sunshine—not at all the flowery perfume she would have expected—and swallowed her surprise. "Just my father and two younger sisters, sire. My mother died in giving birth to a stillborn son." Why was she telling him that?

He glanced down, and then raised his gaze to her again. "I'm sorry." And his eyes said that he meant it.

Torya forgot how to breathe.

Then he turned to the next in line and she let the air out of her lungs in a low whistle.

The officer who assigned her to guard the king's bedchamber said that Rogan had asked for her. But when he came up the tower stairs, escorted by his many manservants, he didn't even glance her way. After they assisted him in his bedtime preparations, the men left and Torya stood in silence on the opposite side of the door from the other guard.

After a few moments, the guard whispered across to her, "Ever done this before?"

Torya shook her head. "Have you?"

The guard nodded. "Some nights it's quiet. Other nights, he makes a fearful noise—dreaming about the curse, I think, or all the people who've died because of him."

Torya expected to feel glad at the dreams, but then she remembered the look in his eyes when he said he was sorry. She reminded herself that he ought to be sorry. He could never be sorry enough for her.

She sighed and settled her mind into the trance of waiting that she'd used when on guard duty in the field. Any sound, any change in the scene before her, and she would come out of it quickly. Until something happened, though, she found that her trances rested her almost as much as sleep did. If only her hand would stop itching. Though it didn't seem to itch as much as it had of late. She puzzled over this until she remembered that it hadn't itched at all during the review, when she'd been speaking with the king. Was that because of her part in his curse? She rubbed the scab on her hand. Why hadn't she noticed that at the time? Then she shrugged. Too many questions and not enough answers. Always too many questions.

Her thoughts were interrupted by a loud creak as the door to the king's chamber opened. "Is the soldier from the Vortex Riders out there?"

"Yes, sire." Torya stepped forward and peered into the darkness beyond the door. He must have doused the candles because the torchlight from the landing only showed a bit of carpet on the floor.

"Leave your spear out there and come in, then."

Torya glanced at the other guard, but he was staring at the wall, refusing to meet her gaze. Had something like this happened before? She suppressed a sneer. Well, at least now she knew why he'd requested her as a guard. Just let King Rogan try something with her and she'd teach him about curses. She leaned her spear against the wall and let her hand brush against her dagger, reassuring herself that it was still there at her side, then stepped into the darkness.

"Shut the door and come over to the bed."

Once the door was shut, the room didn't seem as dark. Moonlight through the open window showed a room much smaller than she'd expected, barely large enough to hold the high, oversized bed. The curtains hanging around the bed were all open and the golden threads in the bedclothes glittered in the pale light.

Rogan sat in his bed, staring at her. "Come away from the door and into the light."

Torya walked around the bed to the edge of the pool of light. Her eyes had adjusted, and she could see him quite clearly. It would be so simple. She glanced toward the window. It was probably too high off the ground to use as an escape route. She wondered whether she could kill him and return to her post as if nothing had happened. The relief watch wouldn't check him until morning, and by then she might even be out of the city.

"Tell me about your family."

Torya brought her gaze back to his face. "Why? What do you care about mere peasants?"

Rogan looked down at his hands as they lay in his lap. "I've seen too many of my people die." He looked up at her. "They will have told you about the nightmares?"

She shrugged. He seemed more Delly's age now, a child, ready to cry for his mother. She gritted her teeth. Well, she was no mother, especially not his.

"They aren't really nightmares. They're real." He pointed at her. "And you know about that, don't you? I saw it in your eyes this morning. What do you know about Our curse?"

Torya made a fist with her left hand, hiding the sore that had stopped itching when she came into the room. What did that mean? That she should stay near him? That she should kill him? But how could she kill someone who just sat there in his bed like that?

"Please." He reached for a robe hanging by the bed and put it on as he slid to the floor. "I can't let myself go to sleep. If I can stay awake, maybe I can end the curse. Tell me about your family. Tell me about farming. Tell me how to make things live, instead of making things die." He stepped toward her and she stepped back. He stopped.

She narrowed her eyes at him. She shouldn't have stepped back. If he had gotten closer, she could have had her dagger out and into his stomach in one move. But he would have cried out, then. She didn't want to die the way they'd kill her if they caught her. But could she kill him in his sleep? Why did he have to be so different from what she'd expected?

Suddenly he lunged forward and grabbed her arm. As suddenly her dagger was in her hand and at his throat. For a moment, they stood there, frozen in their surprise. Then he cleared his throat. "Yes. That would be the answer, wouldn't it?" He shifted from his lunge and moved closer to her. The point of the dagger released a drop of blood onto his neck.

Torya stared at the dark bead. "Let go of my arm, or I'll kill you."

The fingers tightened. "Please. Do it."

"No man, not even a king, is going to— What did you say?"

"Please. I don't deserve to live. If you only knew what I've done." His eyes glittered in the moonlight, and a single shining tear trailed down his cheek.

Torya blinked. He meant it.

"I don't deserve a quick death, but if you take too long, they might catch you." He released her arm, pulled a ring off of one of his fingers, and pressed it into her left hand. "Here. Take this when you go. Tell the other guard that I've sent you on an errand. This will get you a horse from the stables and take you through the gate, as well. You can be far away before I'm found."

The ring burned her, and Torya dropped it on the bed. She backed away, but he grabbed her shoulders with both hands, sobbing as he shook her. "Please, please, please! You don't understand!"

She jerked away from him and ran to the door. As she opened it, she could hear him weeping in great shuddering gasps behind her. But he didn't follow or call out, and she stepped back out of the room. The other guard stood staring at the wall, just as she'd left him. She moved to stand opposite, though her stare was directed at the floor.

How could he beg her to kill him like that? No curse could be so terrible, could it? She thought back to the time she'd been with a group of soldiers hunting through a forest for stray goblins. The man next to her had stumbled onto a carnivorous plant, and before she understood what had happened, it had swallowed him up to his shoulders. The crunching as it ground his bones and the sizzling as it dissolved his flesh were almost drowned out by his screams begging for death. But Torya couldn't do it then, either. She'd killed plenty of goblins, but kill a fellow human? Another soldier had to step close enough to cut off the victim's head and then jump back as the plant reached out a tendril for him as well. The sounds still haunted Torya's nightmares. She shuddered and tried to think of something, anything, else.

Rogan. He may have been born and raised to be a king, but he was still only a man; nay, a boy. What could his advisors have been thinking of to allow him to send the army out to attract the attentions of the goblins of the Flarg? Oh, he'd fought bravely enough the time or two she'd had a chance to see him, but fighting wasn't the only duty of a king.

She remembered the pain she'd seen in his eyes just now and earlier in the day. Pain you had to be up close to see. Maybe he really was suffering for the sake of his people. Maybe he really could have human feelings and still be a king. But what kind of curse could be as terrible as being consumed by a carnivorous plant? What could make a man, or a king, beg for death like that?

Torya was startled out of her reverie by a roar that burned through her whole body, starting at her left hand. The pain almost knocked her into the wall. She looked over at the other guard, who shrugged and smiled at her, as if sharing a joke. But this was no nightmare. Couldn't he feel it? The roar came again, and this time Torya braced herself against the wall. The other guard didn't even move. She stepped to the door, trying to decide what to do with the spear—her left hand burned so that she could neither hold the spear nor open the door with it. Finally she left the spear where she'd leaned it before and pulled on the handle with her right hand. Ignoring the other guard's cry of warning, she stepped over the threshold once again.

Something large and awkward shuffled near the window, only half-revealed by the moonlight. She couldn't see the king, but then, he was probably hiding under the bed.

With another roar, the shape turned and saw her. Eyes that burned with their own light, green and baleful, glared at her. Torya remembered a sick wolf she once faced across the body of a newly dead lamb. But this was taller than any wolf, bigger even than a horse. Then shadows moved at its back: the monster had wings, folded now because of the lack of room. Opened, they would have bumped against the high ceiling.

She reached back through the doorway for the spear with her right hand and brought it up to rest against her throbbing left arm. Then she stepped toward the monster. Part of her cried out at how frail the weapon looked against the bulk before her. With no space to maneuver, she had little chance to use it anyhow. She should have brought her crossbow, but even at close range she doubted that it would have penetrated the plate-mail scales that glinted in the torch-light. The monster grunted, probably agreeing with her about the frailty of her spear, and turned toward the window and the balcony beyond it.

"No!" She couldn't let it escape. She rushed to the windowed wall, keeping as far from the creature as she could. It swung back as she moved, following her progress with its whole body, turning to keep its smoky breath blowing in her direction.

Once she reached the wall, she didn't know what to do next. She could see the other guard peering at her from the doorway, brave while she held the monster's attention. "Send for help! Have someone bring a crossbow!" The beast snorted at her and turned again toward the window. Torya took a step forward, waving the spear. The creature twisted its head to look at her. The spear caught in its nostril and flipped out of Torya's hands. Flame accompanied the beast's roar of pain and Torya scrambled back with singed eyebrows. Out of the corner of her eye, she noticed that the doorway was empty.

The monster's great claws covered its face, but when Torya moved to retrieve the spear, the claws dropped quickly to show eyes overflowing with liquid. Could it be crying? She shrugged the idea away; this was no time for sympathy.

Before she could take another step, the creature backed out onto the balcony and began to turn, the wings opening out into the room. Torya dashed forward and grabbed a wing. The monster turned back, pulling away, but only succeeded in dragging Torya with it as she clung to the leathery membrane.

The unexpected turn brought her across the beast's tail and she banged her shins against the bony plates along its spine. Reacting to the pain, Torya let go of the wing and found herself hugging the monster's back as it moved once more toward the window. She hauled herself upward along the back plates to where the wings sprouted from the shoulders. Grasping the nearest plate with her right hand, she struggled to get her dagger out of its scabbard with the left. At first, the angle was wrong, and then, with a little jiggling, it came free so forcefully that it flew out of her hand.

She froze for a moment, staring at the scaly back and the great wings before her. Then she noticed the itching in her hand. No, not itching: burning, throbbing, screaming, worse and worse now that she'd noticed it. It was so bad she could barely hold on against the shaking and jerking as the creature tried to get her off its back. Suddenly it leaned forward and Torya felt herself slipping down toward its lowered head. She put out both hands to catch herself on the scales and cried out as the rough flesh scraped her skin. But the scrape made the itching stop for an instant. She scraped some more, scraped it all away, scraped until hatred and anger flowed out with the blood, scraped until the scab was torn off and the poison in the bite was gone. Blood covered several scales before she stopped, but at last the itching and burning turned to simple, clean pain.

As she squeezed her injured hand with her uninjured one, a great shudder seized the monster's body and threw her to the ground. Screams overwhelmed her hearing, followed by acrid fumes, hot and cold waves of air, and eye-stinging smoke that she could not escape no matter how far back she scrambled. Just as suddenly, chaos changed to peace. She shook her head to clear it and then looked around the room to see servants standing over something that lay before the window.

Torya struggled to her feet and staggered toward the crowd, which parted at her approach. In the center of the huddle, lying naked on the floor with his blood-smeared back to her, was the king.

As Torya knelt beside Rogan, his head turned and his green eyes stared up at her. "You should have killed me when you had the chance."

Torya sat back on her heels. So that was the curse. And it had taught him how terrible destruction could be. This was a boy who could learn to be a man, to be a king. Just as she had learned that anger and hate bring their own destruction. The two of them had a lot to make up for; she had been as guilty in her way as he had in his.

She looked at her hand. The bleeding had slowed, but this time it would not scab over so quickly. She stood up, staring at the man-boy lying before her. There was no wound on his back, just smeared blood. "The curse is ended. You don't have to die; and you don't have to see anyone else die either. You aren't even hurt. That's my blood, not yours. Bring me a bedsheet." Torya held out her right hand and someone thrust the cloth into it. She spread it over Rogan and knelt again, pulling him to a sitting position. He opened his eyes and pushed with his hands at the sheet. "What are you doing?"

"Covering your wretched hide so you can get up and be a better king than before."

The crowd parted and a man in green came through. "Let me look at him."

Torya rose and stepped back, letting the royal healer take her place. The king clutched the sheet around himself and waved the healer away. "I'm fine. She's the one who's bleeding. See to her!"

Torya held her hand out. "You didn't know what would happen when you started your game of glory. Nor did I when I let a healer bite me." Once her hand was bandaged, she squatted down to look him in the face. "You are going to live, King Rogan, and you are going to start being the kind of king you should be. You've learned what you shouldn't do. Now you have a chance to start doing what you should do."

Rogan's lips curled in what Torya at first took to be a sneer. "Then you, farmer, have to stay and help me."

"Me? How can a farmer help a king?" Torya stood up. She didn't want to stay here; there were people out there ready to try living again, and suddenly she wanted to join them.

"A farmer knows how to make things grow." Rogan coughed. "If I have to stay here and learn, you have to stay here and teach me."

Torya stared at him for a moment. The color was coming back into his face. Maybe it would be all right after all; in fact, it would have to be. She was a practical woman and could recognize an opportunity when she saw one. Besides, she really had nowhere else to go.

"Well, then, it's time we got started." And she bent over to help the healer get the king on his feet.

What Leaf Learned of Goblins

by

Hanovi Braddock

There once was a Great Mother of Savaen who as a child had been called Whisper and as a young mother had been called Brookcharm, but whose name in her later years was Leaf. Among the elves of Savaen Forest, this was one of the high names for aged Great Mothers and Great Fathers of their kind.

Leaf had seen more than a hundred winters, though no human who regarded her would guess that she had attained so great an age. Years do not mark the elves as they mark humans. To human eyes, elves seem young until the very last of their final days. In their last year, their decline is so swift and sudden, like a cut leaf shriveling, browning, and returning to dust, that the elves have but one word to mean "grow old" and "decay."

Even among elves, for whom wisdom is as common as grass, Leaf was counted wise. She spent many of her days in the deep shade of the Emperor Oak, that ancient tree in the heart of Savaen Forest. The Emperor Oak spread its branches high and wide and shaded the forest floor beneath to blackness. It was a holy place, and a place for elves to think wise thoughts. But the folly of wisdom is this: it does not know its own rare nature.

One day, a goblin from the Red Mountains wandered into the forest, and the Savaen elves did as elves anywhere would do. They shot the wretched thing full of arrows. After it was dead, they did not even inspect it closely, but left it where it had fallen. Goblins were trouble, and that was all any elf needed to know. Any elf, that is, except for Great Mother Leaf. When she heard of the lone goblin who had been wandering in the Savaen, she asked the hunters to show her the body.

"What's this?" asked Leaf, taking a carved and painted stone from the dead goblin's clutches.

One by one, the hunters examined the stone.

"A glyph," said one, an elf called Shade.

"A talisman, perhaps," said a second.

"A ward against arrows," guessed the third with a laugh.

"Pity," said Leaf, "that the one who might have answered may answer not."

"Not so great a pity. There is profit in knowledge, Mother Leaf," said Shade, "except in the case of goblins. What do these gray-skinned skulkers ever make but mischief? Long ago our ancestors tried to reason with theirs, but the goblin mind admits no subtle thought."

Bending close to the body again, Leaf said, "He was unarmed. Surely he knew that the forest has eyes . . . and arrows. Yet he came bearing only this stone."

"And still I say there is no subtlety," said Shade, "but stupidity alone."

"Perhaps," said Leaf, taking the carved stone from the third hunter and putting it in her pouch. "But whether carried in craft or foolishness, this stone is a question I would have an answer for."

When a second goblin entered the Savaen, Leaf again asked to see the body. Different hunters had killed this one, but Shade came along to inspect the goblin. This one was female. Like the first, she carried no weapon. In her hand was a stone.

"Much like the first," said Shade.

Leaf took the first stone from her pouch. "Very like it," she said. Indeed, were she to confuse them, she would never be able to say which stone had come from the first goblin and which from the second.

One of the hunters who had shot the goblin said, "She carried it a little before her, as if it were a lamp that showed her the way. And she came cowering with every step."

"And you did not think this curious?"

"I did not stop to think, Great Mother Leaf," said the hunter. "She was a goblin, so I let fly my arrows. The others did the same."

"You credit goblins with no subtlety," said Leaf to Shade, "but how subtle are we ourselves?"

"I see what you mean," said Shade. "We ought not to kill the next, if there is a next."

Savaen elves have neither books nor princes. They are ruled neither by law nor by title; however, an idea that seems right to a few will soon enough seem right to all. So it was that when a third goblin entered the Savaen, snuffling and ducking and casting wary glances that failed to see, it was allowed to come deeper and deeper into the forest while one of the hunters summoned Leaf.

When Leaf saw how the goblin cowered behind his stone, holding it a little aloft and casting nervous glances all about him, she could no longer doubt what the glyph must mean among goblins.

"You ask for parlay," said Leaf, stepping from behind a tree. At the same time, a dozen elvish hunters came into the open, bows drawn, arrows sighted.

The goblin dropped the stone and fell to his knees. "Don't kill! Don't kill! Busjaw comes alone! No jabbers, no stickers, no stabbers! I got nothing! No smashers, no slicers or prickers!" Seeing the stone on the ground before him, he yelped and scrambled to pick it up and hold it out before him with the carved glyph visible. "Busjaw here to talk, that's all. See? The talking mark!" He waved the stone. "Don't kill!"

Leaf stepped forward and held out her hand for the stone. Busjaw rose to give it to her, then knelt again, trembling, to bow at her feet.

"Busjaw is all alone. Got no spikes, no pokers, nothing," he said to the ground, splaying his fingers out for all to see that he held no weapon.

"Is it the same as the others?" asked Shade.

Leaf nodded. "The same mark."

"Don't kill Busjaw," the goblin said again.

"We won't kill you," Leaf said, and the hunters eased their bowstrings.

Busjaw looked around. "Busjaw live! Good, good, good!" He grinned, but he was still trembling.

"Are you a messenger?" asked Leaf, returning the stone to him.

"Yes, chieftess," he said, bowing again.

"I am no chieftess."

"Then take Busjaw to chieftess. Message is for her, from goblin chieftess. Busjaw got to tell your chieftess, or Chieftess Kruuna crack Busjaw head hard-hard-hard or maybe break his jaw another time when he gets back." At those last words, he grinned a lopsided yellow grin, obviously delighted with the thought that he *would* get back, that the elves would not kill him.

"We have no chieftess," Leaf told him.

"Boss, then," said Busjaw. "King, like the city people. The ones that lived over-mountain, in the valley."

"In Oneah?" said Leaf. The great city beyond the mountains had fallen so recently in its war with the goblins that ragged human refugees still sometimes passed through the Savaen. "We have no kings like them, either. Among the elves, all are the same."

"Same?" Busjaw said. He looked warily at the elves all around him. "But who tells what to do? Who cracks head, who pinches ears? Who says, 'This one disobeyed. Everyone throw stones at him now'?" Then his face twisted with fear. "If no chieftess, who does Busjaw give message to? Got to tell message, or Kruuna crack Busjaw's head!" He raised his gray hands to his head as if the blows were about to fall.

"I command no one," said Leaf, "but I am a Great Mother of my people. You may as well give your message to me."

Busjaw looked relieved again. "Good, good, good," he said. And then, in a rush to deliver the message before Leaf could change her mind about receiving it, Busjaw said, "Chieftess Kruuna says for you to come. Follow Busjaw to goblin caves. Kruuna wants to know about a magic thing, and elf chieftess can tell her. Kruuna will give jewels and gold. She promises goblins will not eat you. She says 'Please, please, please' many times, like one who is tortured."

"I will consider," said Leaf.

"Great Mother!" said one of the hunters. "You can't be serious!"

Leaf ignored him for the moment. "You are our guest—" she started to say, but was interrupted by Busjaw's howl.

"Not guest! Busjaw is messenger! Don't eat Busjaw! You said no killing! Not guest, not guest!" He groveled at Leaf's feet.

"I think," said Leaf, "that the word means different things to elves and to goblins. I mean that we shall feed you and give you things to drink. We will give you a place to rest, and no one will bother you."

"No killing!" screeched Busjaw.

"No killing," Leaf reassured him.

"And no eating! No cutting off parts to eat!"

Leaf scowled. "Of course not!"

Busjaw raised his gaze cautiously. "No torture?"

"No."

"Not even a little, for the children?"

Leaf shook her head. "No harm shall come to you."

Busjaw grinned a wavering grin, as if he couldn't quite believe what he was told. "A little torture is okay," he said. "Children expect it." And he let two hunters lead him off to another part of the forest.

"Great Mother Leaf," said Shade, when Busjaw was out of hearing, "how can you even consider going back with such a creature? In every word he speaks, he reveals the nature of goblins. How can you trust for your safety?"

"I can't," said Leaf.

"Then why do you think of going?"

"Young Shade, I have seen much, and I have lived long. It is the privilege of Great Mothers to be considered wise when we speak, and what have we done to earn such consideration?"

Shade had no ready answer. "It is because . . . Well, you *are* wise."

"If that is so, then how have Great Mothers and Great Fathers come to be wise? We have lived long, and we have seen much, nothing more. Now I think to trade the promise of living a little longer in safety for the possibility of seeing a little more deeply. Goblins have long been our enemies, but we have never understood their hearts."

"Sooner fill their hearts with arrows than understand them," said another hunter. "This very goblin, this Busjaw, could scarce be a better example of why goblins are despised. Any good thing that is in the hearts of elves is absent in the hearts of goblins."

"Well argued," said Leaf, "and thus my case is proved."

"What?" said the hunter.

"If we are to know our hearts," said Leaf, "how better than by contrast? If I return, I will know goblins a little better, and by knowing them, perhaps better know ourselves."

None could dissuade her, though not an elf in Savaen who heard of Leaf's determination thought well of it. Even so, since there was no one to command her otherwise, Leaf found herself the next day traveling through the forest in the company of the goblin Busjaw.

While they remained in the forest, Busjaw's manner was as it had been before. He cast worried glances to this side and that, squinting into the shadows and nonetheless failing to see the hunters who watched from every side, and he bowed now and again to Leaf and called her chieftess. But as the forest thinned and the archers were left behind, Busjaw's manner began to change. By the time the two of them were climbing the scrub-covered hills between Savaen and the Red Mountains, Busjaw no longer bowed, and he called Leaf by her name.

Before long, they were climbing the steep approach to the first of the mountain passes, and Leaf said, "Why don't we stop here a moment and rest?"

"No resting!" Busjaw barked. "We go on until Busjaw says to stop."

"Do as you like," Leaf said, sitting on a boulder. "Howsoever briskly as it suits you, go. But I am weary, and I mean to rest."

Busjaw gave two sharp whistles, and suddenly the rocky slopes above the trail and below it were acrawl with goblins. A few brandished knives or axes, but most were armed with sharpened staves.

Leaf reached for the hilt of her dagger.

"Don't," said Busjaw, "or else Busjaw call down hospitality on you. Then everybody free to kill, take your things."

Leaf looked at the crooked yellow grins around her. "I thought Chieftess Kruuna guaranteed my safety."

"Chieftess wants elf alive. You come alive, unless you are bad prisoner and don't do as Busjaw tells you. Good prisoner all right. Bad prisoner becomes guest."

"I'm no prisoner," Leaf said.

"You are Busjaw's prisoner," the goblin insisted. "Or else you are Busjaw's guest."

"Guest! Guest!" said the nearest goblins, crowding in, reaching with grubby hands for the buttons and ornaments of Leaf's clothing.

"Not unless Busjaw says!" the goblin shouted, and he grabbed a pointed stick and whacked its erstwhile owner on the head. "To the caves!"

"To caves! To caves!" cried the others, some of the nearest ones jabbing sharpened staves at Leaf's legs and ankles from behind.

As they went, Busjaw sang a song about his exploits, about the way he had single-handedly defeated a dozen elves and taken their chieftess prisoner. The second and third verses were about the tenderness of elvish flesh, which Busjaw claimed to have tasted many times after his victory.

If Leaf thought of fighting Busjaw and the others, she gave no outward sign. For most of the journey, she suffered their goading without complaint. The one time she turned to snatch the staff from a goblin who was pricking her, she broke it and flung away the pieces before the owner could begin to shriek that Leaf had armed herself. The others, seeing that Busjaw did nothing about this infraction, grew sulky. They also stopped goading Leaf with their staves.

"Busjaw returns!" the goblin announced as he led the way into the goblin cave. "Busjaw brings a prisoner! The elves killed the goblins that went before Busjaw, but Busjaw brings the elvish prisoner to Kruuna! Hooray for Busjaw! Say his name! Busjaw! Busjaw!"

The goblins that crowded into the torchlight of the main passage refrained from singing Busjaw's praises, but Busjaw seemed content with singing them for himself. As he continued to crow, goblin children were throwing pebbles at Leaf's eyes, crying in frustration when Leaf raised her arm to ward off the missiles.

"Tie the guest!" the children urged, and some adults chanted, "Guest! Guest!"

"Not guest!" Busjaw bleated. "For Kruuna!" But no one seemed to hear him.

A grubby hand grabbed at Leaf's sleeve, and then another snatched at her buttons. Leaf reached again for her dagger, and a howl of anticipation arose from the goblins.

"Guest! Guest!"

"Stop!" came a voice from the shadows.

There was silence immediately. Half of the goblins melted back into side corridors, and Busjaw's manner reverted to what it had been in the forest. At once he was on his knees, bowing and touching his head to the cave floor.

"Busjaw obeyed Kruuna," he said into the darkness from which the voice had come. "Busjaw brought prisoner! Busjaw killed elves, captured this chieftess."

"That's a lie," Leaf said. "We spared you when we might as easily have killed you. And I came of my own free will."

Busjaw gave her a look that made it clear: if he were free to do so, he'd declare her his guest then and there.

"What is your name, elf?" said the figure stepping from the shadows.

Involuntarily, Leaf took a step back. This was the biggest goblin she had ever seen. Her head was as round as the moon, and nearly as pale.

"I am Leaf."

"I am Kruuna, Chieftess," said the giant goblin. The golden chains looped around her wrists and neck jingled as she walked, and she wielded a silver scepter like a club. Without looking at Busjaw, she struck the side of his head as she passed. Busjaw whimpered and held his bloody ear. "Are you a chieftess of your kind, Leaf Elf?"

"No," Leaf said, and Kruuna cracked Busjaw again.

"I told you to bring a chieftess!" Kruuna said. Busjaw whimpered, but made no attempt to explain.

"There are no chiefs among elves," Leaf said, "but I am as near a chieftess as I may be."

Kruuna turned a skeptical eye on her. "You know magic?"

Leaf was no wizard. She could call blossoms from the trees in winter or charm game into the open. And she could undo enchantments that were directed against the earth itself. Any elder elf could do so. But that was not so much magic as forest sympathy. Still, she answered, "Yes."

Kruuna grunted. "All right." She tossed a few copper coins at Busjaw's feet.

"Good, good, good," Busjaw said, scooping up the coins and vanishing into the shadows.

Kruuna said, "Come."

Kruuna's chambers were far from the main entrance of the caves. In all the long walk to them, Kruuna did not speak once. Not until she and Leaf arrived in her chambers, hung with stolen tapestries depicting human scenes of hunting and human feasting halls and human musicians and dancers, did she even acknowledge that Leaf was following her.

"You will help Kruuna," the goblin chieftess said, "and Kruuna not kill you. This is more than fair. This is a good bargain."

Leaf folded her hands. "What sort of help do you require?"

"Kruuna is old," the goblin said. She rubbed her face. "Kruuna does not look old, though. Kruuna stays strong. Kruuna's face is smooth, and young goblins cannot take things away from Kruuna. Kruuna can still bash them. Some young goblins try, and Kruuna cracks heads, year after year. Other young goblins wait for Kruuna to get old; they get old first. Kruuna still strong, and young schemers get old and weak." She laughed. "Good trick, yes?"

Leaf had heard of spells for eternal youth, but they were nothing that any elf would take an interest in. "There are advantages to growing old, too," she said.

Kruuna stared at her for a long moment, then grunted. "Advantages? Not for Kruuna. Start to get old and weak, pretty soon some young one is stronger. Some other goblin will have all this." Her hands swept the room to indicate the moldering tapestries, the human furnishings, and perhaps the room itself. Then she clutched the gold chain around her neck. "This is Kruuna's because Kruuna can keep it. Anyone tries to take it, Kruuna bashes them, maybe bashes them dead. But if Kruuna gets old, Kruuna loses everything."

Then she pulled back one of the tapestries to reveal a recess in the chamber and a rough-hewn window that looked out over the valley below. It was not the valley of the Savaen Forest, but the wider expanse of rolling grassy ground. In the distance, Leaf could see the ruins of a human city: Oneah. The furnishings in Kruuna's cave, Leaf guessed, had been looted from the Oneahns when their city fell to the goblins.

Next to the window was a little table, and on the table, an ivory cup. Beside the cup was a box carved of blue stone.

"All these things, Kruuna got because Kruuna is strong," the goblin said. "Killed humans for some. Made goblins give tribute when they killed humans. Got lots of things. The more things Kruuna got from those people, the stronger Kruuna became." She nodded to herself with satisfaction. "Got this cup and box from a young wizard, very long time ago. Wizard was lost, weak with sickness." Kruuna pantomimed a man stumbling along, fevered, half blind. Then she laughed at the memory.

"Kruuna brought him here, gave him food and drink to get better. Took away his things. When young wizard was strong enough, Kruuna tortured him very slow until he showed how to use the box and the cup."

The goblin chieftess opened the box. It was empty. Kruuna cupped it secretively in her hands and spoke a word into it, and when she showed the box to Leaf, the interior was glowing.

"Power for magic," Kruuna said.

Leaf nodded.

"Wizard said power can be used for lots of things, but wizard only had the cup. Oooh, wizard said lots of things, told about lots of magics. Goblins stretched him. Goblins pierced him, but careful, careful. Keep him alive to tell us many things." She picked up the cup. "When cup lights up, put it over the box. That's what wizard said. Then the cup fills up with white stuff, like milk. Drink it and stay young, maybe forever ever always."

Kruuna put the cup over the box, but nothing happened. "Light!" she commanded.

But there was no change to the cup.

"Cup doesn't fill if it doesn't light up first. For a long time now, cup doesn't light up." She shook the ivory cup at Leaf. "You know magic. How can Kruuna make the cup light up?"

Leaf took the cup from the chieftess. "When did it light before? In the morning? At night?"

"Anytime. Sometimes morning, sometimes night." Kruuna's brow furrowed. "Some days, lights up lots of times. Then not for days. Then lots again." She smiled. "When we were fighting humans, light came all the time. Kruuna younger every day, fight stronger all the time."

"I see."

"Leaf Elf understand?"

Leaf traced the profile of the cup from the bottom up. "Wide below for roots," she said, "and slender for the stem. Here at the top, it spreads as branches do."

Kruuna grinned, and her teeth glistened. "Leaf Elf knows magic! Leaf Elf knows how to work the cup!"

Leaf said, "I think so. It's hard to be certain."

"How does Kruuna make the cup work some more? How does Kruuna stay young some more forever?"

"I'm sorry," Leaf said.

Kruuna glowered. "If you help Kruuna, you live. If not, goblins deep in the caves want to have a guest."

"It's not a matter of wanting to help you or not," Leaf said. "But if I understand the cup . . ."

The goblin's brow furrowed. "Need to make sacrifice? Kruuna will do anything. Kruuna makes sacrifices all the time, giving guests to the goblin gods."

Leaf said, "The elves have something better than the cup."

The goblin picked up her scepter and twisted it in her enormous hands. "Kruuna not care what elves got. Kruuna has the cup. Cup keeps Kruuna strong, bashing weaker ones. Just tell Kruuna what Kruuna has to do."

"I don't think there's anything you can do. I think the cup depends on other sorceries, the spells of Oneahn wizards and healers. The box below is like the earth that feeds the roots, but roots alone are not enough. A tree needs sunlight. The bowl of the cup is like the branches of a tree; it bears fruit, but it also drinks in light. Or, in this case, spells. When you destroyed Oneah, when you drove off the people who cast their healing spells, you drove away what made the cup work. It is as if you banished the sun."

Kruuna stamped her great feet on the floor of the cave. "No! Elf lies! I see elf trick, trying to make Kruuna give you cup! First elf tries to make Kruuna think the cup is worthless!" She swung her silver scepter at Leaf's head, and the Great Mother dodged the blow.

"I don't want your cup," Leaf said. "I already told you that the elves have something better."

Kruuna swung again, closer, and had raised her scepter for a third try before the notion penetrated her brain.

"Better?" she said.

"Much better," said Great Mother Leaf. "And if you come back to the forest with me, I will show you."

Kruuna growled. "Not show it to Kruuna. Give it."

"It shall be yours."

Kruuna waved her scepter. "If you trick Kruuna, you die! Kruuna not afraid of skinny elves!"

"I intend no deceit," Leaf said. And so it was agreed.

Thus it was that Great Mother Leaf and Chieftess Kruuna retraced the path between the Red Mountains and the Savaen Forest. And thus it was that they came to stand in the heart of the forest, with unseen elves all about them, elves who marveled at the sight of Kruuna and kept their bows at the ready. And thus did Leaf come to the folly of wisdom, for she showed Kruuna the Emperor Oak with its branches spreading for half a league. She showed Kruuna the bleak expanse beneath, where the tree's shade kept even the grass from growing.

"Here is a thing greater than your ivory cup," Leaf said.

"Tree is magic?" Kruuna's brow furrowed. "Kruuna not see how to carry tree back to caves."

Leaf laughed gently.

Kruuna frowned and squinted, raising her scepter. "This elf trick?"

"Take care, Kruuna," Leaf said. "There are archers about. And, no, the tree is no trick. It is wisdom. It is consolation." Then she explained the tree, and what it meant to elves.

"Here is life," Leaf told the goblin. "This oak is sacred, not because it is tall, though there is no tree in Savaen that is taller. It is holy not because of its girth or the spread of its branches, though no tree casts a greater shadow. We love it, Kruuna, because it lives, and because it dies."

Kruuna shook herself impatiently. "All things die if things get old," she said. "Where is magic?"

"Beneath our feet," Leaf said. "When at last the Emperor Oak dies, when the sunlight again shines on this ground, then the grass will push up from between the decaying leaves. The first dandelions and starwort will grow. And here or there, unlike all the seedlings that spring up into darkness now, acorns not yet fallen will swell in the ground and unfold in the new light. The old oak, dying, makes way for the new."

And Leaf, poor Leaf, wise Leaf, smiled at that. "This is the magic," she said, "that is stronger and better than the ivory cup. We live: that is beauty. And so that others might live, we someday depart. We die. And that, too, is beauty."

Leaf waited for understanding to dawn behind the goblin's green eyes.

Kruuna scratched her head. "That's it?"

"Yes."

"That is better than ivory cup? That is better than be strong and live forever?" Kruuna's face wrinkled in concentration.

"On this very ground, when I am gone," Leaf said, "another elf will stand. Great Mothers before me have stood on this spot, and others before them. This moment is eternal. There will always be one who stands on this earth. A different one, and yet the same. Life endures. The living make way for it." Leaf smiled. "That is the greatest magic: to receive life, to hold it, and to pass it on."

"Where Kruuna is," Kruuna said, "goblin child will be, dressed in Kruuna's clothes, touching Kruuna's things, eating Kruuna's food. That is what Leaf Elf says."

"Yes!" Leaf said. "You understand!"

And Kruuna, chieftess of goblins, cried, "Touching Kruuna's things! Nasty little goblin! No! Smash it!"

But as there were no goblin children to smash when Kruuna raised her club, she aimed at Leaf.

From the foliage beyond the Emperor Oak's great shadow, a dozen arrows flew. Each found its mark, and Kruuna fell to her knees.

"Elf trick," she gasped. "Elves wicked, nasty!" And she broke Leaf's skull with her scepter before she died.

When Shade and the other hunters came to Leaf, she was dying.

"Great Mother," said Shade, "what has come of this?"

"The wisdom," Leaf said, "to know that not all may know wisdom." She stretched out her hand to the barren ground, and she called up the long-dormant grass seed. Her fingers caressed the tender blades, the green hair of the newborn earth.

Then Leaf looked at where the great bulk of Kruuna had fallen. "We have always filled them with arrows without a thought, but now, Shade, we know goblins better."

"And for what?" asked the younger elf. "Great Mother, to what end?"

"That we may pity them," Leaf said, "for what their hearts may not admit. Pity them first," she said.

Her last words were a whisper. "Then fill them with arrows."

DUAL LOYALTIES

by

Glen Vasey

1.

A sunny day. Helana paused before entering the church, closed her eyes, and aimed her face at the heavenly radiance, the only deity she worshiped. She opened her eyes then, muttering a short prayer as she stared directly into the Face. She closed her eyes again and admired, drifted in, the ebon and crimson aftersight, feeling the tingling, radiant massage throughout her lithe form, prickling at her skin, loosening her muscles, warming her bones.

"It is good," she murmured as she opened her eyes again and turned toward the door of the simple, country church.

Koborah, the priest who had raised the girl since finding her wrapped and cradled by the church doorsill, watched the young woman as she entered the church. Sixteen cycles since he had found her, and every day he had sent up thanks to the Face of the Sun. She was his only daughter, born of his only union. His union with the Sun. Every day her presence banished his belief in coincidence, enhanced his faith in manipulable destiny. She was a child of the Sun, if ever there was one. She belonged here. Perhaps, he hoped, even more than he did. Her presence was stronger, he felt. Or would be.

Three steps in, Helana knelt, curled into a ball so that her cheeks touched either knee, her arms wrapped tightly about her torso. She held this position for a slow count of ten, breathing deeply, gently, evenly. Then, gradually, she began to uncurl, deeply feeling the sensations of all of her muscles individually and collectively; inventorying the balances between tensions and relaxation in each and in all; raising her torso, straightening her legs, and spreading her arms simultaneously, in imitation of a sunrise. In all, it was fifteen minutes before she finally stood erect, arms outstretched and fingers splayed, face turned up to the wide casements above the altar. The casements that literally invited the Goddess into Her own Church.

An athletic feat, when done so, thought Koborah. *That simple gesture, which my most devout parishioners complete in fifteen seconds, she devotes sufficient time and energy to make into an athletic feat, an artistic statement, and a gesture of worship all at once. I am fortunate . . . the entire parish is fortunate that she is here. She will be needed here when I am gone.* He shook his head, not liking to think how soon or sudden his departure might be.

He watched her from entry to completion of the gesture with as singular a devotion as the young woman was displaying. *Such grace,* he thought, *in every conceivable meaning of the term. Such an odd, and wonderful, and powerful child. More powerful than she rightly imagines. At such an age, with so little instruction, to have utilized the stones I gave her, like some prodigy upon first touching a musical instrument.*

When she stood again at ease, he spoke: "It is marvelous to watch you, child."

She smiled as she approached him, "I perform only as you have taught me, Father. I feel it as you have taught me."

"You offer me too much of the honor that is yours. I can only hope that I have taught you enough in the time that we have had."

She caught his subtle implication, cast a line to get him to volunteer something more forthright: "I still have much to learn, Father, but we have much time remaining. You are still a young enough man. I look forward to the gentle, continuous unfolding."

He nodded and frowned. "Time is the one thing we may never be certain of having enough of. We make do with what we are allotted, even if we feel we have been cheated in some way." She reflected his frown, so he laughed at the two of them, "Come, my child, there is much that we must do and say. Time is a far less certain commodity today than it was one week ago."

In Koborah's study the two of them were greeted by Rorsa, who sniffed and yapped at the cleric first, then danced about Helana's feet until she was seated, at which point the small, white, winged dog leapt into her lap, spun himself around three times, and plopped himself down as if he'd come there to stay.

Helana stroked him absently, confounded by her onlyfather's unusual solemnity. On reflection she realized that Koboraħ had been prone to such spells lately, and she became suddenly fearful that he might be ill.

But if that is the case, certainly one of the gems of healing could be used to make him well. I could even brandish it. He has taught me this process, I have done it. . . . She curtailed such thoughts by telling herself sternly that Koborah would explain the situation as he recognized her need to understand it. This is important. She must silence all distractions.

Koborah, meanwhile, smiled at Helana and Rorsa as he took a seat on the opposite side of his large, birchwood desk. The dog would be in his lap now if Helana hadn't been in the room. He would miss his pet and protector, if it came to that. He would miss each and every member of his parish. But most of all he would miss his child-grown-woman, upon whom he was about to depend all of his hopes, if she would have them. He, too, had to shake away such thoughts as distractions. There was business to attend to.

"Do you remember the stranger who called upon me last week?" he asked her.

Remember? How could she possibly forget?

She had been cleaning the altar, suffused in the spiritual gestalt that overwhelmed her when she was engaged in even the most mundane of tasks, when a loud knock resounded on the front door of the church. This was unusual in two respects: any of the parishioners would have simply opened the door and entered; and the sounding of the knock had momentarily shattered Helana's serenity, an experience she was remarkably unused to.

Quickly she had set down her dusting cloth and moved to answer the door, fearful that another such knock might disturb Koborah in his study, where he had retreated to write.

A strange, prickly, tingling sensation overcame her as she neared the door, as if a tickle that didn't itch had married an itch that didn't tickle and had borne a brood that suddenly covered all of her skin. Neither pleasant, nor unpleasant, but disturbing. She shuddered once involuntarily, then shook herself intentionally as she had seen Rorsa do after swimming in the creek, wishing she could shake the sensation off like so many droplets of water. It didn't help.

She took a deep breath and noticed that her head had gone all swimmy. Portent of something, but what?

When she opened the door to the stranger she stood transfixed by his long, dark features, his pale gray eyes, his salt-and-pepper hair and beard, his incongruously youthful face. Not that she was attracted to or repulsed by him. It was something quite beyond either, or any mix of those responses.

The stranger smiled and spoke in an oddly accented voice. "Is the padré in?"

"Who?" she asked, nearly breaking the word into several syllables.

"The padré, minister, cleric, goodfather, the deacon of this house of worship, whatever title you may call him by."

She had stared into his smiling eyes for what must have been a long time, unconscious—until later, and only then in recollection—of the yammering and yelping of Rorsa in the study. That should have been an alarming sound to her, coming as it did from the normally equable creature, but she heard it only with her ears. Her mind was doing lolly-loops, sensing dollops of dozens of reactions to this phenomena without really settling on any one of them. Finally she found her voice and made answer. "I'll get him."

When she turned toward the study, Koborah was already out of it, the door closed behind him as he stared at the stranger. Behind the door Rorsa was whimpering and whining to be let out.

"Leave us, child," Koborah said without looking at Helana.

"But Father," she began, "I still have much—"

"Go now! Walk in the fields. Ask the Sun to take you into trance. Care for your spirit."

She had bowed her head and left.

The trance she took on had carried her through to sunset. When she returned to the church, the stranger was gone. Since then neither she nor Koborah had made reference to the visit or the visitor. Until now.

"Certainly I remember, Father."

"He made an image of me in prairie clay. An image for which he required some of my hair. Does that mean anything to you, my daughter?"

Helana shook her head.

"He was a walker, child. A magus of incredible power and ability. Do his intentions become clearer in this light?"

Again she shook her head. Certainly she had heard of walkers before. Some called them gods, others preferred to refer to them as demons, but she knew only one deity: the Sun. Since the Sun gave life, even to the walkers, but the walkers could no way affect the Sun, then surely they were only creatures, like Helana herself, like Rorsa, like the spiders in the kitchen, or the winged horses that swooped across the mesa. Creatures could aspire to divinity or diabolism, but creatures they remained. That the walkers might possess powers that she did not, did not impress her. Many creatures under the Sun's wise and loving diversity were capable of things that she could only dream about, like Rorsa, with his wobbly, comic flight, but that did not make the dog divine.

"He tagged me," explained the cleric. "The clay figurine was his method of creating a talisman. As long as he retains the token he may summon me at will. When that summons comes I will vanish from here, appear by his side, and act as he commands me to act. I will have no choice as to the time of the summons, or in my response to it. It will be when and as the walker commands."

Helana's tense reaction was abrupt and obvious. "Certainly you could have refused him!"

Koborah smiled wanly. "Yes. I could have refused him with my life. Then I would have had no time to prepare you, instead of this uncertain temporal increment my acceptance has permitted us."

"Surely the Sun, if you had called upon Her in such a need, surely She would have protected you!" But she could hear his response to that argument even before he began.

"The Sun nourishes us and helps us to grow," he intoned. "She lights our paths by Day, and comforts us with her reflected glory at Night, via Gohrah, Sister Moon. She bestows upon us gifts uncountable, unaccountable if measured against the slight gifts we deserve. She heals us, offers us succor and surcease in our times of need. She inspires us toward understanding and compassion, giving us the strength and wisdom necessary to protect ourselves. All natural creatures that She made, and feeds, and bestows gifts upon, even as She bestows gifts upon us, are admired by Her equally. It is up to us, among ourselves, using the tools and talents that we have or might make, to strike whatever balance or imbalance there will be."

Helana found herself automatically reciting the catechism with him. Of course he was right.

She bowed her head, her vigor subdued, but her tension in no way reduced. "You spoke of preparing me in this uncertain increment of time. Preparing me for what? How much time can we count on?"

"I'll answer the last first," he said. "We do not know. He could call me as we speak. He may never call me. Uncertain is what I said. Uncertain is what I meant. I did not speak to you of this because I was waiting for the Sun's sign to show me that She was ready for me to prepare you. Every day I worried that I would be taken before the Sun granted me my prayer, but it has not proven so. I found my prayer answered today. Perhaps that is a sign of imminence, perhaps not. The walker himself gave me the impression that it would not be long, that he expected the chance would not be long in presenting itself, but even walkers face surprises, change their plans. I simply do not know."

Helana nodded. "And the other thing? My preparation?"

Koborah smiled serenely upon her. "You are a young and lovely woman, entering that stage of life where you should begin to entertain the thought of taking yourself a spouse, raising yourself a family, making yourself a home somewhere."

Helana sat up straight and spoke with proud certitude: "The Sun is my spouse, the parishioners my children, the church is my home."

Koborah shook his head. "But the Sun is female, and very far away. You may feel Her, but you can never touch Her. Is that the sort of spouse that you could spend a happy life with?"

She returned his smile with that transparent, guileless coyness that is the province of the young. "As I examine myself, I seem to discover that such is my nature. Such is the nature of revelation."

His face grew stern. "Helana, think closely. Are you prepared to serve the Sun before your parishioners, your parishioners before the church, and the church before yourself?"

She paused a moment, not from any uncertainty on her part—she knew the structured response by heart, had memorized it, hoping for this opportunity someday, never dreaming that the day would be so soon—but because this was an oath-taking, therefore not a time for eager answers. Ritual demands concern, respect, conviction, all of these over any fever of emotion.

Finally she nodded. "Sun is cause, I am but effect. I will foremost serve the cause. The parish is community, family; I am but an individual within that group. I will serve the parish without reckoning cost to myself. The church is a shrine to the Sun, and a home to my family. I will keep it secure to the best of my abilities."

Koborah smiled. "My daughter, long have I been certain that you were not abandoned on my doorstep, but were brought here for a purpose greater than any that you might have filled in the company of your natural parents. I believe that the Sun directed them, just as I believe that the Sun directs you now. You do the church and the community a great honor and a great service on this day. The Sun will shine proudly upon your face."

"The honor is yours, Father. It is you who have taught me these understandings."

"Teaching is only half of understanding," he replied. "It is useless without an apt pupil."

Rorsa whined once, briefly, then climbed down off of Helana's lap, plopped himself down upon the hearth rug, and curled up to go to sleep. He had heard the two of them take these tones before. There would be no interesting action. Helana would be too preoccupied to even scratch his ears.

The manner of her preparation surprised her. She had anticipated theological lessons, such as he had given her in the past, perhaps comprised of more arcane instruction. She wouldn't have been surprised if he had produced some scripture previously forbidden to her eyes as a simple acolyte, but now permitted with her ascension imminent. It would have seemed just as natural to her if he had offered for her reading some of his private journals, beginning with the volume he had kept on the advent of his own ascension, perhaps followed by those recounting that blessed event itself.

He did none of these things.

He rose and moved to stand before a pearl-framed mirror. He passed a hand over it and spoke in the Sun-tongue, reciting a pair of couplets that she was able to translate accurately, if unpoetically, even as he spoke them:

> *"Sun-sister, Gohrah, the Dualist;*
> *Often Day-white, often Night-black,*
> *Mistress of radiance and treachery*
> *In clear delineation."*

When he finished speaking the mirror vanished, though the frame remained intact, even seemed to glow with some eerie luminescence. Where the mirror should have been, or, for want of a mirror, where the wall would have been, was a cupboard-like space. Into this space Koborah reached, withdrawing not some arcane text or hidden volume of his early journals, but a small wooden tray compartmentalized by cross-thatched wooden slats. Within each compartment but one resided one or more pearls. The last compartment was elongated and contained a multifaceted crystal of some sort.

Helana recognized the pearls. She had seen Koborah use them, had even been permitted to use them herself, in healing the parishioners of any number of physical ills. She had also seen him use them in other ways, ranging from inspiring proliferation in the parish crops and livestock, to encouraging understandings in the recalcitrant youth or reluctant spouse, to warding off the evils that seemed to have beset some unfortunate family.

Though she had only ever handled them herself in simple healings, she had felt blessed and conspiratorial in all such chances. Using them created such an intense spiritual charm that she was nearly overwhelmed by the sensation of it; she was the only person in the parish Koborah had entrusted with so much as the knowledge of the existence of the gems. Even so, she had never realized that there were so many of them. At least a score of the spherical stones glinted up at her from the dark brown tray.

"We understand the rarity of such things only in proportion to how unusual they are to us," Koborah said. "You have known of these stones a long time, never guessing at how unusual they really are. They combine magic and divinity in a manner that I have never even heard spoken of before, a manner I have never seen described in any of my studies. As far as I know, you and I are the only two who know of, let alone possess, talismans that provide both the power of divine magic *and* the necessary geometric schema to form such energy into patterned actuality."

Helana sat, silent and attentive, not knowing what to say. Koborah was not prone to prevarication or exaggeration, but if such things were really so rare, why should a one such as herself ever even know about them?

"Yes," Koborah smiled as if reading her thoughts, "we are extremely wealthy for a small country church, are we not? We have been blessed beyond any right of our expectations. When the stranger appeared I feared that he had somehow learned of our wealth. I feared that these were what he was after. It was a great relief to understand that it was only a simple cleric that he was seeking."

Helana looked at him. "He would have preferred these things to the power he has gained over you?"

Koborah nodded.

"Then why didn't you give them to him and send him on his way?"

Koborah shook his head and smiled. "These are not mine to surrender. They belong to the parish, not me. Besides, if he felt he required a cleric, then a cleric he was going to have. He wouldn't have changed his mind about that just because he discovered that I possessed something else of value to him. Not even something of so enormous a value as these stones represent. He would have taken the gems *and* still made his talisman."

"Couldn't you have used these somehow to defend yourself against him?"

"For a time, yes. For a very short time. We are rich for a country church, but he was rich for a magus. I could have thrown up a shield against some of his spells, then bombarded him with healing ointments and water-finding spells until he crushed me, and then he would have taken whatever was left of the Sun-stones for his own.

"Any resistance on my part would have antagonized him, reducing the likelihood of him demonstrating any compassion when he eventually uses me and finishes with me. Not that I anticipate compassion for my compliance. Compassion rarely enters the equations of his ilk."

He shook his head as if chasing away uncomfortable thoughts, then looked at his acolyte and smiled. "But we are wasting precious morsels of that valuable and irreplaceable commodity: time. I still have much to teach you regarding the Sun-stones."

He first described to her the manner of their finding and their nature.

Now and again, need as need, and oftentimes as a hedge against future need, he would be engaged in a Sun-trance walk among the fields and suddenly become aware of some hidden glinting. Like as not, on further investigation, he would find the source of the glint to be an opalescent pearl deposited by the Sun, in Her wisdom, specifically for his finding. Thus they were collected.

"They are," he told her, "distilled crystals of solar energy. Bottled mana of the Sun, as it were, each already assigned and prepared for a particular purpose, which is unusual for such things—so unusual as to be unheard of. I have even written to a professor of arcana at the university in Akkat, merely 'suggesting' the 'theory' of the 'possibility' of such a combination within the structure of a single talisman. I received an impressively dismissive missal in response, upbraiding me for lack of logic and my belief in 'fairy-tale absurdities.'" Koborah smiled broadly.

"When I find them" he went on, "a brief and quiet meditation is all that is necessary to apprise me of their potential uses. It is as if they radiate their purpose and methodology to insure themselves against misuse. It is a most singular sort of magic, requiring more of spiritual attunement than of any structured learning of the arts. My own training in such arts is minimal, but you have seen me use the stones effectively. Your training was entirely nonexistent, but when I handed you the stones you used them flawlessly.

"Admittedly, those were the simplest stones. Some of the more powerful among them require the sacrifice of other stones to activate their schema, and one must know . . . ah, but even that becomes apparent with the usage." He smiled again. "Especially, I think, in the hands of one such as you."

"Me?" she inquired, self-consciously.

Koborah smiled. "Child, you do not recognize it yet, but you are gifted beyond redemption."

He told her, too, that he sometimes found them in his night walks: "Always beneath the fullest moon, when Sister Gohrah is most thoroughly pregnant with the radiance of her love for the Sun. But these are rare, and often the most peculiar of the lot."

Helana looked at the pearls in the tray before her. "But I have no way of distinguishing one from the other. I have not your gift of communication with the stones, therefore I do not understand their uses, nor how those uses are to be achieved. They look different from the ones you have taught me to use in the healings. They look solider, more substantial."

"I attuned you separately to each of the stones that you have used," he told her, "because I wanted to familiarize you with the sensations and procedures you might one day be required to master. When I attuned you to them, they responded to your essence as if you had indeed been the one for whom they had been intended. Each such attunement required the sacrifice of an additional stone, but I felt it was worth the price."

Helana frowned. "Then if attunement is to cost us half of our wealth, wouldn't it be better to save all of the stones for your own use, letting the Sun bring such gifts to me as seem to suit Her purposes?"

Koborah smiled. "That is a dilemma I myself have had to consider this past week, wondering all the while whether I would have enough time here to use them all, or even half of them, or whether I would be snatched away, leaving you unattuned and unable to utilize those I left behind. I prayed for the Sun to give me some signal when it was time. Today I received my answer from the Sun. This morning on my walk I found a special stone, one which will permit me to attune you to the lot of them with no sacrifice but the newfound gem."

Helana had no time to ponder the portent of such a discovery before Koborah raised the new Sun-stone above her head and began incanting a prayer in the formal Sun-tongue. She was about to bow her head to receive his benediction when a sudden change came over his face.

She stared in terror as his every muscle tensed, as she had seen the victims of seizure go rigid. His tawny face completely drained of color, even his lips went white, and he visibly fought to retain control of his own actions.

Rorsa suddenly came alert, flying clumsily from his position on the floor and landing on the desk, mere inches from his master's face, a low growl vibrating the dog's entire body.

In a moment Koborah's body relaxed a bit and he grumbled, "By all the gods that never were, not now! Wait!"

Again he held the pearl aloft, no longer speaking, but concentrating intently. The pearl began to glow.

Helana sat fearful, frozen into inaction by a mind that saw no useful options, as a beam of white light seemed to pierce the wall, curving and cracking like a whip as it lashed itself around her mentor's wrist.

Rorsa, not bound in spirit by the distinction between useful and futile activity, flew up into the air, snapping and snarling at the beam of light to no effect.

"Use them!" Koborah commanded, staring straight into Helana's eyes as a second beam of white light and one of red lashed around his neck and remaining wrist. "For the Sun! For the parish! For the church!"

A sudden burst of light blinded the young woman. A clap of thunder knocked over the chair she sat in and threw her to the floor.

When she finally felt able to open her eyes, Koborah was gone. Rorsa was licking her face and whining.

She hugged the dog to her breast, rose, and stared at the pearls in the tray. They all appeared translucent to her, nearly transparent, like those she had handled in the healings. Each seemed faintly marked, somewhere in their depths, by a single turquoise sigil. One of the oddly shaped runes of the Sun-tongue. A different rune in each stone.

She recognized the meaning of each one.

Only then did she commence her weeping.

That night, indulging in a moonlit trancewalk, Helana knelt to recover an object that she had seen glinting in the grass.

A translucent gem. A pearl. A Sun-stone. Koborah had told her that he had sometimes found them on night walks under a full moon.

Helana looked up. The moon was very neatly halved. One side a perfect, nearly blinding whiteness. The other side so dark as to disappear entirely into the surrounding night.

She looked at the gem, read the sigil there. It was the sign of travel.

She looked back at the moon, stared at it a long time. She wondered what to make of it all, what possible interpretations to infer. She couldn't help but believe that her prayers had indeed been answered, but she had no idea how she was supposed to manage such magic with so little experience and training.

Training or no, she knew she would have to try.

*   *   *

The following day she arranged for a nearby family to look after the church in her and Koborah's absence, being politely evasive as to the reasons for the absence. She also asked to look after Rorsa for her, which they were more than happy to do.

Pressing on, Helana didn't make it more than a quarter mile down the road before she heard a clumsy fluttering and flapping of leathery wings. Even as she turned, she was preparing an admonishment to send Rorsa scurrying back to the place that she had left him, but when she saw him he looked so comically earnest that the only admonishment she could muster was to pluck him out of the air and explain that it wasn't wise to wag one's tail while flying.

In recognition of her wisdom, he licked her face.

"Just as well," she told him, "that you didn't try to follow me a half-hour from now. Even I don't know where I'll be by then. How would you ever have found me?"

She hugged him tightly, then set him down to walk beside her.

Before a half an hour was up, she thought, she would have topped the gentle rise that she was climbing, set off through the woods, and found the clearing that was her favorite of all the places hereabout. Once there she would test Sun-stone that she had found.

Logically she had no way to be certain, but in her heart she felt sure that it would work the way that she wanted it to. She understood inherently that the travel spell required her to form an exacting image of her intended goal, but she sensed that forming a mental image of "the place where Koborah was spirited off to," while not in keeping with the letter of the law, would flatter the law's spirit. Why else would the Sun have sent her such a token?

But the linchpin of her logic brought back all of her trepidations. Less than twenty-four hours ago she had taken a solemn oath to put Sun, parish, and church before all selfish urgings. Her arguments that finding and bringing back Koborah was a service to all three could not discount her certain knowledge that she would pursue the same path with total disregard to all of them if necessary. Her true inspiration was her love for her onlyfather, the sense of loss she felt with his vanishment, and the sense of wrong that his being summoned against his will embodied. She knew that she was deserting church and parish in their hour of need, and that Koborah himself would not have approved of the venture.

She answered such forbodings again with the now familiar refrain: *The Sun, at least, approves. Why else send such a token? A token whose intended use certainly could not be misconstrued.*

She ignored the soft but strident voice that echoed round the back of her mind, whispering: "Not the Sun, but the Moon. Not the Moon deep and full with the Sun's unblemished radiance, but Gohrah, the Dualist, full evenly split in her dichotomy, half of Day and half of Night."

A voice that, despite its softness, reminded her so much of Koborah in his pulpit.

A soft purse dangled from her belt and bounced against her thigh with every step. The purse contained the church's entire cache of Sun-stones, as well as the strange multifaceted crystal that Koborah hadn't had time to enlighten her regarding the use of.

Her favorite of all favorite places, lush and verdant. She stood holding Rorsa in the crook of her left arm, the travel-stone in the palm of her right hand. She closed her eyes and tried to remember the feelings that coursed through her when she had used the healing-stones. An odd sensation, she recalled. Rather, an odd series of sensations, electrical and tingly. A feeling of becoming transparent, gaseous, like becoming a ghost. She remembered Koborah handing her the healing-stone, remembered his eyes upon her as she felt herself transformed into a luminescent ether. Remembered her hand reaching toward the ailing farmer, seeing the farmer's illness through her own glowing flesh, seeing the canker shrink, and fade, and finally disappear, the flesh closing whole and new where it had been. A pleasant sensation washing over her, almost entirely ripping her soul from its moorings on this earth. An image of the undiminished brilliance of the Sun sitting like a diamond in her mind, deep in the very center of her mind, suffusing her whole being with its warmth.

Remembering the feelings.

Believing them odd.

Not knowing them to be wholly unique.

So she centered herself in this favorite place. She opened her heart and mind to the message of the stone in her palm. As the first tinglings of the swirling powers enveloped her, she closed her eyes to the lush verdant surroundings and went inside of herself.

A self that seemed somehow detached from herself, felt a rush of gratitude as her nerve endings began to pop with minute electrical charges, as her skin began to glow and she became ensconced in that mysteriously misty feeling of translucency that had accompanied her healings.

This time there were other sensations as well, sensations foreign to her experiences handling the other gems: a cool dampness throughout her being, rather than the suffusing warmth; the tactile pressure of heavy, gently moving air; sounds of subtle movements; a dense, fecund aroma.

She opened her eyes, or had the sensation of opening her eyes; afterwards she was never certain whether this particular sequence of the vision had been internal or external.

Night. Humid, cool. A tangle of plant life more complex than any woods she had ever walked in. Soil soft and springy beneath her feet. The rustle of plants moving, not stirred by the present breeze, but moving of their own volition, to their own purpose. A strangely elongated figure some distance away, watching her in the darkness. Too dark, too far away for Helana to discern any of the figure's features, but she sensed that it was female, sensed that the woman was smiling in the darkness that was barely illuminated by a source of light hanging high in the sky.

Helana looked up to see that the light was cast by a huge but very thin crescent shape directly overhead. A crescent twice or thrice the size of the moon that she was used to, blue and white and brilliant along its sharp-looking edge.

As she stared and puzzled at this strange sight, she was suddenly overcome by a feeling that combined elements of rising and of falling simultaneously. The crescent began to spin crazily toward her.

She shut her eyes then, looked again within her mind. Where she had thought to see the diamond image of her miniature Sun, she saw instead Sister Gohrah, the Dualist, the Face of the Moon neatly halved. Spreading through her entire being, she felt a simultaneous warmth and coolth.

2.

When Helana next opened her eyes, she took in the sight of a devastated glade, blemished as if by war. A solid, very real vision, this. Firm, hard ground beneath her feet. Not another soul in sight. She held Rorsa to her chest, certain now that her spell had worked precisely as she had intended it to. She was amazed at the sensations that had run through her body. They had been so powerful, she was certain that the stone had taken her to the place Koborah had been summoned. She could sense this, though there was no sign now of Koborah ever having been here.

A small crater, charred around the edges as if a flaming boulder had impacted. Nearby, the severed arm of a large bear. The nearly intact remains of a giant spider, ravaged by scavengers only where the exposed flesh remained unprotected, soft. An entire grove of trees blasted down into splintery rubble, as if hit by a tornado.

Helana decided that this would be the center from which she would spiral outward, searching for signs, for clues.

By sunset she was far from the pit, but had discovered nothing illuminating Koborah's fate. What a joke it would be if the magus had sent him home. If he was back at the church even now, wondering what had become of her and the stones. She supposed that he would be angry with her, even as he understood her choice. That was fine. She would gladly accept his anger, even excommunication, if it would only mean that he was now back at the church, safe from harm.

Anything was possible. All she knew for certain was that he was not yet dead. She knew this because she felt it to be true.

Helana clutched some recently gathered berries to her chest as she looked for the best spot to bed down for the night. Rorsa was off hunting the small animals of early evening when Helana first noticed the red flicker of a small fire on a distant hillside.

She sat down where she was and ate her berries very slowly, savoring every mouthful. Investigating the fire could wait until Rorsa returned. Whoever had built the fire wouldn't be moving on in any hurry.

Illith paused in his carving, suddenly aware of the presence of another. He closed the inner eyelid that improved his night vision, then stood to put his back to the fire. He could see no movement anywhere near. He scanned a bit farther, closing another inner eyelid to enhance his distance vision. Still nothing. He listened intently and opened his nostrils as fully as he might, but was rewarded only with the crackling and popping of the logs behind him, the sizzle and spatter of the spitting juices of the meat he cooked, the roasting smells from the same source, and the scent of his own flesh, healing from the scorching he had received from the previous day's damnable sorceries.

Odd, he though, *more strangeness in this strange place. Some magic veil, hiding the intruder from my senses? Or does this stranger approaching possess such power that I perceive them from afar?*

The yelping of a small dog reached him from quite some distance. He focused on the sound, sent his mind's eye out in search of it, watched as the night-scattered shadows flitted past this new vision, stood alert as he focused on a moving patch of brightness within the darkness and followed its pathway, knowing that the small creature in the center of his thoughts was not the one that he was searching for, but knowing that the creature would lead him to the presence he had felt.

Odd again, he thought, while watching the dog take wing and land in the arms of a barely postpubescent human female, *a child, standing at some distance, yet emanating a sufficiently volatile aura so as to disturb my concentration here. A walker?* He examined her closely. *No. Odder still. What is she, then?*

He willed his mental eye back into his head, had it do a backflip dive into his pool of reflections, read the ripples, waited for the waters to still, then asked himself some questions.

The answers he received were the oddest thing of all on this surpassingly strange night. Not only would this unusual creature seek him out quite soon, but it seemed likely that she would not only be unguarded regarding the nature of her powers, she may even be coerced into using them toward his own ends. Perhaps she could somehow provide him with a path back to his homeland. Perhaps she would even be a way to buy back his station once he got there.

Pity the poor child, he thought, but his smile was not compassionate at all.

Rorsa was terribly reluctant to approach the clearing, but at Helana's request had kept his protestations silent enough that the two of them managed to enter it and step into the circle of firelight before their unsuspecting host looked up from the log he was sitting on. Their host divorced his attention from the task he had been engrossed in with a glint of curiosity rather than startlement.

For a long time the three just stared at one another.

Their host was clearly not a man, but a manlike thing: fire-blackened, covered with blisters and running sores wherever its skin was exposed through the tattered and scorched remnants of its clothing. Its elongated skull was adorned on either side of its high forehead with what appeared to be the shorn-off stubs of what might have been horns. The task it had been arrested at was the whittling of a large and fire-scarred bone.

Helana looked upon this creature and experienced a gentle but pervasive thrill. She was widely read, but her experience was narrow. She had witnessed almost nothing beyond the realm of her small human settlement.

The blackened thing stared at his two uninvited guests with what seemed to be wry amusement, his eyes alive with a penetrating intelligence. He gave no indication of feeling threatened at all. He gestured elegantly toward the flames and spoke in a clear voice. "Warm yourselves, if you'd like. My repast, I'm afraid, is dreadfully singular, and I can offer you no libation, but I believe that the meat that I've managed to acquire will be enough to stretch three bellies."

Helana gave her attention to the fire. Above it a large piece of meat sizzled and dripped juice into the flames, radiating a delicious aroma. On the clear ground in front of the fire she noticed a diagram etched into the dirt. A circle encompassing a five-pointed star. A pentagram.

"Travelers or locals?" the blackened creature queried, busying himself with his carving once again.

"Travelers," Helana answered. "I am looking for my father."

The black thing chuckled. "Aren't we all, my dear, aren't we all? If I could just have five minutes alone with the bastard that got me onto dear old Mom, we'd have enough meat on the spit for a dozen uninvited guests." He looked up from his carving. "But I am being indelicate, I am sorry. Perhaps you have fond feelings toward your own. Mine is unknown to me and left me in a bit of a bind. Do you happen to know the name of yours?"

"Koborah."

The black thing shook its head. "Never heard of him, but then, I'm not from around here. Not from anywhere near around here."

"He was summoned here against his will by a magus of some power," Helana went on, noticing a sudden spark of interest in the being's intelligent eyes. "A priest of the Sun, he is. White-robed, golden-haired, cleanly shaven, human."

The black thing threw his head back and laughed and laughed and laughed.

"Pardon my mirth," the strange creature begged when he finally got his breath, "but it seems that your father and I *did* meet. We were intimate, even, albeit briefly. In fact, you could say that he helped make me what I am today: a blistered, homeless, powerless creature, living in an unfamiliar and untenable environment. And you can fairly add that I saved his life, though it wasn't my intent at the time, and he is unlikely to ever entertain any desire to thank me for it."

The odd creature laughed again, either at the bewildered expression on Helana's face, or at some private joke that she was very far from understanding.

He shook his head, held up a hand as if requesting peace. "Not that I harbor any personal rancor against him, I assure you. None of it was his fault at all, just as none of it was mine. It can all be neatly laid at the feet of Gerheart, the magus who summoned him up and controlled him. Your father had no more choice in the matter than I did. Indeed, if it weren't for Gerheart's tricks, I wouldn't be here at all. I'd be safe at home in my study, drinking a miktik and smoking a kalar as I pursued my research."

"You mean the magus summoned you both just to pit you against one another?" Helana asked in horror.

The creature paused. "Oh no, it was trickier than that, much more complicated. How much do you know about the duels of walkers?"

"Only that they can summon creatures to do their bidding without the creatures' consent."

The dark thing cocked its snub-horned head, considering. Could this young human be putting him on? It certainly seemed unlikely that any creature radiating such an intricate power could be so blithely unaware of the other powers that surrounded her. *Then again,* he thought, *there is power, and there is power. I am attuned to all such things; maybe hers is the sort that escapes the walkers' notice, and they hers.*

"I'll try to explain," he told her. "I didn't exactly write the rule book, but I am an expert on how to cheat. In fact, that's my job. You could say that I'm a professional strategist in such affairs. Though that didn't help me much when Gerheart pulled that damnable trick of his."

"First tell me about my father. Where is he now?"

"I don't know for certain. Last I saw him he was on the road to Hell."

"There, there, it's not as bad as all that," the man-shaped thing tried to comfort Helana. "In fact, he'd have been much worse off if I hadn't sent him there."

"*You* sent him?"

The creature sighed. "That's another place where it gets a little tricky. Do you think that you could sit still long enough for me to try to explain the situation to you? It'll take some time, and you must promise not to interrupt, or we'll never get through it. By the time that I am done, I'm sure you'll understand that he and I were both victims of these events, and that there is nothing for it but to accept what is and hope that we each might find our ways back home."

"You're wrong," she said decisively.

She was seated on the log beside her host. The fire had died down, the meat had been devoured, the Sun was beginning to rise, and Helana was feeling reinvigorated despite not having slept all night.

Rorsa, too, had gone sleepless and was lying at her feet, eyes open but droopy, ears perking up at Helana's sudden tone of adamance.

"How's that?" The creature raised the blisters on his forehead where his eyebrows might once have been, causing one of them to burst open, the fluid running down along the side of his nose.

"You said I would see that there is nothing for it but to accept what is and to hope that you each find your way back home."

He nodded for her to go on.

"There is one other thing that I can do. I can help you find your way, then bring him back with me if he is still there."

Again the creature laughed.

During the course of that night, the demon Illith—for such he claimed to be, and so he named himself—had essayed a description of the metaphysical mechanics of a walkers' duel.

Helana had listened intently and had limited her questions to those intended to clarify her understandings of points she believed to be important to her own situation and that of her father. She was surprised at how natural the entire process sounded to her, as if she had always harbored some inherent, internal comprehension of all such things.

Once the groundwork had been laid, Illith brought her to the point of his personal involvement in the duel that had sent her father on the road to Hell, and that had stranded the demon himself in what he could only describe as "this strange green, blue, and white environment."

"I have told you that I am a sort of professional strategist. Normally, when I am called upon by any magus, major or minor, it is only my mental prowess that is summoned. My body remains wherever the calling found it. In what seems an instant, I study the situation as it stands, trace all the lines of power that the calling mage might possibly have access to, then bring to his or her hand the forgotten or otherwise neglected spell that seems most called for by the circumstances the mage finds himself in. Then I am done, and go back to . . . whatever amuses me.

"Gerheart, however, possessed a spell that even I had no idea existed. When his opponent—whom I shall not name for fear of drawing her attention—established her mental link to me, Gerheart seized upon that connection, like a man with a tangible fishing line, and yanked me physically into the fray."

Illith paused a moment, rearranging his small bone carvings upon the log on which they sat. Helana offered them her first intent inspection and noticed that they were tiny replicas of skulls. In that brief span of time, he sent his mental eye out in miniature form to follow the words he had just spoken. He was able, thus, to visualize her reception of them and to follow the minute electrical impulses that described the schematic of her comprehension. He was surprised to see the information processed so rapidly and stored so neatly within the strange sac of brain tissue that is dormant in most humans, but active to varying degrees in all users of magic. He was surprised, too, at the size and sophistication of this portion of her brain. These facts would seem to indicate rigorous practice and schooling in all things magical, but all of the things he was telling her were being tagged and registered as new conscious knowledge. Certainly if she had received any formal training at all, it would have included these bits of information. *An interesting specimen,* he thought, *quite worthy of further study.* He drew his mind's eye back into its socket, and continued his explanation.

"I am a scholar, not a fighter," he went on, "and it took me some little while to adjust to this unexpected change in my environs and situation. I was unable to perform the function for which I had been called. By the time I had adjusted myself, Gerheart had sicced your father on me." Illith smiled. "Your father is a tenacious and persuasive man, a psychically powerful one. I was controlled by him, by Gerheart's engineering, through most of the rest of the duel. In the course of the struggle I was unable to aid my caller, which distracted her from her other involvements. Gerheart even managed to constrain me to aid his own efforts, and my caller grew quite annoyed with me. Unfairly, I might add, since I had lost all but the faintest scintilla of personal volition, as I have said."

He sighed. "This went on for quite some time. During my struggle with your father, who was clinging to me like a psychic bind, I noticed the dark pit that had opened in the earth when I had so rudely been drawn through from my home. It occurred to me that getting into the pit was my only way of returning to where I belonged. With what little volition I could muster, I started making my way toward the pit, intent on throwing your father off of me and making a dive as soon as I could manage.

"Then everything seemed to happen at once. Somehow I managed to throw your father off, but he fell into the pit through which I had intended to make my escape. The pit closed behind him as he fell. My howl of rage at that misfortune was almost immediately transformed into a howl of pain as I was struck by a blast of fire with which my caller had no doubt intended to incinerate both your father and myself. Then, as if the loss of my chance of escape and the blistering of my beautiful hide were not insult enough, my caller sent Boris Devilboon—?"

"Boris Devilboon?" Helena queried, unable to restrain her curiosity.

Illith smiled at the interruption. "Yes. Boris Devilboon. He is the bogeyman invoked by all the mothers of Hell when their brats misbehave. He is our staple inducement to better manners when we are young, and remains our constant fear when we are older. He is often called forth, as he was in this case, to punish my people when they have failed a superior in some act of commanded service. He and his hordes of demons are more likely to maim, or disable, or depose, and so are more feared than any murderer in such a case." Illith shook his head. "Now where was I?"

"Your caller sent Boris Devilboon . . ."

"Yes. You are a good listener. My caller sent Boris Devilboon to shear off my horns, effectively robbing me of all of my magical powers. Then she withdrew, conceding the duel to Gerheart, and with that Devilboon's fury turned away from me, which is, no doubt, why I am still around to tell the tale."

This was the tale that had inspired Helana's adamance that a solution could be found, which, in turn, had inspired the rekindling of Illith's mirth.

Now, in the burgeoning sunlight, Helana reviewed all that she had learned from the long night's discourse, ignoring Illith's most recent laughter for the moment.

"And how, pray tell, do you intend to help me return to my home?" the demon asked her, feigning skepticism, certain that this strange, untutored mageling could indeed assist him in some fashion, willingly or no.

She paused uncertainly, then smiled at him. "You tell me. You're the scholar-strategist, remember?"

"Quite." He looked disgruntled.

"What were your plans before I arrived?"

Illith considered how best to answer this. He decided to do so honestly, the better to gauge her understanding. After all, even shorn of his powers and exiled from his home, he could handle any predicaments presented by any human mageling, even so curious and precocious a one as this.

He gestured toward the pentagram etched in the dirt. "I tried that. It would have been enough at home, or if I had retained the power of my horns, but not here, shorn as I am. I realized that I needed additional energy, more magical power." He waved a hand dismissively at the tiny carvings. "I am afraid, however, that these are weaker than I'd hoped, despite being carved from the thigh bone of a giant were-beast. I am afraid I will need more of these carvings than I could make in a week."

Helana stared at the carvings and made the intuitive leap that they were, to her host, weakened versions of what the Sun-stones were to her. Energy. Like the electrical crawly feeling that came over her whenever she used the stones. "I have something that might help," she said.

The demon brightened visibly. He had sensed the presence of power in her hip purse already, but he didn't want her to know that. He wanted her to offer the power to him. It is always so much better when they offer, unless, of course, you kill them for it, and he didn't want to do that. She was too strange, too curious, too promising to waste.

"Really?" he said. "Let me see its manifestation."

Helana reached into her drawstring pouch and produced a small handful of the Sun-stones.

Illith's shoulders drooped. Without moving, he gave the impression of having stepped back a pace. "I cannot even touch those," he half whispered, half hissed. "They manifest an energy that is the polar opposite of the kind I need."

"Oh."

He frowned and stared at them more closely. He sent out his mental eye to dance about them, as near as it could get without suffering burns from their peculiar aura, and was amazed at what he saw there.

"These stones contain raw energy *and* the schema, or pattern of effect," he said aloud, forgetting to even consider being discreet. "I have never even heard of such things. With such as these, years of study, practice, and procurement could be eliminated. It really is a pity that I can't use them. I couldn't even handle them without discomfort, and they would not activate the magics I require. These are distillations of sun energy. Any other form of energy would be useful to me. The energy of living things would be acceptable. Air and water would be fine. Fire would be nicer, and nether energy would be the nicest of all."

Helana hesitated, thinking of the multifaceted crystal that she carried, knowing that it had special powers, but not knowing how to use them. She was aware that the item was unusual, if not unique, and she knew that such things were usually best kept secret. Her desire to follow Koborah warred briefly with an intuitive distrust at showing so special an item to even so amicable-seeming a demon. The desire to locate and rescue her onlyfather won out.

"I also have this." She withdrew the glittering artifact from her satchel. "Though my father didn't have time to instruct me in its use."

Illith clapped his hands together, his eyes glittering at the sight. "A prism of sorts! My lord, but you are a child of wonders." He knew from its aura that he could not so much as touch the object without suffering for it, much as he would suffer from any contact with the Sun-stones, but he recognized its value and knew its uses. Certainly he could convince this young woman to use it for his purposes.

"Yes," he said, "I think that just might be my ticket to the boneyard."

He described the process by which she would be able to turn one of her Sun-stones into fire energy by passing it through the prism. He would then be able to take up the fire energy and form it appropriately into a spell that would set the pentagram aflame.

"Then we step into it," she asked, "and it will give us an entry into Hell?"

"We?" he asked in response. In his eagerness to get home, he had forgotten her desire to go with him; and in his unexpected fondness for the girl, he had forgotten the uses he intended to put her to once he got there.

"Yes. I already told you that I intend to go with you to find my father. Together he and I will find some method of return."

Illith looked troubled. It was unusual for him to feel any hesitation regarding the uses he might put anyone or anything to. He wondered why this young lady had affected him so strangely. "It would cost you two of your Sun-stones to power the pentagram if we both go," he told her.

"I wouldn't care if it cost me all of them."

Illith frowned. "It just might, in the long run. And perhaps a good deal more than that."

"I am prepared to make whatever payment is required."

Illith stared at her a long time, then spoke in a manner that reminded her of Koborah when he would intone the words of the scriptures. "There be darkness unmitigated by any light. There be voids in which many souls wander, lost and raving. There be dangers that await the suspecting and the unsuspecting alike. There be triumphs and turmoils intermarried so that one can scarce know which might be which."

He shook his head, as if breaking a trance, then spoke to her in a kindly voice and with a pained expression. "You are young, beautiful, and naive. You do not know what you are letting yourself in for."

"But I must do it. There is no other way that I know of to reach my onlyfather."

This troubled him more than he would have believed possible before he had met the child.

"You are principled and honorable. Those virtues will not be rewarded where you wish to go. At best they will be overlooked. More likely, they will be used against you."

"Still, I have no choice."

"Look upon me now. Look close. Look deep. Tell me if you are willing to trust a one such as me, who was raised in this place I am describing. See truly, then speak truly."

She did as she was instructed, staring as intently as she could into his wide, unblinking eyes. When she spoke, she spoke as truly as she could.

"I want to trust you, because I have no other hope. I would trust you completely if I had some power over you, some leverage, because you have been taught and taught again to respect that. I have no such power. I must lay all of my trust in your compassion, which you possess in modest quantities, but possess nonetheless. I must hope that the quantities I see are sufficient to my purposes. My answer is: I half trust you. That will have to do for now. It is my best and only hope."

Illith seemed amused by her response. "You half trust me. That is beautiful, because your charm draws me halfway toward being trustworthy, which is unfamiliar territory for me. Based on that half trust, you are willing to let me lead you into Hell?"

Helana nodded.

"Even as I tell you that I am persona non grata there at the moment, and that the only way I can win my way into the city with you at my side is to present you as my captive, my bribe, my purchase price for buying back my station and my powers?"

"Yes."

"Even as I tell you that given the choice between relinquishing you as ransom to the archduke, or forfeiting my station, I would chose to reclaim my station without any hesitation or qualm?"

"My answer remains."

"And even as I tell you that warning you away like this, when you would be such a pretty prize to return with, has squandered every last vestige of the compassion, honor, and trustworthiness upon which your hope in me depends?"

"Yes."

He rose, his own code of honor—such as it was—fully satisfied by the thrice-warning. Normally he wouldn't have bothered. What was it about this child? He took her hand and kissed it, using the contact to run a probe of sorts through all the tangled branches of possibility this child embodied. Only an iron will kept him from emitting a gasp and shudder. *Incredible,* he thought, *the merest touch, and all the world laid open. This child* does *require more attention than I'd have thought.* "Let us be off, then." He smiled.

Rorsa, perhaps possessing better sense than his human mistress, refused to enter the flaming pentagram, so Helana picked him up and held him to her chest, closing her tunic about his trembling form.

3.

"Would have to land in the outskirts," Illith grumbled as they walked along a narrow ebon path between what seemed two rivers of molten stone.

Helana said nothing. She was totally disoriented. Incapable of speech. Nearly as incapable of coherent thought. Scenes rushed past them in insubstantial but brilliant outlines of red and blue and black. Odd scenes depicted at vertiginous angles so that, no matter where she cast her eyes, it had the effect of peering over a precipitous drop from some unstable ledge. She could not distinguish the real from the imagined, or even be certain that there was any difference at all. Her only solid comfort was the warm, still-trembling weight of Rorsa against her chest.

Illith was talking to her again, but it was difficult for her to focus on his words.

". . . some idea how *I* felt in those damnable environs *you* call home."

She nodded mutely.

They continued on.

"Hold!" he grabbed her arm.

Helana looked around her. The road they had been walking had given way to a vast, boulder-strewn, black plain. Everything still seemed lined in shades of red and blue. Then she saw what had drawn her host's attention.

A ragged band of knobbly-limbed, dwarf-like creatures was moving in their direction, trading raucous, caustic-sounding comments with each other as they drew a bead on their prey.

Their prey—it was not open to question—was none other than

Helana and Illith: two straggling wayfarers who, from the bandits' point of view, had let themselves stray into the wrong territory.

"What can you do?" she asked the demon.

"Nothing at all. I am no warrior, my horns are shorn, I have no energy with which to cast even rudimentary spells, and I can't use yours." With this last he touched her arm swiftly, as if offering an urgent warning that should have been given earlier. "Do not display that other trinket you have, or even speak of it in this realm. You would find yourself quickly stripped of it. It would likely be destroyed." *Which would be a shame,* he added silently, *if it should occur before I'd developed and effected my own plans for it.* He gazed at the creatures closing in on them. "What can you do?" He smiled.

"I do not know." Her hand dipped into her purse, closed on one of the Sun-stones. Immediately she was suffused with calmness. An electrical tingling set up all the fine hairs on her arms and the back of her neck. Her mind exploded with an image of the Sun and Moon negotiating the same sky. "Continue on," she said. She felt as if her will had suddenly been taken over by some normally dormant portion of her brain, some segment of her mind that felt that it could handle this situation just fine, without bothering to consult with the rest of her. It was not a completely unfamiliar sensation. It was the same feeling that she had whenever she walked in a Sun-trance, whenever she felt most at one with the spirits that are beyond.

Illith shrugged and, catching a glimpse of the pulsing deep within her brain, kept pace with her.

Their antagonists fanned out as they drew near. Twenty of them, each clutching a crude dagger, hammer, or hand-ax. Each hurling threats and imprecations toward their intended victims.

Illith was uneasy. In the fullness of his natural form he'd have nothing to fear from such insignificant creatures, but exiled and dehorned he could only trust to direct physical combat and the potential abilities of his inexperienced companion. He knew the intentions of the bandits only too well: first to kill their prey, then to strip the bodies clean and distribute the wealth via brawling, then to feast upon the lifeless forms. He had no idea what Helana had planned, but he hoped it was effective.

Rorsa suddenly pushed away from Helana's chest and took wobbly flight between the attackers and their victims, barking as ferociously as he was able.

Helana used the opportunity of distraction to withdraw from her purse one of the Sun-stones, knowing which one she had by feel, a part of her attunement that Koborah had neglected to mention, or perhaps had never experienced himself. She viewed the entire scene with no sense of alarm, no sign of concern, giving herself over to the urgings of what she was beginning to think of as her second mind.

When the attack came, swift and sudden, all of the pock-marked creatures shambling toward them in a rush, she hurled the pearl in their direction and announced in a clear, calm voice: "I am so happy to see you all."

The beastlings came to a staggering halt, watching the pearl as it began to glow and floated toward them, expanding as it came, like a soap bubble, then like a balloon. It popped over their heads, sprinkling them with its strange luminescence.

The bandits stared at each other, and then at Helana, their craggy faces breaking into smiles that began to twitch from the cramping of seldom-used muscles.

"Balm of Tranquillity," she whispered to Illith, "useful in situations where surgery is required." There was an answering whisper from somewhere deep within her mind. A quiet, but imperative tone that she believed she recognized. An odd but fervent and irresistible impulse came over her. "Watch this," she said.

She beckoned the nearest of the bandits to approach her. He did so without the slightest hesitation, head bobbing contentedly.

"May I see your knife?"

The bandit relinquished his blade to her.

"Your hand?"

The bandit held his hand out in accommodation.

She sliced off the smallest finger of his right hand, feeling a very strange, delicious thrill run through her as she did so, experiencing an image-flash of a cowled female form smiling upon her from distant shadows. She put the finger in her pocket, along with the knife.

"Thank you," she said.

The bandit nodded happily, ignoring the blood running freely from his wounded hand.

Helana gathered Rorsa back to her chest.

To Illith she said: "Let's move along, before they come out of it."

And so they did.

Their next obstacle was a free-roaming band of drudge skeletons.

Her hand fell upon a proliferation spell, and on impulse she strengthened it by sacrificing an additional Sun-stone as she cast it. Even so, she was surprised at the immediacy and intensity of the effect, as the skeletons clattered awkwardly against one another in frenzied efforts at copulation. It occurred to her that using this spell to distract creatures actually capable of procreation could have serious long-term drawbacks.

"These spells seem to have stronger effects here than they do back home," she observed.

"Diametric polarity," Illith observed, himself amazed at the spectacle. "Contrast," he added.

Helana stood listening less to her companion than to the voice in the corners of her mind. She strode over to one of the clattering couples and snatched a finger bone away from a participant. She placed the bone in her pocket with the bandit's severed digit.

Illith smiled at her, as if beginning to understand and appreciate her more. *I had taken her to be unschooled,* he thought, *but clearly, that is not the case. I wonder who her teacher was, to leave no obvious mark upon her conscious memory.*

He reached out to take her hand, as if it were a gesture of friendship, but in truth, he simply wanted to probe her once again. This wasn't just a matter of curiosity; the question could prove ultimately important.

He virtually blanched as the understanding came to him: *Stranger and stranger this story grows. She has no conscious imprint of her instructor, because she has never been conscious of her instruction. The deities themselves, or something so like them as to make no difference, have touched this child. This explains the staggering possibilities that await her. It may well be in my best interests to treat this creature hospitably, if only so that I might monitor her progress.* He then remembered that he was, in theory, marching her to the end of all such progress. *If so, so be it, but surprises* do *occur, and I sense that it might be unwise to bet against such a one as this.*

From the edge of town they could see the huge, black wall that encircled the center of the city. By this time she had pocketed pieces of half a dozen creatures. The zombies she had zapped with a healing spell, causing them a frenzy of pain and anguish as their decaying tissues tried to knit themselves back together. As far as her collection went, all she'd had to do that time was pick up a piece that had fallen off of one of them. The gonfons—ball-like creatures with four stubby legs, long snouts, and very sharp teeth—she had foiled with a spell called Stomach-pump. It had done the job, but only at the cost of having to watch as the gonfons vomited bits of other creatures that she wouldn't want to have seen whole, let alone partially digested. Lacking fingers, one of the gonfons lost his tail to her collection, the bandit's knife coming in handy for that bit of pilferage.

Her pocket also contained the tongue of a banshee that she had zapped with Meditative Stillness, and the kneecap of a rag man whom she'd hit with a double dose: Contentment With One's Lot and Charity. So the kneecap had been given freely, and with undying gratitude. Undying, that is, until the spell wore off. By then she and Illith were well beyond his hobbling range.

"The things you do to them," Illith suggested, "are so unfamiliar to them, the experiences so alien, that they are completely overwhelmed. I bet that's half of what's making your spells so effective here."

Helana smiled, thinking her friend had donned the cloak of the scholar once again, that he was trying to evaluate and establish the *meaning* of the events that were occurring. But in her heart she was beginning to worry now. Here she was, approaching the walls of one of the cities of Hell, the ostensible, perhaps actual, prisoner of a demon resident of that city, with her supply of Sun-stones dwindling to a seemingly dangerous paucity. She resisted the urge to reach into her pouch and count how many remained. It would either be enough, or it wouldn't. Counting them wouldn't change that any.

"But how do you know what to do with the stones, which of them to chose, and how to activate them?" he asked.

"I don't know how to answer that," she said. "It is as if another hand steered mine, as if another mind informed my movements and my thoughts."

Illith nodded, for this coincided with what he had perceived regarding her tutelage. *Not only have the deities been her teachers,* he thought, *they are with her now. If she requires this much of their attention, how could they fail her in the end?*

Rorsa trembled against Helana's chest as they neared the gates of the city. She stroked his head, calming herself as well as him.

"Let me take it from here," Illith said. "This is my hometown and I understand the politics here as well as anyone is capable. Keep your eyes cast down at all times, remember that you are my prisoner and that I will be handing you over to the archduke as ransom for my pardon."

"What do you need to be pardoned for?"

"Failure. Failure is punished here by banishment and the stripping of one's natural powers; no mitigation of fault is permitted. I failed when I was called upon. The shearing of my horns was representative of my banishment and hobbling. I would not even be permitted to enter here now if I didn't have you along. You are my bribe." He smiled then. "Funny thing, I almost wish I were bringing you as my bride." A sudden frown took his face and he looked away from her, wondering what could have possessed him to say such a thing. "You are a very impressive woman," he finally said. "Especially for a worldy."

They had a moment alone in an antechamber adjacent to the archduke's throne room. Illith had just completed his own private interview with the archduke, and it had evidently gone quite well. He had returned, at any rate, with his gleaming horns intact, his beautiful slate gray skin as smooth as it had ever been, and a rolled, signed, and sealed pardon reinstating him to his position in the community. Looking upon him Helana realized for the first time what a truly beautiful creature he was, so much so that she forgot for a moment her anxiety regarding her own imminent interview, during which the archduke would decide what to do with her. During which, too, she would have to decide what to do with the archduke.

The demon looked deeply into Helana's eyes and told her he was sorry. "You thought you recognized in me what might have been a vestigial remnant of that thing that you call honor. You were right. It isn't much, though. It is just barely enough to constrain me to tell you to your face that my ruse of turning you over to the archduke was never a ruse. I intended, from the first that you agreed to accompany me, to use you to gain entry and pardon. I have done this thing. You are now the property of the archduke, and I am again free to take up my station in this city. Three times I told you not to trust me, and you responded that I was your only chance, your only hope. That chance has gotten mighty slim now, that hope mighty ephemeral. Be that as it may, I wish you the best of luck. It wouldn't surprise me as much as it should if you actually did manage to achieve your goal." He hesitated, swallowed with some difficulty, then went on. "If you do, it should be recorded forever in the songs and stories of your people."

Helana reached out and placed a hand on Illith's shoulder, then cocked her head as if listening to something faint.

Indeed she was. It was the same faint voice that she had heard only as a distant murmur when she had taken each of the tokens from her victims, but as she listened now it grew to a clear and steady tone. She understood its origin now and imaged it as a willowy, cowled woman, the dark half of Sister Moon. *Through examination,* she thought, *I am beginning to understand my nature.*

Aloud she said to Illith, "One last thing."

"No," he answered quickly, "I cannot afford to help you in any way now." But her hand was still upon his shoulder, and he could feel the urging pouring through the contact. Not Helana's urging, but the urging of her patron, her tutor, her almost unrecognized deity. Not the Sun she thought she worshiped, but the Sister of that Sun.

She shrugged and dropped her hand, as if she'd been preparing to ask for a meaningless trifle. "I was only going to request that you take Rorsa with you."

Illith closed his eyes and shook his head, but when he opened them, he asked, "Would he come with me?" not knowing what constrained her to beg this boon, only aware that he wanted to afford her any opportunity to escape and so humiliate his hated rival. For the archduke, he knew, had been laying in wait for any opportunity to banish him. Even now, Illith had only received his pardon under constraint of Higher Law.

Helana nodded, her heart pounding. So much depended on this moment. She locked eyes with the demon. "And if you should happen to set him down, and he were to run off, I am certain that he would head for whatever cell they are holding my father in. That one guard we spoke to on our way in as much as admitted he was here."

"I would not be permitted trespass wherever they are keeping him."

"Even if you were innocently chasing after a runaway dog?"

He smiled. "I might. But what then? What am I to do once I discover where he is kept? Surely it is locked and guarded."

"Then?" Helana forced herself to speak calmly, causally, calling upon the image of the halved Moon for strength. "Surely you know that I would ask nothing of you personally at such a time. I know how precarious freedom is in this domain, and how much yours means to you. I would not ask you to risk your freedom for my personal gain. However, if the guards were somehow led to believe that you had overheard a rumor that the archduke was fuming because he'd requested audience with a prisoner who hadn't been delivered yet, and if you were to give them the impression that this man the dog has led you to is the prisoner in question, how would they be likely to respond?"

Illith smiled, at once rueful and appreciative. "Why, they'd hustle him down to the throne room pronto in an attempt to keep their positions and their heads. That would probably get your old man to the throne room, though I don't know why you'd want him there, but I'd be on a hot seat if anything came of it. As the source of the rumor I'd be suspect."

She smiled at him. "Ah, but surely you could pass the suspicion along. If failure here is punished by banishment, if no mitigation of fault is permitted, wouldn't the guards take full responsibility? And if they insist on digging deeper to discover the rumor's source . . . well, isn't there someone in this city whom you would prefer to live without? Wouldn't you be able to name them as the source of this rumor? Even as you relay it to the guards you could be explaining to them that you don't put any stock in it. You could even tell them to ignore the rumor, as long as the source you name is someone they'll feel obliged to respond immediately to."

Illith reach out to touch her hand once more. Again he traced the many paths of possibility that she embodied. Some of the branches ended abruptly in impenetrable darkness. Others of the branches went on and on to unguessable glories. Certainly any help he gave, if he kept it safe enough so that her failure would not implicate him, could pay tremendous benefits as she came into her future power—as her trust in him, and her gratitude toward him grew. He also found that he *wanted* her to succeed, beyond all proportion of the archduke's humiliation or his own future benefits. He was growing damn fond of this strange child.

He smiled at her again. "I have told you that you are an impressive woman. If proof be needed beyond your immediate grasp of the politics of a world so alien to your own, it is evidenced by the simple fact that you have convinced me to act in a situation in which it is clearly safer for me not to." He squeezed her right hand in both of his. "I sincerely hope we meet again one day, both of us free folk."

"And what have you to offer me that I should be willing to grant you your release?" The archduke leaned far forward on his throne, growling and smiling simultaneously, his eyes alive with secret humors, blue flames dancing on his naked shoulders, his whole face dancing in the flickering light of the many fires in the throne room. He was doing his best to be intimidating, but the slight, almost-a-child before him was showing no signs of anxiety.

"I have nothing to offer you, Your Majesty, except for magic trinkets that you could not use." She reached into her pouch and removed three stones. She held these in her palm and extended her hand in his direction. This gesture left only two stones in her satchel. It would be enough, or it would not.

The archduke made a face at her offering, not bothering to examine them closely enough to note their unusual properties. Contempt and scorn mingled on his face with a touch of trepidation. He hurled his baritone voice at her as if it were a javelin. "You dare to produce such—" but his rejoinder was interrupted by the opening of one of the wide, arched doors behind Helana's back.

The archduke glanced up at the entering guard and turned his fury up a notch or two. "What is this interruption of my private audience?"

Helana tensed, afraid to turn and look to see if her father was there with the guard. Whether he was or not, she sensed that this would be her last and best opportunity for making any sort of escape.

"The prisoner you required, Your Grace. The guards have brought him."

"Prisoner? What prisoner? I have requested no . . ." then the archduke screamed, beset by a pain unlike any he had ever experienced.

The three stones in Helana's palm glowed and vanished. She had used two of them to add energy to the one with the sigil for Conscience, a spell normally used to induce its subject to ponder the consequences of deeds and intents, with an eye toward how they are likely to impact on others.

The archduke continued to scream as the guard who had entered took stock of the situation and called upon his brothers to aid him in subduing the insolent girl who was attacking the archduke in his own throne room.

Helana reached into her pocket and grabbed the first thing her hand encountered. It was a long, whip-like thing. Words and symbols leapt into her mind unbidden, incantations she'd never heard or learned leapt from her lips. She drew the object out and brandished it exactly as its shape suggested, calling upon the name of Gohrah and mentally imaging the dark half of the Sun's Sister. She inhaled deeply and intuitively drew upon the dark energy abundant in the very air about her, recognizing in it the flavor and the texture of the dark side of Gohrah's mystery. When the tail snapped at the end of her swing, she let it go. Instantly there were a half-dozen gonfons between her and the guards. The round beasts seemed disoriented at first, but they provided an effective shield, biting and ripping at any of the guards who tried to push past them to get at Helana.

The archduke continued to scream, holding his head and rocking back and forth.

Side doors opened and more guards entered the chamber from the left and right sides of the throne's dais.

Helana repeated her blind pocket-dipping maneuvers, altering her gestures to fit the items being produced, instinctively incanting unfamiliar words, her mind remaining focused on the Moon, breath still coursing deeply in search of the energies that would aid her here.

Within moments the guards on the left were blocked by a band of drudge skeletons, while those on the right found a dark gathering of dwarven bandits blocking their way. Helana was then finally able to cast a glance at the major entry where Koborah stood, an unreadable expression on his face, forgotten prisoner in the sudden melee. Rorsa hovered by the cleric's shoulder, barking furiously.

"Father, come to me!" she intoned, as if these words, too, were part of some spell. She reached into her satchel for her last stone but one, and with it offered him a path of protection through the confusion. Rorsa grabbed the man's shoulder in his teeth and batted his wings furiously until Koborah, clearly exhausted and nearly starved, got the idea and began to stumble forward toward the woman he had raised as a Sun-spirit, but who was obviously now so much more than he had ever imagined her to be.

As Koborah drew near, Helana saw that his face was lined as she had never seen it before. He looked as if he had aged ten years since she had last seen him. "What now, my daughter?" he asked. She sensed that his question went much deeper than a simple query regarding what they would do next. No time. She drew her last Sun-stone into her hand and put her arms around him.

"Home!" she commanded, and the corresponding sigil deep within the stone seemed to blaze with the speaking of the word. "Home!" she said again, and the pearl began to glow strongly, faltered, weakened; the stone began to look as if it were going to turn opaque. The sounds surrounding her, which had faded some with the glowing of the stone, came back to full volume with the stone's weakening.

She could tell that the guards were closing in, that the archduke was regaining control of his mental functions to some degree, but she couldn't spare any of them enough attention to gauge how much time they might yet give her. Her hand darted to her satchel, grabbed the multifaceted crystal. She offered a prayer to both Sun and Moon that her plan might work. She held the crystal above the stone and used her mind to draw energy from the fires in the room, from the stone beneath her feet, and from the very air she breathed. She focused her image of these powers onto the crystal, asked it to bend and blend the energies, and was rewarded with a solid white beam of light that landed on the Sun-stone and made it glow anew.

The archduke roared words now, though she could not make them out. His exclamations were more than mere agony: they were rage at the fates that would permit this woman to produce and wield an artifact, right here in his very throne room, that he would love to see destroyed. He rose to his full height, gathered all of his considerable energies, and prepared to cast a spell that would have not only obliterated her and her friends, but all of his guards and a good piece of his palace as well. At the last minute he hesitated, wondering if it was really the best course for all concerned.

Again he screamed, just as the young lady, the cleric, and the dog faded into insubstantiality. Only then did he strike.

4.

Helana spent the ensuing week in total silence, going about the church and its grounds performing every task of maintenance and upkeep that she had ever performed in her many years of service. She ate only bread; she drank only water; she slept only two hours out of every twenty-four. She was serving a personally chosen and administered penance, and Koborah made no attempt to intervene or to engage her in any conversation.

On the seventh day she bore four buckets of water from the creek to the church; the buckets, two to a side, slung over a good straight stick she had lain across her shoulders.

On entering the church she noticed Koborah standing silently in his pulpit watching her, and she tried not to look at or think about him. She bowed forward, passing the stick over her head to disburthen her shoulders, then performed her ritual sunrise with all of the care and grace that she had ever invested in the activity. On finishing this, she carried one of the buckets to each of the two fonts that stood to the left and right of the pulpit and filled the fonts. For now, the fonts were filled with simple water. Tomorrow at noon, when the Sun streamed through the corresponding portals in the domed roof and shone on their contents, the water would be blessed.

This done, she retrieved the other two buckets and delivered them to their more mundane receptacles, where the water would be used for simple washing and the quenching of more secular thirsts.

Throughout all of these tasks Helana was acutely aware of her father's intense scrutiny of her every gesture.

All tasks completed, Helana moved to the foot of the pulpit, knelt, and bowed her head.

"Forgive me, Father," she began in a voice grown coarse from disuse, "but I am no longer fit to be an acolyte in this fine house of worship. I have had commerce with the Night, and with the powers of Sister Gohrah. I have accepted the inducements that she has offered and have worshiped her in equality with the Sun and the things of the Day. I am not remorseful of this and have no intentions of renouncing such allegiances. Also I have spent the resources of this church in ways that might be interpreted as the breaking of the oaths I have recently taken freely.

"Surely I am an ill choice to become your successor. Despite all that you and the Sun have given me, I find that I am no longer a pure daughter of the Sun. I am no longer fit to be your daughter."

"Rise, child." Koborah's voice sounded worn and weary.

Helana did as she was told.

"Look upon me."

This, too, she did, seeing her onlyfather's face gleaming orange from the glint of the setting Sun's rays that were streaming in through the western portals.

"In some of this you are correct. I relieve you from your duties here, as you have already taken the steps that relieve you from the oaths you spoke. You may not remain here as an acolyte. You are unfit to serve as my successor. You are no longer pure in essence as a daughter of the Sun. Take none of this as criticism. Bear none of it as fault. Truth is.

"I have told you before that I do not believe that you were abandoned but were brought here to some purpose. It was vain of me to believe that I perceived that purpose, especially since I allowed myself to believe what I most desired. I will not compound that folly by passing any judgment on the purpose as it appears to me now.

"Regard all that I or the Sun have given you as justly yours. The gifts were for you, not some false image of you. They were not given under false pretenses, or as the result of any coercion. Nothing that you have done has alienated either the Sun or myself, even as the things you've done have drawn distinctions between us. No attachments were ever made upon any of the gifts you received from us, nor will such attachments ever be made upon any gifts of the Sun or upon any of my own gifts. While it is true that you are no longer pure in essence as a worshiper of the Sun, you remain nonetheless a Sun daughter. And always, no matter what fortunes or misfortunes may occur to either of us, you will ever remain, in all ways but the strictest biological, my only daughter, my true daughter, and, I hope, my closest friend."

For a space, the only sound in the church was the two of them striving to control their breathing so that when they spoke again it would not come out as senseless fragments.

"I must leave here," she finally said.

"You must," he agreed.

"My worship has turned to Gohrah, Sister Moon, the Dualist, the daughter of the Night. I must learn how to treat this appropriately."

Koborah nodded. "Gohrah has insinuated herself so as to give you no choice in the matter. Had I Her power, my own most selfish wish would be to attract you in a similar manner. I do not blame Her. I do not blame you. The Sun instructs me to lay no blame."

"I must go and examine my nature."

"Truth is."

"I will always love you, Father."

"And I, you."

The following night she walked beneath the crescent moon, following no known path, pursuing no known destination. On her back she carried a bag that contained her worldly goods: some clothes, some wine, some bread, some cheese, two books, and a little money. At her hip hung a satchel containing no stones but cradling the multifaceted crystal that Koborah had declared to be hers by right of use and usefulness. In her pocket were the remaining tokens of her journey into Hell; tokens she hoped she would never have to use, but which offered her some strange comfort by their presence.

A glinting in the grass caught her eye. She stooped, reached out, and picked up the gleaming object, drawing it to her breast.

Communication was instantaneous.

Illith looked up from some arcane text he'd been perusing in a dim, candlelit study. Every wall behind him was lined with richly bound books. Several globes within globes covered a table to his right.

"Ah, so there you are." He smiled.

"I am."

"I just wanted you to know that things worked out as well as could be expected on this end. The politics here are still in a state of chaos, the archduke and maybe a dozen others dead, imprisoned, or exiled, but such is ever the way of things here. Politics are flux. I am back, more or less, to the station I occupied before we met, hoping that the new regime will simply leave me alone. So I am content. And you?"

"Content? No. I no longer have any station, but I am glad to be on the way to learning enough about my nature that maybe I will one day find a station to suit. I have no idea what it is that I will say, or do, or be in my many tomorrows, but I am eager for such discoveries."

He smiled again. "No idea?" This amused him, for he had many ideas regarding what she might be or do. There was no end to the valuable uses she might be put to by a trusted guide and mentor.

She returned his smile. "Perhaps one day I'll locate a magus named Gerheart and relieve him of a token or two. Other than that, no. No idea at all."

"Things shall be revealed," he told her. "Keep the stone you are holding. Its luster will fade, but its power of contact will not wane. If you ever

want for anything I might supply, or if you simply feel a need to talk . . ."
He let his voice trail off, knowing well the virtues of a soft touch, understanding the importance of her future trust in his good intentions.
Disturbingly, he felt himself desiring that trust for its own sake, for the
sake of his own good feelings. An unusual experience. One that would
require some future examination.

"Thank you," she said, clutching the communication-stone more
firmly to her breast as she recognized its value and importance to her.

Illith smiled and made a gesture toward the stone. "Just don't let that
bastard Gerheart ever get his hands on it," he laughed, "or on that other
trinket you maintain." And the spell was broken as quickly and easily as
the contact had been made.

She regarded the crescent moon, the dimly lit world. She drew the
crystal from her satchel and used it to cast the moonlight into rainbows on
the darkling grass. A dozen colorful crescents smiling up at her. Then she
returned the "trinket" to her satchel and continued on her way.

A few minutes later she paused when a sound arrested her attention. She
listened intently for a moment, then smiled as she recognized the sound of
an erratically flapping pair of wings drawing near.

DISTANT ARMIES

by

Peter Friend

"Father, I had a dream last night," said Somilar.

Some parents would have shouted or wept or pretended not to hear. But I hadn't become a Merchants Guild councilor by ignoring unpleasant facts, and there was no point crying over spilt beng juice.

"It's nothing to be ashamed of," I told her, squeezing her hand. "We'll go and see a sage today; I'm sure it can be treated easily."

"I dreamt of war," she whispered. "You know what that means."

"It means nothing," I said firmly. "Dreams don't come true—that's just a silly superstition. When I was your age, I once dreamt of a city full of little white-skinned people. Have we shrunk? Has our skin turned horrible colors?"

She smiled a little, as I hoped she would. "It was frightening."

"I know, I know. My dream frightened me at the time too," I lied. I'd never dreamt in all my life.

Normally I went to Sage Verus, a modern young elf whose lizard's kidney balm I found most soothing when my left fangs ached. But today I chose Sage Kinekin. He was so old his claws were falling out and so traditional he didn't trust any potion invented this century, but he was kind and sensible.

"Dreams of war? Oh dear, not again," he chuckled as he examined her. "Well, at your age, with all the changes your body's going through, a little disturbed sleep is hardly surprising, is it?"

"So it's just a side effect of puberty?" she asked, sounding almost disappointed.

"What do you mean, 'just' puberty?" he scolded kindly. "It's the most exciting time of a female orc's life. You're already taller and stronger than your father or I. Your fangs are coming through beautifully, your eyes are bright and red, and you've inherited your dear mother's clear green skin and broad back. You're in the prime of good health."

"So will the dreams go away?" she asked, ignoring his praise.

"Of course they will, given a little time. Take this prescription out to my apothecary—she'll mix you up an herbal tea to help you sleep."

He turned to me after she'd closed the door. "I didn't see any need to worry her, Kalin, but you should know that there's a lot of this dreaming going around at the moment. Of course, many people are so superstitious they won't even admit it's happening—I'm sure we don't see even half the

cases. Just keep Somilar at home for a few days and make sure she gets
plenty of rest. Dreaming isn't dangerous in itself—it won't bring bad luck
or drive her insane or any of that nonsense. All she needs is your love and
support."

"I do love her, more than anything—she's all the family I've got left
now. I'm only worried . . . well, you know how people gossip about this
sort of thing. I have my reputation to consider, my business depends on it."

He glared at me. "It's a mild illness, that's all. Last year every second
child in town caught yellow tooth fever, and next year it'll be something
else again. Go home and stop worrying. You're a normal parent and she's
a normal child."

I bought Somilar a candied rat from a goblin's roadside stall, and we
strolled home along Pundin Quay so we could see the blossoming dassikh
trees. But she seemed more interested in staring up at the barren rocks of
Ironclaw Hills.

"Have you ever heard of any Ironclaw *Mountains*?" she asked suddenly.

I frowned, puzzled by the question. "Even the plains traders don't
describe our little hills as mountains. The Hurloon Ranges are the closest
real mountains, I suppose. There could be another region called Ironclaw
somewhere, over the seas perhaps. You could ask the merfolk navigators at
the Seafarers Guild—they might know."

She grimaced as I mentioned the merfolk. "In my dream, there were
tall crags called the Ironclaw Mountains, with ocean on one side and
plains on the other, just like here. And we were being attacked by the
armies of both sides, including the merfolk."

I laughed uneasily and hugged her. "There hasn't been a war anywhere near here for six hundred years. Ironclaw's a major trading port for
the whole region. Trade's increasing every year, and the plains farmers
and the merfolk fleets are profiting just as we are. Why would anyone
want war?"

"I'm sorry, Father. I didn't mean to upset you. I know it was a silly
dream, but it seemed so real."

After lunch, she fell into a deep and apparently peaceful sleep. I left a
servant watching her and hurried down to the Merchants Guild, anxious to
hear any news of our overdue fleet.

But the Radzali Ocean was still nearly windless according to the sea
eagles. It would be at least two days before our cargoes of spices and elf
glass arrived.

The guild hall was almost empty, just a few bored merchants drinking and staring out the harbor windows. I poured myself a mug of russet mead and joined them.

"Not blocking your view am I, Kalin?" asked the dwarf in front of me.

"Afternoon, Spenggra," I said. "Very funny. I could sit on the floor and still see over your head. How's business?"

"No wind, so no ships, so no business. Today's biggest excitement was selling a grelm of red pearls to a couple of centaurs. I've never gotten my tongue around their dialect—your translation skills were sorely missed. Where were you, anyway?"

"Somilar's a little unwell today," I said. "The sage said it was nothing to worry about."

"Mmm, young Kebwin's come down with something, too. Nothing dangerous. That's children for you—always catching something or other."

When I arrived home, Somilar had just woken.

"No dreams," she whispered, and smiled. "I feel much better now."

So did I.

"Try the sage's herbal tea tonight," I said. "If you sleep well, perhaps you can go back to the academy tomorrow."

But she didn't. A little before dawn, I was woken by her scream, and ran to find her cowering on her bedroom floor.

"They drowned the goblins," she sobbed. "The whole village, even the men and children. The waves got higher and higher, then crashed down on them. It was horrible."

I held her in my arms. "The same dream again?"

"The war's getting worse. Dead mountain people everywhere—orcs and dwarves and goblins, even ogres. We're being crushed between plains and ocean, and attacked from the air."

"Be quiet, darling, be quiet. It's just a bad dream."

"You don't believe it will come true?"

"Of course not."

I sent a servant out to fetch Sage Kinekin. She returned with a hysterical Spenggra instead.

"He won't come," he wailed. "A score of parents have all called for him at once. He says there's nothing he can do, says we're a bunch of superstitious fools." In the many years I'd known him, I'd never seen him so upset.

"Kebwin's dreaming, too?" I asked.

He nodded, blinking back tears. "For nearly half a smallmoon now, on and off. It's an evil omen, I've said it from the start. People are dreaming all over Ironclaw—not just orcs and dwarves, but kobolds, even rock giants. Merfolk, too, I've heard, although they're so secretive it's hard to be sure. It's absolute chaos out there in the streets. The guilds will have to do something."

"We are the guilds," I reminded him.

To my dismay, I discovered Spenggra had not exaggerated the number of people affected—more than a hundred families, pods, and bloodclans arrived at a hastily arranged meeting that noon. On the streets, the gossip was of nothing else.

I'd hoped the meeting might suggest some cure or plan of action, or at least give us a sense of togetherness. It started well enough, with Sage Verus observing that everyone had dreamt of the same war in the so-called Ironclaw Mountains, whatever they were. But the discussion quickly descended into name-calling, wild accusations, and ludicrous threats, mostly against merfolk. Spenggra and I walked out, unnoticed in the hubbub.

"Idiots," Spenggra spluttered.

"They're frightened," I said. "We're all frightened."

"I hope that's all it is. Down by the docks last night, a centaur was beaten unconscious and his mane cut off. And someone tried to set fire to a mulgrain warehouse—not for the first time either, they say. Sometimes I think the dreams are coming true, that we really are heading for war—civil war." He grimaced and took a deep breath. "Sorry Kalin, you need cheering up, not all this gloomy talk of mine. Why don't you bring Somilar over to our clanhome tonight? My wives would love to see you both again, the whole clan would. A little company would be good, and . . . well, perhaps we can stop the children dreaming tonight."

"Your clanhome must have shrunk," Somilar told the dwarves, bumping her head on the rafters for the third time. "It wasn't this small last time I was here."

"That was mistmoons ago—before the firling harvest," an old daywife told her with a toothless grin. "You're growing far too tall, that's your problem. I honestly don't know what Kebwin sees in you."

The roomful of dwarves erupted into good-natured laughter again—the supposed romance between Somilar and Kebwin had been a favorite joke since the pair were toddlers. Somilar rolled her eyes and sat down.

Such a large amicable gathering of dwarves was rare, but today their endless feuds and rivalries seemed forgotten as they polished steel-bound shields with nemoth oil and trimmed great piles of crossbow bolts.

"Big hunting expedition?" I asked Spenggra. "We orcs have an old saying: 'Dwarves only stop fighting each other to fight someone else together.'"

"Wrong—it's actually an old dwarfish saying." He grinned sourly. "We won't provoke war. But if it comes, we'll be ready."

"It'll be us mountain people against the rest of them," said Kebwin. "The dreams make that clear."

"Clear? What's clear about them?" I asked.

"Haven't you noticed who all the dreamers are, Father?" asked Somilar. "Female orcs and goblins and kobolds. Male dwarves and centaurs and merfolk. The biggest and strongest of each race, and all of us young and fit. Perfect soldiers, don't you think?"

"They're just dreams," I said.

She bared her left arm to show a long ugly bruise, and Kebwin lifted his tunic, revealing a bandaged midriff.

"In our dreams last night, we were both hurt. And when we woke, the wounds were real."

The room was silent.

"Well, there'll be no wounding of anyone tonight. We're going to watch you both all night if we have to," said Spenggra, trying to sound stern but stifling a yawn.

"You're already exhausted from this morning," his nightwife told him. "The four of you will be snoring within the hour. Why don't you sleep in the kitchens while we bake tomorrow's shaa loaves? We'll keep an eye on you all and wake you if anything happens."

It was a sensible idea; I was already drowsy myself. The nightwives spread blankets for us on the floor by the great stone ovens, then started their breadmaking. Somilar and Kebwin were asleep in minutes. Spenggra and I lay next to them, watching their faces.

"They'd make a good marriage, if only Somilar was a dwarf," whispered Spenggra.

"They'd make a great marriage, if only Kebwin was an orc," I replied.

The gentle clatter of baking lulled us to sleep.

I woke to daylight and the thick musky smell of shaa loaves fresh from the ovens. The other three were still fast asleep.

"You all slept like fazdrones the whole night through," said a passing nightwife with an armful of loaves. "Perhaps our baking is a cure for dreams."

"Perhaps," I said.

Servants and children were soon running through Ironclaw, first checking then spreading the news—no one had dreamt during the night.

The day passed in fragile peace. No one dreamt that night, either.

Sails were spotted far out to sea the next morning, and by dusk the first of the fleet was moored in the harbor. Ironclaw remembered it was a trading port, and the docks filled with the usual crowds of merchants, scriveners, carriers, prostitutes, and bankers.

The scent of money reminded people that customers were customers, whatever their race. The past days' air of tension dissolved into the greedy goodwill that normally marked a fleet arrival.

No one was really surprised when the night was again free of dreams.

The next morning, the guilds unanimously announced a feast day. People muttered embarrassed apologies for their hasty words of previous days, and shaky trade pacts were resealed with many shared mugs of wine and plates of pickled frogs.

It seemed that the world had returned to normal.

A smallmoon later, I woke shaking in the darkness, my head full of fading images of blurred violence. Perhaps I'd started dreaming, too, I wondered, then realized what that might mean and ran to Somilar's room.

She wasn't there.

I searched the whole house, checking the locks on every door and shutter, shouting her name, over and over again. The servants stared at me as if I was mad. A little before dawn, we found her asleep in her room again, though we'd checked there only minutes earlier.

Her feet were blistered and bloodied as if from long marching, and her hands had become as callused as a stonesmith's. Her face was haggard and exhausted, and we couldn't wake her.

I ran out to the stables, thinking to search the town for a sage who might be bribed or threatened into helping me. From all directions I heard crying, shouting, and frantic footsteps, and I realized the sages could do no more today than they could before.

Instead, I saddled a placid fazdrone and led it to the back door. Half an hour later, I was knocking on the stone door of Spenggra's clanhome, Somilar still fast asleep on the fazdrone behind me.

Kebwin had also dreamt again, and his body, too, was battered and torn as if by long, harsh exertion. His mothers treated his cuts and bruises and tried to wake him, but he was deep in the same exhausted sleep as Somilar.

Both children woke some hours later, but refused any food or even water. They hunched in a corner, hugging each other for comfort, sometimes drowsing, sometimes raving about their dream world.

"I saw her," said Kebwin.

"She's dying, she knows it, but she'll never surrender," said Somilar. "Their sorcery is crushing the very mountains around her, but still she fights on. I will die defending her." Her words were madness, but she sounded calm, almost proud.

"Who are you speaking of?" I asked, desperate for some clue to their delusions.

They smiled bitterly at each other.

"See?" said Kebwin. "Just a few thousand years and they've all forgotten her, forgotten even that there were once Ironclaw Mountains here. Perhaps it isn't really worth fighting for."

"Of course it is," Somilar shouted weakly. "They didn't win. Look around you—we survived, Ironclaw survived."

He nodded and closed his eyes.

"You'll be fine," I told her, no longer bothering to hold back my tears. "The dreams won't come true."

She smiled again and squeezed my hand. "Too late, Father. We were wrong—the dreams weren't the future, after all. The war finished thirty centuries ago, and now it's about to finish again. The Benalish surround us on three sides. They're crowding us toward the cold sea, where the merfolk wait with tridents. They say we orcs are vicious and cowardly. They say they'll exterminate us all."

And so on, for hours—mystical gibberish about enchantments, summonings, curses, and spells. We're modern, rational people—any child knows there's no such thing as magic.

"It's just a bad fever," said Spenggra several times, not even believing it himself.

"No one will take them from us. I won't let them," he said at sunset, making no more sense than the children. Grim-faced dwarves began loading quivers with crossbow bolts, while others hauled huge boulders to block the room's door and window.

"Safe at last. Hard granite and a score of armed dwarves guard us now," he said happily as the four of us were entombed in our tiny fortress. "No one can get in or out."

"If she calls for us, how can we refuse to answer?" asked Kebwin quietly, and fell asleep in Somilar's arms.

What Spenggra hoped to achieve by our incarceration I didn't know. Disease cares nothing for walls and weapons. Keeping watch over the children seemed pointless, though I could think of no better plan myself. When I heard his gentle snoring I didn't have the heart to wake him.

I myself stayed awake, although I, too, was exhausted. Perhaps I might have nodded off for a few moments, for it seemed as though both Kebwin and Somilar vanished in front of me. A trick of the dim light or my tired eyes, I thought, for when I looked again there they were, lying peacefully on the blankets as they had been all along. And then I looked more closely and noticed the blood trickling from Kebwin's ears and the trident in my daughter's neck.

Some would say Somilar was one of the lucky ones. She lives. When I put food in her mouth, she swallows it. She smiles now and then. Sometimes I think she still recognizes me.

Spenggra does not speak of his grief. He spends his days immersed in old books and folklore and giving money to any passing charlatan who claims they can talk to the dead.

I know the merfolk suffered as we did. I saw the smoke plumes over the harbor as the dozens of burning coffins floated out to the open sea.

I heard the centaurs beating the drums made from the hides of their fallen comrades. The sound was like thunder and lasted for days.

The guilds speak of forgiveness, of reconciliation and rebuilding. No one is to blame, after all. I know that.

But tomorrow I take my daughter and ride toward the Hurloon Ranges. The mountains stretch to both horizons, they say, and I for one never wish to see an ocean or a plain again.

BETTER MOUSETRAP

by

Jane M. Lindskold

In a rustic hamlet on the western slope of K'Cur Mountain is Teeka's Shop of Wonders. The K'Cur Mountains are rocky and the roads are poor, yet every year hundreds make the journey, some to buy, some merely to look then go away with tales to tell around winter fires or during the lazy heat of a summer afternoon.

The tales that they tell are of beasts—bears, lions, wolves, apes, and mammoths—made of metal and crystal, their innards a clockwork paradise of cogs and gears and wheels. The eyes of Teeka's beasts are gemstones, and their claws and fangs are polished steel.

On the breast of each is etched a brief poem which is said to be the beast's soul.

One morning when the staff of Teeka's Shop of Wonders were preparing to begin their day, a howl of purest outrage shook the halls.

"Who has scratched my lion!"

Apprentices froze, spoons of hot raisin oatmeal halfway to their lips. Mechanicians paused in their discussions of rasps and sandpaper. Artificers let their patterns roll shut unnoticed.

Again came the cry.

"Who has scratched my lion? I'll have the culprit's head, I swear!"

Teeka stalked into the great hall, where her staff gathered for breakfast and talk before beginning the day. They sat separated by rank and position, but in the face of Teeka's fury they all melded into a group of one. Sallow, gray-haired Andros who rose from his seat at the artificers' table was their voice.

"Your lion, Teeka?" Andros's tones were husky, but friendly. He had joined Teeka soon after graduating from the Institute of Arcane Study and usually counted her as friend, not employer.

"The Emerald Lion," Teeka clarified. "I set its poem on its breast past sunset yesterday, and it was perfect then. This morning I went to admire it and found a deep scratch a finger's breadth in width running from the right shoulder along the flank across the haunch to the tail."

Silence fell and even the innocent felt guilty under Teeka's searching gaze.

Teeka herself looked like one of her artifacts. Skin the hue of darkest ebony contrasted wonderfully with the wild hair like molten gold that tumbled in an undisciplined profusion over her back and shoulders. Her eyes were bright turquoise and ironic, her voice shrill and acerbic. Apparently ageless, she was a mystery to everyone—including herself—and didn't care a whit.

What she did care about were her wonderful clockwork beasts and now one of them had been maliciously damaged.

Andros faced the trembling staff members, his brown eyes more mundane, but his gaze equally searching.

"Does anyone care to confess?" he asked.

No one moved. Several tried not to breathe.

Teeka scowled. "Gospor, Hendron, when you are finished with your meal, meet me in the showroom. Perhaps we can repair the damage."

She paused and surveyed her huddled staff. "I accept explanations, but I have no patience with foolish cowardice. I hope that the guilty party chooses to speak with me or with Andros rather than waiting to be discovered."

Without further comment, Teeka departed. Gospor and Hendron left their unfinished meals and followed. Only when the door was shut behind them did conversation flurry forth.

"I want your help checking the locks in here," Teeka said when she was alone with Gospor and Hendron.

Hendron, the chief mechanician, a portly Benalish with rusty brown hair and dark eyes, rose from where he had been kneeling by the Emerald Lion. His hand restlessly traced the incised patterning of the beast's bulky mane.

"You are certain that you locked up last night?" he asked gruffly.

Teeka nodded, calmer now. "I am. I set the lion's poem in my workshop, then walked him in here as a test. When I left, the jingling of my keys as I locked up gave me an idea for the Silver Courser we've been working on for the viceroy of the Shore."

Gospor, a pretty, rosy-cheeked dwarf, stroked the braided length of her beard. "Have you considered that the damage may have been done by someone other than our staff?"

"Of course!" Teeka snorted. "Nor have I forgotten how the Dragon Engine vanished for a fortnight two Lesser Moons past, to reappear in a locked storage room."

"Or how the Hematite Wolf Pack vanished in entire one afternoon and reappeared that evening with blood on their fangs," Hendron added.

"Just so we are not too quick to blame our staff," Gospor said, satisfied, climbing a ladder to inspect window locks.

Teeka's Shop of Wonders was actually a complex of little shops—private workshops dedicated to individual projects, open-air smithies, smaller forges, a glass-blower's furnace, a sky-lit scriptorium for drafting plans, libraries, living quarters, classrooms, and the elegant showroom wherein finished projects awaited buyers or reposed until those who had commissioned them came to pay and collect.

Hendron stared out a window as if the activity within the compound had given him an idea.

"All of the trouble has been with pieces in the showroom, hasn't it?" he asked.

"Now that I think on it," Teeka said, "that is true."

"Perhaps someone wants to learn your secrets," Hendron offered diffidently. "No thief could hope to profit from selling the clockwork beasts. Your work is too unique."

"True," Teeka admitted without false modesty. "If your guess is right, that would make our enemy either a mechanician or a sorcerer. Have any of you found anything wrong with any of the locks?"

Hendron and Gospor shook their heads.

"Then let's see what we can do about the Emerald Lion," Teeka said, laying an affectionate hand on the beast's brass mane. "And let's stay quiet about what we've been discussing. If someone is trying to steal my secrets, they may have allies in our staff."

Teeka was hardly seen over the next several days. She retreated into her private drafting room and workshop, conferred with Hendron and Andros, worked for long hours with Gospor. The Emerald Lion was repaired, the Silver Courser completed. Life at the Shop of Wonders settled back into something like normal.

When Teeka reemerged from her workshop, she bore on her arm a magnificent falcon. Its plumage was beaten copper and the wires and gears were so skillfully hidden that the artificers marveled aloud. Etched tiny on its breast feathers were the lines:

> "Watcher, Striker, Hunter, I/ From the Heights, All I Spy."

Gospor followed carrying a second falcon, identical to the first except that its plumage was gold. The poem on its breast was subtly different:

> "Watcher, Striker, Hunter, I/ Capturing All In My Glittering Eye."

Teeka pressed a lever hidden within the Copper Falcon's fanned tail-feathers and the falcon came alive. Its faceted topaz eyes sparkled as it turned its head with tiny, halting jerks and assessed everyone present.

In a fey, merry mood, Teeka darted from room to room, allowing all and sundry to examine her prize. Gospor ran short-legged and short-breathed behind her, sharing in the fun. At last they retired the Falcons to the showroom, setting them on aeries made of gypsum plaster built high in opposite corners of the room. From there they appeared to survey the Hematite Wolf Pack, the Emerald Lion, the Silver Courser, and sundry other clockwork beasts with the hauteur of visiting nobility.

The very next day, the viceroy of the Shore arrived with his large and gaudy entourage to claim the Silver Courser. Dismounting from his red silk-caparisoned charger, he raced into the showroom with a boyish enthusiasm at odds with his reputation as a ruthless warrior. The sun had bleached his beard and darkened his skin, and a weapon scar neatly bisected his left eyebrow.

He bowed deeply before Teeka, folding his hands before his face. When he straightened, Teeka had activated the Silver Courser.

It pranced up to the viceroy, a slim, elegant steed with a coat of polished silver. Extending one perfect foreleg, it bowed, mane of fine silver wire brushing the floor with a sound like tiny bells. Then it rose and surveyed the viceroy from eyes of smooth, polished amethyst.

"I am awed, delighted, impressed, stunned!" the viceroy bubbled, skipping with short steps around the courser. "Were it not for the lines for the joints, I could believe some mortal dam foaled an immortal steed! Can something so rich and delicate be as powerful as you promised?"

Teeka smiled, unpiqued. She was accustomed to awe at her clockwork creations. Anything less would have aroused her ire.

"The Silver Courser is indeed the warhorse you desire," she said, stroking its neck. "Its bones are steel, as is its exterior. The clockworks are protected within and warded with charms of my own devising."

She pressed a button concealed beneath the courser's jaw and a panel slid open. Polished gears bit into each other, wheels spun, wires slid in perfectly machined grooves.

The viceroy clapped his hands in delight and asked question after question. Teeka answered them all, and when the panel was shut again, she showed the viceroy two pegs set behind the courser's ears.

"Press the right-hand one and the courser is readied for battle," she explained. "It will bite and kick and refuse to carry any but you. Its hooves become razor-edged and its teeth become fangs. Press the left-hand peg and the courser becomes a steed fit for travel or the hunt or a casual amble."

The viceroy drew a pouch from his belt and spilled forty pink pearls into Teeka's dark hands. They glowed in her dark black hand like new fallen dew drops.

"Tell me, Viceroy," Teeka asked, "in your journeys, have you heard of another beast artificer of my skill?"

"None," he replied bluntly. "Trade caravans cross through my city as the sun crosses the sky and none have heard of your like. There are others, makers of clocks and music boxes, of trinkets and toys, but no other makes beasts that seem to counterfeit life without being heir to life's frailties."

He patted the courser affectionately and the metal horse nuzzled him in return.

"Some say," the viceroy continued, "that not since the days of legend when Urza and Mishra fought their ancient battles has there been an artificer to compare with you."

If Teeka blushed, none could see it.

"No other offers clockwork beasts like these?" She gestured about the showroom. "No others even pretend?"

The viceroy glanced about, studying the wonders. A satisfied smile grew beneath his mustaches as he shook his head.

"I heard of a man who dyed horses and dogs in fanciful colors and offered them for sale, but no one else makes clockwork beasts so fine." His gaze rested on the Copper Falcon. "How much do you want for that lovely bird?"

"It is not for sale," Teeka replied.

"But you have two," the viceroy protested, pointing to the Falcon of Gold. "Surely you can spare one!"

"They are not for sale," Teeka repeated calmly, her turquoise eyes glinting so strangely that the viceroy did not press further.

To salvage his dignity, he pretended to become fascinated with a cobra whose delicate scales were individually hammered from silver, gold, and copper, capturing a fiery rainbow that intensified the brilliance of its slanting fire opal eyes. Its fangs delivered a sleeping potion, making it a subtle guard.

The viceroy paid ten white pearls and a strand of scrimshaw beads for the cobra and departed on his Silver Courser. With a worried frown, Teeka watched the entourage depart.

Several days later, the Hematite Wolf Pack again vanished. An apprentice discovered the theft and told his instructor, who reflected on the wisdom of not bearing the news to Teeka himself, and so told Hendron. Hendron brought the news to Teeka.

Teeka scowled and sent an apprentice to fetch Gospor.

In the showroom, the unfortunate lad who had discovered the theft waited trembling. Teeka dismissed him with a few surprisingly kind words. Then she summoned the Copper and Gold Falcons down from their aeries.

"I hear that the wolves are gone!" Gospor said, rushing in, her beard full of iron filings.

"They are, and now we see how well our experiment worked," Teeka gloated. "We need paper."

"I brought some," Gospor said.

"Then here's the quill," Teeka said.

Her long fingers deftly removed a single feather from the wing of the Copper Falcon. Hendron did the same for the Gold. On command, the clockwork birds extended their right talons and took the quills, holding them as neatly as any scribe.

Gospor slid a piece of paper into position beneath each quill.

"Now, falcons, tell us," Teeka said, rubbing her hands together briskly, "who was in here last night after I cleared and locked the showroom?"

"No one," wrote the Copper Falcon in words that glittered the very shade of its topaz eye.

"No one but the clockwork beasts," wrote the Gold Falcon.

The three artificers stared at the words.

"Someone must have been," Hendron said.

"Perhaps we were not precise enough," Gospor offered with a worried glance at Teeka. "Falcons, who took the Hematite Wolf Pack away?"

"No one," wrote the Copper Falcon.

"No one that I saw," wrote the Gold Falcon.

"Did they just get up and walk away?" Teeka said sarcastically.

"No," wrote the Copper Falcon.

"They did not walk," wrote the Golden Falcon.

"Run? Leap? Creep? Spring?" Teeka asked angrily. "Any form of locomotion known to wolf or clockwork beast?"

"No," wrote the Copper Falcon.

"No," wrote the Gold Falcon. "They vanished."

"Vanished?" Hendron echoed, making a superstitious gesture.

"Vanished?" mused Gospor, turning the page to make certain that she had read aright.

"Vanished," wrote both falcons.

"Into thin air," added the Golden Falcon.

At the very moment that the quills stilled on the paper, there was a sound and a faint stirring in the air of the closed and sealed showroom.

Turning as one, the three artificers saw that the Hematite Wolf Pack had been returned. They ran over to inspect them.

"This one has blood on its teeth," Hendron marveled.

"This one is streaked with a greenish ichor," Gospor said. "Could be goblin blood, if I rightly recall my martial cousins' tales."

"This one is scraped about the shoulders as if it was bitten and shaken," Teeka said grimly. "I wish these beasts could talk or write! I want to make this thief and vandal pay!"

Hendron and Gospor traded nervous glances.

"Who do you think it is?" Hendron asked cautiously.

"As we discussed before, a sorcerer of some type," Teeka said. "If the culprit is trying to copy my craft and enchantments, I'll have my revenge!"

"My people," said Gospor and Hendron simultaneously. They stopped and then Hendron deferred to Gospor.

"Dwarves have long lives and longer memories," Gospor said, "and there are tales that the gods do war using earthly things as their troops in the same way that children rank lead soldiers for mock battles."

"A cult within my people has similar tales," Hendron added. "The heroes of Benalia claim a sacred place within our shifting caste system so that they will be ever prepared to answer the call of the gods."

Teeka studied them thoughtfully.

"I hear your words," she said, "but I cannot believe that the universe is so arrayed."

"No?" Gospor asked, surprised.

"No," Teeka scoffed. "Gods surely have more profound things to occupy their time than playing petty war games. As I see the universe, the gods made the world and its creatures, and then wound it up like some vast clock and let it run. That is the only explanation that makes sense. Either gods are gods with divine interests, or they play at the same games that mortals do and thus are not gods at all. Our culprit must be a sorcerer or petty artificer jealous of our skill. And that is who I plan to entrap!"

Hendron and Gospor shuddered, but they listened as Teeka outlined her plan.

The entire of the Shop of Wonders immediately felt the ripples of Teeka's project. The storehouses were pillaged for gears and wire and wheels in such quantities that the quartermaster wailed that they would be pressed to supply the parts for a butterfly, much less a lion or a bear.

Smithies produced an odd assortment of teeth, talons, bones, scales, and skin. Gospor, Hendron, and Andros nearly vanished from general congress. Their projects gathered dust; their students were delegated to others. Yet, for all this flurry of activity, no one but a chosen few knew precisely what manner of beast was being roughed into shape within Teeka's private workshop.

Teeka herself, it was rumored, had forsaken sleep, but no one could know for certain, for she emerged from her workshop but rarely. When the Emerald Lion vanished for a week, she glowered, questioned the falcons, and stomped back into her workshop. When the jet and bronze leopard that had been commissioned by the princess of distant Parma vanished, Teeka sent a message telling the princess that there had been a delay in the work and did not retract it, even when the leopard reappeared in need of little more than a manicure.

Through a hundred minor crises Teeka continued on her private project and as fall turned into winter, the shop grew accustomed to her absence.

The snows were high all over K'Cur Mountain on the day that Teeka emerged from her workshop and startled the apprentice on duty in the showroom. The day had been quiet—more precisely, the past Lesser Moon had been quiet—for the winter snows had kept all but local visitors away.

To wile away the hours, the apprentice had been doodling a plan for a clockwork polar bear with fur highlighted with crystal and eyes like blue ice. The apprentice blanched and tried to hide her sketch pad when Teeka entered, her golden hair wilder, her turquoise eyes brighter than ever. Teeka only glanced at the drawing and smiled.

"A good thought. See what you can do about the beast's weight. Clockwork beasts tend to sink in snowdrifts. If you solve the problem, we'll make one."

The apprentice blushed. Noticing that Teeka held a small tool kit, she cleared her throat.

"May I help you with that?"

"No, that's all right," Teeka said, her tones surprisingly mild. "Just see that I am not disturbed."

The apprentice watched covertly as Teeka went to the Jetty Leopard, etching something on the beast's breast, just below the soul poem. Finishing, she did something to the activation mechanism. Then she moved on to the Dragon Engine. When she had made her alteration to each clockwork beast in the showroom, Teeka departed.

The apprentice hurried over to the Emerald Lion and knelt to read its poem: "Pride of Verdure/ Pride of Plains." Beneath this, Teeka had added the single word: "Protected." The same legend had been added to each of Teeka's clockwork beasts, from the delicate falcons to the lumbering Dragon Engine.

A spill of paper had been neatly tied to each clockwork beast's activation switch. Glancing over her shoulder, lest Teeka return and find her snooping, she unrolled one and read: "This Beast is Protected. Activate at your Peril. Lease or Purchase plans available."

That evening, beneath a clear winter sky lit only by the misty light of the Greater Moon, Teeka unveiled the rest of her project. Andros stood at her side, looking drawn but obviously pleased.

Gospor and Hendron directed crews that were loosening pegs and bolts in order to slide back the roofs of both the showroom and Teeka's workshop. Both wore enigmatic smiles as they ordered their teams about, refusing to answer any of the queries called to them from the watching crowd.

All but the illest and the youngest of K'Cur hamlet had turned out to watch, despite the cold. They stood outside of the Shop of Wonders, stamping their booted feet, nibbling hot chestnuts and sticky buns, and speculating whether there would be anything worth seeing.

They need not have worried. As the last panel of the roof slid clear, Teeka slipped into her workshop and activated the mysterious new beast. At the first sounds from within, Andros filled the sky with globes of pastel light, and in their glow a mysterious creature sprang into the air.

Sinuous as a sea serpent, but six-legged and stirring up a cold wind from powerful wings, the clockwork dragon hovered over the crowd surveying them from diamond eyes. When it roared, the double row of silver teeth caught the light and saber fangs glimmered like sword blades. Each of its six feet bore six curving steel talons and its lashing tail ended in an envenomed stinger. Heavy bronze scales covered the whole beast, leaving not one point unarmored. On its broad, barrel chest burned one word: "Protector."

"It looks larger up there," Andros said nervously, "but that is because the wings are outspread—isn't it?"

Teeka did not answer, glorying in the beauty of the beast. The gathered throng shouted and applauded. Some fell mute in awe. No one noticed the cold, and when Teeka commanded the dragon into its new lair in the showroom, it was as if the sun had set at noon.

Hot cider was served to those outside and a smaller, private party was held in the showroom.

"Six legs," Teeka said, caressing the protector. "Two for fighting, two for carrying, and two for standing. And those fangs and claws! It was much more beautiful than I had hoped. Thank you, friends, for making my dream come true."

"But such a dream," Hendron said slowly. "I never want to see your nightmares, Teeka."

"It is a protector," Teeka said, hooking her hand around one of the heavy steel claws. "Let our thief make another clockwork beast vanish!"

And so it happened that two weeks later an apprentice ran to tell Hendron that the princess's leopard had vanished and moments later the Protector Dragon had raised its head as if taking a scent and, reaching out after the leopard, it had vanished as well.

"Shall we guess what is happening?" Teeka mused gleefully when she had summoned her artificers to her and sealed the showroom behind them. "Our thief has again 'borrowed' one of the clockwork beasts. Disregarding my just warning, the thief activates the leopard. Now things do not go according to our thief's plan. The leopard stubbornly refuses to obey and the Protector Dragon manifests overhead!"

Quiet fell.

"I wonder what is happening?" Gospor said.

"I wonder if the Protector Dragon will be able to find its way back?" Andros asked, "I set the magic carefully, but still . . ."

"I wonder if we've overreached?" Hendron said.

Teeka folded her long ebon fingers around her mug of hot, mulled wine and said nothing.

"Why did you do it, Teeka?" Hendron asked. "Whoever the thief is, the clockwork beasts are usually returned and we can repair them to make them fit for sale."

Teeka's turquoise gaze met his dark one. "You don't think that I make the beasts for money, do you? I won't believe that. None of you work here for money. We could all retire to some warmer city just on the pearls from the viceroy. We do not need to live in this cold and isolated place. We live here because here is what we need to make the clockwork beasts, and we craft the beasts for love and beauty, for the wonder we bring to people's faces."

One by one, the artificers nodded. Teeka smiled upon them.

"Now some arrogant clod believes that our shop is a storage locker free for the looting!" Her voice rose shrilly. "I won't tolerate that without a fight! Maybe Protector Dragon will fail! Maybe we've lost the leopard, but I will not let anyone abuse my art—our art—art that belongs even to the least apprentice within our halls. I will not let it be stolen for someone else's purposes without offering even a whimper of protest! Protector Dragon is my protest!"

She stopped, aware that she was shouting.

"Our protest, too," Andros said hastily.

"I write the poem that gives each beast its soul," Teeka whispered. "Should I not care?"

They kept vigil all that night, and as dawn was outlining K'Cur Mountain with pink and yellow, first the leopard and then Protector Dragon reappeared. The leopard showed only a faint scuff on one paw. Protector Dragon was battered, but entire and proud.

A scroll had been tied to one front talon. Standing on her toes, Teeka plucked it down, unrolled it, and read aloud the single sentence: "How Much to Lease this Dragon?"

THE FACE OF THE ENEMY

ENEMY

by

Adam-Troy Castro

danforth 95

In the far provinces of Cyrristiii, a year's hard ride from the edge of the civilized world, sits a blasted plain that once teemed like a garden; a place where waters ran sweet from crystal-clear springs, where the skies were brilliant with the promise of summer, and where each vine bore a nectar worthy of the gods.

Once, when this place was known to humankind, it was called Woerishin, a name that means Touched With Perfection; were it on any maps now, it would be called Viroscek, which means the Place of the Damned. But Viroscek is no longer on any maps; nobody goes there; nobody wants to go there. The land is now a black, brittle cinder, hardened by centuries of battle; the waters are brackish, foul smelling, and redolent with blood; the skies are dark and openly hostile to the light; and the only plants are the carnivorous, sucker-mouthed vines that snake from horizon to horizon, growing plump on the flesh of the fallen. The only inhabitants are the two powerful figures who each squat in their castles at opposite ends of this ruined landscape and endlessly send arcane armies to destroy the other.

The battle has been raging, without either side gaining any advantage, for a thousand times ten thousand years.

Until today.

Today, there are no screams of bloodlust anywhere within the borders of Viroscek, no sound of clanking swords, no moist thuds of corpses being trampled by invading horses. Today, when the wizard Xavis peers down upon the land from the highest tower of his battered fortress, the invaders from the south simply fail to materialize, the defenders of the north do not rise to meet them, and the only movement anywhere in sight is the single bedraggled figure approaching through the shadows of dawn.

Xavis is great, and Xavis is powerful, but Xavis is also an old man, who has been old longer than most mountains have stood. He has fought his eternal war for so long that he has forgotten how it started, or what was initially at stake; he has sent forth his whirlwinds and firestorms and undead legions for so many summers and winters that the very blood in his veins has turned black from the bitterness in his soul. It has been centuries since he even remembered the name, or the face, of the enemy whose own fortress blots the southern horizon; it has been longer since anything that enemy could do wreaked from him even the slightest stirrings of fear. But today, as the lone figure from the south stumbles purposefully in his direction, not even remotely slowed by the bones and the craters and the scars of battle, Xavis feels something cold and dreadful clutch greedily at his heart.

Panicking, he draws upon the strength of his land and brings down the lightning, forging it in his hands into the shape of a horse, which crackles and thunders and scorches the earth even as it meekly allows Xavis its lord to mount and ride. The walls of living stone that comprise his fortress sink into the ground, so that Xavis and his mount can pass, and the distance between them and the lone figure disappears in an instant of arching light.

Apocalyptic thunder rocks the landscape as Xavis dismounts, now close enough to see his visitor more clearly. He notes, unsurprised, that the visitor is not human; he might have been human once, but he's fought so many futile battles, and been so frequently hurled between life and death, that almost no humanity remains. Now the visitor is little more than an animated skeleton, bound together by a patchwork quilt of lesser miracles: demon wind drives his legs, mystical fire powers his arms, and things unnamed give strength to his heart. He is no direct threat to a wizard as powerful as Xavis; he's only an automaton, incapable of anything beyond doing the job he's walked so far to do.

Xavis speaks to the hidden forces that animate the wretch: "Give it to me."

And the visitor reaches into his dried, exposed ribs and extracts a scroll that's been threaded in and out and around those bones like fabric on a loom. The scroll is old and dusty and composed of something far more intimate than paper. The visitor hands it to Xavis and then steps back, silent, finished, empty, his entire purpose in life achieved.

Xavis reads the message with trembling hands. There is but a single word written there: a word in a language that Xavis knows, but which has not been spoken anywhere in the world since long before the war between him and his enemy began. The script is ancient and ornate, ruled by its loops and flourishes, a calligraphy so complex that readers not as wary as Xavis could lose their minds and their souls in all the beautiful permutations of the letters. Xavis, of course, fails to see its loveliness. He's lived beyond his ability to appreciate beauty; he only sees the message, which leaves him gasping.

After a moment he looks up and, with a single peremptory gesture, causes the ground to rise up in the shape of a hand and crush the visitor in a grip of dirt and stone. The visitor does not scream. He dies, as he's died a thousand times before: silently, and obediently, his powdered bones salting the earth beneath him.

As for Xavis, he simply mounts his thunder horse once again . . . and gallops off toward the south to greet his eternal enemy for the very last time.

The horse is born of the lightning, and it races across the ruined landscape with a speed that beggars thought, reducing the ground in its wake to fused glass, causing clods of flaming soil to scatter in every direction like thousands of miniature comets. And yet Xavis rides the reins hard, whipping the beast, cursing it for its laziness, damning its inability to reach the enemy's fortress in less than the heartbeat the journey actually requires. Still, if Xavis suspects a trap, there is none. Nothing tries to stop him. None of the enemy's legions of fire rise up to block his way; no hurricanes of ice descend to force him back; no rains of poison blood plunge down to slay him as he rides. The enemy's lands remain open and accommodating, like the door to the house of a friend.

Xavis pulls up short before the enemy's castle, which is now and always a mirror-image of his own: its once brilliantly jeweled façade now black, scarred and pitted from the uncounted years of assault by the forces at his command. As he dismounts, he reclaims the life he's bestowed upon his mystical steed, sending its substance back into the skies where it belongs, then he examines the crumbled edifice before him and takes a distant, desperate form of satisfaction in noting that it wouldn't have stood for very much longer. The magnificent stone walls are latticed with cracks, and the eastern tower lists dangerously from the damage done by the acidic vines at its base. Just to be sure that this isn't some sophisticated illusion, designed to lull him into carelessness, Xavis summons the mana of the ground in order to call more insistently to the stones in the tower walls, and though he half expects the tower to resist him, showing strength it would not possess without the hidden will of the enemy holding it upright, that is not what happens. Instead, the tower crumbles; the walls sink into the ground in an explosion of shattering stone and mortar; the dust of the ground billows upward in a cloud that blots out the resentful light of the sky.

Xavis waits until the last fragments come to rest and shudders, his newborn fear pulsing like a second heart at the base of his spine. He considers merely destroying the rest of the castle and riding off, content at last to be done with it, but there are rules to such events, which bind him as tightly as the heaviest chains. He must enter, and confront the enemy, in this, the moment of his victory.

The castle door lies open, waiting for him.

Xavis walks through the door, passing through one corridor with walls of ice, and another with walls of flame; descending an ever narrowing stairwell deep into the molten bowels of the earth; passing through water, and stone, and time, and barriers that only wizards know; until at last he comes upon the vast underground chamber that could only be the enemy's sanctuary. The room is cold and black and large enough to house entire kingdoms of its own, with great stone walls that radiate darkness the same way the sun radiates light. It is also almost entirely empty, and so it takes Xavis only an instant to spot the forlorn, withered figure seated on a throne at the farthest wall. The enemy: an old, old man, far more aged than Xavis, with a face gnarled and pitted from the furrows the years have worn in his skin, and eyes well-accustomed to lifetimes spent dwelling in the borderland between omnipotence and failure. And as Xavis freezes, horrified, wondering how closely that wasted face mirrors his own, his endless, immortal enemy . . . smiles.

"You have come," says the enemy in a voice swallowed whole by the great stone walls.

"I received your message," Xavis says, indicating the parchment. His own voice doesn't sound much healthier. He pauses, stunned, wondering how long it has been since he last spoke as a simple man, instead of a wizard rendered great and terrible by the magical forces at his command. Against his will, he coughs, eliciting an unwanted chuckle of understanding from his enemy; then, furious, humiliated beyond measure by being seen showing even that tiny moment of weakness, he continues, "A word I did not even know was in your vocabulary, one I never thought I'd hear. Total, unconditional surrender, with no pleas for mercy, no expectation of even being permitted to live. I dared not believe it . . . but the closer I approached your castle, the more I knew it was true."

"It is true," says the enemy. "I have withdrawn my defenses and dispatched my legions and returned all my remaining power to the earth. I am nothing now but a sack of aged flesh rattling with brittle bones. The worst I can do is go on drawing breath. You may kill me, or torture me, or do what else you will; whatever you choose, I shall meekly accept as just and not stir myself to fight."

"You are still alive only because I want to know why."

And for what must be the first time in millennia, the enemy laughs: not the last, bitter, defiant cackle of a defeated foe, spitting in the face of death, but the robust, arrogant laughter of a conqueror, closely hoarding a secret more powerful than any magically summoned army. The laugh is by far the worst sound Xavis has ever heard, and he has heard soul-vapors, and blood-music, and the roar of unnamable things summoned forth from places far worse than Hell; the shrieking moss, and the rains of blood and steel, and the clouds that fall like stones; and the way the very stars hiss with dismay from the incantations that crackle on his tongue. Xavis has long imagined himself well beyond the neophyte days when any sound could make fear rise in his throat, but as the laughter rises to fill the chamber, the shattered castle above it, and the scorched landscape about that, the unease that has plagued him since the moment of his enemy's surrender finally blossoms into full-fledged terror.

"Because," says the enemy, "my dear Xavis, my true war was never with you. For all your cunning, all your power, all your self-important delusions of free will, you've never been anything more than just another inhuman creation of mine. You never had any past beyond the clay I used to sculpt you, never any blood beyond the humors I employed to fill your veins, never any life beyond that which I initially tapped from the sun and the earth and the sky, never any purpose beyond the greater war you've yet to fight. You are a weapon, Xavis: created by the skill of my hands, forged by a thousand lifetimes of battle, and tempered by all the hatred in your unliving soul. Each and every terrible plague I bestowed upon you was naught but a means of compelling you to become more and more terrible in return; our entire war naught but the millennia-long spell I used to conjure you. And now that I've done, and you're finally the creature I once envisioned, you might finally be strong enough to meet my true opponent: the one who will now become your opponent; the one so terrible that even I had not the will to face him."

Enraged, horrified, tormented, appalled, Xavis extends his will deep into the surrounding earth, gathering up all its energies, all its cold crushing weight, all its terrible capacity for destruction . . . hugging them close to him, and giving them shape . . . stoking the result to firestorm intensity in the cauldron that is his unliving, inhuman heart . . . and launching it against his hated creator in a single instant of white-hot terror and despair.

It is the single most powerful spell ever cast: one capable of shattering continents, or commanding stars.

But to Xavis, it feels like nothing at all. . . .

Much, much later—possibly even centuries later, for it might take Xavis that long to recover from the truth about himself—he emerges from the darkness of his enemy's throne room and climbs the westernmost tower to stand beneath the sun of the land he has finally conquered.

He still looks older than time, but the frailty that had begun to overtake him is gone, replaced by an awful strength that leaves no room for hope, or compassion, or humanity. There is naught in his eyes but emptiness, naught in his heart but the terrible awareness that the worst is yet to come. He looks down upon the now oddly peaceful land of Viroscek, and he gauges the time he's been gone by the grass seedlings just beginning to sprout where, for so long, no life was ever permitted to grow. And he stands there, not moving, not caring, not doing anything at all but waiting, as the days turn to nights and the nights turn back to days.

Somewhere, farther away than even his eyes can see, a new host is approaching.

HORN DANCER

by

Amy Thomson

Hamu's thoughts were heavy and deep as he waded through the thick new snow on his way home from the Long Night's Calling. His injured hock ached in the fierce cold of midwinter. The despair that had plagued him all winter enveloped him like a thick cloud. He was tired, more tired than ever. Even his singing had lost its power. Weighed down by worry, he had not hit the resonant high notes with his usual force. The other bulls had noticed. Several had tried to sing over his refrain, challenging his authority as lead bull.

It did not bode well for him at the next Mating Festival. This last one had been disastrous. His hoof had slipped during his final match, and he had fallen heavily, injuring his hock. He had won, but only barely, and his hock still hurt. How would he fare next fall, in the competition for the favor of the Mothers? Losing was unthinkable, but he faced the prospect of his loss in status, and the loss of the gifts showered on him by the Mothers he had lain with. He might, perhaps, last a few more seasons, sliding down the ranks, studding lower-status Mothers, but eventually he would be forced to leave the mountains and seek a living among the yumans, or become a beggar, living off the charity of the Mothers and the leavings of other bulls.

He looked up at the sharp, snowy peaks, their lofty heads shrouded in clouds, and closed his eyes in pain at the thought of leaving. He had heard of bulls who had chosen exile, but he couldn't do it.

The long, slow, ignominious slide into poverty was equally unthinkable. He had seen the old bulls, no longer strong enough to maintain a place in the rankings. They hung around the edges of other bulls' territories, like mournful ghosts, living off what the other bulls gave them out of pity, munching dreamwort until their saliva ran green with it.

There was only one honorable way out. The Morningstar Falls were close by. He would not be the first aging bull to take his life by leaping from the top of the cliffs. If he died now, as lead bull, the Mothers would mourn his passing. It was better than becoming an exile or a beggar.

He crunched through the new-fallen snow deep in thought. Then his foot caught on something. He stumbled and nearly fell. He stopped to see what had tripped him. It was a yuman female, her hairless skin as cold as ice.

"Huuuu!" he breathed in amazement, his breath clouding around him. What was a yuman doing up here in the middle of winter? And a female at that?

He knelt to examine this puzzle more closely. She was alive, but barely so. Leaning closer, he caught a scent that made his nostrils flare in surprise. His hands explored beneath the layers of her clothes, feeling the firm swelling of her belly. She was with child!

He wrapped her tightly in his red cloak and carried her home, the Morningstar cliffs forgotten. She needed warmth, hot liquids, and food— and quickly—if he was to save her and the baby she carried. What had brought her up here in the dead of winter?

He reached his cave and quickly stripped off her clothing. She was thin, even for a yuman. Her rounded abdomen stood out in painful contrast to her ribs. She had not been eating well. He shook his head. How could the yumans let a pregnant woman starve? He set her in the warm water of his hot spring pool. The cave and its hot spring was one of the privileges of being lead bull. After making sure that she was safe, he turned and stoked the fire. Using a hooked stick, he pulled a heavy clay dish of stones out of the coals. He took the blackened tongs out of their reservoir of water, removed the lid from the dish, and began dropping the hot stones into a water jug. They sizzled as they hit the water and sank, heating the water to boiling.

She was coming around by the time the tea was ready. Carefully he propped her head up and set the cup against her lips.

"Here, drink this," he said. "You need the warmth."

She drank, tentatively at first, then more eagerly, draining the cup. When he came back with a second cup of tea, she was sitting up.

"You're a minotaur," she said, using the yuman's term for the Hurloon.

"You're a yuman," he replied. "What were you doing in the Hurloon Mountains in the middle of winter?" he asked. "You nearly died, and your baby with you."

She looked away. "It would have been better that way."

"Huuuu!" Hamu exclaimed. "You yumans are strange. Why die when you're carrying life? What about the baby?"

The yuman looked away. "I wouldn't have lived to see it born," she said. "I had no money, no food, and no place to stay. Dying of the cold is a better death than starving."

"Why didn't your people take care of you?"

The yuman's jaw tightened. "I have no people."

"Huuuu!" said Hamu. "How could such a thing happen?"

"I was an acrobat with a theatrical troupe. I made the mistake of sleeping with the manager. When I got pregnant and couldn't hide it anymore, he fired me." She looked up, her face tight with anger. "He didn't want his wife finding out who the father was. He abandoned me in the village of Morningbrook. I tried to find work, but no one would hire me, not when they found out I was pregnant.

"I ran out of money and was begging on the streets. Three days ago the Morningbrook watch ordered me to leave town. They don't want beggars there. I looked up the road and saw the morning light on the peaks. It looked so peaceful. I thought that these mountains would be a good place to die."

"Well," said Hamu, "you can stay here until you and the baby are ready to travel. I'll go get you some more tea." He stood.

"But—"

"Yes?"

"All I have with me are the clothes you found me in. I can't pay you."

Hamu shrugged. "If you had money, you wouldn't be spending the winter in a Hurloon's cave, now would you?"

The yuman shook her head. "But I don't even know your name."

"Nor I yours. My name is Hamu. Yours?"

"Ikenet."

Hamu nodded. "Ikenet," he repeated. "I'll fetch more tea and make you some porridge."

After a few days, they fell into a routine. Hamu fixed breakfast for both of them and went off to gather firewood and patrol his territory in the morning. Ikenet would have lunch ready for him when he came back. In the afternoon, Hamu would show Ikenet how to weave the tight grass baskets that the Hurloon were famous for. Near sunset, Hamu would climb to the nearest ridge for the evening singing. His deep resonant voice echoed across the mountains, harmonizing with the other bulls. Ikenet would have tea for him when he returned. It was enjoyable, but there remained an inexplicable tension between them. Ikenet seemed oddly furtive.

Then one evening he came back from his singing to find Ikenet in his bed. She was naked. He stared at her in puzzlement.

"Why are you in my bed?" he asked her.

"To pay for my keep," she replied, "If you think I'm ugly, then we can do it with the lights out. The baby won't get in the way."

Hamu tilted his head, even more puzzled. "I don't understand," he told her. "What are you talking about?"

Ikenet looked startled. "Don't you want to have sex with me?"

Hamu stared at her incredulously for a moment, then threw back his head and roared with laughter. "Huuuuu! You yumans are so strange! That would be like a hill giant mating with a dwarf! Besides, I'm not in rut right now. I'd really rather have a nice hot mug of tea."

"I'm sorry Hamu, please forgive me." She wrapped a blanket around herself and scurried to the fire, where she started heating the water. She dressed while the tea was steeping. As she poured the tea, he saw her wipe her eyes with the back of her hand. She brought him the cup of tea.

"There, is there anything else you want?" She seemed awkward and fearful.

"Sit down, Ikenet," he told her. "What's the matter?"

Ikenet sat down, looking huddled and small, as though he were about to strike her. "Why are you so nice to me?" she asked in a small, frightened voice. "What do you want me to do?"

Hamu stared at her, wishing he knew more about yumans. She was so different from the female Hurloon he knew. None of them would act like this.

"I don't understand, Ikenet. Why should I want anything from you?"

"Then why did you save me?"

"Ikenet, I couldn't leave a pregnant female in the snow, not even a pregnant yuman. The Goddess would never have forgiven me, and neither would the Mothers. You're welcome here."

"But how can I repay you?"

"Repay me for what? The food I eat comes from the Mothers' fields. I have more than I need. And besides, you do pay your way. You make me lunch, you make me tea in the evenings. You keep me company. I like having you here."

Ikenet straightened; she seemed less fearful. "You don't want anything?"

"Just your friendship. You're welcome to stay here until you and the baby are ready to travel."

After that, Ikenet seemed less wary, but occasionally he would see her giving him an appraising glance. He would nod reassuringly and go back to whatever he was doing. Slowly, she began to trust him.

Then one evening, Hamu was grooming his heavy winter pelt, scattering combfuls of hair in piles on the floor. He was trying to reach an awkward spot on his shoulders when Ikenet took the comb from his hand.

"Here, let me do it," she said, and began combing him. Hamu relaxed under the gentle tug.

"Thank you," he said when she was done. "I can never quite get at that patch of fur."

Ikenet began gathering up all the scattered combings and nodded. "It was pretty matted back there. I hope I didn't pull too hard," she said as she stuffed a handful of fur into a sack of combings she had collected from his previous groomings.

"No, it was fine. Ikenet, why are you doing that?"

"Doing what?"

"Saving my hair."

Ikenet looked down, embarrassed. "I wanted to spin it into yarn and make a blanket for the baby. You don't mind, do you?"

Hamu laughed. "Of course not, little one. I'd be honored to have you use my hair to keep the baby warm."

"My parents were weavers, before—" Ikenet began.

"Before what?" Hamu prompted.

"They were killed by goblins. I was off gathering firewood. When I came back, they were dead and our house was a smoking ruin. After that I had nowhere to go. A band of traveling jugglers and musicians found me begging by the roadside and took me in. They taught me to do acrobatics and tumbling. When that group disbanded, I joined another one, and then another, and here I am."

"I'm sorry," Hamu told her, laying a hand gently on her shoulder.

Ikenet shrugged. "It's all right," she said, patting his hand. "How about a cup of mint tea?"

As she was brewing the tea, she remarked, "What I'd really like is some rock gazelle's wool. It's so soft. I could mix it with your fur and make a lovely, warm blanket for the baby."

"I've got twelve pillows and two mattresses stuffed full of it," Hamu said. "I gather it in the spring and give it to the Mothers during the mating festival. The Mothers use it for weaving and stuff pillows with it. You're welcome to use the stuffing for a blanket."

"You stuff pillows with it?" Ikenet asked incredulously. "Rock gazelle wool is very expensive. The orcs have killed most of them off."

"Not here," Hamu told her. "Orcs are nasty creatures. You won't find any in the Hurloon Mountains. But there are lots of rock gazelles. I gather seven bags of wool every spring."

He got up and lifted the lid of a huge carved chest. "Here," he said, shaking out a massive ceremonial robe of rock gazelle wool. He looked at the elaborate white maze-like spirals set against the red ochre background and remembered Makura's skilled hands working the loom, and then remembered those deft hands on his body. "The Great Mother made this for me herself," he told her, "after I secured her favor as consort five years ago."

"Oh, Hamu!" Ikenet breathed. "It's a masterpiece! Look! I've never seen such beautiful work! A robe like this would fetch a king's ransom."

Hamu looked down at the floor, embarrassed and pained by her praise. This summer he was going to lose the Great Mother's favor. He would probably have to leave this robe behind if he went into exile. Beautiful as it was, it was bulky and heavy. Besides, he would have no reason to wear it.

"I'm glad you like it," he told her. He would give it to Ikenet when he lost his consortship next summer. She could sell it in one of the yuman towns, and she would have enough money to support her and her baby for a long time.

"Perhaps," she suggested, "I could help you gather more rock gazelle wool next spring. Then you would have even more to give the Mothers. And maybe I could keep a bag of it for myself."

Hamu laughed at her sly, wheedling tone. "Of course, little one. Perhaps even two bags." He paused. "I'm glad you're here, Ikenet. It's good to have a friend."

Ikenet looked up at him. "I'm glad I'm here, too, Hamu."

The next day, Hamu and Ikenet went down to the river to gather willow branches for making baskets. On the way home, Hamu slipped on a wet rock. His injured hock buckled and he fell.

"Hamu! What's the matter?" Ikenet said.

"Huuu! It's my hock," he told her. "I've hurt it again."

"Let me help you up."

She helped support him all the way back to the cave. Hamu was surprised at the wiry strength of her small body.

"Here," she said as she eased him onto a comfortable couch by the fire and propped up his leg. "You sit there. I'll go get some snow."

"What for?"

"To pack around your hock and bring the swelling down," she told him.

She packed his hock in two buckets' worth of snow and then wrapped it with a long stretch of toweling. "I'll need some arnica, some comfrey, and some bearberry."

"There's some in that chest over there," he told her. "How long do I have to keep this ice on? It's starting to melt and run down my leg."

"Keep it on until the skin is numb," she told him as she rummaged in the herb chest. "Ah, here they are." She opened a jar and sniffed it critically, then reached in and crumbled some of the herbs between her fingers. "Good, the arnica is nice and fresh. We're going to need quite a bit of it to make that hock better. And here's some thyme, and some elfwort."

"Will it—" he started, then paused.

"Will it what?"

"Can you make it better by next summer?" he asked, trying to hide his anxiety.

"I think so, it's just a bad sprain. I've treated similar ones before this for the acrobats. Normally I'd use a healing spell, but I can't cast one now. It might be bad for the baby. What happens next summer?"

"The Mating Festival," he told her. "The bulls compete for the favors of the Mothers. I hurt my hock last fall. It's never completely healed."

"You didn't stay off it long enough," she said. "You're not to go outside of the cave for a week. And after that, you're going to have to be careful of it for another couple of months. Once I've recovered from having the baby, I'll cast a healing spell on it, if you still need one."

"But what about my evening singing? And who's going to gather the firewood."

"You can sing from the mouth of the cave for the next couple of weeks, and I'll take care of the firewood," Ikenet told him. "The baby isn't due for almost three months. You'll be well enough to haul firewood by the time I need help."

So Ikenet took over most of the outside chores, while Hamu did the inside ones. It was hard at first, letting Ikenet do all his work, but once he got used to it, it was rather pleasant.

Winter eased gradually toward spring. Ikenet's belly began to look like the full moon. While Ikenet worked at the loom she had made, Hamu would gaze at her belly in wonder, occasionally touching it with a shy hand. One day the baby kicked while he was touching her belly. He took his hand away as though he had been burned.

"Are you all right? Did I hurt the baby?" Hamu asked anxiously.

"No, Hamu, the baby just kicked. That's all. They do it all the time."

"Huuuu!" he said with a look of wide-eyed awe.

"Haven't you ever seen a pregnant minotaur?"

"Oh, no. A pregnant Mother lives in the Grandmothers' labyrinth until her baby is born."

Ikenet shook her head. "The Hurloon seem very strange to me," she said. "How did the Mothers and the bulls come to live separately?"

"It has always been this way among the Hurloon. We bulls are too dangerous and violent to be trusted near the Mothers."

"But you're not violent, Hamu. Indeed, I think you're very gentle."

"Ah, but you're a female, and carrying a child. How could anyone bear to hurt you or cause you trouble? But we bulls are always fighting each other. We live widely separated, each on his own territory. During the winter months we avoid each other, communicating only through our singing. In the spring and summer we fight almost every day, defending our territories and preparing ourselves for the Mating Festival. After we are chosen by a Mother, we are taken away to her house and live there for the next two moons, while we help the Mothers create life.

"Then we return to our places in the mountains, laden with gifts from the Mothers, and have our own festival. It is the only time bulls are together at peace, gentled by our time with the Mothers. We exchange gifts, drink, and sing together, celebrating the Mothers' generosity. Then we go back to our mountains and prepare for the winter."

"It's a lonely life," Ikenet said.

"It is the life that I have, and I have lived it well," Hamu told her. "But I have enjoyed your company these last few moons. I think it will be harder for me when you go. But at least you have helped me make my hock strong again, so that I have a chance to retain my place as the Great Mother's consort."

Ikenet stood and stretched, placing her hands against her back.

"Does it hurt again?" Hamu asked her. "Would you like me to rub it for you?"

Ikenet nodded and settled herself against a stack of pillows. Hamu sat behind her and worked his thumbs along the small of her back.

"Thank you, Hamu. That feels wonderful. Tell me about the Mating Festival."

"We bulls spend most of the last month of summer grooming ourselves, getting ready to fight, and practicing our singing and dancing. Then, when the moon is new, we don our best festival clothing and come down into the Mothers' village, singing and dancing. The Mothers are waiting for us in the darkness. They come forth from the village, bearing torches and singing. Then they drape us with garlands of wheat and flowers and lead us out into the newly harvested fields, where we lie with the Mothers to bring renewal to the land."

"But I thought that all the bulls had to fight for the privilege of mating," Ikenet said sleepily.

"Huuuu!" Hamu said. "Yes and no. That is the only chance for bulls to mate without fighting for the privilege, but very few offspring result from it. Mostly it helps bring the Mothers fully into heat. The next morning the bulls are ushered into their quarters and left to groom themselves and prepare for the rest of the festival. That evening each bull sings and dances for the Mothers, and the Mothers show their favor by tossing colored ribbons which the bulls pin to their ceremonial capes. After the singing and dancing comes the fighting. Once the fighting is done, the

Mothers come forward in order of seniority and select their consorts for the next two months. Usually—" but he stopped, realizing that Ikenet had fallen asleep.

A chuckle rumbled deep in his chest. He picked her up carefully and put her to bed. She stirred and smiled in her sleep. He stroked her hair with one massive hand, then pulled the covers up over her. He was glad to have found Ikenet. His life had been so lonely. He would be sad when she had the baby and went away.

"Hamu," Ikenet was saying, "Hamu, it's time. I need your help."

"What?" he said, blinking sleepily.

"The baby's coming, Hamu. You have to help me have the baby."

"The baby? What should I do?"

"Heat some water for tea and help me make that dried grass into a bed."

Hamu began hastily flinging large handfuls of dried grass into a pile.

"Slow down, Hamu. Having a baby takes a long time. I'm afraid it's also rather messy. We'll need that pile of clean rags over there."

So Hamu helped her make a bed to deliver the baby on. Then he walked with her up and down the cave, fed her warm tea, massaged her back, and supported her during her labor pains. It was a long, weary night, indeed, and Ikenet's labor lasted well into the morning, but at long last she delivered a baby girl.

"She's perfect, Ikenet!" Hamu said as he gently cleaned the baby. "Look how tiny her toes and fingers are."

At last Ikenet persuaded Hamu to give her the baby, "Oh, Hamu, you're right, she is perfect," she said, stroking the baby's fine dark hair.

"What will you call her?" Hamu asked, but Ikenet was in the midst of another contraction. "Are you having another baby?" Hamu asked as he lifted the baby from her arms, freeing her to push.

"No, Hamu," Ikenet gasped, "just the afterbirth. It's the messy part I was warning you about."

The afterbirth was soon delivered, and Ikenet took the baby again.

"Can I call her Hamu?" Ikenet asked him.

Hamu shook his massive head. "No, that's a male name. It wouldn't be right for someone so small and perfect."

"What would be a good name, then?"

Hamu held the baby, considering. He remembered the Morningstar cliffs. How Ikenet had saved him from them. He thought of the morning star, glowing pink in the morning light, as pink and perfect as this little one.

"Well, she's beautiful, and she came in the morning. We could name her Malanai, after the morning star."

"Malanai," Ikenet said, tasting the word. "I like it. Little one, your name is Malanai."

Malanai grew and flourished. Soon she and her mother were going with Hamu to collect the rock gazelle wool that lay in drifts on the mountain meadows. Once, Hamu caught one of the delicate creatures and brought it to her. Ikenet admired it and swiftly combed the gazelle's shaggy side, raking out half a dozen handfuls before Hamu let it go. It bounded off, shaking itself and shedding a few more tufts of wool as it went.

Soon they had almost a dozen bags of wool. Ikenet set about picking and carding it while Hamu began practicing for the spring fights.

"You should stay near the cave while I'm away," Hamu told her. "I'm afraid of what might happen if you met a rogue bull."

"How can I tell whether it's a rogue bull?" Ikenet asked him.

"It's simple. Any other bull is a rogue," Hamu said. "We start getting very aggressive about now. Some might attack you merely because you're a yuman in the Hurloon Mountains. Not all of them would realize that you're a Mother."

"I'll be careful."

Two days later, Ikenet was gathering mushrooms with Malanai strapped to her back. She was no more than a bowshot from the mouth of the cave, among a patch of trees. She heard a rustling noise and looked up to see a red-eyed bull minotaur preparing to charge.

"Yuman!" he roared, and hurtled toward her. Quick as light she leaped upward, grabbing a tree branch, and swung out of the way of the bull's first rushing charge. Malanai began to cry. The bull roared again and shook the tree. Ikenet hung on as the branches whipped from side to side. Then the bull leaned his massive shoulder against the trunk and pushed. The wood shrieked and groaned in protest as the tree bent under the bull's weight.

Hamu's angry roar rumbled across the clearing. The bull pushing the tree didn't look up. Hamu struck the bull squarely in the side, hurling him against another tree.

The intruding bull shook himself, snorted, and faced Hamu, arms wide, head held low. There was a deep growl, like a distant avalanche. Ikenet glanced up anxiously at the surrounding peaks, before realizing that it was the bull, speaking to Hamu. Hamu replied with a low rumbling roar and a deep, resonant, almost musical snort. He tossed his horns contemptuously.

The two squared off, circling each other warily. Hamu backed away until he was in the clearing, then bellowed a challenge. The intruder charged. Hamu sidestepped with surprising speed and grace, catching the other bull by the horns and twisting hard. The minotaur went down. The impact shook the branches of Ikenet's tree.

Despite the force of his impact, the other bull rolled swiftly to his feet and closed with Hamu. The two bulls stood there, grappling with each other, powerful limbs straining for a long frozen moment. Ikenet watched, holding her breath. Suddenly the stranger hooked a swift hoof around Hamu's fetlock, and pulled upward. Hamu stumbled and nearly fell, but broke free of the other's hold just in time. Before the intruder could recover, Hamu charged, butting low with his horns, catching the other bull just below the ribs. The air whuffed out of the other bull's lungs. Hamu grasped the bull by his brawny shoulders, hooked a broad cloven hoof around the other's leg, swept him to the ground, and pinned him.

The intruder yielded.

Hamu stood and watched as the other bull departed. When he was out of sight, Hamu turned back toward Ikenet's tree. He seemed so angry that Ikenet was afraid that he would attack her, but he merely reached a hand up to help her down.

"Are you all right?" he asked her.

"Yes,"

"And the little one?"

"She's a little shaken up, but that's all. Thank you, Hamu. You saved our lives. Are you hurt?"

"From a young upstart like that? Hu!" Hamu said dismissively. "He won't be bothering us again, but you'll have to be careful from now on. I don't want you going out of the cave without me."

"Hamu—" Ikenet began to protest, but just then Malanai began crying. "All right, Hamu," Ikenet said. "Oh dear, she's wet again. I'll need some fresh moss and another diaper."

With Hamu off fighting much of the day, Ikenet was bored. She began exercising, trying to get her birth-stretched body back into shape. One day Hamu returned to find Ikenet walking on her hands back and forth across the cave mouth while Malanai slept blissfully in the sun. He stared at her, head tilted, and began to laugh.

Ikenet rolled gracefully out of her handstand. "You liked that, eh?"

"Huuuuu!" Hamu said. "It was very funny."

"Can you hold your head very still?" Ikenet asked.

"I think so."

"Good, then hold out your arm like this." She went into a crouch, bracing one elbow on her thigh. "Hold it steady and stay very still."

She stepped on his outstretched palm, then up to his shoulders. He felt Ikenet steady herself and grasp his horns. Her feet left his shoulders and he felt her weight on his horns.

"Does that hurt?" Ikenet asked.

"No. What are you doing?" Hamu asked, rolling his eyes upward in an attempt to see what she was doing.

"A handstand on your horns." She swung down onto his shoulders and leaped lightly to the ground. "Thank you, Hamu. I've been wanting to do that for months," Ikenet said.

"Huuu!" Hamu said, shaking his head. "What a strange thing to want to do!"

Ikenet shrugged. "I'm an acrobat. I used to do handstands on the backs of galloping horses. You have such broad, tempting shoulders, and those horns are just made for doing handstands."

Hamu shook his head again. "You yumans are so strange!" he said, rumbling with laughter.

As the spring lengthened and warmed into summer, Ikenet continued to work on her acrobatics, and more and more often, Hamu worked with her.

"You know, Hamu, it's a shame that we can't take this on the road. We'd be a very popular act," she said one day as she was balancing one-handed on his broad forehead.

"Hu! What a strange idea!" he said, but he was obscurely pleased at the thought of performing, though he wouldn't want to leave his beloved mountains.

Hamu also began practicing his own dances. Ikenet sat in the mouth of the cave and watched, offering helpful suggestions. His dancing had always been the weakest of his skills. He had always danced alone before, trusting to some inner instinct. Now Ikenet, with her performer's eye, helped to hone his performance, enhancing his impression of strength and power. Hamu felt the difference when he danced. The difference carried over to his fighting. He won more easily now.

"You've found your center," Ikenet explained. "It helps you move better."

One day, as he was dancing, Ikenet joined him, her small figure spinning about him like a baby whirlwind dancing in the wake of a hurricane. He picked her up and set her on his shoulders. She laughed and vaulted off, then backed away and with a light swift stride ran toward him. He lowered his head, and she grasped his horns. He flipped her back over his head, and she somersaulted to the ground, then circled him with joyous backflips and cartwheels. Malanai, watching from her blanket, clapped her hands and laughed. Hamu scooped up the baby and twirled her around at arm's length. The baby laughed and cooed with joy.

At last they stopped. Laughing, Ikenet took the baby from Hamu.

"Huuuuuu! I wonder what the Great Mother would have made of that!" he said.

"Well, she'd certainly remember it!" Ikenet said.

Hamu rumbled agreement. "She won't have seen anything like it before, that's certain." He grew thoughtful. "I think she would have enjoyed it, though. She loves new things. I'm the only consort that she's ever taken more than once. She told me once that it was because I was always surprising her. Imagine, me, surprising the Great Mother. Hu!" He shook his head, "It's a shame that she'll never get to see us dance like this."

"Why won't she?" Ikenet jounced Malanai on her hip.

"Huuuu," Hamu sighed, "No yuman has ever set foot in the village of the Mothers."

"Why not?"

"No yumans have ever made it past the bulls on the mountains. We are here to protect the Mothers' privacy. If they need to trade, they go, suitably escorted by eunuchs, to one of the yuman towns beyond the mountains."

"It's a shame I can't go. I'd really like to see the Mothers' village."

"It's a nice place, but I prefer the mountains. It's quieter, more peaceful, and freer than the village. You're not missing much."

"Still, I'd like to see it," Ikenet said. She looked a little wistful, and Hamu thought that perhaps she was lonely. He sighed. She was fully recovered from giving birth. In a few months, when Malanai was a little bigger, she would leave, perhaps finding another group of performers. He would miss them.

The summer ripened. Malanai grew into a happy, cheerful baby, watching everything with wide blue eyes. She was extremely fond of Hamu. She would lie in the minotaur's arms, staring up gravely at him, twisting her plump baby fists into his thick white fur. She shrieked with pleasure when he nuzzled her with his broad nose.

One afternoon, Ikenet was spinning wool with her drop spindle, just inside the mouth of the cave when an unfamiliar bull minotaur came out of the forest and into the meadow below the cave. Ikenet scooped up Malanai, and hid inside.

The intruder bellowed a challenge that echoed off the mountain peaks. Ikenet made sure that the baby was safe, then peered out from behind a pile of rocks. He was a big, powerful-looking bull, with wide, black-tipped horns and a broad red streak of fur running down his back. His face was covered with the intricate maze-like patterns of scars that marked a senior bull. Ikenet recognized him immediately. Hamu had talked of him often. This was Herhoona, Hamu's most formidable rival.

Hamu emerged from the forest a few minutes later and roared a response to Herhoona. The two bulls squared off, snorting loudly and resonantly through their nostrils. Herhoona struck first, quick as a snake, but Hamu shook off his grip. They backed and circled, then Hamu closed, grabbing Herhoona by one horn and a shoulder. He pivoted neatly, pulling Herhoona off balance, but he rolled out of the fall, bouncing to his hooves just out of Hamu's reach. Herhoona feinted right, then grabbed Hamu's nose, forcing his chin against his chest and shutting off the flow of air. Hamu backed away, but Herhoona maintained his suffocating grip. Then Hamu surged forward, tossing his head and hooking Herhoona's fetlock with his left hoof while grabbing and twisting Herhoona's elbows. He broke Herhoona's grip and the two fell into a grim clinch, circling and trying to throw each other in various ways.

Then Herhoona, his sides coated with sweat, hooked Hamu's leg with his hoof pulling it off of the ground. Hamu, struggling to stay upright, kicked forward, freeing his foot. But it was too late. Hamu fell heavily. Before he could get up, Herhoona stepped forward and, raising one heavy hoof, brought it down on Hamu's hock. Ikenet heard the wet pop of breaking bone and Hamu's huff of pain. Herhoona tossed his head contemptuously at Hamu, then strode off into the forest. Ikenet ran forward as Hamu struggled to rise.

She bent to help him, and Hamu snorted and lunged at her, swinging his horns.

"Hamu, it's me, Ikenet," she said, backing out of range of those dangerous horns. "I'm here to help you."

The angry light died out of Hamu's eyes. "Ikenet," he said, "leave me be. You should go. Take my ceremonial cape with you. Sell it. It'll give you enough money to take care of the baby."

"What about you?"

"The wolves will come tonight, or maybe tomorrow night. They'll take me. It's an honorable death. The others will sing of me when I'm gone. The Mothers will mourn my passing."

"Hamu, please. At least let me look at your hock. Perhaps I can heal it. Lie down." She put her hands on his massive chest and pushed gently. Hamu lay back against the grass and let her look at his injured leg, which was already swelling.

"It's broken," she said at last, "and badly. I can heal it, but—" She paused. "It won't be as strong as it was before."

"How much weaker will it be?"

"I don't know," Ikenet said. "It could only be a little bit weaker, or you could have a limp for the rest of your life. You'll be able to walk, though, and probably run and even dance."

"Huuuu," Hamu breathed thoughtfully.

"At least let me try, Hamu. I owe you two lives: mine and Malanai's. Please, let me try. You can always die an honorable death later, if it doesn't work."

"All right," Hamu said. "What do you want me to do?"

"We'll have to work right here," she told him. "I'll go get what I need."

Ikenet ran back to the cave and came back with an armload of blankets. She pulled out a battered amulet and held it out for him to see. The designs were worn and the stones were dulled from long handling and age, but its lines were still graceful.

"It was my mother's. She was a healer."

"What is it?"

"An amulet of Kroog. It's a healing artifact. I tried to sell it in Morningbrook, but no one wanted it. They didn't believe it was real."

She lay down beside Hamu. "I'm not very good at using it," she said. "Lying down seems to help."

Ikenet placed the amulet on her abdomen, just below her navel. Then she placed one hand palm down against the green grass and rich soil of the meadow and gently rested the other just above Hamu's injured leg. She closed her eyes and breathed deeply.

"Breathe with me, Hamu," Ikenet told him.

Hamu forced his pain away and focused on breathing when she did, using deep, long slow exhalations. Ikenet's hand felt like a small patch of warm sunlight on his leg. He breathed again. With each breath the pain of his hock receded. He closed his eyes and became conscious of the ground beneath him, the sweet grass, the fertile soil, and beneath that the bones of the Hurloon Mountains that he loved so well. He breathed deeply, drawing on the strength of those mountains, their long, green slopes, their steep, jagged cliffs, and their towering, snow-covered peaks. He felt their strength flowing into him. The surface of the soil seemed to become as insubstantial as water. He floated above the bones of the mountains, like a waterbug on the surface of a mountain pool.

He awoke to a dark, star-filled sky and the smell of wood smoke. For a moment he lay there, puzzled. Why was he out here, under the stars, instead of in his own snug and friendly cave? Then he remembered Herhoona and the fight. He flexed his hock experimentally. There was no pain. He sat up.

Ikenet sat, wrapped in a blanket, beside a small fire. "How is your leg?" she asked him.

"All right, I think. What are you doing out here?"

"Keeping watch. I couldn't move you and I didn't want the wolves to think you were waiting to die."

"Hu! Little one! And what were you going to use to fight these wolves?"

Ikenet held up a long, stout staff. "This and a torch. But the night has been peaceful. There's enough food this time of year. They don't need to concern themselves with a tough old minotaur like you."

"Or a tough little mouthful like you," Hamu added with a pleased chuckle. "Why don't we go inside where it's warm and comfortable?"

He rose. Ikenet moved to help him, but he waved her away. He took a few experimental steps.

"It's a bit stiff and sore, but it works," Hamu said.

"I'm glad," Ikenet told him. "The healing went well, but it will be a few more days before we know if there is any permanent damage."

Ikenet scooped up the baby and the three of them started back up the slope to the cave.

Hamu's hock was weak and shaky by the time they reached the cave. He slid gratefully into his chair while Ikenet made him a huge bowl of porridge. He ate it, surprised at how hungry he was, and then limped to bed and fell asleep.

As the days passed, Hamu's hock did improve. Within a week it was no longer stiff, but the joint was very weak. Ikenet helped work out exercises that would strengthen it, but despite their hard work it was apparent that it would still be weak enough to affect Hamu's ability to fight, especially in the long, physically demanding tournament.

"What am I going to do?" Hamu asked her. His leg was trembling and tired from the half hour he had spent pushing against the cave wall. "It's only three weeks till the Mating Festival. I won't be ready to fight. Perhaps I should have let the wolves take me."

Ikenet had been playing peek-a-boo with Malanai. She looked up. "Why don't you dance with me at the festival? You told me that it would really surprise the Mothers, and you can't win the fights this year."

"Well, yes, but—"

Ikenet set a gentle hand on his arm. "Hamu, you have nothing to lose."

"But the dancing is a tradition that goes back for centuries. What if the Mothers are offended?"

"Hamu, can you win the fighting this year?"

He shook his head. "But no dancer has ever won the festival without also winning the fighting for as long as I can remember."

"Which is why you need to try something extraordinary," she told him. "It's risky, but it's the only chance you've got."

"Huuu," Hamu inclined his head. "You're right. We'll try it."

"Good."

So they began practicing, slowly, gently at first, testing to make sure that Hamu's leg could stand the strain, then with more intensity, until just a few days before the festival Hamu was dancing as fast as he could, while whirling Ikenet around him as he turned.

"I think we're as ready as we can possibly be," Ikenet said.

"Good, I want to spend the next two days resting and grooming myself for the festival. Then we're going to have to start down the mountain. It takes a day and a half to get to the Mothers' village, and my injury may slow me down a bit, so I'd like to take a little bit of extra time to get there."

Despite his claim that he wanted to rest, Hamu spent the next couple of days in frenetic activity. First he washed his furry pelt with soapwort, lathering and rinsing it three times. Then he and Ikenet combed his snowy white fur until it looked soft as a cloud. After that, he clipped away the hair on the front of his neck and down onto his upper chest, leaving it short and smooth. He carefully left a fringe of longer fur along his lower jaw, leading to his beard. Then he burnished his hooves and horns with a soft piece of oil-soaked leather until they gleamed. Next, he dyed his forelock with red ochre and emphasized the elaborate tracery of cicatrices on his face with a paste of yellow ochre mixed with ground henna. Once the henna paste was washed away, the scars gleamed like burnished bronze.

"Well?" he said, turning before Ikenet's appraising eye late in the afternoon of the second day. "How do I look?"

"Magnificent," Ikenet told him. "The Mothers will be overcome with desire when they see you."

Hamu seemed to swell with this praise. "I hope so," he said, then deflated again as worry conquered his pride. "Oh, Ikenet, I hope so."

They started out early the next morning, eating a substantial breakfast and gathering their things before the day was more than a promise in the sky. As soon as it was light enough to see, they set out. Hamu took one last searching look around his cave, sighed, and turned his face resolutely toward the Mothers' village.

Ikenet touched his shoulder as they crossed the meadow below the mouth of the cave. "Don't worry, you'll be back."

"Huuuu, I hope so," he said.

They made good time that morning and were soon following the Morningstar River as it rushed down to the fertile valley of the Hurloon, sheltered by high snowy peaks from the outside world. Occasionally they caught glimpses of other bulls, but they kept their distance from each other.

Then, as they rounded a bend, they saw a bull resting just off the path in a warm sunny spot. Ikenet tensed, expecting a violent confrontation.

"It's all right," Hamu told her. "It's old Uharoo. He's no harm to anyone anymore."

As they drew closer, Ikenet could see that the old bull's fur was patchy, ungroomed, and there was a froth of green saliva on his muzzle.

"Dreamwort," Hamu informed her. "The old ones chew it to forget the present and remember the past."

As they passed, Uharoo glanced up at them with eyes dulled by age and drugs. His eyes widened for a moment at the sight of Ikenet and her baby, but he lapsed back into dreams after Hamu laid a half-empty sack of grain beside him.

"Five years ago, Uharoo was one of the best bulls at the festival," Hamu told her as they rounded a bend and the older minotaur vanished from sight. "He was injured in the tournament and never recovered. He didn't come to the festival last year." Hamu shook his massive head. "I'd rather die a clean death than let that happen to me. If I lose, I'll go back up to Morningstar Falls and throw myself over the edge. My bones will lie among those of the proudest and strongest bulls of the Hurloon."

Ikenet touched his arm. "But that won't happen to you."

"If I'm lucky, it won't happen for many years. If not, then—" He shrugged. "It is as the Goddess wills."

They camped that night along a rushing stream and arrived at the Mothers' village in the middle of the afternoon.

"Good," he said, "we're early enough to ask for a boon from my consort. Stay behind me."

They walked through the streets of the village. Female minotaurs paused in their work to watch them pass. Children began following them, staring at Ikenet and laughing. By the time they arrived at a great house in the center of the village, a crowd was following them. Hamu knocked on the thick wooden door. It creaked open and an old, grizzled minotaur peered out.

"Hello, Arnam. Please tell the Great Mother that her consort wishes one final favor before the festival begins."

The old minotaur nodded, and the door creaked closed. They stood waiting a long time, then the door creaked open again.

"The Great Mother will see you now," the old minotaur said. His voice was surprisingly light and mild.

They were led through a vestibule where other servants washed Ikenet's feet and Hamu's hooves with warm, scented water. Then they were led through a maze of passageways and into a central atrium. Water splashed in a small fountain, and roses twined around simple wooden columns painted with red ochre. On the walls nearest them was a beautifully painted mural of a fruitful harvest being gathered, threshed, and stored. On another was a portrait of Hamu looking proud, fierce, and dignified. Ikenet looked at it and smiled.

The Great Mother was seated on one of the minotaur's narrow, slanted chairs in front of a marble bas-relief showing female minotaurs in earnest discussion. She had tall, lyre-like horns and a proud, dignified carriage. She was wearing a heavy necklace made of golden sheaves of wheat and a pleated linen wrap skirt that began just beneath her heavy breasts and fell to the floor. Her wide round eyes were alight with intelligence and curiosity as they regarded Ikenet.

"Greetings, Consort," she said, inclining her head with regal grace.

"Greetings, Great Mother," Hamu replied, bowing gracefully. He lowered himself before her. "I come to ask one final favor of you before the festival begins."

"What favor is that?"

"I ask that you shelter my friend Ikenet, a yuman female, and her child. She is necessary to my performance at the festival."

"I see. Is this another surprise, Hamu?"

"I hope it will please you, Great Mother."

Just then Malanai began to fuss. Ikenet began rocking the baby to quiet her.

"Is that a baby yuman?" the Great Mother asked. "Let me see it."

Ikenet came forward and handed Malanai to her. "I'm afraid she's cranky and tired. It's been a long trip."

The Great Mother nodded, acknowledging Ikenet's words, and unwrapped the baby's blanket. Malanai regarded her, too fascinated to fuss. The Great Mother peered closely at the baby's feet.

"Huuu! Such small toes, and so many of them!" the Great Mother said. She called over several of her female attendants and they came over to look at the baby. Malanai cooed and babbled and reached out to touch

the Great Mother's nose. The Great Mother nuzzled her, and Ikenet
screeched with laughter. The Great Mother laughed back. Ikenet glanced
at Hamu; he winked at her.

"Great Mother," Hamu said, "the hour grows late. I must go and prepare myself for the festival. Will you shelter Ikenet and her baby until the
festival is over?"

The Great Mother looked thoughtfully at Ikenet. "Do you mean any
harm to the Hurloon and their sons?" she asked Ikenet.

"No, Great Mother," Ikenet said. "If my presence creates difficulties,
I can go back into the mountains and sleep under the stars until Hamu
needs me."

The Great Mother shook her head. "I cannot turn away a mother and
her child. Please, stay here and be welcome."

"Thank you, Great Mother," Hamu said. "Please—" He paused, suddenly awkward and shy. "Please. How is your son?"

The Great Mother smiled. "He is strong and smart, and he has his
father's ability to surprise me." She paused, measuring her words. "May
the Goddess show you her favor during the festival."

Hamu's ears stood straight up. "Thank you for your blessing Great
Mother, and for the news of our son. And—" he looked down, shy and
embarrassed "—I enjoyed being your consort. I hope that the Goddess
favors me with your kindness again." With that, he turned and left.

The Great Mother watched him go. Ikenet had learned to read the
minotaur's expressions, and she thought she saw concern, worry, and
fondness in the Great Mother's eyes.

"You must be very tired from that long trip," the Great Mother said
kindly. She clapped her hands, and two young female minotaurs stepped
forward. "Ikenet and her baby will be my honored guests during the festival. Please show them to the apartments near the nursery, and see to her
needs."

They led her to a sumptuous apartment, then attended her in the bath.
Malanai was the center of an adoring crowd of young female minotaurs,
who were as fascinated by the baby's toes as the Great Mother had been.

When her bath was over, she was shown back to her room, where an
excellent meal was served. As she was finishing it, the Great Mother
came in.

"Greetings, Great Mother," Ikenet said, bowing.

"Please, call me Makura. Only males use the title." She paused, and
then spoke as though she were imparting a great secret. "Tell me, how is
Hamu? He was injured last fall, and I had heard that he might not
recover."

Makura's voice was soft with concern, but Ikenet hesitated, unsure how to answer this question. "He has recovered from that injury."

Relief lit Makura's wide eyes, and the tension went out of her body. "Good." She laid a hand on Ikenet's knee. "We Mothers are supposed to be impartial in our choice of consorts, but I am not. I am—fond of Hamu. I was glad when our union bore fruit. Our son is strong and beautiful, and more, he shows Hamu's gentleness and intelligence." She laughed. "Imagine, describing a bull as gentle! Especially such a fighter as Hamu!"

"He is gentle, though," Ikenet said. "You should see him with Malanai. He practically worships her. He loves to hold her, and she's very fond of him."

Makura's eyes widened in surprise. "You let him hold your baby?"

"Of course. He helped me give birth to her."

"He did?" Makura said, even more amazed. "You let a bull witness the mystery of birth?"

"There was no one else to help me," Ikenet explained. "Once I got him calmed down, he was a very good midwife."

Makura looked thoughtful. "It is good that you are only a yuman. Any Hurloon who violated the mysteries in such a way would be torn apart by oxen."

Ikenet swallowed, nodded, and resolved not to speak to anyone of Malanai's birth.

Makura stood. "I must go and prepare for tonight. If you wish to watch, I have left instructions with the servants to let you onto the roof."

Then Makura rose and slipped out the door. Ikenet lay back against the pillows and closed her eyes. She was tired, and the next two weeks promised to be very trying.

Several hours later, she was wakened by the older male minotaur who had greeted them at the door. "The Great Mother asked me to let you know when the procession was about to begin. Would you like to see it, ma'am?"

"Yes I would. Thank you, Arnam."

She bundled the sleeping Malanai up and followed Arnam onto the flat roof of the Great Mother's palace. The sun had set, and there was only a dull flare of orange behind the mountains to the west. Overhead the stars were coming out. In the streets, Ikenet could see the vague shadows of minotaurs hurrying about. Twin fires burned in low cauldrons flanking the eastern gate of the village. One by one, the Mothers lit their torches and proceeded out of the gate in a double file, singing as they went. Their voices were as rich and resonant as the males, but sweeter and higher in pitch. Then, in the distance, one by one, the bulls came filing out of the fields surrounding the village, singing in reply, their voices like huge, low-pitched horns, blending together in song. The females scattered into the fields. Each one greeted a bull, lighting the torch that the bull carried. The females draped the bulls with garlands, then they danced and sang, formally at first, slowly revolving about each other. Then the singing intensified and the dance sped up. They moved closer to each other, until their torches were a single whirling flame. One by one the torches were doused, and the entwined minotaurs vanished into darkness.

"Thank you, Arnam. It was very beautiful."

Arnam nodded. "Yes, I like to come up onto the roof and watch. It's the only way I have of sharing in the festival." There was a note of powerful yearning in his mild tenor voice.

"But why—"

"I'm a eunuch, Ikenet. Only the strongest and best males are allowed to become bulls. The Grandmothers geld the rest of us, and we stay behind to serve the Mothers."

"Oh, Arnam, I'm sorry. I didn't know."

Arnam shrugged. "It's my lot in life. Most of the time, I never notice, but tonight—" He paused. "Tonight I would like to be out there, with Makura."

Ikenet listened in silence, not knowing what to say.

"Hamu is my half-brother. I was glad when he won the right to be Makura's consort. He makes her happy."

Ikenet nodded. "He's been very kind to me and to Malanai. I want to do everything I can to help him do well at the festival, but I'm afraid I'll do something wrong and hurt his chances."

"Huuu," he said with a thoughtful nod. "I'll see what I can do. The baby will help. The Hurloon love babies. Take Malanai with you whenever you go out."

"Thank you, Arnam."

"It's nothing, little one. You and your baby please Makura, and that pleases me."

With that he escorted her to her room. Ikenet nursed Malanai, tucked her in, and then went to bed.

She was wakened by Malanai's laughter. Two serving girls had crept in and were playing peek-a-boo with her. She sat up, smiling. At least Malanai wasn't going to lack attendants while she was busy with Hamu.

She took the serving girls with her to mind the baby when she went to find Hamu. The bulls were quartered outside of town, in a maze of temporary shelters built near a large arena. The serving girls retreated to the safety of the seats of the amphitheater, where Malanai was the focus of attention. Ikenet threaded her way through the bulls' quarters to find Hamu's stall. It was a frightening walk. The bulls roared at her, and the stink of their individual privies was overwhelming. Several of the bulls, maddened by their close quarters, charged her, making the thick timbers of their stalls shudder.

She hardly recognized Hamu when she found him. He looked like some wild animal in a cage. His neck was swollen and his eyes were red and wild. He roared at her and snorted through his red-lined nostrils, not seeming to recognize her. She stepped back from the door to his stall, her stomach tight with fear.

"Hamu, it's me," Ikenet said.

Slowly the wild light in his eyes died as he came back to himself. "I'm sorry, Ikenet, it's this place. It makes me crazy. All I can smell is other bulls, and it makes me want to fight anything I can get my hands on."

"I came to see if there was anything I could do to help you get ready for tonight."

"Huuuu," Hamu said, considering. "I need to get out of here, away from this smell, where I can think. There's a lake about a mile from the village. Perhaps we could go there, and you could groom me. I'll meet you by that clump of willows south of the village in a few minutes."

Ikenet went back to reclaim Malanai from the serving girls, who were surrounded by a curious crowd of onlookers. Malanai was beginning to fret, but she quieted as soon as Ikenet picked her up. The females were sniffing the air, nostrils flared wide and upper lips curled back.

"You smell like the bulls," one of the servant girls told her with a giggle. The other females burst into raucous laughter.

"I'll be glad when the festival is over and Makura loans her bull out to stud!" one of them said. "I didn't mate last year because of the baby."

The others laughed again, and one of them sidled up to her, sniffing deeply, clearly aroused. Ikenet blushed and glanced down, wondering how to save the situation. Just then Malanai started to cry. She pulled her shirt aside and gave the baby her breast. Malanai settled down, slowly waving her feet in the air as she nursed. The minotaurs watched, fascinated by her tiny feet, so different from their own broad cloven hooves.

"You yumans have such strange and complicated feet. It's amazing that you can walk at all, but it must be nice, not getting kicked all the time by those little hooves," one Mother remarked.

"Those hooves must hurt!" Ikenet exclaimed sympathetically.

Several Mothers rolled their eyes expressively. The others laughed. Soon they were talking about their own children. Ikenet listened for a while, then slipped away to join Hamu outside the village.

Ikenet spent most of the morning and a good deal of the afternoon washing and combing Hamu's fur until his white pelt shone brightly in the midafternoon sun. Then she returned to the village, washed off the smell of Hamu's rut, and slept the rest of the afternoon away.

At last the sun slipped below the mountains. Ikenet accompanied Makura to her booth in the front of the amphitheater. She watched in fretful boredom as the youngest bulls performed, trying to make up for their lack of skill and experience by dancing as quickly and frenetically as possible to the drumming of the eunuchs. The Mothers around her clapped politely, but the only favors tossed came from the low-status Mothers high up in the stands. Those favors that fell short were passed to the aisles and carried forward by eunuchs, who tossed them to the sand.

At last it was time for the senior bulls to perform. A fresh set of more experienced musicians replaced those who had performed for the cadet bulls. There were flutes now, and several stringed instruments. Ikenet slipped like a shadow past the reeking pens filled with anxious, brooding bulls to Hamu's stall. He was nervous and fretful.

"Are you ready?" he asked, anxiously.

Ikenet nodded. "You look magnificent," she told him.

He was splendid. His fur was carefully brushed, and his massive body was draped in ceremonial robes.

She brushed out the fur on his neck. He relaxed under the quiet hiss of the brush strokes, until a round of applause and cheers came from the stands. He craned his neck anxiously.

"Don't look," she advised. "It will only make you more nervous."

So they waited in the dark of the stall until finally it was his turn.

"Huuuuu!" he said. "It's time. Follow me."

Hamu waited until the arena had been raked smooth, then strode out into the empty ring as though he owned it. Ikenet, watching from the sidelines, was amazed by his presence. He walked three times around the ring so that everyone could get a good look at him, his arms held wide, showing off the rich treasures he had won during his career. He began to sing, a low, rich, throbbing melody about a bull on his lonely mountain remembering the delight that his consort had given him. The Mothers in the stands listened with rapt attention. Even the clamor of the bull pens quieted while Hamu sung.

Then, in the waiting silence, he slipped out of his garlands and ceremonial robes and stood clad only in a short, red kilt, his fur gleaming in the flickering torchlight. Ignoring the furtive shapes of the children who gathered up his fallen raiment, he nodded gravely to the musicians and began a droning discordant chant that echoed in the silent, waiting amphitheater and made the hair on the back of Ikenet's neck stand on end. The musicians joined in, first the flute, then the strings, taking his harmony and enlarging upon it. Finally the drums, throbbing a beat under the powerful boom of his resonant voice, improvising on the rhythm he had set.

Then Hamu began to dance, his feet picking out a complex pattern as he whirled around the ring, his arms upraised. The muscles in his legs rippled as he leaped a second time around the ring, leaps so high and so soaring that he seemed to hang for a moment in the air. Then he spiraled inward to the center of the ring and paused, drawing himself up into a proud pose, one hand extended.

Ikenet, watching, was so entranced that she almost forgot that this was her cue. She came bounding into the ring, turning handsprings, leaping from her last one onto Hamu's outstretched hand, and then up to a handstand on his horns, legs spread wide in a split. They held that pose for a moment while the audience absorbed this new spectacle. Ikenet rolled out of her handstand and down to the ground, where they began to dance.

Ikenet whirled and spun around Hamu, the packed dirt of the amphitheater firm under her feet. She cartwheeled out to the edge of the ring, paused a moment, then ran toward Hamu, leapt and caught his lowered horns. He tossed his head, throwing her high into the air, where she spun in a triple somersault. She landed lightly and leaped for his horns again. After the last of several spectacular leaps and somersaults, Hamu picked her up and lifted her up over his head with one arm. Ikenet swung herself up to a one-armed handstand on his broad palm and posed there for several dozen heartbeats before somersaulting off to stand beside and a little in front of Hamu, arms outstretched, chest heaving from exertion.

The audience sat silent for a long moment. Then Makura threw a long, feathered streamer to his feet. Hamu picked it up and draped it over one shoulder and across his chest. The low-status females high up in the stands began applauding, then the rest of the audience joined in. Favors rained down on Hamu like colored snow, piling up around their feet in drifts. The applause went on and on. Hamu picked Ikenet up and held her over his head again.

"Hu! I think they liked us," Hamu said.

"I think you're right," Ikenet said, tousling his fur affectionately.

They filled their arms with Hamu's favors, leaving what they could not carry for the children to collect and bring to Hamu's stall. Arnam was waiting for them at the exit of the ring.

"Did my dancing please the Great Mother?" Hamu asked.

"Very much. I don't think I've ever seen her so pleased."

"And you, Arnam. Did you like it?" Ikenet asked.

He nodded.

"Thank you, brother," Hamu said. "Please tell the Great Mother that I am happy to have surprised her." Arnam nodded, then escorted Ikenet back up to Makura's booth.

Makura was the center of an excited crowd of female Hurloon.

"Ikenet!" Makura called as Ikenet stepped into the booth. The crowd around her parted to let Ikenet and Malanai through. She could see the Hurloon females' nostrils flare as she passed and realized with a flush of embarrassment that she smelled strongly of aroused bull.

"That was wonderful!" Makura said, handing her the baby. "I've never seen a bull with such grace and control!"

Ikenet shrugged. "He's a good dance partner: strong, smart, and quick. I wish—" She paused, biting her lip. "I wish we could perform together more often."

"Perhaps after the festival, it might be possible to arrange some performances," Makura said. "I'm sure most of us would like to see it again."

"Thank you," Ikenet said, but her throat was tightening with sadness. She had been thinking of performing among humans. This was the first time that she had performed in nearly a year, and she found that she missed it. She missed humans; she needed to be among her own kind, though she would miss Hamu and the other minotaurs.

Malanai awoke and began to fret. She needed to be put to bed. All this activity was trying for a baby used to only two people for company. And she was tired, too. It had been a stressful and exhausting day. She felt as tired and cranky as Malanai.

"Please excuse me, but I think I should put the baby to bed." The Great Mother excused them, and Arnam followed her out of the stands and escorted her back to Makura's house.

"You really gave them something to talk about," he told her with a low, rumbling chuckle.

"Good," she said, yawning.

Arnam showed her to the bathhouse, where she quickly bathed herself and the baby, settled Malanai in her crib, and then slipped into bed and fell deeply asleep.

Makura and her entourage went out to watch the first day of fighting. A series of rings had been set up and the cadet bulls were fighting, their fur gleaming in the morning sun. Small clusters of young males and adolescent females watched avidly, while the older females stood apart and gossiped, occasionally glancing up as a young bull performed an especially tricky or complex maneuver.

Ikenet left Malanai with Arnam and slipped off to Hamu's stall. He was almost as nervous and irritable as he had been the first day. She groomed him into calmness, then knelt to examine his hock for swelling and puffiness. "It looks good," she said, running her hands over it. "How does it feel? The dancing didn't hurt it?"

"It's about the same as it's been, no worse, but not much better, either. I don't fight until this afternoon, when the young bulls have finished. It shouldn't be much of a fight, though. I won't fight any really experienced bulls until tomorrow."

Ikenet nodded; Arnam had already told her that. "We were a big success last night. Everyone's been talking about it."

Hamu nodded distractedly. "That's good."

"Is there anything I can do to help?" she asked.

"You already have," he said, clasping her small, strong, five-fingered hand in his massive four-fingered one.

Ikenet smiled. "Good luck, then."

"Thank you, little one."

The young bulls finished their fights as the stars began coming out; the rings were raked smooth in preparation for the next round. The senior bulls entered the arenas, groomed and massive. Hamu was matched with a large, younger bull, spotted black and white, with black-tipped, upcurving horns.

"That's Huharna," Arnam told her. "He's slow, but he's very strong."

Ikenet nodded, never taking her eyes from the bulls as they circled, each looking for an opening. Malanai recognized Hamu. She lifted her chubby hand and pointed. "A-ooo!" she said loudly.

Hamu glanced up and Huharna charged. Hamu nimbly sidestepped the charge and caught Huharna by the horns and pivoted into him, pulling Huharna over one hip and throwing him to the ground. Swiftly, Hamu pinned him, and the judges declared him the winner. He tossed his head defiantly and snorted loudly.

"A-ooo!" Malanai said again, excitedly. "A-ooo! A-oo!"

"She's certainly won that one's favor," one of the Mothers remarked. Ikenet strode to the edge of the ring so that Malanai could see him. Hamu trotted over and bowed, first to Makura, then to Ikenet. He held up his hands and Ikenet handed him the babbling baby. Hamu lifted her up and shook her gently. Malanai squealed in delight. The watching Mothers gaped and murmured in astonishment. He lifted her several more times, then nuzzled her gently. Malanai caroled in delight and grabbed a handful of his white beard. Hamu gently detached her hand and gave her back to Ikenet. Then he trotted out of the ring.

The ring was raked smooth by two older boys, and two more bulls lumbered into the ring. It was a good fight, closely matched, but the women were too busy talking about Hamu and the baby to take much notice.

Hamu won his second fight that evening almost as easily and quickly as his first. Makura was extremely pleased; she chatted and laughed brightly. Ikenet, too, was relieved. It looked like his hock wouldn't prove to be a problem.

The next day was overcast, the sky threatening rain. The fights started at noon in the big amphitheater. Watching, Ikenet could see that these fights were much harder than those of the day before. The bulls were bigger, quicker, and more cautious. They circled a long time before grappling, and their opponents were much better at slipping free, or twisting a grip to their own advantage. She watched five other fights with a sense of growing uneasiness.

At last it was Hamu's turn. His opponent was a black bull with a white face and chest. They circled, snorting defiance at each other. Each attempted several feints, which the other shrugged off. Then Hamu rushed his opponent, attempting to grab his shoulder and one leg, but the black bull stepped backward, pulling Hamu into a clinch. They remained in that clinch, straining, pushing back and forth across the ring. Ikenet watched Hamu's injured hock, looking for signs of strain. Suddenly his leg buckled, and he was forced backward across the ring. It threw his opponent off balance, and Hamu managed to throw him to the ground and, after a brief struggle, pinned him. Ikenet leaned back against the hard wooden bench with a sigh of relief.

Hamu strode out of the ring with no trace of a limp. She handed Arnam the baby and fled out of the stands and to his stall.

Hamu was sitting in his stall flexing his hock experimentally.

"How is it?" Ikenet inquired.

"I don't think it's injured," he told her. "It just suddenly buckled. The muscles couldn't take any more strain."

"I'll rub some liniment on it."

Hamu shook his head. "No. You've done enough already. I don't want to lose face with the other bulls."

"Hamu—" Ikenet began, but Hamu looked at her, and she stopped.

"I can rub the liniment on myself," he told her. "It'll be all right. It only has to last through a few more rounds. If I can beat Herhoona, the rest should be easy."

Ikenet nodded. They clasped hands wordlessly, then Ikenet ducked out of his stall and headed back to her seat. She was turning a corner in the narrow maze of passageways when a massive hand clamped down on her shoulder.

Ikenet looked back and up and realized with a thrill of fear in the pit of her stomach that it was Herhoona. His eyes were red with rage, and his breath was coming in deep, angry snorts.

"Yuman," he said. "You don't belong here." His fingers tightened painfully on her shoulder. She could feel the bones grinding beneath his fingers. Only a little more pressure and one of them would snap.

"Herhoona, I'm the Great Mother's guest," she gasped, her eyes watering with pain. "If you hurt me, Makura will have your head on a plate."

"Ikenet, are you all right?" It was Arnam, somewhere around another corner.

"I will not forget, yuman," Herhoona said. "Hamu will pay." The grip on her shoulder vanished. By the time she had blinked the tears of pain away, he was gone, the ache in her shoulder the only proof of what had happened. She was suddenly very glad that she had left Malanai in the stands.

It started raining as the last fight of the afternoon began. When they returned after dinner, the bulls' ring was a muddy mess, despite the best efforts of the ring tenders. The next few fights churned it up even more. By the time of Hamu's fight, the footing was slippery and treacherous. Ikenet stiffened as Hamu's opponent came into the ring. It was Herhoona. He looked at her and snorted derisively. Hamu came in. He acted as though Herhoona were no more of a threat than one of the young, inexperienced bulls.

Herhoona circled, looking for an opening. Hamu tossed his horns and beckoned him forward. Herhoona shook his head. They continued circling in the torchlight. Ikenet glanced up at Makura. She was looking on with rapt attention, her fists clenched in the pleats of her skirt.

Herhoona charged. Hamu sidestepped and tried to trip him, but Herhoona shook Hamu's foot loose, pivoted, and grabbed Hamu by the horns. Ikenet gasped as Hamu sank to the ground, throwing his head forward and pulling Herhoona off balance. Herhoona teetered, nearly going over, then let go of Hamu's horns. Hamu sprang up, but slipped in the mud. Herhoona was on him immediately, grabbing his horns and pulling forward. With a roar and a shake of his head, Hamu slipped free, grabbed Herhoona by the horns, and tried to throw him over his hip. Herhoona rolled and grabbed Hamu in a choke hold from behind. Hamu reached back with one foot, trying to hook one of his opponent's legs, but Herhoona shifted his stance and hooked Hamu's other hoof. Hamu went down, but rolled out of Herhoona's grasp before he could pin him. He scrambled to his feet and lunged at Herhoona, trying to throw him off balance before he fully regained his footing.

Snorting and struggling, the two clung to each other, their bodies slick and gritty with mud and sand. Their hooves churned the mud as they fought for purchase. Hamu got his forehead against Herhoona's chest and began to push up and back.

It almost worked. Herhoona was backing, slipping in the mud, fighting to break the hold, when Hamu's injured hock buckled again. Herhoona grabbed his horns and pulled forward, pulling Hamu into the mud. Herhoona quickly pinned him, grinding his face into the dirt.

Ikenet slumped back in her seat. Distantly she heard the judges declare Herhoona the winner. She heard Herhoona roar with victory. She saw Makura's proud muzzle dip dejectedly toward her open hands as Hamu got up and gave her one last, longing look before limping out of the ring. Ikenet reached out to touch Makura, to give her comfort, but then Makura sat up straight as though determined not to show weakness, and Ikenet let her hand fall. She picked up Malanai and headed for Hamu's stall.

Hamu was sitting, staring at the ground just in front of him, his hands lying limply in his lap. His fur was plastered with gritty mud.

"Oh, Hamu," Ikenet said with a sigh of sadness. "You fought well."

"But not well enough," he said. "I've lost everything."

"No, Hamu, not everything. You still have me. You still have Malanai. And someone will choose you as their consort."

"But it won't be Makura," he said. He looked up at her. "It isn't because she's the Great Mother, you know. It was at first, but now—I don't want anyone else. To all the others, I'm just a bull, a way of getting children, but to Makura, I'm Hamu."

"Oh, Hamu. I know that she's sad, too. I saw her when you lost. It was as though she had lost everything, too."

"Huuuuuuu," Hamu sighed. "What am I going to do?"

"You could come with Malanai and me; we could perform for my people. I know we'd be successful. It's not a bad life, and you'd be with two people who care about you."

"Huuuuuuu, I suppose," he said, but his voice still sounded hollow. Ikenet's jaw tightened in sudden anger at the minotaurs for the way they had treated Hamu.

"Come on," she said, "let's get you cleaned up, and then I want to

look at your hock." It might take a long time, but Ikenet was determined
to stay with Hamu until he healed.

It was late when she returned to the palace. The gatekeeper yawned sleepily
as he let her in. She padded to her room, where she tucked Malanai into
bed. She stroked her sleeping baby's dark silken curls and then gathered her
things, picked up a small oil lamp, and headed for the bathhouse. She
scrubbed down, rinsed off, and then slid into the warm dark water, wincing
as she put her weight on her bruised shoulder. She let out a grateful sigh and
gave herself up to the comfort of the hot water. It had been a very long day.

She heard the clack of hooves on stone and opened her eyes. It was
Makura, carrying an oil lamp.

"I heard you come in," she said. Even in the middle of the night she
was as proud and poised as a queen.

Makura lit four large candles set in a bronze sconce. They filled the
room with a warm honey-colored glow. She washed herself, rinsed, and
slipped into the bath with Ikenet.

"How is Hamu?" she asked as soon as she was settled.

Ikenet sighed and shook her head. "Defeated."

Makura looked down at the water for a long moment. "Huuuuu," she
sighed, her breath rippling across the surface of the water. "I wish—" She
paused, then looked up. "Will he recover?"

"I think so. I've asked him to come with me and perform for my people.
We'll be leaving right after the festival."

"What!" Makura exclaimed. "But what about being a consort?"

"He doesn't want to be anyone else's consort," Ikenet told her.

"Oh," Makura said, and looked down at the water again.

"He said that you're the only Mother who treats him like a person.
You know," she continued, "if you two were human, I'd say that you
loved each other, but the Hurloon don't seem to allow that sort of thing
between bulls and Mothers."

"No," Makura said, suddenly aloof. "We don't. The bulls are too different, too solitary, too uncivilized."

Ikenet pushed herself up to sit on the edge of the bath, wincing as she
strained her bruised shoulder.

"What happened to your shoulder?" Makura asked. "Did Hamu—?"

Ikenet looked down at her shoulder, at the bruise in the shape of a
minotaur's hand. "No, Hamu would never do such a thing. It was
Herhoona," she said, and then told Makura about his threats, then about
how Herhoona had injured Hamu and how she had healed him.

"Thank you for telling me this," Makura said, when Ikenet was done. "I apologize for Herhoona's rudeness. The matter will be dealt with."

As Ikenet slipped out of the bath, she looked back to see Makura staring thoughtfully down into the dark water.

Out of politeness, Ikenet went with Makura to the last day of the tournament, but neither of them were very interested. Herhoona won the tournament. He danced around the ring, roaring his victory. Makura bowed her head, acknowledging his victory, but Ikenet saw that her nostrils were contracted in distaste.

That evening, the bulls, in all their finery, paraded out of their stalls and lined up in the main square in order of ranking in the tournament. The Mothers, elaborately groomed, dressed in their finest clothes and draped with garlands of flowers, came, each out of their own house, carrying baskets of fragrant herbs, which they strewed in the streets, singing as they went. They converged on the main square and stood in a line facing the bulls, also in order of rank.

When they were in place, a delegation of Grandmothers came forward, their horns draped in black, carrying sickles made of beaten gold, symbolizing their power over life and death. Ikenet stood with Arnam, amid the eunuchs and children of the village, to watch the selection.

One of the Grandmothers lifted a bull's horn to her lips and blew.

"Mothers and bulls," she said in a loud, resonant voice. "The festival is drawing to a close. It is time for the Mothers to select their consorts. May the Goddess guide them to choose wisely."

Makura stepped forward, amid a clamor of horns and drums. She was massive and regal, wearing her crown of flowers like a queen. Herhoona seemed to swell with pride and expectation. Makura nodded acknowledgment, then strode past him and past half a dozen other bulls to stand before Hamu.

"Grandmothers, sisters, daughters, and sons," she said. "Although others surpassed him in the tournament, our son Hamu surprised us all by bringing with him a stranger, a yuman Mother, whom he had found in the snow, great with child. He took her in, controlling his violent warrior's temperament in order to care for her and the child. Even in the excitement of rut, he was controlled enough to dance with the yuman and gentle enough to play with a baby.

"We have all seen Hamu fight in previous years. We know that he is a fierce warrior of great skill and strength. A brother bull tried to cripple him so that he could not fight. Despite that injury, he fought with the heart of a great warrior. We can ask no more of any bull than Hamu has given us. So I choose Hamu to be my consort. Not only because he can fight, but because he has shown great intelligence and control."

She motioned to Arnam, who led a baby minotaur forward. The baby looked like a sturdy three-year-old with a calf's broad forehead and wide round eyes. Makura took the child from Arnam. "Hamu, this is your son, Amahu." She held Amahu out to him. He took him from her arms and looked down at him with wonder and awe while the villagers murmured in amazement.

"Huuu!" he said. "He looks strong like his father, and wise, like his mother. Thank you," he said, giving the child back to Makura.

She turned to Herhoona, who stood shamefaced and angry at the head of the line of bulls.

"Herhoona, not only did you seek to cripple Hamu for your own advantage, but you also threatened and injured a guest under my protection. I ask that Herhoona be given to the Grandmothers for judgment. We need our sons to be good fighters and strong warriors, but Herhoona's viciousness endangers the Hurloon. If our bulls start crippling their brothers, then who will be left to protect us? If a bull endangers someone under a Mother's protection, how soon before he strikes a Mother?"

With a roar of rage Herhoona charged. Hamu stepped in front of Makura to protect her, but three other bulls brought him down before he could reach her. They held him while the Grandmothers conferred briefly. One stepped forward and, with a flash of her sickle, cut his throat.

"He threatened a Mother and her child," she declared as Herhoona's life blood pooled around her hooves. "For that, the punishment is death." She turned and strode back to the other elders, leaving a trail of bloody hoofmarks on the stones of the square.

Ikenet picked up her traveling staff and took the lead of the pack mule that Makura had given her, laden with fine weaving and beautiful carvings that would fetch a good price in the human towns. She stroked Malanai's silky curls, checking to make sure that she was secure and comfortable in her sling. She then turned to Hamu, who stood beside Makura in the doorway.

"I'll be back next summer to be your horn dancer," she told him.

Hamu nodded. "Huuuu! We'll do even more impressive stunts," he agreed.

"You'll always be welcome here," Makura told her. Hamu bent his head down to nuzzle her neck. "And if you see any other women who might be interested in becoming horn dancers—"

"I will bring them with me," she said with a smile. Ever since the end of the festival, Ikenet had been besieged with requests to find other horn dancers.

"Hamu," Ikenet continued, suddenly serious, "without you, Malanai and I would have died. Thank you."

He looked up, suddenly solemn. "And without you, my bones would be whitening in the sun at the bottom of the Morningstar cliffs."

He reached out, and they clasped hands one last time, then Ikenet pulled the mule's lead rope and set off. She looked back one last time and saw Hamu and Makura standing in the doorway nuzzling each other, oblivious to the rest of the world. She smiled, happy at her friends' happiness, and then turned her face to the morning sun, eager to be on her way.

SHEN MAGE-SLAYER

by

Laura Waterman

S it down, cub, and let me set the record straight. Joerrin came to us in the fall, not the spring, of my second season as lead huntress. She was, indeed, a strange-looking creature. She was almost furless, except for long flowing locks, like a horse's tail, on the top of her head. Those locks, by the way, were a deep rich brown, like the earth, not the yellow of sun-lilies. Her eyes weren't black, either, but brown like her hair.

No one really knows why she came. At first she watched us from the outskirts of the pride. Thirran went out to challenge her, of course, for she was plainly not of the pride. She fled before him, so everyone thought she would leave, as all other outlanders do. She didn't. She came back and watched us. Again Thirran went out. Again she fled, and again she returned, just like a loner asking acceptance into the pride.

The pride considered this. No one had ever heard of an outlander being allowed into a pride. Yet none had ever heard of an outlander who asked admittance, either. Vacu argued against it, as the newcomer was puny. Farnip (you know how persuasive he can be) argued that the exotic creature would increase our store of knowledge, simply by telling us about herself. He also pointed out that the risks were minimal. Once she was among us, there was no way such a puny animal could inflict any real harm on the pride before she was torn limb from limb. So we agreed to bring her in.

As lead huntress I was, of course, chosen to escort the newcomer into the community. So, in full ceremonial dress, I went out to greet her. Looking back now, I believe that she really did not realize the honor I did her. She knew very little about our ways. Later, she told me that she had talked to another creature who had seen a loner accepted into a different pride and had tried to copy what he told her.

At first, she fled before me, too. I don't know if it was confusion on her part, or if she was startled by the ceremonial garb. (I do make a commanding figure in my feathers and paints, and as we learned later, she certainly did startle easily.) I stopped and waited. Then, when she realized that I wasn't pursuing her, I again approached slowly, calling greetings to her.

I quickly discovered that she didn't know our language. So we used hand signals and pantomime, the usual sort of thing, to exchange names and to determine that she did, indeed, wish to join the pride.

We had quite a time after that. It didn't really take long for her to learn our language in a rough sort of a way, though her mouth simply wasn't formed properly to pronounce some words. Soon we were communicating quite well. Joerrin then fell to the tasks set for her with a gusto. She had very long, very mobile digits, though her claws were not retractable and therefore very weak. She was particularly good at fine tasks. In fact, she did the paintings on my shield here.

What I remember most about those weeks, though, was how curious she was. She wanted to know everything about us. She gladly gave us knowledge of her own civilization and eagerly answered all of our questions. She could never seem to get enough of hearing about us, though. Nothing would do but that she sit down and talk with each and every individual in the pride. She even sat with old Garrac, though everyone knows he's a senile old relic. She listened to his ramblings for hours on end.

We all could have been quite happy together, though she wasn't much of a hunter. (I took her out after we learned that she was female. She was good at spotting prey that was out of smelling range, but she couldn't have brought down a rabbit.) The menfolk were all terribly interested in her. I do like to keep them happy: it keeps them out of trouble. Remember that, cub, if the tasks of leadership ever fall to you. You have to give the men something to do besides guarding the children while we women are out hunting. Otherwise you come back to all kinds of mischief.

Then that other one came. I'm fairly certain that it was of her species, and from its mane I believe that it was a male. He quite literally appeared on a hill just north of our camp late one afternoon. It was upwind and there was a good stiff breeze blowing, so he couldn't have gotten there through sheer stealth. One minute the horizon was clear, the next he was just standing there. Needless to say, the pride was alarmed. In my agitation, I nearly did one of the sentries in with an overly strong swipe of my paw for what I perceived as incompetence. In fact, the only one who didn't seem surprised was Joerrin. She did seem a bit sad, but it was as if she had expected the stranger to come sooner or later.

Calmly, she got up, stretched, and walked toward him. He called to her in her language and she answered back. Then, with her following, he walked off toward the plateau in the west, leaving the pride in turmoil.

Now I know that this seems a bit silly now. She was not of our people and she didn't live by the same instinctual urges. We had gotten used to Joerrin, though, and had come to think of her as one of us. Frankly, we had almost forgotten that she was an outlander at all. Her behavior, then, was inexplicable. The stranger had not offered battle, nor had challenged Thirran. He hadn't even tried to be sly about it. He had simply appeared, and she had, quite willingly, walked off with him. Thirran wanted to go after the outlander and rip him to shreds, but everyone argued against it. We didn't know what he was up to, and we couldn't imagine why Joerrin would just walk off with him. No one wanted to risk the security of the pride for one female who behaved so strangely, no matter how interesting she was. Farnip thought that the stranger, having taken the only one of his kind among us, would depart and leave us alone. Vacu, though, pointed out that we didn't really know that they were of the same species. They looked similar enough, but then all outlanders do look alike. Vacu thought that the stranger was some sort of sorcerer, who cast a spell to steal huntresses. She thought that Joerrin, for some reason, was more susceptible to the spell. I doubted the truth of that argument, having felt nothing myself. However, I have always believed that a known hazard is less dangerous than an unknown one. So I told the pride that I would track the two, see what they did, and report back.

By the time all this was decided, the sun was setting, so I set out immediately. I needn't have hurried. They had gone no further than the plateau, and as I arrived, they were standing at opposite ends of it. I took my time approaching the two, discretion being the better part of valor, and I made certain that I stayed downwind.

By the time I found a place from which I felt I could safely determine what was happening, a fierce battle was well underway. Joerrin, it seems, was a magician, as was the other. Vacu did have that part right. The outlander wasn't interested in our huntresses, though. He wanted to kill Joerrin. The two fought a battle of magic on that plateau. I watched for a time as the brightness of their clash outshone the sun setting behind them.

They created monsters to fight for them and cast strange spells which warped the air. Joerrin's creatures, though, were different from those of her challenger. They cast no shadows and were less substantial. At certain angles, they were completely transparent. I didn't think that was a good sign for Joerrin, but they seemed to fight just as well as the monstrosities of the other wizard.

I was about to go back to the pride and tell them to flee before the mages lost control of their hideous fighters and the monsters came to feed on us. Then Joerrin brought forth a creature that stopped me in my tracks. It was me. Not me in the fleshly sense—I was still hiding behind a bush watching the fight—but someone, or something, that looked, smelled, and acted exactly like me. She was shadowy, though, like the other beings that fought for Joerrin. That other-me sprang into battle and used one of my favorite moves to decapitate a great hulking thing.

Joerrin then brought forth replicas of more members of the pride. As I watched, all the members of the pride—Thirran, Farnip, Vacu, and even silly old Garrac—sprang to her aid. (It was odd; that other-Garrac appeared to cast spells that seemed to blind the attacking monsters. I know that he always brags of having been a wizard in his youth, but I had thought that was nothing more than the dreams of the decrepit.) Then, one by one, the other-pride all fell in battle. It was a very odd sensation. I knew that these were not my pride any more than the one who bore my scent was me. Yet watching them die in the clutches of those horrors was profoundly disturbing. It was even worse to watch my own death.

The other-me had been fighting quite well. She had killed a number of creatures, but was mostly concentrating on the sorcerer. She used the forest that he brought up around him as cover. Weaving her way around his defenses, she attacked him from behind several times, jumping back into the cover of the trees before he could retaliate. She was leaping at him from a branch when, by chance, he turned and saw her coming. He pointed at her and a lightning bolt sprang from his finger. It struck her in midair, throwing her back against the trees. Her charred body was lifeless before it hit the ground. I gasped, numbed by this vision of my own death. Perhaps I was delirious, but I believed that the scent of the corpse did not change to one of death. It seemed to slowly fade away, as the body itself grew less and less substantial, melting into the shadows until it was no more.

The battle went on a bit longer. I was, frankly, in shock, and probably couldn't have moved if I had wanted to. Little by little, Joerrin seemed to be tiring. More and more, opposing monsters would break through her lines of defense and bat her about before she was able to do something to dispatch or distract them. Finally, several got to her at the same time. I don't believe she would have survived that attack.

Suddenly, she was gone, and all her fighters and defenses with her. A second later the other wizard also left, taking his entourage with him as well. I sat alone and shivering on the edge of the plateau for the rest of that warm night, unable to rouse myself.

With the dawn came exhaustion and sleep. When I awoke late that evening, I was back among the pride. They had seen the strange lights, heard the sounds of the battle, and dug well in, awaiting my return. The next day, with the sounds of battle gone, some of the huntresses had gone out to search for my remains, assuming that I had been caught up in the conflict and killed. Finding me alive but deeply weary, they carried me back to the pride.

I'm not entirely certain how the rumors started. I know that, immediately upon my return, I wanted only to forget. I told no one what I had seen and went out alone on long hunting trips, trying to purge my spirit of the horror I had witnessed. I first heard the story almost a year later.

Garrac was telling the history of the pride to some of the new cubs. I saw that he was gesturing toward me, so I wandered over to find out what part I played in his story. He was telling them about Joerrin, so I sat and listened. Strange as she was, I did miss her, and I still do. Then he came to the time that she left us and his story diverged entirely from fact. According to him, Joerrin had been ensorcelled by a terrible, evil wizard. He had the little ones all trembling in terror at his description. I was so amused by his exaggerations that I didn't stop him. That was a mistake. It gave those cubs the impression that what he was saying was true.

Then he told them that I had challenged the magician. I was, frankly, curious as to why Garrac thought I would be suicidal enough to challenge such an archetype of evil. (Bring down one grizzly and everyone gets an inflated view of your abilities.) So I let him ramble a bit longer. His version of the battle was quite entertaining, though not at all accurate. According to him, it was Joerrin who spent the battle cowering behind a bush while I single-handedly fended off the "magical attacks" (whatever they were) of the sorcerer. Eventually, of course, as with all good stories, good triumphed over evil, and the brave warrior slew the dastardly magician. Garrac decided to give it a tragic twist, though, and claimed that Joerrin was killed by a magical backlash created by the death of the wizard.

By that time I had heard enough. Garrac's yarn had no basis in fact, and I could not allow him to present it as history. So I made him stop and told them that neither he nor anyone else was ever to repeat that ridiculous pack of lies ever again. (I was still new to the ways of leadership and thought that tactic would work.)

Of course, the story did not stop there. It was repeated over cook fires and whispered in the backs of tents. I've tried repeatedly to stop it, but it seems to have developed a life of its own. Over time and repeated tellings, it has slowly changed. Now the tale you sing to me has left the truth far, far behind.

I'm sorry, cub. Joerrin was not my blood-sister. I did not fight an evil wizard to free her soul. And the magician did not turn her into a sun-lily as his last vengeful act. I know that those flowers grow only on that plateau, but they grew there long before the battle.

So, no, the "Ballad of Shen Mage-Slayer" would not be an appropriate addition to the historical chant of the Cat Warriors. It is fiction, not fact. If you must add anything, then tell of Joerrin, pride-friend, and sing that, somewhere, we fight for her still.

DEFENDER

by

Edd Vick

B inyen's last citizen had slipped off in the night centuries ago, a fact that greatly bothered the city's resident gargoyle.

"I was only trying to help," he muttered for—well, it would take weeks to count up the number of times he had said it. "How was I to know his dog was so fragile? And anyway, it certainly *looked* as if it were attacking him."

He was perched on a ruined building in an abandoned city on a ledge halfway up the Muraytt Mountains. One day he finally grew weary of standing sentry over a hall nobody would ever use again, so he creaked and he stretched and tiny cracks appeared all over his body.

When he was limber again, he straightened up and scanned the horizon for any sign of life, any city he could stand sentry for. First he looked north, into the great white plains of ice. But they were empty. Then he looked west, straight down—almost—to the endless blue ocean. But no ships, no watery dwellings, did he see. Then he turned south to look over the forests and swamps. But because he was so high in the mountains, he did not see the forest peoples' cities, which are green, or the dark swamp villages. He saw life aplenty, birds and such, but no people he could guard. Heart sinking, he turned his gaze east, up into the mountains, expecting to see nothing more than ruins like the one he was now so eager to escape.

But there, from a cave high up in the side of a cliff, he saw a wisp of smoke rising to blend with the thin clouds far above. *There!* he thought. *That is where I will find humans, with their squabbles and their scraps, their clamor and their hunts and their games and their battles!*

He lifted one foot from the roof, then the other, snapping the vines that had grown over his body during the centuries he'd faithfully guarded the ruined city. Gathering his strength, he launched himself into the air, flailing his stiff, barely responsive wings. He fell hundreds of feet before recalling the patterns and rhythm of flight. The air caught him then, and he glided far out over the Muraytt foothills for several minutes before turning his attention once more to gaining height. After many minutes of struggle, he flew past his city and then soared higher, and higher yet, where the air was thin and his labored breath misted away.

Slowly the cave mouth grew before him. It was bigger than he'd expected at first. Finally he hung before it, wings aching in their effort to keep him aloft, and stared in awe at the entrance. It was a cleft, a giant fissure in the side of the mountain. He saw no path leading up to it, no way for humans to reach the cave, yet still that curl of smoke drew him on.

He landed just inside the mouth of the cave. The light of the sun penetrated only a few steps into the recess. The cave's ceiling was more than five times his height above him. An errant breeze blew some of the smoke back into his face. He sneezed, then sniffed at it thoughtfully. Why would someone be burning sulfur? Had some hermit blacksmith set up shop in this inaccessible place?

He'd once heard of a thing called a "volcano." "Can this be one of the fiery mountains?" he wondered aloud. "But that must be nonsense. Sensible rocks know better than to burn, and this has always seemed a reasonable, no-nonsense kind of mountain. There *must* be someone here, people I can defend from—well, from whatever comes along."

The gargoyle determined to see for himself who it was that had taken up residence in so inhospitable a place, so he walked into the cave, carefully stepping between stalagmites and over fallen rocks. He wondered again how anyone could use this as an entrance, so strewn was it with obstacles. Perhaps a tinkerer had repaired one of those flying machines from the days of the artificing brothers, one of those ornithopters. The gargoyle, who was very old indeed, had even seen one of *them* flap by his city in his time.

Finally the passageway opened out into a huge cave, where he paused. Dismayed, he looked around. There was no sign of life. Where were the people? More to the point, where were the buildings? Did this smoke just herald some weary mountain climber who slept and cooked on the bare stone? Following the scent of sulfur, he picked his way toward the back of the cave, which was suffused with a gentle red glow.

His footsteps echoed back from the walls around him, and he wondered why no one had challenged him yet. Surely the noise of his passage would have brought someone out. Could they be hiding, fearful of his size and obvious power? He walked further.

And that is when the back wall of the cave moved.

She was huge and she was ancient and she was so hot that the air around her shimmered a deep scarlet and stank of brimstone. In short, she was one of the fabled dragons of Shiv, thought long gone from the civilized lands. But then, the gargoyle realized, his land was hardly civil any longer. Its last citizen had left long ago.

"What are you doing here?" The dragon's voice was a rumble of stone on stone. "This is *my* cave."

The gargoyle backed away, stumbling on a bone that rolled under his foot. He fell back against a stone column and gasped. Looking up, and up, he said, "My pardon, Mistress Dragon. I was merely looking for—for a town."

The great head turned to regard him from one baleful eye. "Up here?"

"Or a shack. Anything. I just wanted to see somebody."

"You see me." There was something horrible in her dry amusement.

"Humans!" he wailed. "Or dwarves or kobolds. Even orcs. People who build dwellings! Castles. Houses, halls, shops, stables, something over which I can stand guard."

The dragon laughed, a deep, terrible sound. "Dragons and cities have never been the best of friends, little beast. We fight, the two of us, them for survival and me . . . for prey!" And with that she pounced, as quick as lightning.

He took a step and she was on him, caging her claws around him and bathing him in her fire. He breathed it in, the heat and the odor and the taste of her. He hunched down, waiting to be roasted.

Not melted. Roasted. He had lived all his life among humans, a frail and easily broiled people. He saw the fire and he felt the heat, and so like a human he cowered.

To his surprise, he lived. When the wash of flame subsided, he stood up again. His skin glowed sullenly, not nearly as brightly as the dragon's, but painfully. He felt it all the way through—the incendiary heat of his skin muted to a summery warmth at his center. Then he felt something else, something from the granite around him. A kinship.

He backed up against a column of stone. "Mistress Dragon, I mean you no harm. Let me go back to the lands of men, and I shall bother you no more. If you fear that I'll lead anyone here—"

"Me? Fear you? An insignificant flea about to be dashed into so many shards?" The dragon's grin widened at the thought, then was suddenly wiped away as she flicked out a massive paw to strike him. The column at his back crumbled, and he skidded across the cave floor in a cascade of stone. In another instant she was on him again, slashing at him with tooth and claw.

He lay there against the rock, fearful once more for his life. How long could anything mortal last against such an onslaught? But then, once more, he felt that familiar well of power, like the one he'd drawn on back in his own safe little city.

He drew on that force. Between one blow and the next, he pulled into himself a portion of that strength, that brotherhood of stone with stone, and he stood. And standing, he raised his head and returned her stare for stare.

The dragon reared back. "What *are* you made of?"

"Rock," he whispered. Then he said it aloud. "I'm made of granite, like your cave. You can no more hurt me than you can pull your home apart."

"Can I not?" Flicking out a massive paw, she swatted him down again. "You shall see what I do to this cave!" She held him for a moment, then sprang to her feet to slam her body into the cave's ceiling. Her scornful laughter washed over him as her flames had before, but this time he lay and stared back at her calmly. Rocks, from small shards to stalactites larger than he, rained down around them both and pounded into him. She did it again, laughing all the while.

Ceiling met floor. Boulders smashed and crashed down. Pebbles clattered and skittered to the ground. The fine mist of dust that hung in the air was tinted the same red as the rest of the cave. Finally, all was still and quiet.

The Shivan dragon snorted, a brief burst of flame, and shook to rid herself of the bothersome boulders that had fallen on her. She dredged up a ton or so of rock and let it sift through her claws, looking in vain for any sign of life. "Invade my home, will you?" Then she turned her back and settled herself against a wall, slitting her eyes against the dust. For an hour she sat thus. Finally, satisfied that the invader was dead, she lowered her head and slept.

All was silent once more, save for an insistent *tip-tap* of water dripping from a stalactite. Then, with a patter of stones, the gargoyle pulled himself slowly to his feet. Reeling with pain and confusion, he stumbled as silently as he could to the cave's exit. Once there, he prepared to throw himself into the air. He would go back to his ruin of a town and there allow the vines to slowly cover him. It was best that way, in a world devoid of civilization.

Spreading his wings widely, he stepped to the edge of the sheer cliff. The westering sun was full in his face, throwing his shadow deeply into the still-intact dragon cave. Then, slowly, he lowered his arms. He refolded his wings. He sat on the verge.

For all her fury, the dragon had not truly managed to hurt him. His granite wings were whole. No limb was broken. There were no rips in his rocky skin as witness to her awesome fury. Her savage assault had not even chipped so much as a toenail. Quite the contrary. He had drawn strength from this mountain, this home of hers, as he had from so many other dwellings in the past. He felt—at home.

He was a guardian. His life's duty was to keep homes and the people who lived in them safeguarded, and while doing so they would be as much his fellows as if he were just another native. His strength came from duty, from honor, and from stone.

For hundreds of years he had guarded a dead city. Now, he could have a cave to guard, a cave with one inhabitant. Oh, she would be angry. She would most likely bake him and swat him and stomp on him. But he knew—he knew!—she would not be able to hurt him. She could no more rend him than she could tear this mountain in twain. Like him or not, she would have to put up with him as long as she called this cave home.

The gargoyle sat and waited. Dragons flew by night, he knew, and this one would need to have her cave watched while she was gone.

He just knew she'd grow to appreciate him in time.

THE OLD WAY TO VACAR SLAB

by

Michael G. Ryan

The horses were dead and still Spirokai's party moved on toward the execution site in the desert. They dragged themselves from the arid mountains, a band of four haggard captors leading one prisoner by the rope around his neck, led by Spirokai of the Split Skull. He placed the first massive footprint in the shifting sands and the others followed his uncompromising back into the heat.

Ophelia stumbled and fell, picked herself up again, fell once more. No one helped her, and for that she was silently grateful. She'd seen the others "help" the prisoner back to his feet when the Abuser, as they called him, slumped to the ground. They dragged him upright again by the thick rope wound round his throat like a garrote. The Abuser choked and gagged, but he found his feet again. Ophelia didn't know how the man maintained his strength. The heat surely sucked him dry of will and hope; it was having that effect on Ophelia.

Someone, she thought, *should have done the decent thing and buried a sword in his heart days ago and have done with it.*

It simply wasn't the way of the Kenlefian shamen; an offender was punished at the holy site or not at all. So it was written (or so Ophelia was told by her brother) and it had always been the custom—the Abuser would either die for his crimes at the ruins or he would go free. Ophelia had her doubts that either thing would occur; she suspected the Abuser would die long before the execution party reached Vacar Slab. In fact, there was a strong possibility that *none* of them would make it. Their original party had consisted of eight—two had been killed in a hostile confrontation with Ærathi marauders in the foothills just outside of Kenlefia. One more had died from a lethal snakebite after lingering for over a day. And the last to die, the one whom Spirokai had called "Teeth," he who carried nearly all of the precious water supply, had plummeted yesterday into a deep canyon from which the others had not been able to extract his corpse. Below them, Teeth's two-handed sword, spilled from its sheath in the fall, taunted them. The torn waterskins bled their contents into the dry ground at Teeth's feet, and those which still held their precious fluid were as indifferent and unreachable as the sun above. Ophelia knew this situation disturbed the others far more than just the loss of the water—custom demanded a proper mummifaction of the body to ensure the soul's transit

to the Otherworlds. But there was no time or opportunity—the remains of
Teeth were left to rot in the blistering heat while the survivors staggered
on toward the completion of the execution. Teeth would have to find his
own way to the Otherworlds.

Spirokai raised one sunburned hand to signal a stop on the desert's
edge, and Ophelia collapsed thankfully. The horizon shimmered and
sweat ran down her forehead into her eyes, blinding her with her own precious salt. Cleatin, the gray ogre warrior who had assumed primary control of the prisoner, shoved the Abuser down into the sand and stood stoic
guard over him as if the prisoner might miraculously find the will to
escape.

"How are you doing?" Methos asked. Ophelia shielded her eyes and
looked up into the face of her older brother, who had convinced Ophelia
to come on this suicidal pilgrimage. He smiled wearily at her, and she felt
her chest constrict with the intensity, devotion, and affection that only
Methos could bring out in her so forcefully. She was here for him, and for
no other reason; Methos, lost in his zealous religious fervor, had been so
persistent, so convincing, and so righteous, that Ophelia had never
thought to ask him how much he really knew of the passage to Vacar
Slab. Methos, who had found the Kenlefian Old Ways satisfying and
thought Ophelia would find inner strength there, too. Methos, who meant
to bridge a gap in their relationship by enlightening his little sister.
Methos, who had been wrong about everything.

"I'm not going to make it," Ophelia answered as Methos came to his
knees next to her. They both looked over at Spirokai, who stalked the
sands like a crazed duneclaw, impatient to be on the move again.

"You can make it," Methos whispered. "Then you'll witness holy
justice at Vacar Slab. You just have to hold on."

Ophelia ignored the reference to the execution. "How much further?"

"A few days."

"We'll run out of water, Methos. There was a creek in that canyon
where Teeth fell. We should have—"

"We can hunt desert beasts," her brother cut in. "We can drink their
blood, if necessary. All that matters is reaching Vacar Slab and doing the
will of the shamen. It is the Old Way. Spirokai will get us there."

Yes, but how many of us? Ophelia wondered, yet kept her silence.
She could see in her brother's firm jaw that Methos still believed, despite
the loss of the horses, despite the searing heat, and despite the four deaths.
Worse, Methos trusted Spirokai of the Split Skull to get the Abuser to the
execution site, even if it meant drinking hot blood.

Ophelia could not look anywhere without staring at the pacing

commander of the execution party. Spirokai was a member of the
Viperdeau, the warrior clan serving the Kenlefian shamen, but this alone
did not make him unique. There were whispers among the nonbelievers
that he might have even once been an Akron legionnaire, but Ophelia
doubted that—he gave no indication of being sufficiently disciplined for
such service. It was not his mysterious origins, however, that made him
unique. What made him memorable and—to Ophelia—horrifying was
the jagged red scar slicing like a part across the top of the warrior's bald
head. It was deep and wide enough to place a finger in, and it dipped
down to just above his left eye. Methos had told Ophelia that the Lords
of the Viperdeau had not expected Spirokai to live, and Ophelia
believed him—the warrior's brain must surely have been cleft in two.
Yet Spirokai had survived the axe wound delivered in the chaos of battle by an insane frost giant, though Ophelia believed it had left him
insane. The Viperdeau warrior frequently degenerated into shivering fits
that immobilized him; he could barely speak, often falling back on sharp
gestures to convey his desires. And he was possessed of a cold determination, a single-mindedness which drove him forward relentlessly. It
made him reckless, and this scared Ophelia. Spirokai would persevere
across the desert even if everyone else, including the Abuser, died
around him.

"It's too far," Ophelia said suddenly, looking from the scarred warrior and out into the desert. "Your shamen should have created a closer
holy site. Or maybe they should abandon holy sites altogether. After all,
no one's had to go to Vacar Slab for more than five years. Why do they
even need it?"

Methose shook his head sadly. "You don't understand," Methos said.
"We can't 'create' a holy site, not even if the desert should swallow
entirely the one we know. The Old Ways speak only of Vacar Slab as the
place where—"

Spirokai snapped his fingers suddenly, commanding the party
into motion. Methos rose, offering his forearm to Ophelia, who
took it reluctantly. She adored her brother, no matter how differently they saw the world, but his business of the shamen and their
Old Ways was becoming too consuming. When Spirokai snapped,
Methos, Cleatin, and D'Bray—the standard bearer—jumped. All
three fell into a ragged marching order behind the Viperdeau warrior, Cleatin in the rear tugging on the rope tied around the
Abuser's neck. The desert yawned before them.

"It's too far," Ophelia said again, but no one was listening to her. She
was an outsider, suffered only because of her relationship to Methos.

Knowing she had no allies and no hope of returning through the mountains alone, she joined the others as they moved into the sands.

The sun blinded Ophelia and scalded her exposed flesh as she forced herself to place one boot before another. Each step sank her to her ankles in the hot sand, threatening to burn her feet like potatoes cooked amidst the coals; it kept her moving. Each minute stretched impossibly into an hour; each hour took her further into the afternoon. She counted her paces, head down to spare her face the full blast of the sun's heat. With a titanic effort, she resisted the desire to gulp greedily from her sole waterskin. By midday, she thought she had truly achieved self-control, and she was proud.

It was then that D'Bray, the standard bearer who carried the dated flag and the implements necessary to conduct the execution, collapsed and died.

"Dehydration," Methos said as he rose from next to D'Bray's body. The party was clustered around it, Ophelia behind her brother, Spirokai and Cleatin across the corpse from them. The Abuser had crumbled into a panting ball as soon as the party halted; evidence, Ophelia thought, that the prisoner was never going to survive long enough to be killed at Vacar Slab. Watching the man struggle for breath, she felt his misery.

"More water for the rest of us," Cleatin whispered dryly, and stooped to remove D'Bray's waterskin. It barely sloshed. "I'll carry this."

Spirokai stepped forward then and snatched the skin away from him. Surprised, Cleatin offered no resistance.

"You," Spirokai slurred, his tongue stumbling on the word, and he pointed at Methos. "Get flag. Get shovel."

Methos nodded and removed the backpack from D'Bray's corpse, then recovered the dated flag of Kenlefia from where it had fallen from the standard bearer's hand. "We must shroud the body, Spirokai. His soul must be aided to the Otherworlds."

Ophelia swallowed, about to protest—it was too hot, there was no shade, they needed to be pressing on—when Spirokai began to shake.

At first his hands began to tremble as if from intense cold. The shiver traveled up his arms, the muscles twitching and tightening, pulling his elbows into his belly and his vibrating hands to his chin. His head bowed until his trench of a scar was pointed at the others like a hieroglyph drawn in blood. In mere seconds he was on his knees, the long sword at his hip rooting itself in the sand as he fell.

Ophelia began to move forward to aid him, but Methos touched her shoulder. "It's the wound," he murmured by way of explanation. "It will pass."

And it did. An agonizing minute passed during which Ophelia, Methos, and Cleatin watched and waited as Spirokai knelt in the sand, possibly praying but for the violent spasms which racked his muscular frame. The Abuser seemed too far gone to even notice the incident. Then it was over. The Viperdeau warrior rose back to his feet effortlessly, almost majestically, Ophelia thought, and nodded to Methos as if nothing had happened.

"Wrap," he said, pointing at D'Bray's body.

"But—" Ophelia began.

"It is the Old Way," Methos said gently.

Cleatin was already producing needle, thread, and a large ball of yellow-white bandages from his backpack as Ophelia bit the tip of her tongue into silence. She cast a dark look at Spirokai, who did not acknowledge it. The scarred warrior simply raised D'Bray's nearly empty waterskin to his lips and drank from it.

"I'll tend to the prisoner," Ophelia spat. She turned away from the corpse and the party; still, she could feel her brother's pleading eyes burning like the sun upon her back. She shrugged it off as best she could.

The Abuser lay with his knees up to his chin, his bare, reddened forearms locked around them, and one cheek in the rough sand. Ophelia marveled at the man's incapacity to feel pain—the ground was nearly hot enough to cook on. She sat him upright.

"Have a drink," she said, taking her waterskin from her belt. She gestured with her head toward D'Bray's body. "I've learned my lesson about trying to conserve water. Here."

The Abuser took the skin slowly, suspiciously. He was a thin man with dark hair and stubble on his face. Ophelia thought he was young, perhaps not even twenty. It was so hard to tell; the first time she'd seen the Abuser was the day the man had been brought from the Cages after weeks of underground imprisonment. He'd been dirty and scrawny, and there had been whispered suggestions that he be fattened up for the trip across the desert. These suggestions had been ignored by the shamen.

"You are a decent one," the Abuser said after he had drunk. "You are not Kenlefian."

"I live there," Ophelia answered. "But I don't follow the shamen, if that's what you mean."

"I did not do it, you understand," the prisoner blurted out suddenly. "I courted a powerful shaman's daughter. That is all. The shaman did not approve, and so sent his other daughter, the child, to lie about me. To say I did terrible things. I did nothing, you must see, but they took me away just the same. It is written in the Old Ways that the word of a shaman cannot be a lie." The Abuser sighed. "Of course, ancient shamen *wrote* the Old Ways. It could even be said that the shaman did not lie—it was his youngest daughter who told the lie for him. And now I am to die."

Without fully understanding why, Ophelia found herself believing the prisoner. The Abuser's tale dovetailed neatly with her opinion of the Kenlefians' influence over her brother, confirming her suspicion that there was something sinister about the whole religion. More than anything, she *wanted* to believe the story. It was the ammunition which might save her brother from becoming involved beyond rescue.

"Tell me." The Abuser broke into Ophelia's thoughts. "What will they do to me at Vacar Slab? How am I to die?"

Ophelia looked over at Methos and Cleatin as they tightly wrapped D'Bray's body in the bandages. From Methos's backpack jutted the shovel he'd removed from the dead standard bearer.

"You really don't want to know," she answered.

"Perhaps I will not make it to my execution at all," the Abuser said.

Ophelia knew he was suggesting that he might die in the desert, but a new idea was forming in her head. Dying was not the only way the Abuser could avoid death at Vacar Slab. "Perhaps you won't," she agreed thoughtfully, just as Methos and Cleatin rose from the body, their work finished. D'Bray had been aided into the Otherworlds, according to the Old Ways, and it was time to move on.

"I'll talk to you again later," Ophelia promised and, recovering her waterskin from the Abuser, joined her brother as the party reformed into their marching order once more. Cleatin snagged the Abuser's rope, tugging him to his feet, and they continued on their way, leaving D'Bray's mummifying corpse in the baking sand behind them.

Camp. The sun finally fell and Spirokai halted the party for the night. The shelters had been lost with the horses, too heavy for any of them to carry, so they were left to arranging their thin bedrolls beneath open sky. Ophelia had thought the heat would vanish with the sun; it was not so. The ground seemed to pulse with the warmth it had stored all day and the cooler night air called it forth. In the moonless darkness, Ophelia still felt the sweat run down her back beneath her leather armor.

Cleatin pounded an iron stake into the ground, tied the Abuser's rope to it, and then set about building a cooking fire. The Abuser lay nearby, oblivious to the activity around him. Ophelia wanted to go to him, but Spirokai hovered just beyond him, a threatening shadow darker than the night. Ophelia could hear the Viderdeau warrior gulping greedily from a precious waterskin—the sound made her wish dearly for a weapon other than her dagger, though she knew she wouldn't use it even if she had it. *Spirokai,* she thought, *should have to replace every drop he drinks with a drop of his own blood.* But it would have to be someone with warrior skills who extracted that price, not Ophelia.

Methos joined his little sister as Ophelia stretched out her bedroll and took off some of her armor. Beneath the leather she wore a thin blouse and breeches, more appropriate clothing once the burning sun was gone. She sighed with relief.

"Feeling better?" Methos asked, his voice tired. The miles were showing in his eyes; Ophelia thought that her brother might be prepared to give up this dangerous journey, if only to save his own life. One more day in the sun could kill him.

"I had a chat with the Abuser earlier," she began. "He told me about his crime."

Methos nodded. "Terrible thing he did."

"He says he didn't do it."

"Of course he would say that."

Ophelia considered her next words carefully. "I think he might be telling the truth, Methos." She avoided mentioning the ahaman the Abuser had identified. "Maybe he should be taken somewhere outside of Kenlefia to be judged, somewhere not so emotionally connected to his supposed crime. Maybe he should not be taken to Vacar Slab."

"It has already been decided," Methos said. He was trying to be diplomatic, Ophelia knew by his tone. "It was decided by people more qualified to judge than you or me. The Old Ways say that the shamen speak only the truth—they are protectors of honesty and integrity."

"I believe you," Ophelia said, though she did not, "but even shamen make mistakes."

"They don't." Methos smiled. "That is the wonder of the shamen— it's what makes them leaders. The Abuser would naturally try to convince you of his innocence because you're the only one here who doesn't entirely trust his prosecutors. He's playing on you because you're an outsider. But you can be inside, Ophelia. All you have to do is—"

At that moment, Cleatin screamed.

Methos leaped to his feet, placing himself between Ophelia and the battle suddenly raging across the fire from them, and drew his sword. Ophelia jumped up, one hand flashing to her dagger; she knew it was a pathetic weapon, but it was all she had. Even the Abuser looked ready to defend himself, crouched in preparation to leap as far as his restraining rope would permit him.

The monstrous shelled creature had six legs, three to a side, and four huge pincers, two situated close to its head, and two midway down its worm-like back. Its tail was coiled above its ten-foot long frame, tipped with an ugly stinger that dripped venom. The stinger had been plunged through Cleatin's body, suspending him in the air above the monster. Ophelia knew he wasn't alive; the stinger had emerged from his chest near his heart, but more horribly, the monster had torn off one of Cleatin's legs with a razor-sharp pincer. Two feelers, extending from the creature's head, danced over Cleatin's body in search of any remnants of life.

"Duneclaw!" Methos hissed, and ran forward.

Spirokai was already there. He planted his feet firmly in the sand before the monster and swung his long sword savagely down from above his head as if wielding a sledgehammer. Sensing new prey, the duneclaw snapped at the Viperdeau's legs with its forward pincers. Spirokai did not retreat. His first blow split the protective armor atop the duneclaw's head; the second sheared off one of its feelers. A pincer narrowly missed closing on his leg between the two swings, but when its feeler flew off into the night, the monster became enraged with pain. The pincer holding Cleatin's leg dropped its prize; its tail twitched and flung Cleatin himself across the camp into the darkness. All four claws as well as the poisonous stinger came to bear on Spirokai as he battered away at the monster's head. Ophelia didn't know if it was the bravest or the stupidest act she'd ever seen.

Methos joined the battle, his own sword arcing down and neatly removing the duneclaw's other feeler, effectively blinding it. Ophelia felt her heart surge; she had just come to the realization that Spirokai's death would free the three survivors to go their own way, abandon the voyage to Vacar Slab. Now Methos was in danger—Ophelia could lose her brother and ally and be left alone with the mad Spirokai.

"Methos!" she cried out. "Don't—!"

Her brother looked over at her, his concentration shifted away from the frenzied monster before him. It was only for a moment.

One pincer closed at Methos's waist.

"No!" Ophelia screamed. It came to her in frozen flashes, like lightning on a clear night: the glint of the pincer's sharpened edges in the firelight, Methos's eyes turning back toward his attacker, the scissors-like claw closing with a terrible finality. And then the spray of water as the pincer snapped shut on Methos's waterskin, narrowly missing his belly. Ophelia thought, for a painfully long moment, that she was seeing blood splash over her brother's body. Then Methos was hacking away at the duneclaw again, and the truth sank into Ophelia's awareness. *Water! Just water!* She wanted to laugh aloud.

Spirokai took a running step forward and leaped into the air, his feet coming down together onto the monster's back, making a hollow ringing sound as his boot heels struck the bony armor. The monster's tail-stinger wavered in his scarred face, but he battered it away. With a decisive stroke, he buried his sword to the hilt between two panels of the duneclaw's head-protecting shell. The monster made a pitiful noise, something between a squeal and a grunt, and its pincers sagged to the ground. Its stinger drooped. It was dead.

There was nothing but the sound of their hoarse breathing. Ophelia ran to her brother but stopped short when Methos raised his hand. They looked at each other; Methos looked down at the water stains on his body, the *last* of his water. A pang of guilt stabbed at Ophelia—the loss of Methos's water was her fault. She had distracted her brother from the fight.

"Go see if Cleatin's skins survived," Methos said softly. "Then we'll wrap him."

Ophelia nodded. *My fault.* She hurried to Cleatin's crumbled form, mindful of movement out in the darkness that would signal the approach of another duneclaw, and searched the gray ogre's body. There was no water, only a burst and tattered skin. She held the destroyed skin out before her, a quiet panic beginning deep in her gut. No water left. Her eyes drifted to find the Abuser staring at her from nearby.

"We are all destined to die," the Abuser said. He sounded resigned. "It is only a question of when."

Ophelia was floundering for a response—*any* response which would counter the prisoner's claims—when Methos joined her. He was carrying the bandages necessary to mummify Cleatin's remains. In his other hand he bore Cleatin's leg.

"We have to flee," Ophelia said without preamble. Methos moved past her to the body. "We have to go back or look for water. If Spirokai blocks us, then we'll need to do something—"

"We need to post guards," Methos said. "I'll tend to Cleatin and take the first watch. I know you don't wish to participate in the customs of the Old Ways, sister, and I respect that. I won't ask for your help with Cleatin. But we can't leave. Even if I wanted to, Spirokai wouldn't permit it, and I cannot contest him. He is Viperdeau. He may even have been a legionnaire once—do you know of their skills in battle? He would kill us before he would allow us to leave with the prisoner. We would have to leave without him, and I would then have abandoned my duty to the Kenlefian shamen. I could never go home."

Ophelia said nothing. She could not tell if Methos was agreeing with her or not. It didn't matter; he was not about to act in opposition to the dictates of the Old Ways.

"Will you take a watch?" Methos was beginning the task of wrapping Cleatin's corpse.

Ophelia looked across the way to where Spirokai of the Split Skull cleaned his bloodied sword. They would never be free as long as Spirokai pushed them on and on into the desert, heedless of their condition. The Viperdeau would drink all their water and drive them forward until each of them ended up as Cleatin, D'Bray, and the others before them. Something would have to be done.

Her eyes found the remains of the duneclaw, its pincers and tail now half-buried in the sand. She looked back at Spirokai and an idea came to her: a barbaric but necessary idea.

"I'll take a watch," she said to Methos. "Wake me when it's my turn."

They were moving again just after dawn. Ophelia had assumed control of the Abuser, though she suspected Spirokai had some misgivings about an outsider being so closely involved in the execution activities. But there was no other choice—Methos was already burdened with the shovel, the bandages, the flag, as well as his own equipment and bedding. Spirokai had scorned the idea of taking responsibility for the Abuser—Ophelia imagined it was because of vanity, the superior warrior refusing to be saddled with the menial labor of tending a prisoner. So the task fell to Ophelia, who took it willingly. Only this way could she be sure that the Abuser was no longer the abused, that he was treated like a person instead of baggage. She believed she saw gratitude in the prisoner's eyes as she led the man across the desert behind Methos and Spirokai.

It had been a long night and a long watch for Ophelia. She had worked diligently yet quietly throughout her watch to cut open the tail section of the slain duneclaw lying barely ten feet from the sleeping Spirokai. Her dagger was not up to the task; she was forced to saw instead of slice, cracking off bits and pieces of the monster's shell to gain access to its insides. No one stirred. At length the plating gave way to what Ophelia had hoped she would find: the stinger's poison sac. It was nearly empty, but it was enough, she thought, to do the job. She drained the lethal fluid from the sac into her empty waterskin, which she then stowed in her backpack. To hide her handiwork, she replaced the cracked bits of shell as best she could, like a sickening jigsaw puzzle, and covered the broken section with a few scooped handfuls of sand.

By then it was nearly dawn and the others were stirring. It would have to wait until tonight, she decided, as soon as their next camp was pitched and everyone was bedded down . . . then she would dowse her dagger in the poison and stab the sleeping Spirokai in the throat. If the wound didn't kill him, the poison most certainly would. It would free the rest of them to abandon Vacar Slab. They could seek out another city, the three of them, where the Abuser could be judged impartially. Or they could just release him and go on about their own business. It didn't matter to Ophelia. All that mattered was getting away from the Old Ways and taking her brother with her. It had been a mistake to get involved with them in the first place.

Methos fell frequently, more often than did Ophelia, who was becoming worried about her brother—the battle with the duneclaw had taken a lot out of him, and today he wasn't looking very well. In fact, he looked *ghastly*. There was no water left, nothing to get them back across the desert even if they fled. The Abuser staggered along behind them, his dark hair hanging down over his eyes and the sun burning the back of his neck. No one spoke; they all simply followed Spirokai's rigid back as he plodded relentlessly onward. Ophelia wondered what he would do if they all simply stopped walking. Would he carry them? Kill them?

"We should walk at night, sleep during the day," she mumbled to Methos as they walked. "Just because he can keep going in any heat doesn't mean we can."

Methos wheezed an unintelligible response.

The skin on Ophelia's forearms began to crack from dryness. She scratched herself once and could still see the white marks left by her trailing fingernails two hours later. She licked her lips but felt no moisture.

"Storm," Methos groaned sometime later. It was well after midday; the sun had done its worst to them and they were still going. A few scattered rocky outcroppings dotted the horizon now like islands in a sandy sea. Methos pointed off toward a small cluster of them and Ophelia saw the storm. It was like a cloud descended to the ground—it was a wall of whipping sand, gyrating in on itself, a stretch of storm fabricated from seemingly nothing. It was very far away and difficult to tell how big it was; Ophelia guessed it was two or three miles long. It was impossible to tell how deep it was.

"We'll miss it, I think," Methos volunteered. He seemed to wobble before Ophelia's eyes. "Or it'll miss us. It depends on how you see things."

His eyes rolled back in his head and he pitched backward into the sand.

"Methos!" Ophelia stumbled forward, kneeling next to her brother. She looked up briefly at Spirokai—the Viperdeau had halted but had not turned back to offer aid. A cold loathing burned into Ophelia's chest; she could not wait to bury her venomous dagger in the mad warrior's windpipe.

"Must've fallen down," Methos said thickly. He tried to shield his eyes from the sun above, but his hand didn't seem to understand the command—it kept falling back at his side. He looked at it as if it were a traitor. Ophelia moved until her own body cast a shadow over her brother's face.

"Thirsty," Methos said.

Ophelia's chest hitched up; she was afraid she was going to cry. How could she deny her brother? "You have to hold on until Vacar Slab," she said, not knowing if the words she spoke were true. "There'll be water there."

The Abuser came up behind Ophelia's shoulder—she could sense the man there.

"Take my blood," Methos said. "It'll keep you alive."

Ophelia recoiled, shaking her head violently. The action made her dizzy. "No! I'd rather die!"

The thought of bleeding her brother into a waterskin made her stomach flop over with nausea. Not her brother. "We should have bled Cleatin," she said carelessly, though the vision of doing so was equally disturbing.

"Poison," Methos mumbled; Ophelia thought he meant the duneclaw venom hidden in her pack before realizing her brother's true meaning: Cleatin had been poisoned by the monster. His blood had been tainted and would have been useless, even deadly.

"I won't do it," Ophelia said firmly. She realized then what she was acknowledging: her brother was about to die. Despite the blistering heat and her own dangerous level of dehydration, Ophelia felt the tears spring unbidden to her eyes. Her brother was about to die.

"Take my blood," Methos said again. His eyelids fluttered. "It is written. It is . . . the Old Way."

"I don't believe," Ophelia sobbed. "No. I'd rather have *you* drink *my* blood."

She drew her dagger, intent on slashing open her own wrist to offer to her brother, when the Abuser's hand restrained her. Ophelia looked back angrily into the prisoner's face, but the Abuser's expression of genuine sorrow stifled Ophelia's outrage.

"He is too far gone," the Abuser whispered. "If you do this thing, you will both be dead."

Ophelia turned back to Methos; her brother's eyes were closed and his breathing was ragged. With one hand, he reached up and found Ophelia's face. He brushed it with his fingertips.

"Remember to wrap me," Methos breathed. "I'll wait for you in the Otherworlds."

"I love you," Ophelia told him. Her tears fell from her jawline onto Methos's sunburned face. "Tell me you love me."

Methos grimaced, maybe smiling that all-knowing smile which Ophelia remembered from their childhood together in the castle. He died without speaking again.

They wrapped him, Ophelia and the Abuser, though neither held any belief in the Kenlefian superstition about life after death. Ophelia cried during the entire process, thinking that if she believed Methos would return from the dead if not wrapped, she would never do this. That was how much she wanted her brother alive again. The Abuser kept her going, taking responsibility for covering Methos's face with the bandages. Ophelia was grateful; she knew she wouldn't have been able to do it alone.

Spirokai approached. He pointed at Methos's backpack, the shovel jutting from it, and the dated flag. "Give."

Ophelia picked up the pack to hand to him, a vision dancing through her head of surging forward, yanking out the shovel, and smashing it across the Viperdeau's face. She trembled with emotion—the poisoned dagger, the shovel, any weapon, just to kill him, to make him suffer the way he had made Methos—

Spirokai took the backpack and retrieved the flag himself. He checked the pack for the rest of the wrapping bandages before grunting with satisfaction. His uncompromising gaze fell on the Abuser. "Take him."

Tonight, Ophelia promised herself as she wiped the tears from her face with the back of her hand and went to pick up the Abuser's rope. *Tonight you die, Spirokai.*

They walked.

Twice during the boiling afternoon Ophelia thought she saw a figure following behind them on the horizon. Both times her heart leaped—Methos was alive! It was all a mistake!—but both times the figure vanished from her sight like a teasing mirage. She occupied her attention by tracking the sandstorm Methos had spotted earlier, but looking at it in the distance made her think of her brother and her heart ached anew. They moved amongst the rocky outcroppings, Spirokai occasionally pausing to growl nonsense sounds at them. Ophelia got the message nonetheless—hurry up. The Abuser fell every hundred yards. When he wasn't falling, Ophelia was. Spirokai never stumbled, never missed a step. Ophelia was beginning to believe the man was inhuman.

The sun went down for the second time during their pilgrimage across the desert, but Spirokai did not gesture to halt and pitch camp. Without pausing for so much as a rest stop, he kept going, pushing ahead deeper into the sand and rock.

"Are we to sleep soon?" the Abuser gasped from behind Ophelia. The two of them trailed Spirokai by many feet, a new breeze carrying their voices away from each other. Ophelia imagined she could feel her lungs becoming brittle and the poison in her backpack seeping like acid through the leather and into her flesh. They *had* to stop soon. She had thought of nothing but Spirokai's death for the last mile.

"I don't know," she answered truthfully. Her lips touched one another on the word *know* and the pain lanced through her face. They were cracked to the point of bleeding; she could taste the salty copper flavor of her blood with her tongue. "I'll find out what he thinks he's doing. Spirokai!"

The Viperdeau stopped and turned to face the pair as they staggered up to him. Ophelia could not tell if the sun had done any more than give the warrior a deep tan; he didn't seem affected by weariness or thirst. *Perhaps,* Ophelia thought foolishly, *I should have my skull split open, too. It seems to help.*

"When are we stopping?" she asked.

"Not," Spirokai snarled. "Close. Hours. Keep going."

Ophelia shook her head. "We can't make it. We have to rest."

Spirokai touched the hilt of his sword with his hand. "Keep going. Or die."

Kill me, Ophelia thought. *Just get it over with.* But she didn't say anything. She didn't care if she died now, but she wouldn't die without first seeing Spirokai bleeding to death at her feet. If she let the Viperdeau kill her, there would never be vengeance for her brother, freedom for the Abuser, or peace for her own soul.

"All right," she conceded. She gestured. "We're coming."

Spirokai turned and trudged off, leaving the two stragglers to catch up.

"He means to kill me this night," the Abuser said in the growing darkness and wind.

"I mean to do the same to him," Ophelia muttered so softly that the Abuser didn't seem to hear her. "It's the only way we'll get away."

Sand blew painfully into her eyes and she stopped to rub them clear. The Abuser coughed sharply behind her and fell. Ophelia paused to help him up again; when they turned Spirokai had vanished into the darkness and the whirling sand.

The storm! Ophelia realized.

"Run!" she shouted at the Abuser, throwing the rope to him that he might move more quickly. "That way!"

"What—?" the other began, but Ophelia was already upon him, whirling him about and propelling him off past an outcropping. As if to aid them, the storm descended on them in earnest. Ophelia heard Spirokai bellow somewhere not too far away—she wondered fearfully if the Viperdeau could track them at night in whipping sand.

"He's coming!" she called to the Abuser. "Run faster!"

They both fell at once, the wind seeming to place a foot in the middle of their backs and plowing them to the ground. Ophelia took a mouthful of sand that, but for its consistency, was no drier than her tongue. She spat, her tired body protesting as she dragged himself back to her feet. The Abuser came to help her. Gritty sand tore at them, chafing red and raw spots on their exposed flesh. It forced their eyes shut instinctively; they breathed in short gasps and only through their noses to avoid inhaling too many particles. A few were unavoidable, and they gagged and coughed as they fought the winds.

They ran together through the darkness and the sandstorm, holding one another's hands. Ophelia's memory flashed back to her childhood, running with Methos across a make-believe battlefield a thousand miles across Dominaria. She tried to smile at the Abuser, but all she could manage was a weary grimace.

Once, they thought they saw Spirokai in the blowing sand—a figure lurched past them in the blackness without spotting them. Ophelia thought it was too small to be the Viperdeau, but they hid anyway, crouching behind a solitary boulder until the shape had moved on. *Maybe sand marauders,* Ophelia worried. Then they continued their blind flight. It felt to Ophelia as if her skin had been whipped from her body, and each new blast of sandy air aggravated her open sores until she felt like screaming. It was a struggle just to avoid folding in on herself like a child.

They stopped what felt like years later at the base of a huge outcropping, where the Abuser sank to the ground. "I cannot run anymore," he gasped. "Let me die here."

Ophelia felt a flare of anger—she would not allow the Abuser to die, not after all of this. Then she said, "Let's climb, look for shelter. A cave or something. Come on, take my hand. You can make it."

She didn't think the Abuser would do it. But he did. Ophelia held him tightly to give him reassurance and they assaulted the outcropping with the last of their energy.

The storm, both protective and cruel, seemed to sense that they had reached the end of the line. It began to slack off, the blowing sand settling back down to the desert, the wind retreating until it was just a breeze. Ophelia climbed up a few feet, then reached back to help the Abuser join her. After searching the immediate area for any shelter, she climbed up again and they repeated the process. In this way they climbed until they had reached the top of the outcropping.

"Here," Ophelia breathed. It was pitch-black around her. She could barely see the Abuser as the man reached out one last time to take her hand. "We're above the storm here. And Spirokai will never find us atop an outcropping. He only thinks one way, and it isn't *up*."

They fell down together behind a great boulder. The sky yawned starless above them, and for a moment Ophelia thought it was the right time to die. She almost settled back and waited for it—but then her senses returned. She sat up and drew her dagger. With it, she cut the rope free from around the Abuser's neck.

"You're free," she whispered. "In the morning we'll get away from this place. We'll get out of the desert and back to civilization."

The Abuser sighed and touched her arm. "You are the decent one," he said. "Yes. We will go."

"Travel at night, sleep by day," Ophelia said wearily. She felt an overpowering sleepiness coming over her. So much tension seemed to be oozing out of her. "We'll make it together."

The Abuser said something else, but Ophelia didn't hear him—she was already asleep.

She awoke slowly, as if climbing a rocky outcropping of dreams to reach wakefulness. The sun was already up, but she was shielded from its direct rays by the shadow of the boulder. Drifting sand had half buried her legs, and as she shook them free, she turned to wake the Abuser, formulate a plan for survival.

The Abuser was gone.

A blizzard of thoughts and emotions, as ferocious as any sandstorm, tore through Ophelia in that moment of realization: He *abandoned me after everything I gave for him. He'll never make it moving during the day. He doesn't trust me.* She remembered the distant mumbling of the Abuser just before sleep came last night. *Could he have said he was leaving? Why couldn't he wait?* The desire to descend into despair washed over Ophelia, but the energy to sink simply wasn't there. She'd have to go on alone, as she realized she'd been doing since she began on this unpleasant journey into the desert.

Then she heard the sound. It was a regular, steady chopping and sucking repetition, and it came from beyond the boulder where she had slept. Stiffly she rose and peered around the rock, restraining the hope blossoming in her chest that she would see the Abuser there.

The top of the outcropping was ringed with many boulders like the one Ophelia hid behind, and together they formed a crude but natural border for the level sand plot which covered the outcropping's summit. Dotting the sand like marbles dumped haphazardly from a child's bag were skulls, dozens of them, human and humanoid. There were no other bones, only the fleshless heads of long-dead people, black eye cavities staring into white-hot infinity. Next to each skull was a pole, atop which was mounted a flag that fluttered in the dry wind. The sun pounded down from above, bleaching the skulls and fading the execution dates from each of the flags which had been planted to mark a particular burial. For though no other bones were visible, Ophelia knew as she stared that the rest of the bodies were there beneath the sand, where the victims had stood while their captors buried them up to their necks in the ground. This was the place where prisoners were brought to be wound into mummifying bandages and then baked beneath the blazing desert sun. This was where Methos had said holy justice would be done. This was the execution site, Vacar Slab.

Spirokai was here.

The Viperdeau warrior did not look up from his grisly task. The flag the party had carried across the desert was rooted nearby, its date clearly legible even from where Ophelia hid. Spirokai turned from his left to his right, grunting with the strain as he hefted another shovelful of sand to pour into the hole at his feet. The Abuser's head lolled to one side, his eyes closed, his mouth gagged by yellow-white wrapping bandages, as the sand covered his shrouded shoulders. Only his head was visible, his chin resting on the ground before him. Spirokai poured more sand and packed it down with swift blows from the shovel—the Abuser did not flinch as the metal thudded down close to his face. Ophelia could see a second hole, empty, just feet from the first one, and a chill ran down her back.

Sweat beaded on her forehead as she retreated into the boulder's shadow. There was no doubt that Spirokai knew she was here—he had obviously come and taken the Abuser in his sleep. She thought she could probably skitter down the side of the outcropping without being discovered, but conscience tore at her. It would mean deserting the Abuser. Her distress from just moments ago, when she had thought the Abuser had left *her,* would not be forgotten so easily.

Her hands shaking, she fumbled open her backpack. The poison. Removing her dagger and the waterskin, she stabbed the blade into the leather near the skin's ties. When she withdrew it, a slimy yellow fluid glimmered all along the dagger's edge. It would have to do. She felt as if she were suffocating. She and the Abuser, they were both going to die here at Vacar Slab.

She thought she heard pebbles banging from somewhere below, but when she leaned forward and glanced down the face of the outcropping, she saw nothing. The sounds of shoveling had stopped behind her—Spirokai would be coming for her now. Ophelia put her feet under her and swallowed back the nausea rolling up from her belly. *Five minutes,* she consoled herself. *Five minutes and it'll all be over.*

She tossed down the waterskin and poison seeped from the dagger slit. More pebbles bounced down below. As she turned to move out onto Vacar Slab, it occurred to her that the sounds she was hearing from below could only signify one thing: somehow, some way, Spirokai had slipped behind her and was coming up the outcropping's face at this very moment.

The idea stalled her for a breath, and in that breath Spirokai reached around the boulder from where he had been burying the Abuser. He grabbed Ophelia by the throat.

"You traitor," the Viperdeau hissed as he dragged Ophelia out of the shadows and into the sun. Ophelia's feet left the ground as Spirokai hefted her into the air, whirling her toward the second hole, the vertical grave. "You die with Abuser."

The grip at her throat was throttling Ophelia. She feared that the mad warrior's thick fingers were popping the tiny bones in her neck as she struggled to free herself, and her heartbeat came rushing to her temples with a fury. Her vision swam. With a mighty effort, she stabbed blindly with her dagger hand, slashing at the exposed flesh of Spirokai's wrist. She could feel blood running from her nose.

The impact sent bursts of intense pain burning up her arm, and her fingers released the dagger reflexively. Her shoulder throbbed as well, but the choke hold vanished, dropping her to the scalding sand. She tried to land on her feet, but took a staggering step back and her heel connected with one of the many skulls dotting the execution site. She went down.

Spirokai howled with surprise when the dagger buried itself low on his wrist, sliding neatly between his bones and bursting out the far side with a thin spray of blood. He disengaged from Ophelia, retreating a few paces toward the second hole, and turned his hand over. He displayed no obvious pain; Ophelia guessed his severely damaged brain would take many minutes to acknowledge even the most devastating of wounds. The tip of the blade cast a tiny shadow that stretched as far as his knuckles, and on that tip Spirokai saw what he was looking for: a trace of duneclaw poison glimmered in the bright sunlight.

Without changing his expression, he withdrew the dagger from his wrist and, with a casual overhand throw, pitched it over the side of Vacar Slab. The metallic banging of its journey down echoed back.

"Traitor," he growled again.

Ophelia had made it to her knees. She watched the dagger, her only weapon, turn end over end until it was out of sight, her mind hypnotized by the horror of the situation. The poison hadn't killed Spirokai. Maybe it would eventually, but it had not done what Ophelia had hoped for. The Viperdeau was still alive and about to kill her. Spirokai towered over her, an unstoppable, inhuman monster of murder. From behind Ophelia came the sound of sudden movement, something approaching. The possibility of a hungry duneclaw sprang to her mind.

Spirokai drew his long sword and raised it to hack at Ophelia's legs, to incapacitate her until she could be buried. The sword glinted briefly in the blinding sunlight; Ophelia focused on it, aware that she was seeing her last impression of this world or any other. It was over.

Before the blow could fall, Spirokai began to shiver. The blade trembled in his hands, then slipped from them to land with a thud in the sand behind him. His legs shook. His knees began to buckle. His splayed fingers rose to awkwardly cover his face as he degenerated within seconds into immobility.

It was all Ophelia needed. She pulled her feet under her and launched herself at the shuddering Spirokai, aiming for his stomach. Her shoulder caught the Viperdeau squarely beneath the ribs; the warrior reeled backward, stumbling over his sword, and took a misstep. Sand gave way beneath his boot. Still in the throes of his spasm, Spirokai fell into the hole he had dug for Ophelia's execution. His chin cracked sharply against the ground at the grave's edge.

A shadow fell over Ophelia as she lunged for the Viperdeau's fallen sword. *The duneclaw!* Ophelia thought frantically. She snatched the blade up, rolling to avoid the shape as it raced past her, its own sword, a two-handed weapon, raised above its head.

Ophelia hardly recognized the figure after its days of rotting beneath the blazing desert sun, but there was no doubt in her mind—it was him, the one they hadn't been able to retrieve from the canyon in the mountains. Ophelia saw the torn and emptied waterskins dangling from his belt like flayed flesh, saw the sole remaining waterskin that banged against his hip with a rhythmic slosh, saw the man's yellowed mouth as the thing bore down on Spirokai in the hole. It was Teeth.

Spirokai's fit left him like an expelled breath and he looked up just as the dry and withered corpse of Teeth reached him. The Viperdeau's eyes bulged, and Ophelia saw in those eyes, for the first time, what she had always believed Spirokai was incapable of experiencing. In those eyes, she saw fear.

"Sto—!" Spirokai began to order. Teeth was directly in front of him, his weapon raised. The Viperdeau looked down, exposing the top of his head to the corpse, refusing to face it in that last moment, leaving Ophelia with the mixed impression that Spirokai was only afraid of what he could see. But Ophelia would never know.

Teeth's two-handed sword thundered down and the length of the blade buried itself deeply in the Viperdeau's bald head. It crossed his old scar to form a jagged letter X in his flesh and bone, a bright red marker, before a wave of blood burst forth from the new wound and obliterated it from recognition. Spirokai did not cry out; he twitched once, his hands rising halfway to his head as if to grasp and wrench the blade free. Then they fell back again, down into the hole next to his sides. His eyes closed as the blood washed over them.

Teeth released the sword, leaving it buried in Spirokai's skull, and limped forward, dropping down into the hole with the dead Viperdeau. Ophelia rose cautiously, the sword of Spirokai of the Split Skull held out like a thwarting holy symbol before her. When the corpse emerged from the hole again, Ophelia waved the sword in what she hoped was a menacing manner.

Teeth took no notice of her. The dead man fumbled gracelessly with Spirokai's backpack, unlacing it and clawing inside after its contents. He withdrew the last of the burial wrapping bandages Methos had carried across most of the desert. He sagged to the sands of Vacar Slab and began to wrap his decaying legs. His scorched, disintegrating face turned toward Ophelia.

"Uterwurldz," Teeth said slowly, his tongue dried to uselessness in his mouth. He tugged the bandages across his thighs with finality.

Ophelia stared, frozen in wonder and horror. She did not know what words to say or what actions to take. It was impossible for her not to fear Teeth's vengeance against those who had not seen to his proper burial wrapping, though the dead man seemed placated after murdering the party's leader. Even so, Ophelia could not contain her terror and amazement—here was living, or almost living, proof of the Old Ways. Here was a bit of evidence that Methos's faith had been well placed.

The thought of her brother lanced grief through her and prompted her forward. She hesitated, then knelt next to Teeth as the supine corpse drew the bandages across his death-bloated belly. She touched his remaining waterskin almost fearfully. Teeth raised his head; Ophelia met his eyeless stare. It was a stare from beyond life, from beyond Ophelia's understanding of the world. Slowly, the corpse gave the wrapping over to the living— he pressed both the bandages and the waterskin into her trembling hands.

Ophelia worked quickly, not looking at Teeth's face again until she was ready to wrap the head. Then she could not wait any longer. She took a breath.

"Teeth," she breathed. The rotted face came up. "Teeth, is Methos waiting for me in the Otherworlds?"

The monstrosity before her cocked its head as if listening to a distant wind, as if seeing a distant sun. An answer came back—it nodded gently.

Ophelia nodded solemnly and bound the corpse's head as quickly as she could. In moments, Teeth had finally made the journey to his proper grave.

The task finished, Ophelia turned and crawled across the sand, mindful of the array of skulls about her, to the Abuser's side. She felt as if she had no energy left; so many superstitions were dissolving inside of her that she felt as if she were empty, in desperate need of refilling. It was impossible to believe that she would find the strength to take the shovel and extract the Abuser from his grave, but it had to be done. Old Ways or not, Ophelia still believed that all men were prone to lie and that the shaman who had convicted the Abuser had done so through his youngest daughter. She looked for the shovel.

"Ophelia." A faint whisper.

The Abuser.

Ophelia crawled to him, careful not to push sand into the prisoner's face. The Abuser rested with his eyes closed, his chin buried in the sand nearly to his lower lip. He had worked the gag of bandages free with his tongue, and it lay like dead flesh in the sand before him. He didn't open his eyes as Ophelia neared.

"I'll have you out as soon as I can," Ophelia promised. "The shovel is here somewhere. I have water now, too. Let me—"

"I am dead already," the Abuser croaked. "I am enlightened enough to know. You go. You have been decent to me. You are a good woman."

Ophelia shook her head, but the Abuser's eyes opened and Ophelia saw in them the truth of the matter: the Abuser was taking his last breaths. She felt her overworked heart wrench weakly.

"I wanted to tell you last night," the Abuser said quietly. "But you were sleeping. I will tell you now."

Ophelia had the sudden feeling that she didn't want to hear. A gnawing in her mind said that a terrible truth might be revealed. If the Old Ways were true, then perhaps, just *perhaps,* no shaman could lie, even through another. She knew that she could not bear to hear the Abuser say that he had committed the terrible crime of which he was accused.

"It's all right," she said. "I don't need to know."

The Abuser smiled. "You must. It is important to me that someone know. I am to die."

Ophelia stiffened herself. It was the only decent thing to do. "Tell me."

"I wanted someone to remember," the Abuser said, "that my real name is Markus. I have a name. I am Markus."

It made Ophelia's throat constrict. "Markus," she said. It was very close to the name Methos. "I'll remember. And I'll see you in the Otherworlds, Markus."

The Abuser's eyes closed and it was over.

Ophelia took Spirokai's long sword after deciding to forego a search for her lost dagger. She retrieved Teeth's skin of water from near his corpse and her own waterskin of poison from behind the boulder, stopping the leak in it with the last few inches of the burial bandages: there were none left over. She looked around her once, almost ready to be afraid again, and then thought simply: *It doesn't matter. Not now.* After a minute's contemplation, she removed from the sand the dated flag marking Markus's execution and broke it down into kindling, which she stuffed into her backpack. Let Dominaria wonder what this man's crime had been and when he had been killed. Let Dominaria wonder.

Many hours later, long after Ophelia had left Vacar Slab behind, the sun descended and Spirokai of the Split Skull opened his eyes. Faint signals of pain came from the terrible wound in his head, but he had experienced such pain once before—it would fade soon enough. Even a fallen Akron legionnaire knew the difference between short-term and long-term agony. Life was both and neither.

He began to extract himself from the grave.

ABOUT THE AUTHORS

Hanovi Braddock was born in Tucson, Arizona. He did not spend years fishing on an Alaskan trawler, fighting oil rig fires in Texas, sailing a small boat alone across the Atlantic, or teaching agronomy in Gabon. He wishes he had, because that's the sort of thing one is supposed to include in a writer's biography. Instead, he went to college, changed his major five times, and finally settled for a B.A. in Humanities, which was the next best thing to a degree in Major Undecided. Two decades later, he still doesn't know what to specialize in. Braddock's previous stories have appeared in *The Leading Edge*.

Watch for his **Magic: The Gathering** novel, *Ashes of the Sun*, coming in spring 1996 from HarperPrism.

Adam-Troy Castro made his first professional sale in 1987, to *Spy* magazine. Since then, he's sold about forty short stories, encompassing humor, mainstream, fantasy, science fiction, and horror, and including prominent contributions to the magazines *Dragon*, *Pulphouse*, *Science Fiction Age*, and *Fantasy and Science Fiction* and to the anthologies *Deathport*, *The Ultimate Witch*, *Adventures in the Twilight Zone*, *Book of the Dead (volumes III and IV)*, *The Ultimate Super Hero*, *South from Horror*, *It Came from the Drive-In*, and *100 Vicious Little Vampire Stories*. His original short story collection, *Lost in Booth Nine*, is available in both trade and hardcover editions by Silver Salamander Press.

Born in New York City to two wonderful but slightly mad people, **Keith R. A. DeCandido** was given a steady diet of Tolkien, Le Guin, Heinlein, and Wodehouse when he was too young to know better. This damaged his psyche to such a degree that he was forced to go into the SF/fantasy field professionally—

that, or face years of overpriced therapy. He has coedited three anthologies: *The Ultimate Alien*, *The Ultimate Dragon* (both with Byron Preiss and John Betancourt), and the forthcoming *OtherWere* (with Laura Anne Gilman); his articles and reviews on SF, fantasy, and comics have appeared in *Creem*, *Publishers Weekly*, *Library Journal*, *The Comics Journal*, *Horror*, and *Wilson Library Bulletin*; and his short fiction can be found in *The Ultimate Spider-Man*, *The Ultimate Silver Surfer*, and the forthcoming *Two-Fisted Writer Tales*. He still lives in New York City with his lovely and much more talented wife Marina Frants, where he edits books, writes, plays percussion, and indulges in the eternal but futile quest for more sleep.

Kathleen Dalton-Woodbury is the wife of a chemical engineer and the mother of three girls and two cats. She earned a B.A. degree in mathematics and an M.E. degree in mechanical engineering, both from the University of Utah. She is the director of the Science Fiction and Fantasy Workshop, a national network for new and aspiring science fiction, fantasy, and horror writers. She edits and publishes their monthly newsletter, for which she writes a marketing column. She also teaches a writing course for East High Community School and serves as an assistant systems operator for the science fiction areas on GEnie. She has worked as a fiction editor for *Mindsparks*, a small press science fiction magazine. She collects cards, dragons, unusual names, and information about her ancestors.

Peter Friend is a New Zealander who writes a lot of humorous articles and depressing short stories. The articles tend to sell better for some reason, but he's had fiction published in *Aurealis* and *Interzone* magazines. He also draws, paints, and animates cartoons in the vain hope of becoming a living art treasure one day. In real life, he's a computer analyst.

Stonefeather Grubbs, ninth level sage at the Library of Leng in the catacombs of Lat-Nam, is . . . oh, you mean in *this* universe? Sure, why not? At the age of fifteen, Grubbs began his spectacular midlife crisis in Baltimore, Maryland—his realistic life expectancy at this point being no more than thirty—and has diligently nurtured it through the following quarter century. If he keeps this up, he'll live forever. Now in Lancaster, Pennsylvania, he's remained successfully married to the artist Lucyan Latham for going on fifteen years and is the wise and loving father of two children, Eowyn and Gwydion. Lawful chaotic.

Jane M. Lindskold's novels include *Brother to Dragons*, *Companion to Owls*, *Marks of Our Brothers*, and *The Pipes of Orpheus*. Lindskold has also published short stories in a variety of collections including *Dragon Fantastic*, *Journeys to the Twilight Zone*, *Christmas Bestiary*, *Warriors of Blood and Dream*, and *Heaven Sent*. She is the author of a biography of Roger Zelazny for Twayne's American Authors Series. A former professor of English, Lindskold has a new novel due out in June of 1996, two other novels on the block, and is deeply involved with the development of *Chronomasters*, a CD-ROM computer game.

It was August '94 when **Sonia Orin Lyris** picked up her first **Magic** deck. She had successfully resisted for nearly a year, taking seriously the whispered warnings of **Magic**'s addictive potential, and sneering at those who toted notebooks of cards wherever they went.

"It's only a game," she said as she shuffled her first deck. Then, her brow wrinkling delicately: "Explain this banding stuff to me again."

Now she carries around a cigar box full of decks, dice, and life counters and thinks that a "cappuccino blast" counters one cappuccino or destroys a cappuccino already in play.

"Chef's Surprise" emerged from that intriguing quote on the Granite Gargoyle card, which had been nagging at her for some time. She feels much better now.

Lyris's fiction has appeared in *Asimov's SF magazine*, *Pulphouse*, and *Expanse*, and in the anthologies *Infinite Loop* (edited by Larry Constantine), *Cyberdreams* (edited by Gardner Dozois and Sheila Williams), and *New Legends* (edited by Greg Bear).

Watch for her **Magic: The Gathering** novel, *And Peace Shall Sleep*, coming in fall 1996 from HarperPrism..

Michael G. Ryan was born and raised in Decatur, Illinois, and he tries not to brag about this. After attending the University of Illinois at Urbana-Champaign (studying in those potentially lucrative fields of philosophy, psychology, and English), he went to work as an editor for the National Council of Teachers of English. A chance letter to Wizards of the Coast secured him an offer to serve as an editor for **Magic: The Gathering**; both his mother, Irma, and his boss at NCTE, Zarina, encouraged him to accept the offer—one should always wonder when your mom and your boss want you to move away.

Mike now works for Wizards of the Coast and lives in Seattle with his girlfriend, Melody Alder, and their two cats, Scath and Selena LaGur. He has previously published in *Dragon, The Duelist, VideoPhile, The Baldwin County Current,* and a number of other publications.

Michael A. Stackpole is an award-winning game and computer game designer who was born in 1957 and grew up in Burlington, Vermont. In 1979 he graduated from the University of Vermont with a B.A. in History. In his career as a game designer he has done work for Flying Buffalo, Inc., Interplay Productions, TSR Inc., West End Games, Hero Games, Wizards of the Coast, FASA Corp., Game Designers Workshop, and Steve Jackson Games. In recognition of his work in and for the game industry, he was inducted into the Academy of Gaming Arts and Design Hall of Fame in 1994.

While Mike shares his hero's lack of height, he has never been hung-over, has never fought a metal engine of Justice and, alas, is violently allergic to cats.

Amy Thomson is an award-winning science fiction writer, critic, and fan. Her first book, *Virtual Girl,* a novel about robots, artificial intelligence, and homelessness, was published by Ace. Thomson's second book, *The Color of Distance,* is an alien contact novel set in a rain forest. In addition to her fiction writing, Thomson has also been a short fiction critic for *Locus* Magazine and a reviewer for the *Seattle Times.*

While pursuing an ideal career as a quantum mechanic, **Glen Vasey** makes a living as town friendly-guy and whenever-he-can writer. He has published several short stories in the anthologies *Book of the Dead, Still Dead,* and *Obsessions.* A fourth story has appeared in the incredible new magazine *Phantasm.* In the works are *The Innocent Assassin* (a New York crime story), a novel based on the **Magic** universe, and several other great ideas. Glen also spends time collecting books, doing the parent thing, collecting books, playing **Magic**, collecting books, and just generally enjoying life.

Robert E. Vardeman has written more than fifty fantasy and science fiction novels in the past twenty-one years. Recent publications include a novelette in Fred Saberhagen's anthology *Armory of Swords* and the fantasy trilogy *The Accursed*. He plays **Magic** (with more enthusiasm than skill) and lives in Albuquerque, New Mexico, with his wife and son.

In 1986, **Edd Vick** moseyed to the Great Northwest from Dallas, Texas, with a ton of books and the budding MU Press. Now ensconsed in one of the most livable cities in the U.S. and propelled by more than mediocre amounts of Dr. Pepper, Edd & MU/ÆON have come to publish such comic delights as *The Desert Peach* and *Those Annoying Posr Bros*. He occasionally writes and too infrequently draws cartoons for fanzines like *Mainstream* and *TAND*. For a living he manages Half Price Books in Edmonds, Washington.

Edd lives in a shameless den of bibliomania, braving torrents of rain and hordes of latte drinkers with Bounder the Neurotic Cat and the lovely, talented Amy Thomson. This is his first fiction sale.

Born in Massachusetts, in the middle of a blizzard, **Laura Waterman** beat a hasty retreat down to Miami, Florida. After twenty short years she again braved the arctic north and moved to Chicagoland. There she and her husband Paul now faithfully serve the desires of their many cats. These generous felines actually allow Laura to hold down a job (somebody's got to buy the tuna). Thus she holds the exaulted position of secretary and writes as a form of escapism.